A FAMED/DISTRESSED LOS ANGELES POPSTAR MUST CONFESS TO A DARK SECRET FROM HIS PAST—A SECRET SO TERRIBLE IT COULD DESTROY EVERYTHING HE'S WORKED FOR—IF HE IS TO SAVE THE LIVES OF HIS LOVED ONES.

Chris Flowers, one of the most famous and beloved popstars in the world, wants nothing more than to keep playing shows and creating art for his dear fans. Nearly finished with an album, and only days from playing a major show, Chris receives a fateful phone call threatening to expose a dark secret of his past that could ruin him. The sinister voice demands Chris to "Confess" or else... When the lives of loved ones from Chris's past—the very people he left behind to pursue stardom—become involved, Chris must decide how important his career truly is for him—and if he's willing to sacrifice lives for it.

Early Praise for Limelight

"A compelling and intriguing peak into the underbelly of the music industry and the price paid for fame and immortality. The pages fly at the end as betrayal, secrets, and revenge are exposed!"—***C.S. Dodds, author of Fractured***

"A pacy, confident debut novel - we'll see more of Joshua Crosson!" —***Judith Cutler, author of Murder the Boys***

"An intriguing debut novel from a promising writer. A fascinating account of the evils of obsessing about fame. Well written, if unlikeable, characters kept me reading till the satisfying end."—**Valerie Keogh, author of *The Lodger***

"Crosson grabs you from the very first chapter in this raw—and oftentimes tragic—exploration of one man's struggle for meaning beyond his fame. Throughout its various twists and revelations, LIMELIGHT will keep you hooked until its explosive end."—***Nicole Hackett, author of The Perfect Ones***

Excerpt

The voice had the abnormal deepness of someone using a voice changer.

Chris was momentarily chilled by the malicious sound of the voice, but that quickly changed into outrage. "Excuse me? Who's this?"

Out of his periphery he felt Andrea glancing from her cell to him, mild concern disturbing her cool affect.

"Don't worry about that," the voice said. There was a patience and a dark confidence to the voice that Chris didn't like. It was like the voice was in control, not Chris. "I know what you did," the voice said. "Five years ago."

That was when Chris truly felt out of control, for the first time since his addiction years. He was lost for words. An icy chill ran down his back. This voice—whoever it was—was claiming to know things no one should know.

"Who are you?" Chris asked yet again, trying to keep his cool.

The voice said, "You will confess, Chris. I promise you I'll make you confess to what you did..."

LIMELIGHT

Joshua Crosson

Moonshine Cove Publishing, LLC
Abbeville, South Carolina U.S.A.

First Moonshine Cove Edition February 2023

ISBN: 9781952439506

© Copyright 2023 by Joshua Crosson

This book is a work of fiction. Names, characters, businesses, places, events, conversations, opinions, and incidents are either products of the author's imagination or are used fictitiously. Any resemblance to actual events, locales, conversations, opinions, business establishments, or persons, living or dead, is entirely coincidental and unintended.

All rights reserved. No part of this book may be reproduced in whole or in part without written permission from the publisher except by reviewers who may quote brief excerpts in connection with a review in a newspaper, magazine or electronic publication; nor may any part of this book be reproduced, stored in a retrieval system or transmitted in any form or by any means electronic, mechanical, photocopying, recording or any other means, without written permission from the publisher.

Cover image public domain, cover illustration and design and interior design by Moonshine Cove staff.

About the Author

Joshua Crosson lives in a small town in the beautiful Pacific Northwest. He attended college in his early twenties, wasn't sure what he wanted to study, dropped out, and is now returning—this time to get a nursing degree. He has a passion for helping others in need and has always believed good writing has the power to connect and help other people. He's loved writing ever since he was a small boy. While writing can sometimes be a challenge, his passion for it has never died. He's heard other writers use the term "writing as therapy" and believes the expression is a good fit for him too.

He loves a good crime story, is a sucker for anything Daniel Woodrell, Stephen King, Silent Hill (video game series), Life is Strange (also a video game series), and Andre Dubus III. He's also fond of the TV shows Breaking Bad, True Detective, and can't resist a good Forensic Files episode.

He prefers stories, including his own, a little more on the dark side and has a particular fascination with antiheroes. He loves to explore and write deeply flawed characters.

When he isn't reading or writing, he's working as a CNA at an assisted living facility, visiting with his parents at his childhood home, playing video games and watching movies with his brother and sister, drinking too much coffee, learning Portuguese, or spending quality time with his fiancé.

Limelight is his first novel. He's currently finishing his second novel.

More at: https://joshuacrossonwriter.com

https://www.facebook.com/joshuacrossonwriter

Acknowledgments

Lauryn Heineman: For all your help over the years. Your developmental feedback, your enthusiasm, and your encouragement have been invaluable to me.

Darryl Oliver: For your help with my query letter. I'd still be stuck in the querying phase if it wasn't for you. I'll be needing your help again soon, my friend!

Michael Sanders: For the ferocious line-edit. You cut the fat and tightened the narrative. The book is a smoother read because of you.

Laura Dragonette: For the meticulous proofread. You helped clean up the book, spotting and fixing mistakes I missed. I'm thankful for your keen eye and attention to detail.

Monica Crosson: Mom, you taught me the love for creative writing and have been inspiring me since I was a child. You've read and critiqued countless of my writing projects and drafts over the years. After reading the first draft of this book you told me to "tear it apart." And I did. You never pull any punches, always encourage me, and it's you I'm most of all grateful for. Thank you.

PROLOGUE
2018

Chris Flowers walked down the backstage halls, his wingtip shoes clicking against the hardwood floor. The buzz of preshow activity was in the air. Out front, janitors ran their mops over the floors between the seats while backstage workers milled around idly chattering and sound operators tweaked levels on the amps. Lighting techs stood on the stage and ran the light board operator through the light check: left stage lights, then right stage lights, then house lights illuminating and just as suddenly vanishing, as if they were in a haunted house.

The dressing room door was open a crack, and music was spilling out. Chris didn't enter immediately. He stood for a moment on the other side of the door, listening, the music demanding his attention. People said Tray's music gave them goose bumps. In Chris's experience, when a musician's work gave you goose bumps, you knew they were an artist. Chris had goose bumps right then.

He peered through the crack, a strip of light warm on his face, and with one eye watched in awe as the kid's long, slender fingers sculpted sophisticated guitar chords and riffs with the ease of a far older master guitarist. Then, on top of it all, the kid voiced those haunting vocal harmonies that melded seamlessly with his insane guitar melodies. Chris had heard the kid play a thousand times before but still couldn't believe what he was hearing was an original song from an eighteen-year-old.

Chris entered, and Tray stopped playing.

"Hey, kid. Why ain't you out there mingling?" It was Tray's ritual before every show to go out and mingle with his fans, a habit the kid had borrowed from Chris.

Tray was hesitant, nervously scratching his teased blond hair.

Then he said, "I just wanted to be alone for a bit."

Tray's tropical-blue eyes darted away from Chris's gaze.

"Something wrong, buddy?"

Tray shrugged. He picked at his guitar's tuning pegs. "I don't know. I was just thinking."

"About what, kid?"

Chris noticed the color had washed out of Tray's voice. Tray's face darkened, and Chris's eyes narrowed in concern.

"Just thinking about everything." Tray gestured around him when he said this. "Being, you know, famous and all." He looked down, then met Chris's questioning gaze. "Does it matter?" he finally said.

"What?" Chris asked, wondering where this was coming from.

"Does it matter?" Tray asked again, sounding genuinely curious.

Chris had to think about it a moment.

He recalled something Tray had said during a talk show interview: *Chris Flowers has taught me so much, ever since I first got to LA.*

"Of course it matters," Chris said reassuringly. "Look, I know this must be overwhelming for you, you getting all this attention at such a young age."

I love how Chris honors his fans, Tray had continued during that talk show. *How happy he makes them. Chris is so genuine and selfless.*

Praise for the young megastar echoed in Chris's mind: *I love you, Tray! You're a lifesaver, Tray! Thank you for existing, Tray!*

On and on like that.

Chris beamed. "People love you, kid. You make so many people happy."

Tray looked away. When he looked back, Chris saw with surprise the tears in his eyes, the despair in the kid's face.

Tray suddenly stood up and ran into Chris's arms.

"Hey, hey. It's okay, kid." He wrapped his arms around him and patted his back. "It's okay."

Tray sniffled, brushing back his tears.

What had Tray been thinking about that was bothering him so much? The kid had everything going for him.

Chris rubbed Tray's back and the back of his neck, Chris's black hand contrasting against the kid's milk-pale skin.

Chris pulled away from the embrace, gave Tray's flushed cheek a pat. "You're helping so many people, giving them joy. Remember that, kid."

Tray's eyes brightened, inspired, humbled. He smiled, nodded in agreement.

"Go on out there and give 'em some love."

Five minutes later Chris left the backstage bathroom, face in his cell phone. Tray's mother, Marianne, approached, and Chris shoved his phone back into his pants pocket. Marianne looked so much like her son. She was tall, thin-lipped, with those big ocean eyes and soft blond hair. She was wearing a T-shirt with her son's image on the front.

"Hey, Chris, you seen Tray?" She glanced over her shoulder.

"Yeah, he's out mingling with his peeps."

Marianne smiled warmly, the pride for her son unmistakable on her face. "Shoulda figured. The theater managers are asking for him. I better go grab him."

"Nah, I got it," Chris said. "Was about to go check on him anyway."

As Chris approached the front doors, he heard the rumble of Tray Mansfield's fans through the floor, feeling it vibrating up and into his bones, humming inside him.

He stepped outside. Two burly bouncers guarded the main entrance, conspicuous in their sunshades as the sun was setting. Tickets weren't being taken yet, the head of the endless line cordoned off by a metal gate. A sea of people stretched forever down the sidewalk. Faces glowed in the old-timey marquee light that read: *Tray Mansfield Live! Benefit for Youth Homelessness!* Other solo artists and well-known bands were also listed, but Tray's name had the top billing.

The sky was an orange and violet swirl above the tall, curved palm trees and the neon lights of Sunset Boulevard. The Boulevard's traffic was heavy, a rushing river of streaming yellow headlights and glowing red brake lights, many of the cars following the arrows to the concert parking in the back. Chris thought the line of people must stretch at least half a mile, curving around the Pavilion and weaving through that vast parking lot where guys in orange directed incoming concertgoers.

Tray was standing on the sidewalk, cradling his guitar, a long metal fence separating him from the men and women and children, with the Boulevard traffic rushing by at his back. Many of them had tears in their eyes. Some were visibly trembling. Bodyguards in black were trying to keep fanatics from leaping over that endless fence. It was like the Second Coming.

Tray broke the wall between himself and his fans, reaching over and shaking seemingly endless hands. Headlights from the traffic rolled over Tray, hot and yellow.

Chris was smiling at Tray. The whole time he was smiling.

Tray suddenly spotted Chris, waved.

Chris waved back.

A car, out of sync with the rest of traffic, had swerved left, almost hitting someone in the other lane, then swerved hard to the right. Straight for Tray. Then the grotesque, wettish slapping sound of a vehicle striking flesh and bone.

Chris's heart suddenly raced. His eyes bugged out. He tried to scream, but no sound emerged.

It was over in the blink of an eye.

Chris was running. The crowd was a screaming, chaotic mess.

The vehicle had come to a stop on the curb, blood streaking the car's hood. Chris rushed, stepping over Tray's beloved acoustic-electric that had shattered into a dozen pieces, and knelt in the gathering pool of blood.

The kid's right arm was mangled, bone sticking out. He was still under the car, only his chest and head showing. A deep gash ran nine inches from his forehead and across the right side of his face.

A black guy, clearly drunk, stumbled out of the bronze Nissan. There was the *clink!* of a whiskey bottle hitting the still-hot tarmac. The gold-toothed man with thick, dark hair stumbled toward Chris. The man looked truly apologetic, tears in his bloodshot eyes. He kept muttering, "Oh God, oh God, oh God." He squeezed his head between his palms like it was the end of the world.

Now the bodyguards couldn't stop the people from leaping over the fence. Others, tears streaming down their petrified faces, were on their cells dialing for an ambulance. Some were even filming.

Chris crouched, half on his knees, his cream-colored suit jacket and his slacks now blood-soaked, with Tray's bleeding head on his lap.

Marianne had found her way to his side. She knelt behind Chris, letting out a bloodcurdling scream that chilled Chris to the bone, a sound he'd never forget, as her brain took in what her eyes beheld.

She reached out a hand in vain, screaming, "My baby! My baby! My beautiful baby!"

Tears burned in Chris's eyes as he stared, shocked to his core, into the kid's dying face. "Kid, I'm right here. It's okay. The ambulance is coming. Kid? Tray? Please God. Oh, please God. Tray! Tray!"

Chris cried the kid's name over and over and over as the shadows of the crowd gathered around him.

TUESDAY, JULY 15, 2023
CHAPTER ONE

Chris stood in near dark off to the side of the stage, chewing his lips, fidgeting, eager to come on. There was a round of applause from the audience as a woman wearing a long black dress walked across the stage in matching black heels that clicked with each step. She stood in the spotlight, her thin lips trembling as she was about to speak into the standing microphone. Stage light illuminated the tears burning in her eyes.

She cleared her throat. "Hello. Welcome."

The chattering of the audience went quiet.

"Thank you all for coming. I'm Marianne Mansfield." Marianne sighed, her voice quivering. "As you all know, my son . . ." She paused, pursed her lips.

Chris's heart ached as he watched a couple tears rolling down Tray's mother's cheek. He wiped sweat off his palms and onto his bright sky-blue suit jacket, took slow breaths through his nostrils to calm himself and catch his breath.

Marianne couldn't quite bring herself to say her son's name and the word "death" in the same sentence. She simply said, "We're gathered here this evening because of him."

Eyes in the audience grew wet. Chris looked away, pity welling in his soul, as Marianne's tears mixed with her mascara, making her eyes seem darker, softer, and even more sorrowful.

"It was a rare thing, the genius my son had." Behind her a banner was drooping from the wall.

Chris could barely read it from this angle, but he knew what it said: *Tray Mansfield Foundation for Young Artists.*

Marianne's sadness emanated from her in dark waves. She sniffled, looked down, wrung her hands together.

Chris shifted uncomfortably, wanting to leave. But he stood there, trying to whip that encroaching guilt back, trying to keep tears from his own eyes.

"I'm sorry," Marianne said, choking on her words, then she turned away. She put her hand to her trembling mouth, cleared her throat, then said, "Sorry," once more, hiding her pain behind a sad, grateful smile. "I'd like to thank the Wyburns for letting us rent their reception center in beautiful West Hollywood." She looked offstage to her left, at Chris, her face crossed by a genuine smile of warmth and appreciation as she gave the merest nod to him. "There's a certain someone I'd also like to thank . . ."

Chris smiled at her from the half dark, the shame leaving his face yet lingering in his gut.

". . . He's contributed over a hundred million dollars to the Tray Mansfield Foundation for Young Artists. Chris Flowers."

Chris's name was like lightning to the audience, sparking a thunder of applause. The stage light was waiting for him. He took a deep breath, trying to banish the black stain of guilt on his soul, and walked across the stage, the spotlight melting shadows and making his bright blue suit glimmer. His pain numbed as the spotlight's warmth and brightness embraced him and as the audience's eyes fell on him. Any residual guilt he felt left at that moment, replaced with a relieved smile. He approached Marianne, who was slapping her long fingers together—the same long fingers Tray used to have, fingers designed for guitar genius—clapping like the rest. He gave her a gentle kiss on her tear-streaked cheek, then wrapped his arms around her in a tight hug.

I'm sorry, Marianne, he thought. *I'm so sorry.*

The spotlight and the applause pulling him away, he stepped from Marianne's slender arms, approached the microphone, then took a deep breath. The sound echoed, silencing the brightly lit and cavernous reception room. Two hundred faces stared at him, some of the most famous faces in the music industry.

Chris gave them an appreciative smile. "Thank you. And thank you all for coming."

A respectful silence fell over the glittering crowd of musical artists and their managers, producers and engineers, people from A&R. They stood in their shimmering suits and dresses, raised solemn toasts of champagne in glittering glass flutes.

Chris spotted his wife, Andrea, at the front of the crowd, glowing in the black strapless dress and high heels that so many of the younger women wore, tucking her straight, white-blond hair over her ear. She smiled gently at him, raising her tall glass. Chris smiled back somberly, gave her a quiet wink.

Then he put his lips to the buzzing microphone, every sigh, every click in his throat echoing across the banquet hall—heard by the farthest ears way in back by the tables of food. "It was heartbreaking what happened. He will be forever missed. Tonight, we honor his name. The money donated will go to scholarships to young artists around the world."

Chris's eyes were pulled to a large easel on the stage to his right. A two-by-three-foot canvas sat on the easel. Chris braved a momentary glance at the picture of the eighteen-year-old with the wavy blond hair and shy smile. A long, slender hand squeezed the neck of an acoustic guitar. Round, piercing blue eyes seemed to flash at Chris from across the stage. Chris fidgeted, those eyes somehow glaring accusatory at him.

He faced the crowd again, smiling pitiably. "Tray would be happy knowing this money is helping so many people achieve their dreams."

Applause erupted, drowning out Marianne's cries of woe. Chris turned to her and pursed his lips, feeling another rush of pity at the fresh tears running down her cheeks. He wrapped his arms around her tenderly, holding her, relishing the clapping and whistling from the audience. The guilt was there again, but the applause drowned it out as he averted his gaze from the picture. Arm around her shoulder, Chris walked Marianne to the front of the stage where they basked in the audience's love.

* * *

Chris chatted briefly with Dennis Niles, a rock star who kept tapping his tobacco-leather boot to some imagined beat, while they picked through the food at the buffet tables. Then he turned to Becky Valentine, his eyes drawn to the country/pop star's trademark sparkling earrings. They talked about maybe doing another music video together while they plated up on the barbequed chicken and steaming vegetables.

Chris went from group to group, mingling with music managers and rap stars, record producers and talent scouts who picked at their plates of salad, took careful spoonfuls of French onion soup and chowder, and ate chicken, lamb, and pork kebabs off skewers.

By dessert, conversation had quieted into a gentle cacophony. Chris was picking at a plate of cheesecake and gabbing with rap star Mike McLoughlin when a chattering group shifted in response to some unseen direction, revealing a set of easels holding canvas prints. Candles were massed shrine-like around the easel legs. Marianne had spent hours fussing over the easel positioning, making sure every picture could be clearly seen, that none would be overlooked. She had spent that entire afternoon working with the frenetic energy of a mother who couldn't let the world forget about her son.

Mike McLoughlin's famous voice faded as Chris stared at the prints of Tray Mansfield performing on endless stages throughout the world—starting with his big break performing a stunning, original song on *America's Got Talent* when he was fourteen that left the judges bleating praise. Then, the rising star in London, Barcelona, in his home city of New York, and Japan. In every picture, Tray's passion-filled face shone in the spotlights, and the crowds were caught in an eternal moment of joyous fever with their hands raised to the sky and mouths open to forever praise his name. The last picture showed Tray on a quiet stage, a close up on his face, eyes staring directly into the camera.

Chris's stomach soured as he felt those eyes burning into him, so he excused himself, set his uneaten cheesecake down on one of the buffet tables, and walked away.

Later, Chris found himself in a mindless conversation with one of the A&R managers, the guy blotting some pecan pie from his jowly face and asking about potential projects using the money donated to Chris's foundation. Chris's mind started to wander when the guy asked to be kept in the loop for young talent.

He made his way over to his wife, Andrea, and Marianne Mansfield, and overheard them talking. Marianne was eating homemade ice cream out of a paper bowl and was asking Andrea, "So how's the album coming along?"

Chris wasn't sure if Marianne meant his album or an album Andrea had in the works—Chris had yet to hear whether Andrea was planning a new album. He assumed Marianne was talking about the former.

"It's going good," he said, surprising the both of them by swooping in and interjecting, cutting off Andrea's response even as he wrapped an arm lovingly around her.

"Oh, speak of the devil!" Marianne said. "You announced the name of it pretty recently. What was it?"

"*Forever Sober*," Andrea said, a little too eagerly, Chris thought, like she was trying to beat him to the punch.

He also noticed she seemed stiff under his arm. Was it something he'd said?

Andrea had been acting a bit off lately. But Chris chalked it up to the poor response to her last album. If he were blunt, he'd say, between mixed critical reviews, unenthusiastic word of mouth, and the consequent drop in sales compared to her four previous albums, it was a flop. But he reminded her that, flop or not, the album had still sold millions of copies.

"I'm excited to hear it!" Marianne said. Then her eyes grew sad, wandering over to one of the easels with her son's canvas pictures on it. "I just wish Tray was still here so he could hear your new album, too."

Andrea sipped her champagne and nodded somberly.

Thoughts of Tray were so painful, like barbed wire tightening around Chris's heart, that—while bobbing his head solemnly to Marianne's laments—his thoughts turned to that brand-new album.

This album wasn't like the previous fifteen. This one was special. Very personal. After six years clean of heroin, he had finally felt able to write songs about those dark years of his addiction. The tracks thus recounted a lot of pain and sadness, yet all in all the album ended on a hopeful and positive note—it was called *Forever Sober*, after all—with his recovery and subsequent healing. The album was nearing completion. Not just nearing, he was days from finishing it.

"I heard, I think it was on your Twitter or something, Chris, about all the other artists you said were being featured on the album." Marianne mustered a weak smile to accompany the words. "That's something Tray would've freaked over."

"He would've been the first person I called, Marianne."

She smiled as if her heart had melted, and Chris was glad he could at least say something to make her feel better—even if he couldn't bring her son back from the dead.

Andrea was quiet and continued to sip her champagne, and Marianne, who must've noticed this, suddenly focused her attention on her. Chris gave her a cheery squeeze and she seemed to loosen up, leaning her head tenderly against his chest.

Then Marianne asked, "So what about you two?" She was smiling sweetly at them. "Everyone wants to know if you two will be putting out a record together at some point."

"Nah," Chris said absently. It just came out without him really thinking about it. And he immediately regretted it, feeling Andrea stiffen like a board under his arm.

Marianne gave him a slightly surprised look.

He sucked his teeth, then tried to soften his words. "I mean, not right now. But yes. Someday. Absolutely."

"That's great," Marianne said, appearing satisfied, smiling with anticipation.

Andrea became sullen, chilly. Chris felt like he was holding an ice sculpture.

Marianne turned her head when someone called for her, and she apologized to Chris and Andrea, then excused herself.

Chris and Andrea stood alone together for the moment. He gave a quick glance at the people around him, wondering if they could feel the sudden tension between him and Andrea, but they seemed preoccupied with their desserts and conversation. Still, Chris felt bad, regretful, and smoothed back her hair and tried to give his wife's forehead a loving kiss. She slipped out of his grasp just as his lips brushed her skin, walking pointedly away from him. She was no longer sipping but gulping down her champagne, heading to a drinks table to pour herself another tall glass.

Chris sighed, felt bad for even making such a promise. He understood she was in a fragile headspace after all that stuff with her last album, yet it seemed like there was something. But he wouldn't find out here and now. He didn't want to make some big scene at the banquet, so he decided it best to wait until they got home, where they could talk about it.

As Chris was racking his brain thinking of ways to make his wife feel better—taking her out to eat someplace nice, going to a show, or on a trip—his wandering eyes spotted a strange face near the entrance of the room, someone who appeared to be glaring at him. Chris, peering over famous faces, thought he recognized him. The man had greasy, curly black hair. His weak jaw was smoked with a neatly trimmed beard. He was sneering.

Is that . . . ?

Chris sidled through suit jackets and shimmering dresses, inched carefully past plates of dessert and raised glasses of champagne. He reached the entrance door just as it shut. He slipped outside after the fleeing man, giving the two brawny security guards a hot glance. Instead of doing their job, the two muscle-bound white guys were sipping beer and chatting up a couple of curvy blond pop stars who were pretending to be interested. He would see that they were canned before the end of the night. But right now, he wanted to make sure he'd seen the person he thought he saw. Scanning up and down the busy street, he spotted the fleeing man jogging breezily down the sidewalk. The man stopped suddenly, as if sensing Chris's attention, the setting sun casting bloodred light on his face, a cruel smirk buried in dark beard.

"Rich?" Chris muttered to himself, startled, furious.

Rich turned his back on Chris and continued jogging to wherever he had parked.

*   *   *

Chris checked the rearview mirror several times on his drive back to Beverly Hills. He wasn't worried so much about being tailed, more curious as to why Rich was snooping around the banquet. Was it a threat? Was he trying to intimidate him? Was it a reminder of sorts? A way Rich was saying, Hey, I ain't out of your life yet! Chris had to admit he hadn't thought about Rich in months. Chris tried and struggled that whole drive home to keep Rich out of his mind, for he wasn't worth another moment's thought.

Driving his favorite car, his bright yellow Ferrari, he turned onto Hill Street, his street, minutes from home. The western sky was rosy with sunset. Tall hedges, immaculately cut, lined both sides of the street. Colossal houses loomed against the darkening sky. Driveways and garages were filled with flashy sports cars much like Chris's: Lamborghinis, Ferraris, Mercedes-Maybachs, belonging to the movie stars and pop stars who had earned the fortune needed to live here.

This was home, and Chris loved it. One of his favorite things about this place was its warm summer evenings, and tonight was the kind of night he loved to drink in on a drive home. And yet he couldn't relish tonight's beautiful sunset as his mind returned to the chill between him and his wife. She still hadn't spoken to him. Not a word since the banquet, and it made the air-conditioned car's interior feel even chillier. She sat sullenly, slightly drunk, staring out the window at the gated estates rolling by. Chris tried to break the ice by telling her about seeing Rich at the banquet. She apparently hadn't spotted him, and Chris felt she should know. But she answered in blunt sentences, her voice dull. "Wonder what he was doing there. Shouldn't he be in physical therapy or whatever after all that shit seven, eight months ago?" She didn't sound concerned, or even curious. Just sad. So Chris let it go, and pushed Rich out of his mind. Chris had nothing to worry about from him.

Andrea withdrew into silence again and Chris looked over at her despondently. It was darker out now, the evening sky opaque with the sunset a smoldering fire on the horizon, the oncoming headlights of every passing car revealing her glum features. The corners of her mouth hung down, and her eyes seemed dark with gloom. Chris felt like he needed to do something, needed to comfort her, and so he wrapped his arm around her bare shoulder, pulled her toward him. But she resisted, shrugged his arm away—like she was repulsed by his touch.

"Hey, you okay?"

"Yeah."

"Did I say something?"

She didn't speak for a moment. Finally, she said, "No."

* * *

Chris lived in a two-story mansion atop a hill in the heart of Hill Street. His newly replaced roof rose above his neighbors' A-frames and flattop roofs, like a proud finger pointing into the night sky. He'd bought the place when he was thirty-two years old, loving the spot. The only problem he had was the old mansion itself, originally an estate owned by some famous musician from the 1930s. A movie producer had acquired the estate after that but didn't touch even a blade of grass on the property for years. That all changed when Chris moved in. It started with gutting out all the old, ugly utilities. New marble tile and marble flooring was installed. The heavy Louis XV furniture he tossed out, replacing it with sleek, Scandinavian-style furniture. New oak doors and new windows. A thorough cleaning and then repainting of the neoclassical limestone façade. Chris hired people to do these jobs, and every time he returned home from a tour more work had been done, the home all the better for it. It was his sanctuary, though at the moment it felt more like a chilly mausoleum.

The house felt frosty, like an icy wind had blown down the oval-shaped entry hall and up the curving white marble staircase, sucking out all the home's warmth and security. Chris offered to blend her a fruit smoothie to complement the banquet's heavy dinner, but Andrea just shook her head, changed into her swimwear, and went for a dip in the swimming pool. Chris drank a smoothie alone in the ballroom-sized living room and checked his social media. He talked with his manager, Jeff Bentley, over the phone about the next day's recording session. He took some selfies and posted them online, watching them swell with Hearts and Likes and Comments. It took some of the bite out of the frostiness in the air.

It wasn't until bedtime when Andrea did open up, though it was the merest of cracks.

She was lying in the massive king-sized bed in her black silk pajamas, smelling faintly of chlorine, makeup rinsed off and still-damp hair tucked behind both ears, watching videos on her cell phone. YouTube videos about Chris, the voice of the peppy host growing louder as he moved from the bathroom into the bedroom, flicking off the light, freshened after his shower. The host was talking about the upcoming release of his new album, his first in three years, tracks about his recovery from heroin addiction and on and on.

It wasn't just the fact that she had been watching, almost obsessively, a lot of videos about Chris lately—why, he didn't know—but it was the look he caught on her face as he entered the bedroom, white bath towel wrapped around his waist. Her cell phone light glowed on her bitter, scowling features.

"What's that look for?" he asked gently, concern in his voice.

She kept her eyes glued to the screen. "Nothing," she said, nonchalant, still not revealing to him the thing—whatever the hell it was—that was bothering her.

Chris slipped into some silky pajamas and crawled into bed. He'd finally had enough and asked her straight up, "Why won't you talk to me?"

She rolled her eyes at him, like he should know already. "What, are you kidding?" Her voice was sharp. "What you said."

"About what?"

"About an album. With me. Or even a song with me. That'll never happen, will it?"

"I said I'd do it, didn't I? You're doing backup for *Forever Sober.* And getting credit for it."

Andrea shook her head, sighed sharply, the air growing chillier between them. She picked at that fat, sparkling rock on her wedding ring with nervous, uncertain fingers. "Hm. Well, it's *always* about you anyways." Andrea turned off her cell phone and tossed it on the nightstand with a hard *clunk!*

Chris's face turned ashen, stunned. "What? What're you talking about?" She had never said anything remotely like that to him, and it hurt.

"You know exactly what I'm talking about."

She stretched out, facing away from him, scooted as far to the edge of the bed as she could without falling off. She sighed, a sound filled with despair, sadness, bitter disappointment. They had only been married half a year and yet it felt like their marriage was already some hollow Hollywood sham. What had gone wrong?

Chris tried getting her to talk about it, repeating her name. First with a voice that was soft and gentle, thinking maybe it truly had been a dream of hers for them to do a record together, maybe something she was expecting in the future.

"Andrea."

But as that single word hung in the air without any response from her, his tone grew increasingly annoyed. As he kept thinking about it, he realized that what was really bothering her was in those four short words she'd flung at him earlier. *It's always about you.* Which was untrue.

"Andrea. Andrea."

Still nothing. Then with an exasperated sigh he gave up, flicked off the lamp, then lay there in the dark, brow furrowing as the hurt of her words buzzed like relentless flies in his skull. The chasm in the space between them seemed to grow chillier and chillier with each passing minute. He didn't think he'd even be able to get to sleep with all this drama on his mind, until eventually he started to drift off.

Just as he was on the brink of sleep his eyes fluttered open, his ears catching a suspicious sound. He sat up in bed, checked the time on his cell, and realized only a half hour had passed. Andrea was still turned over on her side, gently snoring now, the sound that had snapped him out of his doze slightly louder than her snoring, coming from outside. He peeled back the curtain from the window on his side of the bed, the window overlooking the moon-washed front lawn and the driveway and the trickling fountain. Chris noticed a car was parked near his driveway gate, its idling engine the noise he'd heard. He couldn't make out what kind of vehicle it was, not from there, could only see the pool of headlights on the road through the bars of the gate. It wasn't a sight or a sound he liked. It was nameless intention out there. He'd had the not so infrequent surprise visits from fanatics, but even they had the courtesy of hanging around the gate only in daylight.

Driven by irritation and curiosity, he found himself creeping barefoot down the marble staircase, hand sliding down the wrought iron banister, and wishing he owned a gun. He grabbed a steak knife from the kitchen, stuck it in his pajama pocket, and it lent him a small courage as he crossed the lawn to the driveway and the front gate. He puffed his shirtless chest out, firing up his confrontational self as he neared the gate and the idling vehicle on the other side of it, the gravel driveway still warm beneath his bare feet. Though the vehicle was buried in the moon shade of one of the hundreds of tall, gnarly oak trees that lined this street, Chris could make out the vaguely boxy shape of it. It looked like a hearse, albeit a taller and wider one. It was idling on the opposite side of the street, the tinted driver's side window facing Chris. Whoever it was inside must have spotted Chris because the vehicle suddenly screeched off down the road.

Chris let out a loud, "Hey!" as if that might make the driver stop and turn around.

He did, however, manage to catch a glimpse of the back of the vehicle, a Chevy Suburban. He didn't catch the license plate number, but there was no need to. He knew, with a sinking feeling in his gut, who drove a black Chevy Suburban. He just stood there for a moment in the warm moonlight, the steak knife useless in his hand. He realized Rich must've followed him home.

CHAPTER TWO
2008

Chris slammed his foot on the gas pedal, and his El Camino growled into the blazing air. He kept muttering, "Momma, Momma," and squeezing the steering wheel. His heartburn hit him then, that burning tightness in his chest, that sour taste in his throat. His heart seemed to beat faster and faster the closer he got to home. His breath came in gasps as the El Camino sped down Campbell Street, the street he grew up on, and pulled up to his old house. It was a small house on a poor street, a house his momma had kept meticulously clean. He'd heard somebody once say that there was no such thing as a nice yard in South Central LA, but that wasn't true. Many of the other houses nearby were surrounded by piles of trash. But at his momma's house, flowers bloomed in flower boxes, windows were washed, the tiny patch of green yard pristine. He banged open the screen door and rushed down the long hall, sweat rolling down his face, and into the tiny, square living room where he found the neighbor, Mrs. Williams, sitting next to Momma. His eyes burned with the threat of tears.

"Hi, Mrs. Williams," he said.

"Hi," she said, her face creased with worry.

Momma had her head in her hands, like she had a migraine. She got bad ones. More and more lately.

Mrs. Williams pulled Chris aside and Chris trembled, anxiety humming in his chest.

Mrs. Williams wrung her dark hands together. She flicked back one of the long dark braids that hung down her back. She cleared her throat, and when she spoke, she lowered her voice, out of Momma's earshot.

"I look out the window, and there's your Ma, in our backyard. She said she was lost."

When Mrs. Williams had called him, she only said that something was wrong with his momma and to get to the house as quick as he could. He glanced over the neighbor's shoulder. Momma was still holding her head in her hands as if it hurt.

"My father-in-law used to get lost in his yard too." Mrs. Williams's voice was gentle, yet ominous and filled with warning. "Had Alzheimer's. Slowly lost all his memories. And by the time he died, he couldn't even remember his children."

Chris squeezed his eyes shut; he wouldn't—couldn't—accept what she was suggesting. "It's not that. She's been really stressed lately."

"I'm just saying—"

"She's only fifty-seven!" he said, a little louder than he meant. Then he took a deep breath, trying to slow his heartbeat.

"I know since you moved out and all that you can't be with her as much, but I can keep an eye on her."

Chris smiled at Mrs. Williams gratefully. "I appreciate that. I don't live more than five miles from here, honest." He had just moved into an apartment with his pregnant wife, Maria. He had been at band practice when he'd received the frantic call on his cell phone, Mrs. Williams having found his phone number pinned with a Costco magnet—where Momma worked—to the fridge.

"You should . . ." Mrs. Williams paused, then leaned and lowered her voice further out of Momma's earshot. "Maybe get it checked out or something."

Chris looked away, considering it, but didn't think his momma would go for that. He chewed his lower lip, trying to convince himself. *No, it ain't that. It ain't that!*

"Money's been a problem for her. She's been really stressed." Chris's words sounded hollow to him, and he realized he'd been trying to convince himself for months now, even as his momma's strange behavior had become more frequent and bizarre, that nothing serious was wrong with her. However, she had never gotten "lost" right beside her own house before. Then Chris said, though he didn't believe it, "I think she'll be fine. Really." He looked at Momma. "I'm gonna stay here the rest of the day and tonight too. Keep an eye on her."

"Okay," said Mrs. Williams.

Then her warm smile faded, and she looked Chris up and down in a way that made him feel uncomfortable, her concern suddenly transferred from Momma to him.

"How are *you* feeling?" she asked.

"I'm fine. I'm good."

Her doubtful face softened with sadness. She looked from Momma to him like she was connecting dots.

"Okay," she said sadly.

Chris tried to smile for her.

She then patted his arm comfortingly. "I'm just next door. If you need anything just give me a holler."

Chris smiled appreciatively. "Thanks, Mrs. Williams."

Chris's broken smile faded completely when she left, the screen door smacking shut. Dread returned to him—a blackness, a dark feeling that seemed to creep into his bones. He stood on the outer edge of the living room for a moment, thinking about what Mrs. Williams had said about her father-in-law. But he couldn't bear to think about that happening to Momma.

He broke into a cool sweat as he crossed the sweltering living room, approaching her. Momma was hunched, her head still hanging in her hands, her fingers rubbing her temples in circular motions like she was trying to alleviate a tension headache—or perhaps trying to quell a terror spreading in her brain.

"Momma?"

She raised an eyebrow, looked at him. "Hey, darling."

"You got a headache, Momma?"

"Yeah, baby, a big ol' one. It's kicking my ass."

Chris went into the kitchen and dug out some migraine pills, then ran a cool glass of water. He sat down next to her and handed her the glass of water and the fat, white Excedrin pills.

"Here, Momma."

She glanced at the offered pills in his cupped palm, then at him, her face crinkling with embarrassment, pride.

"No, baby, I don't need to be taking nothing. I already took some, I think." She scratched the tangle of kinked black hair that raged wild from her head. Silver-gray flecked her hair like shavings of aluminum.

Momma hadn't even combed her hair that morning. She always combed her hair.

"You think?" Chris said, thinking back to what Mrs. Williams was saying about her father-in-law getting lost in the yard. "When did you last take some migraine meds, Momma?"

Her eyes went up in thought. "I took some this morning, I think."

"You *think*. Are you just making stuff up, Momma?" Chris said, concerned, but smiling because she did that. Sometimes she just made up stuff when you offered her anything, her pride overriding her concerns for her own health.

"I don't think. I know."

Chris looked at her skeptically, then said, "Momma, please, for me. Just take them."

She just squeezed her eyes shut for a moment like she was contemplating it. Then, relenting, she took the pills and sipped the water. Chris sighed, feeling small relief. He also thought that maybe Mrs. Williams was right and that maybe he should take Momma to the doctor to see what they had to say. Maybe he could convince her. He sighed, already feeling how hard that battle might be. She was too proud. She would rather wait for something to get really bad, until there was no other choice but the ER.

"Momma, what happened today?"

She'd never done anything like this before. There were other weird things that happened, but he always figured, well, *stress*. She had been under a lot of stress with the money issues. Bills were stacked half a foot high on the coffee table.

"I don't know, honey. I was watering the plants and then . . ." She stopped talking for a moment, and her eyes darted. It was painful watching her, like she was struggling for the right words.

"Momma, Mrs. Williams said you was lost in her backyard."

"Oh, no, I wasn't lost."

"Momma?" Chris said, skeptically, a lump forming in his throat. She wasn't even looking at him, like she was a little girl trying to hide something. He gently grabbed her hand. "Momma, look at me."

She looked at him slowly. Her golden-brown eyes looked spooky somehow in the sunshine that was slanting down from the living room window. The first thing Chris noticed was the fear in her eyes. He then knew she had been thinking the same things Mrs. Williams had put into words, perhaps had even been thinking that she should go to a hospital or something, but had been too stoic—or too afraid—to say anything to anyone, particularly her son.

"Momma, Mrs. Williams was telling me about her father-in-law. And he used to get lost in the yard too."

"Stop it, I wasn't lost," Momma said, shaking her wild, kinked head of hair.

"He had . . ." Chris didn't want to say the words and sucked his lips in even thinking about saying it. "He died from Alzheimer's, Momma."

"It's not that. It's just the stress is all. Just the *stress.*" *Ah,* he thought, *she blames the stress just like me, the both of us liars.*

Chris sighed sadly, frustrated. He wanted to keep believing that. He wanted to keep believing it was because of stress that she lost her car keys, that it was because of stress she was having problems responding to people, that it was because of stress she was withdrawing more and more, that she wasn't getting dressed up in her favorite bright summertime clothes or that she wasn't going out on walks anymore. Looking at her uncombed hair, Chris summoned up a horrifying premonition. That eventually she would stop taking care of herself completely, that the lawn would grow inch by inch, the windows would go unwashed, the bright flowers in pots all over the house she loved so dearly would die simply because she couldn't remember how to take care of those things anymore.

"I know you've had problems with money. I can help, Momma."

"Oh, stop!" she said gently. She squeezed his hands back and then looked at him warmly and smiled. "You have enough to deal with, honey. Living in your own place and having a wife. And you two are gonna be having a baby."

That brought a grin to Chris's face, his soul stirring with equal amounts excitement and worry thinking about that. However, right then, he was more concerned about his momma.

But Momma pinched his chin, reminded him, "You don't need to be worrying about me."

Tears in his eyes, Chris grabbed her dark hands again and gave them a gentle squeeze. "But I do worry about you, Momma."

She smiled at him. Then she reached out and touched his cheek. Then she looked at him the way that Mrs. Williams had before walking out the door.

"Baby, what's wrong with your face?"

Chris shook his head, trying to shake her hand away. "Momma, it's nothing. I'm fine."

"You ain't eating right."

"I'm eating fine, Momma. Don't worry about me."

"I have peanut butter and some blackberry jam. I think we have some blackberry jam left." She stood up, joints crackling. "I'll make you a sandwich."

Chris didn't argue. There was no point. He smiled at her as she walked to the kitchen and pulled out a plate. She pulled down some peanut butter from a cupboard, set it on the counter beside the plate, then opened the fridge. Chris ran his fingers through his shoulder-length blond-dyed dreads, feeling flustered. Momma stared at the fridge for a moment, then pulled out a jar of red jam.

"Sorry, it was strawberry, not blackberry."

Chris looked at her, feeling growing disquiet, and watched as she set the jar of preserves on the kitchen counter. She moved jars around on the sun-touched countertop, the July sun spilling through the kitchen window. She slid the jar of peanut butter from the right side of the plate to the left, then back again. Then she just stared at the jam, like she didn't know what to do with it, like she couldn't remember how to even open the damned thing. She just stared down at it, a butter knife waiting useless in her hand. Chris stood up, muscles tightening with alarm, his deepening worry drawing him toward her.

"Momma?"

She didn't say anything, like she couldn't hear him—or was too embarrassed to even answer him. Too embarrassed because she couldn't remember how to open the jam jar.

"Momma?" Chris said a little louder.

She snapped out of it, turned, and looked at him, her eyes looking strange and glassy. Then they cleared up, like storm clouds suddenly vanishing.

"It's okay. I ain't hungry," Chris said. Then he sighed. He couldn't stand it any longer. All he could think about was putting his momma in his car right then and there and taking her to the nearest hospital. He didn't care about costs or anything like that, he would find a way to pay for it. He looked away, trying to fill himself with courage. Finally, he looked at her and said, "Momma, Mrs. Williams said maybe I should take you in."

"Take me where?" she asked, her voice defensive.

She suddenly remembered and opened the strawberry jam jar defiantly and began slabbing on thick layers of jam and peanut butter, mixing the butter knife into both the peanut butter and strawberry jam jars. As a kid Chris hated when she did that, but it didn't seem so important right then.

"To the hospital."

"I ain't going to no hospital!"

"Momma, just listen?" Chris said, trying to keep his voice from shaking. "They will do some tests on your brain. Some scans and stuff. Just to make sure."

"Make sure what?" she said, voice getting hotter, hands shaking with growing irritation.

"That it's nothing, you know, serious."

"It's stress," she growled, tossing the peanut-sticky butter knife, sending it bouncing across the countertop, trailing peanut butter.

She looked at Chris, her eyes wide with terror. He knew for certain then how afraid she truly was, so afraid of going to the hospital because they might actually find something.

"It's just to make sure," Chris shouted, not meaning to.

Her nose wrinkled, her brow sharpened, and she sucked in her lips. She looked away from him, as if trying to hide her shame and terror. She wiped her mouth with a trembling hand.

Chris felt tears bubbling up, feeling like he was being torn apart from the inside.

He wanted to drop down onto one knee as he said, "Please, Momma. Please." Then he waited for her to say something.

WEDNESDAY, JULY 16, 2023
CHAPTER THREE

Chris hadn't forgotten about what Andrea had said the night before, and thinking about it in the coffee shop drive-through soured his mood a little. Yet he swallowed his pride and bought them both coffees and breakfast muffins that morning at their favorite coffee place. He also bought an extra coffee and some egg-and-cheese sandwiches for Bob and started cruising toward the park to fulfill yet another weekly ritual.

The guy went simply by Bob, and Bob was currently living in the park by the Catholic church. Chris pulled up to the curb where Bob was sitting on the park bench in the rising sunlight reading the morning paper. Bob was in his late fifties, balding, in tattered clothes, and had a small train of suitcases that held his entire life. Bob's face brightened seeing Chris's Ferrari, and he thanked Chris as he accepted the coffee—black with three sugars—and the sandwiches in their greasy wax paper. Bob used to live in Hollywood, strung out on dope and alcohol, said he was a failed musician. He had a battered Epiphone acoustic guitar amongst his suitcases. Sometimes Chris would sit with Bob and strum on that old Epiphone. He found playing guitar was like riding a bicycle, something you never quite forget. But he didn't play guitar so much anymore, the music he wrote now being mostly electronic.

Chris knew all of the very small homeless population in Beverly Hills. Several times a week he would bring a different one boxes of secondhand designer clothes, food, sometimes cash. Homelessness wasn't as bad in Beverly Hills as it was in the rest of Los Angeles County, but he did what he could for the homeless here who could stand being amongst the uber-wealthy. Part of Chris believed that was why the homeless population was so small here, because the homeless were too embarrassed being amongst extremely rich and successful people.

As Chris was chitchatting with Bob, he noticed in his peripheral an Escalade creep out of the woodwork and park on the curb down the street a ways. Then the front door clicked open to reveal a man peering down the massive eye of his camera, snapping off shots of Chris's philanthropic deed. It seemed so many of the paparazzi drove in style, this guy on his morning rounds probably making thousands just for the pictures he was taking now. Chris wasn't a stranger to the paparazzi, and he even recognized this guy. But Chris did as he always did, pretended the guy with his camera wasn't there.

Rich wouldn't take pictures like that. Rich hated famous and successful people, and would only take pictures to ruin you, to hurt.

Chris told Bob he had to go, that he was heading to his studio to record, and he pulled off the curb and back onto the street.

The whole time Chris was chatting with Bob, he was thinking about what Andrea had said the night before.

It's always about you.

She seemed reluctant to be cooped up with him on the drive down Sunset Boulevard, as if she wished she would've taken her Porsche that morning, but Chris was glad she'd been there to see that—to witness his act, a complete contradiction to her accusations. He cruised down the vibrant Sunset Strip, the Hollywood sign looming hopefully in the distance like a beacon for dreamers. As they passed endless bars and theaters and comedy clubs and recording studios on both sides of the street, he found himself running his tongue over his teeth, refortified, a point proven.

But his self-assurance didn't last long.

About ten minutes from his studio, which was right off of Sunset Boulevard in Hollywood Heights, he received a phone call.

It wasn't from anyone in his contacts, but as he cruised the palm tree-lined street, he wrinkled his brow, glancing from street to phone, street to phone, vaguely recognizing the number, although he couldn't remember from where.

"Chris Flowers," he said, answering the phone coolly.

There was silence at first. Then a voice came on, and it said, "You piece of shit."

The voice had the abnormal deepness of someone using a voice changer.

Chris was momentarily chilled by the malicious sound of the voice, but that quickly changed into outrage. "Excuse me? Who's this?"

Out of his periphery he felt Andrea glancing from her cell to him, mild concern disturbing her cool affect.

"Don't worry about that," the voice said. There was a patience and a dark confidence to the voice that Chris didn't like. It was like the voice was in control, not Chris. "I know what you did," the voice said. "Five years ago."

That was when Chris truly felt out of control, for the first time since his addiction years. He was lost for words. An icy chill ran down his back. This voice—whoever it was—was claiming to know things no one should know.

"Who are you?" Chris asked yet again, trying to keep his cool.

The voice said, "You will confess, Chris. I promise you I'll make you confess to what you did—"

"I don't know what you're talking about. Bye."

Then Chris immediately hung up, cutting that demonic-sounding voice off. Then, to Chris's horror, his phone started ringing again. Same number. He promptly refused it, then blocked the number. He felt immensely better then, but his sweaty hands trembled around the steering wheel.

"What is it?" Even Andrea seemed to have, for the moment, stopped taking her frustrations out on Chris, narrowing her eyes at him, concerned seeing Chris spooked.

But Chris covered it up as quick as he could, tightening his grip on the steering wheel, relaxing his twitching face muscles, taking slow, quiet, deep breaths through his nose. He refused to address the voice and what the voice had implied. He wasn't going to bring it up, not now and not to her.

So he shrugged it off and said, "Some fanatic. Got a hold of my number somehow. Blocked him. Won't have to worry about that no more."

The last part was true, he hoped. God, he hoped.

* * *

When the Ferrari pulled up to Studio One, Andrea immediately stepped out, face deep in her cell phone, leaving Chris alone in the car as she walked through the sun-drenched studio entrance. Chris turned off the ignition and realized his fingers were sweaty, and his jersey was starting to soak through. He tugged on it to air it out, trying to push that phone call out of his mind. But when he stepped out into the fiery breeze, he was nervous and alert, puffing out his chest, eyes darting this way and that behind his aviator sunglasses. It was then his flitting eyes spotted the black Suburban, and he finally knew who made the call.

The Suburban was black as death idling on the curb on the opposite side of Sunset, traffic flashing by. Its windows were tinted, the vehicle's occupant hidden. It sat there for a moment like a dark reminder, then sped off and disappeared into traffic.

CHAPTER FOUR

Chris had used backing vocals in many songs before. He firmly believed they were an essential part of crafting the perfect pop song. But he had never recorded with Andrea before—at least not before they were married. He told her on their blissful honeymoon six months back that he wanted her on the album. He had been drinking club soda, she had been drinking red wine, and she spilled her wine all over the bed, she was so excited. She had been in the studio a dozen or so times since then, adding harmonies, a few call-and-response, doubling—fattening the melody line with her sweet voice, making those choruses sound full and powerful. It seemed to be coming easy for her so far, her being a singer and an artist in her own right after all.

But on that day at the studio, Chris couldn't help but notice the way she clenched the typed-up page of lyrics, the way the corners of her mouth and eyes twitched, the tenseness in her voice as she laid down tracks in the recording booth. Chris, for the past three years, had spent endless hours in that same booth, baring his soul. Andrea was usually on point, only needing three or four takes to get the perfect track, and her mood was generally carefree. But there was something prickly in her aura that day, and she was now needing to do six, seven, eight takes—and still not getting it. She would sip her honey-and-lemon water, trying to open her throat, all the while with that troubled look on her face. Ever since the night before.

She started recording compilations too. While Chris didn't know what her process was on her solo albums, here she'd never needed to make comps. Comps were like a Frankenstein's monster of multiple takes. Chris once spent a month on one track desperately trying to piece it together one word at a time. Even with his engineers, Monte and Frankel, trying their best to work their magic, it ended up being a wasted month with Chris scrapping all those chopped-up takes and starting over. That was one of the reasons the album had been taking so long on Chris's part. Chris would sometimes work all day, or week even, on a lead vocal track only to scrap it later on. So yes, Chris was guilty of making compilations too. But still, being so close to finishing, he couldn't help but feel his blood run hot, sweat breaking out on his forehead, watching Andrea framed in the recording booth windowpanes and surrounded by mics and Monte and Frankel at the mixing board trying to do a patchwork job of her blundering vocals.

Talking to her through a microphoned headset, his own voice swimming in his head, Chris tried to guide her, politely asking her to rerecord this line or that line. She was getting frustrated, too, though Chris knew, thinking back to what she'd said—*it's always about you*—it had nothing to do with not performing well. She would tell Monte and Frankel to stop the track, then she would take some deep breaths behind shut eyes, looking lost somehow, like something was bothering her and wouldn't let go. Then she'd nod at them and would try again, only to repeat the process.

When Chris couldn't handle it anymore, he told her to take a break and swapped places with her. From the recording booth windows, he could see Andrea on her phone and the eager faces of Monte and Frankel, and his manager, Jeff Bentley. Chris only had a few tracks to finish and was confident—perhaps overly so—that he could bust out his very best work in a few attempts. He'd gone in with this intent before, trying to get his best work done in the first few takes, only to go downhill from there, unending hours pulling him down, his face sagging with exhaustion.

But on that day there were other reasons he kept losing the vibe.

Hearing his voice crack during a take, he told Monte and Frankel to stop the track and go back so he could do a retake. He tried again. And again. He was trying to refrain from using comps. He was one of the biggest and brightest pop stars in the world, goddamnit, and he should just be able to get it in one take. He messed up, again and again, until sweat soaked his armpits, plunking off him and into the studio carpet. A tenth take, eleventh, twelfth, and he was still trying to nail this one vocal track. He messed up yet again, and in a flash of anger he struck out at nearby microphones. Andrea glanced up from her phone, Jeff uncrossed his arms, and Monte and Frankel just glanced at each other. Then someone asked if he needed a break.

Chris took a break, and Andrea went back in the booth. He had on headphones, trying to listen, trying to stay present, but he realized he couldn't stop thinking about that black Suburban. It was like a distant storm looming at the edge of his mind and slowly moving in, closer, closer. And he kept trying to blink the thoughts away, trying to remain focused on the task at hand, trying to keep his ears perked as he listened to Andrea doing a take—waiting for little slips so that he'd inevitably have to ask her to do a retake.

Then his manager's shadow fell over him like a warm, dark blanket.

Jeff was eyeballing Andrea dubiously, as if trying to figure out what was wrong with her. He'd always said Chris didn't need her. That it was superfluous having her on the album with all the other celebrities featured. Jeff also said she wasn't a hundred percent sober like all the other featured artists, that she did, even if only occasionally, drink, and wouldn't that somehow steal thunder from the album's theme, given its title? But Chris wanted her on the album. He had promised her, and she had been so excited to be a part of it.

Jeff glanced from Andrea to Chris, the look on his face going from dubious to concerned. Seeing Chris frustrated in the studio while working was nothing new to Jeff, though Jeff seemed to realize something else was going on.

The polished oak-paneled walls were decorated with silver, gold, and platinum records, all Chris's, and he tried to soothe himself with their presence, but still his hands fidgeted, his legs trembled, and sweat rolled down his shaved head.

Then he felt a tap on his shoulder and saw it was Jeff trying to get his attention, Jeff's cool blue eyes narrowed with worry. Chris peeled off the headset.

"What's up, man?" Jeff asked.

"Hm?"

"You seem distracted."

Chris realized that although he didn't even want to talk about it, he desperately needed to tell somebody. Who better than Jeff? Jeff had been Chris's manager for nearly fifteen years, had seen Chris through his darkest days of addiction. Jeff was also one of the only other people who knew about what happened with Tray Mansfield five years ago.

Chris sighed, then opened up. First, he told Jeff about seeing Rich at the banquet the night before. Jeff nodded, patient as always, sometimes scratching his cropped gray hair, occasionally puffing his vape pen, the replacement for a three-pack-a-day habit. If not for the face-lift, Jeff would probably look a decade older than his sixty-two years.

Chris could see once again that Chevy, black as cancer, idling behind his gate and the headlights like phantasms moving through the trees as it sped away.

"He followed me home, man. He knows where I live."

But Jeff didn't seem particularly worried about that, just pursed his lips, shrugged. "He knows where lots of celebrities live. It's part of his job. Besides, you got cameras."

Both points were true. Chris had taken a lot of comfort in his cameras the night before. He had cameras hanging from every corner of the mansion. But when Chris thought about that phone call, he now wished Rich had tried something last night, had tried attacking him—*round two!*—or had tried getting close to Andrea. Though things seemed tense between him and Andrea now, Chris still wouldn't let Rich get anywhere near her.

"Little shit's out of the hospital."

"Yeah," Chris agreed.

"He's got nothing on you. The great immortal Chris Flowers."

Chris tried to take comfort in that, but he still hadn't told Jeff the worst part. It was making his stomach hurt just thinking about it. And as he told Jeff, he lowered his voice conspiratorially. Monte and Frankel had headphones on and were bobbing their heads to one of Andrea's takes, which Chris could hear faintly coming out of his own headphones wrapped around his neck.

"Actually he does have something on me."

Jeff wrinkled his brow, looked at Chris curiously.

Chris suddenly felt sick to his stomach, wondering, *How? How could this be?*

"He knows about, you know, that business five years ago."

Jeff looked nervous now, shooting quick glances toward Monte and Frankel. "What're you talking about?" He lowered his voice now too.

"He called me just before I got here."

"Called you? How'd he get your number?"

"I don't know, man. I've been asking myself that." Chris realized he hadn't even touched his phone once since arriving. It was still in his pocket, like it was possessed.

Chris could almost hear that devil-like voice in his head.

"He was using this voice changer or something. Trying to hide his voice."

"Why?"

Chris just shook his head, had no clue. He wondered if Rich had seen the cop car cruise up to Chris's gate the night before. Chris had called the cops right after the Chevy had sped off. He knew Rich's reputation, and he felt better when the officer arrived and offered to cruise the nearby roads throughout his shift that night to give Chris peace of mind. Chris had slept a little sounder knowing that cop was out there. The cops all loved Chris, and they—especially Detective Sergeant David Bradford at the Beverly Hills Murphy Street precinct—were all also well aware of Rich Howard. Chris promised himself after the recording session he'd call about hiring a crew of bodyguards to keep a constant watch over the mansion. He felt he couldn't be too careful with what was going on.

And that was when that ugly, horrible voice came back, carrying with it the darkness of the past, and suddenly Chris wished he would've broken the man's neck instead of his wrist back in November of 2018.

"He told me to confess."

Jeff's eyes lit up. "You serious? Or what?"

Chris tried to swallow but his mouth was dry, his tongue like sandpaper. "I don't know, man. I hung up on him."

"Good," Jeff said, looking a little relieved. He then narrowed his eyes, frustrated. "How could he have found out?"

"I don't know."

"Is this his way of getting back at you? Has to be. Listen, we don't need distractions. Not when we're so close to being done with the album and with the world tour coming up. Ignore him."

But how was Chris supposed to ignore something like that? How was he supposed to sleep, even with bodyguards, with that voice haunting his dreams?

Jeff must've caught the fear on Chris's face, because he leaned in closer and said with reassurance, "Look, man. I don't know how or why he knows what he knows, but if he had proof then wouldn't the world know by now? He's nothing. And you're Chris-motherfucking-Flowers."

These small words of comfort began to swell as the hours passed. Chris kept hearing those few sentences in his head—especially the last—and he realized maybe Jeff was right. Jeff had to be right.

By the end of the recording session, Chris found himself smiling even, regaining a little confidence, an enthusiasm that Rich's unctuous voice had ruthlessly stolen from him. He was able to push that voice back into the shadows, where it largely remained for a while, though still with the occasional rustle like rats in the walls.

CHAPTER FIVE
2008

Chris put a hand over his kneecap and pressed to stop his leg from jumping. His momma fidgeted in the chair next to him, stress lines around her eyes. She heaved a deep sigh. The exam room felt too small to Chris, crushingly small. His eyes flitted from wall to wall, each plastered with brain scan images, some of the images in gray and others in color. His nose wrinkled at the smell of disinfectant in the air. He could taste its sickly sweetness on the back of his throat, and it made him want to puke even more. His darting eyes caught Momma's hand trembling on the chair's armrest. She was squeezing it as if for dear life. Chris grabbed her hand, rubbed the back. He looked at her nervous, twitching face, and when her eyes caught his she tried to smile, though the smile seemed off and broken. He smiled warmly for her.

The door opened, and Chris's heart jumped. The doctor entered, her gray hair neatly tied up in the back. Her lab coat whispered in the cool air, and her sweet perfume mixed with the disinfectant cloyingly. She tapped her fingers on a yellow folder she was holding. Chris couldn't read her face, but Dr. Roth wasn't smiling.

"So, we got the results of the MRI back," she said.

Chris couldn't read the tone of the doctor's voice—or maybe it was a glum tone and Chris just didn't want to hear it?

"What's it say, Doc?" he asked.

Momma tensed up. Chris could feel it as he held her hand, her hand locking up like death.

The doctor said something, but Chris didn't hear it, or maybe he didn't want to hear it.

"Mr. Flowers?"

"Hm?"

"Did you hear what I said?"

Momma's hand was limp. He looked at her, her face pale and drained of color. She looked frozen, her eyes wide, her flesh clammy. Chris felt heat flush his face, an inner darkness swallowing him.

"What's that?" he said.

"Early-onset Alzheimer's," Dr. Roth repeated sadly. She cleared her throat, opened the yellow folder, and pulled out brain scans.

Chris couldn't say anything at first. It was like his tongue was pinned to the roof of his mouth. He felt his skin going from hot to cold, fire to ice.

"I'm sorry to have to tell you this," Dr. Roth said, sounding genuinely saddened, but also stoic. It was clear to Chris she'd done this before and often.

"You're sorry?" he said, not understanding. It was like the doctor had just handed them a death sentence. "Fix it," Chris said, still not understanding, not even wanting to understand. "You're a doctor. Fix it!"

Dr. Roth chewed her lips, her eyes shining with sadness. "It's not that simple." She showed Chris the MRI scans. There were three of them. She raised one at a time saying, "This one's a healthy brain, this one's your mother's, and this one is someone with severe Alzheimer's."

Chris looked at the brain scans. They looked like thermal images, in different colors of hot and cold. He looked at the severe one and saw a big black mass that looked like it was eating away at the brain, swallowing it, devouring it. He looked at Momma's and saw that there was a darkness there but not as bad as the severe one, and the healthy one only had a tiny bit of black.

"What's wrong with my momma's brain?" Chris asked, pointing at Momma's brain scan.

Dr. Roth swallowed, pointed at the scans as she spoke. "Her brain scan shows mild cognitive impairment."

"Mild?" Chris said hopefully.

But the hope seemed lost on the doctor.

Chris squeezed his momma's hand as if the contact might pass that bit of hope to her, but her hand was cold.

Dr. Roth looked at Momma, continuing, "What's happening to your brain, Mrs. Flowers—"

"Miss," Momma corrected. The first thing she had said in a bit, and it felt good to Chris that she said something, saying Miss as if it were a badge of pride.

"Miss. Sorry. There's some cortical shrinkage, enlarged ventricles, shrinking hippocampus . . ."

Chris furrowed his brow, eyes darting at the strange phrases. "Sorry. I dropped out of high school and haven't bothered to do much brain studies lately." His voice was dripping sarcasm, though he hadn't meant it to come out like that. It was his pounding heart and his frantic brain that were making him say things differently.

Dr. Roth said something about amyloid plaques.

"What?" Chris said.

"Protein fragments that the body produces normally. In Alzheimer's, these fragments accumulate between nerve cells to form hard, insoluble plaques that keep nerve impulses from transmitting normally. That affects thinking and behavior."

Chris still didn't know what the hell she was talking about. He just felt his heartbeat starting to pick up, getting faster and faster.

"Early-onset Alzheimer's is most likely inherited. Did either of your parents have Alzheimer's, Miss Flowers?"

"No," Chris said, even though he didn't know. He didn't even want to know. He hadn't known his grandparents much, only in fragments of childhood memory.

"Yes," said Momma. "My daddy."

Chris looked at her, outraged, but not because he hadn't known that about his grandfather. He was just outraged at this whole situation. He swallowed a lump in his throat, trying to accept all of this. But it felt like the room was spinning, the way he felt after a bad drunk or too much dope, like he was on a boat on rough waters.

"Okay," Dr. Roth said, nodding.

"Solutions, Doc! What can we do?"

Dr. Roth sighed sadly. Chris hated the sound of it. He squeezed his momma's hand, hope wilting inside him.

"There's medicine we can give you, Miss Flowers. It's regular medicine we give to Alzheimer's patients in all progressions of the disease. Also you should be getting exercise and doing things that will help sharpen your mind, like word games, puzzles."

Dr. Roth's words trailed off. She continued to talk, but Chris had stopped listening. He heard only his own breathing. A cold drop of sweat rolled down his face. He was staring at the doctor's saddened face, the mole on her chin, her regretful blue eyes.

Words jumped out of Chris's mouth, cutting off whatever the doctor was saying. "How long? Before you . . ." *Die,* he was trying to say, but couldn't.

Momma wasn't even reacting, just staring into space.

"After diagnosis," Dr. Roth said, pausing, pursing her lips. She shook her head. "It varies, and I just can't say precisely. Some a few years. Some over twenty years."

Chris felt insulted by the ambiguity of the doctor's answer, and rage blossomed in his chest. "This is bullshit, Doc! She's only in her fifties!"

Dr. Roth nodded sadly. "It is uncommon. Mostly Alzheimer's is diagnosed after sixty or sixty-five."

The doctor was talking again, but it sounded like she was underwater, or very far away. She was saying something about caregiving and retirement homes and nursing homes. Then Chris heard his momma nearly shout, "I ain't staying in no resting home!"

Chris, numb after so much emotion, left the exam room still holding Momma's clammy hand. The hospital's glass entrance doors slid open and sad-faced people poured in and out. Chris wasn't ten feet away from the hospital, outside, when his heart skipped a beat. Reality was being swallowed by a darkness that started at the edges of his vision until he heard Momma's voice trying to break through the swirling blackness, telling him to "Sit down! Sit down!" He felt a warm curb under his ass and stared helplessly at the sun setting behind the shoulders of an apartment complex. He felt chilled even in the summer dusk. He sucked in his lips, eyes watering.

"Momma." He looked at her. She was sitting beside him, the hospital doors opening and closing behind her, someone being rolled out in a wheelchair. His momma was trying to remain as dignified as she could, her lips a tight line, her chin up. Chris wondered if she was trying to be brave for him.

He didn't know all that the doctor was talking about, about plaques and stuff, but he did know what was going to happen. He looked at her, and he knew that it was going to get worse, that there was no cure. Her brain would eventually look like the scan that Dr. Roth showed, the severe Alzheimer's brain, the one with the all-devouring blackness. He looked into her eyes and tried to imagine what that would be like. He tried to imagine what suffering she would go through. He tried to imagine what it would feel like to wake up and not be able to remember your own son. Tears overflowed, and he started to weep. He was overwhelmed with sorrow for her.

But Momma just sighed, as if trying to keep her strength for the both of them.

"I'm so sorry, Momma."

"It's okay, honey."

"I'm so sorry this is happening to you, Momma!" Panic shattered him, and he sat there broken and weeping tears in the dusk light, sanity leaving him. "Was it me?"

"No, no."

"Was it something I did?"

"No, it was nothing you did, baby."

She squeezed his hand, and they sat there like that for a while.

CHAPTER SIX
JULY 2023

The one thing that bothered Chris, that threatened to spoil his renewed confidence, was a small shift in Andrea's behavior. Her chilliness was one thing, as was her frustration as she blundered through her takes. But then she started making suggestions for changes, which was not her place as a backup singer. She had always been sunny and eager to help contribute to Chris's dream project, but now it was like she was trying to take control of it. She would suggest a third harmony here, or a double up there. A couple of times she would experiment on her own without even saying anything, and Chris, who had to wonder if she wasn't doing this on purpose, had to rein her in. "No, let's just stick to what it was," he would tell her, or, "No, 'Drea, we're leaving it the way it is."

Jeff, to Chris's surprise, started getting outright impatient with her, crossing his arms, frowning, pacing, sucking on his vape pen, whispering ever-more-unpleasant observations into Chris's ear. "The dumb bitch hasn't earned the right to make suggestions on an album she barely has a part in." While Chris agreed with his manager and was just as anxious as Jeff to get the album finished, he also wondered if what he had said about Rich earlier had gotten under the guy's skin.

Toward the end of the day's session, as she was recommending yet another harmony, Chris's patience reached its end. "'Drea, either we do it my way or not at all." He was trying to sound calm and steady but could hear the frustration in his growling voice.

Andrea took a sip from her tin flask of honey-infused water, then said, "Well, whatever, I guess I'm just the third wheel anyways." Chris knew this cut was meant for him, probably regarding the night before and whatever it was that was eating her. For the rest of the session she turned into a sulking, gloomy creature.

They finished up early that afternoon, Chris having a meeting with Marianne Mansfield at two. Everyone agreed to meet the next day to bust out the last of the album. Chris was surprised when Andrea called a limo to take her home, another new behavior for her. Chris gently offered to take her back, a part of him feeling bad for getting impatient with her in the studio, another part of him feeling like she was this ticking time bomb that he needed to defuse. Marianne also only lived about ten minutes from Chris; he could easily take Andrea home first then drive to Trousdale where Marianne lived. While Andrea kindly refused his offer, it was clear in her face as she climbed into the limo that she was relieved not to be riding home with him.

On his way to Marianne's, driving past the fancy white modern mansions with smiling families cooling off in lake-sized swimming pools, the savage sun flashing behind the gum and mesquite and cypress trees, Chris tried to push thoughts of Andrea from his mind. But their honeymoon kept coming back to him. It had been his idea to go to London, but he wasn't thinking about their trip to Buckingham Palace or the British Museum. No, he was thinking about their suite at the Lanesborough. It was in the evening, and he and Andrea were sitting on the bed talking the dreamy talk of newlyweds, and she was sipping red wine. That night he'd told her he was going to dedicate the album to her and that he wanted her to sing on it, too. That's when she spilled her wine on the golden sheets and they had laughed.

He couldn't help but feel he had hurt her. Somehow.

But he wouldn't think of that. He pushed those thoughts out of his mind as he did those of Rich—though he would occasionally check his mirror as he cruised down Loma Vista Drive.

He tried to think about the next couple days. Tomorrow, for instance, the last recording session for the album.

The last session.

He could hardly believe it. He could feel the excitement in his bones. It seemed crazy that he'd spent three years, *three years* of his life, on eighteen tracks. Eighteen tracks of pure gold though. The kind of stuff that would make other artists clench their fists with envy. The kind of stuff that would live forever.

He tried to think about that. And he tried to think about tomorrow morning's press conference where he would finally reveal to the world the album's release date.

And he tried thinking about the big show on Friday night.

Yet, even as he was buzzing about all he had to look forward to, his heart skipped like a broken vinyl record when he arrived at Marianne's at the end of the cul-de-sac. It didn't have anything to do with Andrea or Rich—though those situations certainly weren't going away anytime soon. He used to come to Marianne's home much more often when Tray was alive, but the sight of it now, the afternoon sun licking the glass walls and glazing the electric-blue waters of the oversized pool and the patio with the barbeque, brought with it the burden of painful memories. Memories of the home filled with the sounds of that young prodigy playing guitar in his bedroom, writing music, his whole life ahead of him.

When Chris entered, he heard someone playing guitar in a bedroom and had to shake off an eerie familiar feeling. Marianne had remarried several years ago, her husband a guitarist in a famous rock band. The guy was very good, but no genius, no Tray, that was for sure.

While Chris and Marianne plopped down in the living room to discuss their annual Tray Mansfield Tribute, that electric guitar continued its muted wail and was occasionally married with the crooked singing coming from Marianne's husband.

Marianne had made Chris a cup of coffee while she sipped at a glass of red wine.

Pictures of Tray were everywhere in the living room, hanging from the walls and on nightstands and on the coffee table. It was like an eternal wake. There was also a framed master's degree in music that Tray had received at seventeen, and a framed MacArthur Foundation so-called Genius Grant by the mantelpiece. A colossal portrait of him hung above the fireplace, grinning down at Chris, soulful blue eyes and wavy blond hair. Chris felt like the walls were watching him. He tried to shake off his discomfort and sipped his coffee.

Suddenly, in the middle of discussing the date of the second annual Tray Mansfield Tribute, Marianne blurted, "He got out."

"What?"

Her eyes flicked up, filled with a growing anger. "Andre Childs, the bastard who killed my son. He's out of prison. Got out yesterday. I saw it on the news." Then she said through gritted teeth, "Five years wasn't long enough for him."

Chris felt like he was itching all over, his skin on fire. He bit his lips, wrangling with the dark feelings he felt inside. "Marianne," he said, putting a comforting hand on her shoulder. "The lawyers fought for more. That man. It wasn't him who killed your son. You know that."

She looked away and said glumly, "He might as well have."

He patted her knee tenderly. "The tribute, Marianne."

Marianne, like she didn't hear him, pulled a yellow pill bottle out of her jean pocket and popped a handful, apparently not caring whether Chris witnessed or not. Chris didn't know what she'd taken, but the way she tightened her mouth around the pills, the way she squeezed her eyes shut, he knew she had to be waiting for the dreamy effects of a couple of Xanax or an Ativan or some other antianxiety medication. She washed the pills down with her wine, licking red from her upper lip.

"Marianne," Chris said, feeling worried.

"It's nothing, just some antianxiety stuff. It's been helping me."

"A whole handful? And with wine?"

"A couple. It's fine," she said. She shook her head, looked at that massive portrait of Tray hanging over the mantel of the fireplace. Her eyes grew distant, like she was looking at some faraway island. "Why, Chris?"

Chris shook his head, wanting to change the subject, trying to get away from this. "Marianne, I don't know why—"

"He cared about people. He loved so much. And people loved him. All he wanted was to make people happy with his music. And he was so brilliant."

"I know he was."

"A prodigy. Taking college-level classes when he should've been in middle school." She shook her head. "I just can't get over it."

"You never really do,"

His face prickled, his cheeks flushing red, and guilt and sadness weighed him down until he wanted to just lie face down on the floor and never get up, never have to look at Tray's mother, this poor pain-wracked creature, and to never have to look at the portraits of her dead child ever again.

He managed a weak smile. "So, I was thinking we could have the tribute around the holidays—"

"I hate him."

Chris knew she meant Andre Childs. Images of the man flashed through Chris's mind from that day five years ago: the door opening and the fifth of whiskey clinking onto the still-warm tarmac, Andre's ticket sucked out of that dented Nissan and fluttering in the evening breeze, his big gold teeth, bloodshot eyes, muttering how sorry he was, oh dear Christ, how sorry he was.

"How about late December?" Chris said.

Marianne looked at him, and a sudden warm smile spread across her face. "You really were his biggest idol. Bigger than Lennon." It looked like the pills were taking hold of her, her eyes getting slow and oily, a dreaminess relaxing her face—darkness calming inside her, at least for a brief time. Her husband all the while kept playing and singing his tormented melodies in the other room.

"So around December, Marianne? The holidays?"

He finished their meeting early after they decided on having the Tray Mansfield Tribute Concert in December, during the holidays.

He sighed deeply as he walked out the front door and crossed the emerald front lawn heading to his screaming-yellow Ferrari in the driveway, parked behind the shiny black Beamer and the silver Audi.

Approaching his car, he spotted something on his windshield. He thought it was bird shit at first. But on closer inspection he saw that his left wiper was hugging a tightly wrapped baggie of white powder against the windshield. Chris's heart almost stopped. He frowned at the baggie, threw a hot glance up and down the street again.

He followed me, he thought, his face burning beet red, furious. *He followed me and he put this here!*

Chris wanted to snatch it, get it off his car before anyone could see it, but decided to call it in instead.

A skinny young officer arrived, asked a few questions, then donned rubber gloves and put the baggie of powder into a larger Ziploc evidence bag. Chris figured it to be cocaine, unless it was white powder heroin. Both Marianne and her husband came out to see what was going on. Marianne was blinking dreamily, and her husband, finally released from the call of creativity, peered with concern through a curtain of pristine long black hair that gleamed in the sunlight. Chris reassured them it was nothing, just someone harassing him. They gave him a few gentle affirmations before disappearing back inside.

"Can't you do anything about this, Officer?" Chris checked the officer's name tag. "Officer Vincent? Is there anything at all you can do?" Chris's voice was tinged with desperation.

Officer Vincent's bald head gleamed in the sunglow. Chris noticed scabs dotting the man's bald head and face, like he'd been picking at himself a lot lately.

"We'll do what we can, sir." Officer Vincent clawed at a gnarly-looking scab under his left eye—hidden by a thick pair of sunshades. He wrinkled his nose a lot, and Chris noticed his nostrils were crusted with dried blood.

Then the officer pulled off his sunglasses, bloodshot blue eyes glinting with recognition.

"Yeah?" Chris said.

"I know you. You're that famous singer."

Chris nodded.

"Cool," Vincent said with a grin, then put his shades back on.

Chris couldn't help but look again at the blood crusting the officer's nostrils—little red flecks of it.

In a moment of inspiration, Chris started to say, "Do you think you could . . ."

Officer Vincent picked at that red sore beneath his left eye. "Hm? What?" He sounded worried.

Tail me, Chris wanted to say, *and catch that bastard Rich red-handed.*

He'd had a text from Jeff as his meeting with Marianne ended, informing him that a security service, at no little cost, would soon have three bodyguards on rotation, swapping shifts, in front of his mansion day and night. The bodyguards would remain there for the foreseeable future, at least until this bullshit with Rich was figured out. Chris even thought about hiring some extra bodyguards to tail him, and while they would've prevented this little number—planting drugs on his windshield—Chris knew they didn't have the power that Officer Vincent here had, the power Chris needed. The power to arrest the little bastard, toss his ass in jail, out of sight, out of mind. And, most importantly, out of Chris's life.

But his stomach knotted, the rest of the words he wanted to say to the policeman dying on his lips. Watching the man pick at those sores on his face, Chris knew Vincent had his own demons to feed.

"What?" Officer Vincent said again, a hint of paranoia in his voice now.

How much longer will the dude have this job before the department catches on and fires his ass? Chris wondered idly.

The twitchy officer, Marianne's hatred—either was disturbing enough to kill the plan birthing in his head, that there was another way to solve the problem of Rich that didn't involve jail. Maybe it was because paying people to do bad things brought back monsters he'd rather leave buried in the past. He looked at Vincent again, even felt a moment's pity for the skinny, bald man staring at him behind his sunshades.

Chris shook his head. "Nothing. Forget about it, man."

Officer Vincent sniffled, like his nose was runny, and gave the Ziploc bag of white powder a strange, hungry look as he walked back toward his cruiser, tapping on it with a spidery hand. He shot a few suspicious looks over his shoulder at Chris, then climbed into his cruiser and drove off.

* * *

Chris felt better when he arrived at Chris Flowers Automotive, his car club and collection. He had bought the warehouse on East Murray Street, just fifteen minutes from his mansion, seven, or eight years ago, and it was one of his favorite spots. Every weekend the place was packed, Chris hosting some event or other. Walking down the long, cozy hall to meet the camera crew at the lounge that afternoon, he passed endless posters with his face on the front, some for exclusive events and some for Tray's first memorial at the Wyburn Center.

But right now, Chris didn't stop to think about Tray. He just kept walking, hurrying through varnished oak doors until he finally made it into the lounge.

Thoughts of Marianne popping pills and sobbing faded, and he felt his soul being injected with elation as a camera crew followed him out of the lounge and into the cool, colossal garage that housed his collection of four dozen sports and muscle cars. The air smelled of fresh wax and engine oil. Chris ran his fingers along the pristine bodies of sports cars that looked like spaceships. The camera crew was doing their weekly special on him and his cars called *Chris's Cars!*

Chris smiled lovingly as he approached one of his souped-up muscle cars, the camera crew orbiting him. He patted the old black Dodge Charger from the 1960s, gleaming in the steady bright fluorescents. "I'm asking this one to marry me," he said, flashing a grin over his shoulder at the camera behind him, the camera glued to him like a leech.

Two other cameramen circled around, capturing additional shots of the cars in the muscle car section.

One of them kept sniffing at the seemingly out-of-place El Camino.

Chris smiled sadly as he approached it, memories echoing in his mind when he touched the cool beige hood with its black stripe running down the middle. "Sticks out like a sore thumb, I know. Bought it when I was in my twenties. Friend gave me a deal."

"Do you still drive it?" the camera guy asked, pointing the camera into Chris's face.

Chris snorted. "Sentiment won't let me throw it away. But nah, man, I wouldn't drive this ol' thing around no more."

He climbed into a half dozen different cars—the camera crew climbing in with him—and the garage door yawned open like a giant mouth onto the outside driving track. Chris tightened the chin strap of his driving helmet, urging the camera crew to do likewise, then he ripped around the stacks of tires used to make the walls of the winding course. Then he slammed his foot on the accelerator, jerked the steering wheel to the left then to the right again, fishtailing, brakes squealing in the July air. Heart-pounding excitement zapped thoughts of Marianne and Rich and Tray away. The camera guys giggled like children, trying to hold the cameras steady on Chris as he did donuts, the world turning into a spinning blur. Chris did a final donut then stopped the car, the brakes smoking, the smell of burnt rubber in the air. Chris turned his helmeted head and faced the camera's eye, smiling wide, his heart racing but in a good way. It was just him and the camera, the rest of the world melting away.

On his way home, riding the buzz from his day at the car club, thinking about that episode of *Chris's Cars!* spreading like a field of bright flowers on the internet, his eyes would jump into the rearview mirror. No black Suburban, but he couldn't help but check. As thoughts of Rich returned to him, that good buzzing feeling he felt inside ebbed away yet again.

* * *

Smack! Smack! Smack! Chris's gloved fist sunk into the black punching bag, sweat running down his bald head and down his back, his gold boxer trunks soaked. His cell phone alarm beeped, and he crossed his scuffed gym room, peeling off his scarred rubber boxing gloves, and pressed stop on the time clock. The time was stopped at 1:00:08. A solid hour of curls and push-ups and running his fist into the punching bag left his body feeling jacked and pumped, ready to take on anything. He needed the workout to loosen up for where he was going. It was past seven, the sun hanging low over Hollywood Hills.

He cooled his body with a long, cold shower, his aching muscles soothed. He took his time getting dressed, climbed into dark blue jeans, white sneakers, and a black silk jersey T-shirt. He checked the time again. Closing in on eight. He felt a lump in his throat, feeling guilty and worried, realizing that he was milking the sunset as an excuse to delay. He knew the later he arrived, the less time he would have to spend there. They didn't impose visiting hours, but they wanted you to leave at a reasonable time.

Stop it! he thought. *Move your ass!*

His sneakers snapped as he walked, echoing down the cavernous, gleaming hallway. Red sunbeams slanted through giant windows, shining on Chris's concerned face as he approached the living room on his way out the front door. He heard the crisp sound of videos playing on a cell phone. He peeked around the corner and saw his wife curled up on the couch. Her face was aglow, watching old videos of the two of them on her cell phone. It wasn't unusual for her to do, chill on the couch and watch and rewatch videos of them, videos of them dangling lovingly off each other, zipping jokes and rolling their heads back laughing into the golden sunshine. By the sound of it, she was watching one of Chris in his gym room months ago, boxing his heart out.

There's my man! Look at my man! cried her loving voice from the cell phone video. *Here, take the phone, babe. Show me how to box!*

Then Chris heard his own voice guiding her through elbow jabs at the punching bag, and then Andrea throwing herself into the workout with enthusiasm, taking a few swings, laughing and then humbly mocking her deficiencies.

I can't get it like you can, babe, she said.

Both had posted tons of videos like that on their social medias. He would feel a warmth, almost a goofiness inside, a brimming confidence seeing his views skyrocketing into the millions and tens of millions. He felt he could almost bathe in the warmth of the praise he received.

Andrea hadn't looked up at him. She just continued staring at the videos with a glare on her face.

"Hey," he said, trying to grab her attention.

She finally raised her face out of the blue-white glow of her cell phone. She blinked at him curiously, miserably.

"I'm visiting Momma," he said. "Her birthday."

He had told her a few weeks back that his momma's birthday was coming up. She knew all about his momma, as did the rest of the world, and had listened intently and compassionately when he had first told her. But now her face was stony.

"Okay," she said, coolly.

Chris leaned down, kissed her pale cheek, and told her, "I'll be back in a bit." Then he walked out the front door.

The swimming pool's blue night-lights glowed, and he sighed deeply, breathing in the chlorine-perfumed air. His eyes searched the front yard, looking for Rich. Nothing.

He moved slowly, hesitantly, his footsteps taking him into the garage. The palm trees in the front yard swayed in the warm evening breeze. Chris climbed into his Ferrari, cruised past the trickling stone fountain, and punched in the gate code. Sitting there, waiting as the gate slowly opened, he felt his wife's eyes on him. He glanced into the rearview mirror, saw curtains stirring behind the window.

He took a breath, then drove off, the gate squealing shut behind him. He kept checking the rearview mirror when a pair of headlights seemed to follow him all the way into town. He pulled to the curb, his heart pounding. He sighed in relief seeing the headlights belonged to a silver Dodge that passed him. Then he pulled back out onto the street and kept driving.

* * *

Chris bought flowers every year at Fawn's Flowers, a high-end florist shop on Rodeo Drive. It was a little after eight when he entered. He walked down the sweet-smelling aisles until he found a bouquet of daffodils, the petals flaming orange and yellow. He recalled, painfully, how much his momma had loved her daffodils, all of the bright flowers of her well-tended garden.

As he was paying for the bouquet, the cashier, a young woman he didn't remember seeing last year, was blushing, her mouth agape, and she was preening her brunette ponytail. She looked young, early twenties, and she gushed that it was him, it was really him, it was *the* Chris Flowers. She told him she was going to the show Friday night as she handed him his change. Before leaving, Chris took a bright orange card from beside the cash register and scribbled his famous, coveted signature and slid it to her. He could see through the panes from outside that she was pressing it to her chest like it was a love note.

Chris got onto the I-10 and drove west until he reached Santa Monica. It was about a twenty-minute drive to the nursing home. He drove down Madison, past the conveniently located ER, and turned down Lime Street. Lime Street wound its way around a small bluff overlooking the ocean.

Chris passed through a gate, showing the security guard his ID, and parked in the parking lot behind the massive structure looming on the cliffside with the magnificent view of the beach and ocean below. The air smelled heavily of the sea. A few dark, winged shapes flapped against the nearly full moon and squawked, their cries swallowed by the vastness of cliff, sky, and sea.

Chris was parked in the shade of an oak that blocked out the moon's cool blue spotlight. The radio was still on, and he was listening to the DJ's voice, glued to the leather seat.

"I hope you're all having a phenomenal night! That last one was another Chris Flowers tune from his last album, *Forever Golden*. I can't remember how long, but I know the title track of that album was number one on the charts for-freaking-ever! A beautiful song! Chris's new album is still in the works, though last month Chris revealed in a Tweet that it's going to be called *Forever Sober*. Everyone's excited about that!

"Now, a song from Bailey Carter. This kid has some talent, man!

Twenty-two years old and already his newest single at the top of the charts! Here it is."

Chris groaned and flicked off the radio, a dull anger flaring in his gut. The new kid, Bailey Carter, was already a megastar, produced an album a year, and Chris hated him. That was another reason Chris and Jeff had agreed for an autumn release, because Bailey's new album was coming out in November, and they wanted to beat the kid to the punch. Chris took a deep, reassuring breath in the silence of the car, reminding himself that he was still one of the biggest stars in the world, always would be, and thought it would be impossible for the kid to top what Chris had spent three years creating.

Chris stepped out of the Ferrari, could taste the salt in the air and hear the waves lapping the beach below. As Chris headed toward the entrance, he hung his head, feeling bad he had blown the entire day at his track, being filmed driving his cars when he knew he should've spent the day with his momma. Because they didn't have specific visiting hours here, Chris could've spent all afternoon and evening with her if he'd wanted. He used to, even five, six years ago. But it seemed every year his visitations had grown not only less frequent, but briefer and briefer. He tried to push away his guilty feelings, tried to push away thoughts of Rich, and he pushed open the twin glass doors and entered the massive three-story nursing home.

He entered the lobby area, an older woman with curly grayish-reddish hair kindly acknowledging him behind a large desk. She didn't jump up with fanaticism, or even get bright-eyed like that young woman at the flower shop. She glanced at him a couple times as she was checking him into the guest list on her computer, smiled. Chris remembered her from last year. She was used to seeing celebrities pass through here.

It cost ten grand a month to keep his momma here. He'd bought her a private room on the first floor with a stunning ocean view. He'd considered a dozen other memory care facilities, even a nice one in Alaska, but wanted to keep her close by.

The carpet, a floral design, swallowed his sneakers' footfall. He passed an on-site restaurant with mahogany tables and candlelight. Chris could hear clanking dishes, the chefs cleaning up after dinner. He saw steam billowing from the kitchen door. One janitor was running a mop over the dark hardwood flooring of the dining room, and another was stacking chairs upside down on the tabletops.

Chris passed a small library, a beauty salon, and an art studio. He passed a TV room, the elderly residents lounging—some of them loudly snoring—in leather recliners and watching the evening news on a seventy-five-inch flat-screen. Somewhere around here were two spas, a fitness center, and even a movie theater. Chris reminded himself, as he walked down the hall, cradling the bouquet of daffodils, that this place was the best of the best. His momma was in good hands here.

As he continued down the hall, walking by residents' rooms, each marked with their names, Chris passed a familiar face. She was a short, chunky woman in blue scrubs. Her hair was shorter since Chris had seen her last, a year ago. It was boyish short now, with blond highlights. She squinted at him but didn't say anything.

Chris walked past mustard-yellow chairs and coffee tables with vases overflowing with flowers. The walls were decorated with oil paintings of flowers done by renowned artists specifically for this facility.

He arrived at a room at the end of the hall, the name *Flowers* written on the door.

The door was cracked open like the other doors, so staff could do their fifteen-minute checks. Chris took a few deep breaths, his fingers crinkling the cellophane of the bouquet, wrestling with sinister feelings reawakening from dormancy. It'd been a year to the day since he had last been here, but it felt even longer. His hectic life had always kept him on his toes, and it always seemed like he never had much time to think about his momma.

He took a final deep breath, mustering up his courage, then entered the room.

He felt like a little boy in a haunted house. His momma was propped up in bed, watching an old game show rerun on her personal flat-screen TV. He approached her.

She looked older. Her eyes looked paler. Her wrinkles were etched deeper into her flesh.

She squinted at him. "Who's that?" she asked, sounding groggy.

"It's me, Momma."

He stood at her bedside, but he had to avert his gaze. He glanced out the window with its breathtaking view of ocean and night sky and dark clouds trying to erase the moon.

"Who? Is that Carl?"

Chris looked at a picture on the nightstand. It was his momma's favorite picture. In it, she was holding Chris when he was a tiny brown little baby. His momma was wearing a summer dress. The picture had been taken by Chris's dad, who he'd never met. His dad had left Momma for someone else. All he knew about his dad was that his name was Carl.

"No, Momma, I ain't Carl." He was struggling to look at her. He kept his eyes on the nightstand, noticing two empty one-ounce paper cups. His momma had already taken her night medicine.

He remembered he was still holding the daffodils. He handed them to her. She took them and focused on the orange and yellow petals.

"For you, Momma."

"They're . . . wow."

"Nice, huh." Chris noticed balloons tied to her bed. They said *Happy Birthday* on them. Chris figured staff had thrown her a birthday party earlier.

Is she worse?

Her skin seemed waxier, and the circles were really dark under her eyes.

"It's me, Momma."

"Who? I ain't remembering things right these days."

"It's Chris, Momma." He grabbed one of her hands, rubbed it with his thumb.

"Chris." She furrowed her brow, like she was trying to put a puzzle together. But then a clarity, even though it was weak, filled her eyes. She looked at him. "Baby?"

"It's me, Momma," he said once again, trying to keep the thickness of tears out of his voice.

Her cheeks suddenly burned red. "Oh baby, I'm sorry."

Chris kneeled down, patting her hand reassuringly, shaking his head. "You got nothing to be ashamed of, Momma. You remember what day it is today?"

She shook her head, oblivious to the balloons floating above her.

"It's July sixteenth. Your birthday, Momma. You know I wouldn't miss your birthday! Do you remember how old you are?"

She pondered for a moment, rolled it over in her mind. Then she said, "Twenty-nine?"

Chris chuckled humorlessly. "You're not twenty-nine, Momma."

"Oh, how old am I?"

"You're seventy-two."

Momma leaned in, squinting. "What, honey?"

"Seventy-two years old today, Momma," Chris said, louder.

She sunk back, as if the weight of the answer struck her like a fist. "Oh my, that's up there, ain't it."

"Yeah, it's up there, Momma," Chris said, blinking back tears.

She didn't say anything for a moment. Then her eyelids sagged. Chris thought it must be her night meds tampering her down. He watched her, concerned, holding his breath.

Then suddenly her eyes fluttered open. *She must be fighting the meds.*

She stared at him drowsily. "Who're you?" she asked, her voice an exhausted croak.

"Momma. It's your son."

"You ain't my boy. Liar. You trying to replace my boy?" Her eyes became glassy and accusatory.

Chris felt sick. She was definitely worse. "Momma, ain't no one replacing your boy."

She stared at him, perplexed, like she was looking at a stranger.

Chris felt his face burning hot. He smiled cheerlessly. He gave her hand a pat.

"Get some sleep, Momma." He hoped she could find some semblance of peace in her dreams.

She didn't say another word after that. Chris was glad for that. He quietly dragged a blue armchair over by the bedside so he could sit with her. She didn't seem to notice him, just sleepily watched some seventies game show on TV. The volume was low, so Chris grabbed the remote off the nightstand and turned it up a couple clicks so she could hear it better, but not loud enough to disturb the other residents. His momma used to love watching that kind of stuff, even before she got real sick. But he couldn't focus on it. He crossed then uncrossed his legs.

You trying to replace my boy?

Chris was happy when he heard snores coming from the bed. He turned off the TV, approached her, gently moved some of the gray hair off of her forehead, and gave her a kiss.

"I love you, Momma."

Then he flicked off the lamp and left the room.

* * *

He was walking back down the hall, but didn't make it far. He realized he was trembling all over, his heart fluttering in his chest. He couldn't breathe and stopped for a moment. He leaned against the wall, beside one of those oil paintings of flowers. It felt like his chest was caving in, and he started taking deep breaths through his nose, trying to calm himself. His legs lost their strength, and he had to take a seat in one of the hallway's decorative armchairs. He held his head in his hands, continued taking deep breaths, fighting tears.

Someone came down the hall, and through his spread fingers he saw a pair of legs wearing blue scrubs.

A voice was trying to reach him through his panic. Something clutched his shoulder. He shot up, startled, furious.

It was the unit manager, Annie Hart, drawing her hand back, the hand she'd tried to place comfortingly on Chris's shoulder.

"Sir?" she asked, concerned.

"Don't. Just don't."

"I was just seeing if you were all right . . ."

"No, goddammit! Do I look like I'm all right?"

The compassion melted from her face. She was glancing down the hallway. Chris followed her gaze and saw a few of the elderly residents were staring at him with confused and scared eyes. An old woman was visibly trembling.

Annie looked back at Chris, her face stonier. "Sir, I'm gonna ask you to keep it down. We have people here trying to sleep."

You trying to replace my boy?

Chris couldn't get those words out of his head. Was she worse than last year? She often forgot who he was, but she'd never said those exact words before.

"This isn't fair!" he shouted, more heads—staff and residents—turning.

"Keep your voice down, Mr. Flowers. I'm not going to ask you again."

"I . . ." Chris controlled himself. He couldn't allow himself to get kicked out. To his surprise, he started sobbing uncontrollably for a moment.

Annie's compassion returned, and she sighed sadly.

"Momma. My poor momma."

"She—" Annie was trying to find words for him. "She loves you, Mr. Flowers."

"Yeah, right!" Chris said, his voice catching fire again. He kept breathing through his nose, trying to stay calm. A little more quietly, he added, "She don't remember me. She said her boy was being replaced."

"Maybe sometimes it doesn't seem like it, but she does love you."

"I heard all this shit before."

Annie's face hardened. She waited a moment, then said, "She calls you, you know."

Chris sniffled back his tears, stared at her in utter confusion. "What're you talking about?"

"She has you in her contacts. She has moments. Moments of clarity. And she's tried calling you. But you don't answer. And you haven't been here in a year."

"What're you getting at? And what business is it of yours?"

"It'd mean a lot to her if you visited more. If you at least took her calls."

"Do you know how many calls I get on a daily basis? Her calls got buried under the others."

"Then why can't you at least visit her more often? I see people almost as famous as you coming in every day. Busy as you. They make time."

Chris had to bite back his growing fury. "You have no idea what kind of life I live. You don't get it."

She gave Chris a look of disgust. "Okay. Whatever you say, Mr. Flowers."

Strength had returned to Chris's legs, and he was able to walk out of there now, feeling Annie's eyes boring into his back as he headed toward the exit.

He stepped out into the cooling night air and into his car. He started the car but only let it idle. Of course he'd known that his momma had been calling. He was her only contact, her only family left.

He'd lied to Annie.

He even remembered deleting all the nursing home voicemails. Deleted them without even listening to them. With all these dark thoughts gathering momentum in his head, he wept, and wept. Then he left.

* * *

He was feeling wounded on the drive back, so he pecked around on the radio for a bit, a guilty pleasure, trying to find his own music, listening to the DJs talk about him and his prominence, his immortality. But hearing a lot of Bailey Carter, he decided to just plug his phone into the auxiliary. He got back on the I-10 and took that to State Route

2, and was back in Beverly Hills, soothing himself with his own tunes. Listening to his music brought him back into the present. He reminded himself that in the morning he had the press conference when he would reveal the album's release date, set for October. He reminded himself that he had an album to finish the next day. He kept telling himself that the new album was going to be a record breaker.

He turned onto Oak Street, five minutes from Hill Street, tapping along to one of his tunes, realizing how much better he was feeling the closer he got to home.

That was until he caught a lone pair of headlights, like yellow demon eyes, in the rearview mirror, and his pleased grin twitched and died on his face.

CHAPTER SEVEN

He could see Rich's Chevy clearly in the moonlight. Rich was following him. Chris wondered how much of this was just pure intimidation. If this and the coke planted on his car were all punishment. Chris hated to admit he felt intimidated, but he did.

Rich had been known to camp out near celebrities' homes, hang out of planes and helicopters if only to get just a single shot of a movie star cheating on their spouse, or a long-sober rock star sneaking sips from a bottle of Jack.

Chris was approaching that left onto Hill Street, could see the street sign in the moonlight. But instead of turning he slammed on the brakes, coming to an abrupt stop in the middle of the street. The Suburban slowly crept up, and Chris could feel the growing heat of the headlights on the back of his neck. The headlights hovered behind him, reflecting off the rearview mirror, burning Chris's eyes. Then the lights floated out of the rearview mirror. The Suburban crawled around Chris, ominous as a faceless hearse. The dark shape of Rich's head behind the driver's wheel glanced Chris's way. Though Chris couldn't see them, he could feel those hateful, beady eyes boring into him.

The Suburban pulled ahead of him.

Chris, catching a clear look of the license plate, quickly dug a tiny red notebook out of the glove box, flipped through the pages of spontaneous lyrics that came to him in the middle of traffic, and scribbled down the license plate number.

Chris wasn't surprised when Rich didn't turn down Hill Street. The creep must've already caught on to the security guards.

Chris took a picture of the scribbled license plate and texted it to the security company so every guard posted to his house would have it for reference. But until Rich did something—and it had to be something really crazy—it wasn't much use. The license plate number would just sit in his phone. Still, Chris felt better having it on him. In fact, as he pulled past the security guard, nodding at the burly man sitting behind the wheel of a black parked car guarding the estate, Chris had the burning desire to give the license plate number to someone dangerous.

I know what you did. Five years ago.

Hearing that demonic voice in his head sent his heart to pounding.

He pictured a hired gun pointing a silenced pistol in through Rich's driver's side window and letting off a few hushed shots. That would end that.

Andrea had texted about an hour earlier that she had her personal chef, Amy, over to make them a homemade pizza and that there were leftovers in the fridge. Chris found himself sitting at the giant mahogany dining room table eating a couple slices of the parmesan chicken and broccoli pie. He popped a tall can of kombucha, glancing at the windows every now and then.

Funny how people can affect you, Andrea had once said. It was during their honeymoon. She'd finished her second glass of wine and words came easier to her. She looked at Chris with trusting eyes. *You know what Rich said to me once? He was depressed. Really depressed. I wrote a song for him and played it for him. When I'm done he just smirks at me, and says, 'All right, just get the fuck out of here, I don't need to hear your stupid song.'*

Chris gave his can of kombucha a squeeze, denting it, remembering how Andrea's eyes glassed over with tears.

He hated seeing it when I started getting successful. Know what he said? He once told me, 'You really think you're that important? You're a speck of bacteria in an ocean! No one cares about what you create!' It felt like nails were being driven into my heart.

Chris took a long, hot shower, letting the water soak into him and relax him, washing away the day's grime and sweat and fear. He felt relieved to be back within the safe confines of his house, now with outside guards watching the place, felt good to climb into pajamas and slide into his silky bedsheets. The bedroom was air conditioned, sucking away the heat of the day, and cool beams of moonlight shone through the windows, making the twenty Grammys on their twin shelves gleam a creamy blue. The moon also shone on Andrea's beloved Taylor acoustic guitar leaning against the wall. Chris figured she must've been picking away while he'd been gone.

She was wearing a silky nightgown. He curled up against her. He could tell she was awake. She wasn't breathing the deep, measured, rhythmic breaths of one who's asleep. She also had a little bit of a snore when she was asleep, though he never mentioned it to her. He was trying to force himself to doze but still couldn't shake the stress of the day.

Then Andrea's voice rose out of the dark. "Chris?"

"Yeah?"

She was quiet a moment. Then, finally, she said, "Do you really love me?"

Chris furrowed his brow. The seriousness of the question forced him to prop himself up on his elbow so he could look her in the eye.

She turned over, facing him, lying on her back.

"Of course I love you. What kind of question is that?"

"Why?" she asked. "Why do you love me?" Her eyes bore into him through the gloom, searching for something. Chris didn't know what.

It felt like nails being driven through my heart, Andrea had said on their honeymoon. *He liked making me feel worthless.* She had wiped a tear away.

Chris felt his chest puffing up, feeling protective for Andrea all over again. "I love you because you're kind, because you're talented, beautiful, passionate, all that good stuff."

She wrinkled her brow, struggling to believe him.

He brushed her blond hair out of her face and gave her a long kiss to prove his love without words. She slowly relaxed. His tongue explored her mouth, then her tongue explored his. Chris liked the way she melted in his arms. With his kisses he hoped to stitch together the unhappy rift that had been growing between the two of them the past couple days. He hoped tomorrow she would be happy and smiling and ready to bust out the last few hours of work on his album.

This album was going to break records, Chris thought as the kiss turned into groping, his erection trying to poke through his pajamas.

He rubbed her hardening nipples in circular motions through her silk nightgown.

Soon enough they had peeled out of their nightclothes and he was sinking into her, finding a rhythm. Like music. He was out of condoms, so he did what he always did in that situation, pulled out as he was about to spurt.

But Andrea snatched his cock, gripped it firmly, protesting, "No, *inside* me. Come inside me."

Chris stared at her, confused. He'd never heard her say those words before.

She put him back inside her, and Chris squeezed his eyes shut, pursed his lips, wrestling with ecstasy. He saw nine months flash by and a screaming child emerging from her bulbous belly into the world and into their lives.

He pulled out again, fighting the resistance of her thighs tightening like a fleshy vice around his waist.

He backed away from her until he was sitting on the edge of the bed, sweat on his brow, his cock going limp, desire dying.

Her ragged breaths slowed. "What? What's the problem?" she asked.

"You really want a kid?"

"Yes! Of course!" A tinge of heat in her voice.

Chris imagined it, a year from now, having to drop whatever he was doing—writing, recording, working out—to have to tend to this screaming ball of need and want. A kid wasn't something you could put in a nursing home either, out of sight, out of mind.

That thought just reared its ugly head, bitter and harsh. But there it was. And Chris had to look away for a moment to hide his shame.

"I'm not ready yet."

"But you said so. Remember at dinner with my mom?" She was talking about a month earlier when Andrea's mom, Carly, who looked a lot like Andrea, only with streaks of gray in her blond hair and wrinkles around her emerald eyes, had flown in from Tennessee and stayed with them and asked if they were planning on giving her grandchildren soon. "Remember what you said?"

"But I didn't mean right *now*. I meant someday. Besides, you're thirty-five. We don't need to rush. And what with how busy our lives are. Do you think it'd be fair to the kid to be raising him right now?"

He saw dimly in the shadows Andrea's face change from bewilderment to a look like he'd just sunk a cold blade into her back.

She jumped bare naked out of bed and stormed to the closet. She flicked on the closet light, the corner of the room lighting up, and slipped into some jeans, a long-sleeve shirt, and some sneakers.

"I said we would, didn't I?" Chris said, panic growing.

But she ignored him.

Chris jumped back into his pajama bottoms and hurried down the stairwell after her.

She was already in the garage, about to climb into her Porsche.

"Andrea?" he called after her.

"Please, I just want to be alone right now!"

He stood in the driveway and watched the gate shut after her red Porsche passed through, and he listened to its engine fading into the warm, sweet-scented night. The security guard was probably looking at her passing by asking, *What the hell?*

Chris wanted to jump right into his Ferrari and follow her, then thought better of it, knowing there was nothing he could do or say to make her come back. He just stood there, half-naked, helpless, trembling.

CHAPTER EIGHT
2008

They had been playing a game of Scrabble for three days, leaving it on the kitchen table overnight to be picked up the following day. Chris put a fist under his chin, waiting for Momma to make her move. She sat on the opposite side of the table, the word game between them and half-eaten sandwiches and mostly drunk glasses of milk at their sides from lunch. Chris rubbed the bags under his bloodshot eyes, his eyes sore from the past few restless nights, the crying spells. Warm July sunshine poured in through the kitchen windows down on their game. Chris looked down at the words already constructed on the game board: Bean, Fog, Rap, Jam. Simple three- or four-letter words. Then he looked at his momma. Her eyes were narrowed with desperate concentration, her fingers rubbing her temples.

"Come on, Momma," Chris encouraged gently. "You can do it."

"Honey, I'm trying," she said.

"What about that B in Bean. Do you have an E or a D? You can make the word Bed."

Momma stared at the game board for a long time, just kept staring, then she picked one of her word pieces up, put it down again. She wrinkled her brow, picked a piece up, then put it down yet again.

It was like teaching a child, only nothing would stick. Chris tried to help her, but Momma would shoo him away from trying to peek at her letters, or she'd bury her letters under her arms. Momma was right. What was the point in her playing if he was going to help her?

Mrs. Williams arrived, her long, thick braids rolling off her slender shoulders, a kind smile on her face. She brought over crossword puzzles and Mad Libs, some algebra too.

"I heard algebra is good for the brain, so."

Chris glanced at the front door, wanting to bolt already. But he looked at Mrs. Williams, feeling guilty. He swallowed a lump in his throat, said, "Thank you so much for your help."

"Don't mention it, kid."

Chris pulled out his wallet.

"No, no," Mrs. Williams protested, waving a hand in the air between them.

"It's fine. I want to." He held out a hundred-dollar bill.

She didn't take it. "Put your money away. I know you ain't rich."

"We're doing better." He meant his band, The Last Luminaries. They had gone through several band names and would no doubt change the name again until they found something that all three members could live with. There was something about this new name that had a ring to it Chris liked. "We're playing serious," he said, "and we ain't doing too bad." The first part was true.

"That's great. But really." Mrs. Williams's eyes softened. "My husband's dad went through this, remember?" She patted his cheek. "I know what you're going through."

Chris nodded, tried to keep the tears from his eyes. He put the money back in his wallet.

Mrs. Williams pecked him on the cheek, a motherly kiss. "Now go," she said, her voice firm and gentle. "Just don't forget us little people when you hit the big time."

Chris gave his momma a kiss on the head, patted the dark, kinked hair that he'd had to remind her to comb that morning.

She was still staring intently at the game of Scrabble, shaking her head helplessly. "I don't know why it's so hard. Didn't used to be so hard."

"Don't give up, Momma. I love you."

"I love you too, honey."

Chris couldn't leave fast enough. Tears welled as he screeched down Campbell Street in his El Camino. A hot breeze kicked empty beer cans down the sidewalk and paper bags up into the air, the litter of other despairing souls. Chris drove past makeshift shelters: tents and cardboard houses, bicycles with tarps thrown over the top. He drove past homeless people in ragged clothes passed out on the sidewalk or curled up in alleyways. At a stoplight, Chris gave a few spare dollars to an old man talking to people who weren't there.

Fifteen minutes later he turned onto Clancy Street and pulled up to a little house boxed in by a rusty chain-link fence. Manny's new house. Manny's dad owned Luis's Heating and Air Conditioning and said he'd help Manny make payments for a new practice place as long as Manny worked for the company. Manny's parents were always supportive of them, though Chris knew the music the band played, an eclectic mix of rock and rhythm and blues, wasn't their cup of tea. They played a whole bunch of covers from James Brown to Marvin Gaye to Prince to Genesis and Santana, and all the while Chris struggled to find his way as a songwriter. With time, Chris felt he could become something great. Something truly original.

The front door opened after a couple knocks, and Manny poked his warm brown face out, grinning tenderly. His dark eyes, seeing Chris trying to hold back tears, went from sparkling with affection to crinkling with concern.

"Hey, man. You okay?"

Chris didn't answer, just ran into Manny's arms, almost knocking the guy back. Manny smelled like whiskey. It was Saturday after all. Later, they were sitting on the beer-stained couch in the living room. A sticky, foamy tape sealed the cracks of the windows and the front door. The house was soundproofed, so much so that Chris couldn't even hear the intermittent passing of cars on Clancy, couldn't hear the gangster rap being blasted out the windows of neighboring houses, couldn't hear the barking dogs or the occasional distant gunshot. A drum set sat in the corner. Speakers and amps were strewn about haphazardly. Chris's guitar and Daryl's bass guitar were all already there waiting for them, sitting neatly on their guitar stands.

Chris and Manny sipped on a fifth of Bacardi, a good dent already in it before Chris had even taken his first slug.

"Momma has Alzheimer's," Chris revealed, sniffling back his tears.

Manny shook his head, scratched the long black hair he kept in a ponytail. "Shit, man." Manny took a swig of Bacardi, passed it to Chris.

Chris took a dissatisfied sip, wiped his lips, then glanced around hungrily.

Gotta be some dope around here somewhere, Chris thought hopelessly.

"When'd you find out?"

Nothing on the coffee table but a stack of *Men* magazines. The one on top exclaimed: *Summer's Here!* A shirtless, muscled, dark-haired man grinned shyly at Chris on the cover.

"Two weeks ago."

Manny took the bottle, swigged. Then his eyes creased, perplexed. "She at her place by herself?"

"My neighbor's watching her. She's really nice." Chris glanced around desperately.

Just an old cotton swab with heroin residue would work! he thought.

He could stick that in a pipe and smoke it.

"She's been watching Momma during the weekdays while I'm at work."

"What about your momma? Can she still work?" Manny took a swig from the bottle. He looked at Chris curiously, noticing the way Chris kept glancing around.

"Yeah, she can still work. For now. The neighbor lady has been driving her. At least until . . ." *Momma loses her mind completely,* Chris thought, tears returning.

Manny patted his shoulder. "It's all right. I'm here for you, bro."

Manny offered the whiskey.

Chris looked at it. Unable to stand it any longer, he asked, "Please tell me you got some dope, bro?"

"Of course," Manny said.

Chris's hope faded when Manny started rolling a joint. "No, no. I don't mean *that* dope."

Manny set the dime bag of weed on top of his *Men* magazine. He nervously scratched his black goatee. Chris noticed how clear Manny's complexion was now, face a little fuller, eyes a little brighter.

They'd both been clean for three weeks, the worst of the withdrawal symptoms fading on that day two weeks ago when Chris had taken his momma to the doctor, the same day Mrs. Williams had called and seemed to notice how sick Chris looked. Up until around six or seven months ago Chris had only drank and smoked weed. After that, well, Manny and Chris often shot up together, and they usually got together a little earlier, before Daryl would get there, so that they could get high.

"Why can't we just sip on the whiskey?" Manny said weakly.

But Chris could see the same hunger in Manny's eyes, Manny desperately trying to fight it. The same craving for a shot of dope. A shot of heaven.

Chris wiped tears from his face, until he saw the tears roused Manny's pity, making Manny scrunch his face up in sorrow. Chris allowed them to roll a little bit then. "Please, Manny. For me. Call your guy. I just need to forget. Just for a bit."

"I promised Maria I wouldn't let you."

"Please. If you care about me, you do this for me." It just came out. Chris was disgusted with himself.

But it struck a chord with Manny. Manny's skeptical eyes softened.

"I've got money," Chris said, unable to believe he almost gave a hundred to Mrs. Williams when he could spend it on dope. He guessed he'd been secretly hoping she'd reject his generous offer. He saw Manny scratching the back of his neck, unsure about all this, but Chris reassured him. "You don't have to shoot up, bro. And I won't say anything to anyone about you buying for me."

Manny sighed, disappointed. Then said, "Fine."

Manny kept scratching his face nervously as he talked with his guy on his cell phone:

"Yeah, yeah. Perfect. Thanks, 'Dre. I'll meet you in—"

Manny was standing near the kitchen area, talking in hushed tones, though Chris could hear everything he was saying. Then there was inaudible cussing coming from the other end of the phone.

"Shit, sorry, sorry," Manny said. "Forgot."

Chris wondered if the drug dealer was pissed off about Manny using the dude's name over the phone.

The name echoed in Chris's mind:

'Dre.

'Dre.

Like Andre? he wondered.

When Manny got off the phone, Chris handed him the money, then Manny drove down the street to make the pickup. Chris spent no more than ten minutes alone, swigging Bacardi, before Manny came back with a tightly wrapped baggie of black tar and fresh needles. Manny said he had some cotton swabs. He grabbed an ancient spoon from the kitchen and bent it with his thick, callused drummer's fingers.

While Chris cooked the heroin on the spoon after mixing it with a little water, Manny kept glancing at Chris, the looks growing harsher. But Chris just kept Manny in his peripheral vision as he stared at the bubbling black tar. He couldn't wait to be *gone.*

Chris stuck a needle into the heroin-soaked cotton swab on the spoon, filled it.

Manny silently tied a tourniquet around his lean bicep.

But Chris pushed his dear friend out of his mind as he pushed the needle in, piercing his rising blue vein. He pressed the plunger until the needle emptied itself out into him, then he unsnapped the tourniquet tied to his upper arm. Manny was holding a lighter under the spoon, cooking up his own shot. The dope rode Chris's blood and spread throughout his body. His skeleton was buzzing. It felt like the sun had poured some of itself in liquid form straight into his chest and that sunshine was spreading its bright love. Momma's face faded from Chris's mind, and he grinned, feeling sweet relief that he couldn't see her in his mind anymore.

The last thing he heard was Manny's voice getting further and further away, yelling, "Chris! Chris! Chris!"

Then all was darkness.

THURSDAY, JULY 17, 2023
CHAPTER NINE

Chris had had sleepless nights before, especially on world tours, with jet lag, differing time zones, endless cups of coffee, a thousand hotel rooms, and a thousand shows, but it was nothing like this. He tossed and turned all night, wrestling with sleep, attaining little moments of it accompanied by nightmares. He would stir from a fevered dream, his bedsheets soaked with sweat, and he would peek out the window, seeing nothing but the moonlit wasteland of the wee hours. A warm, jasmine breeze sighed through the giant potted bougainvillea and through the palm and oak and fig trees. Chris would sit on the edge of his bed, his pajamas sticky with his perspiration and his cell phone glowing on his nerve-wracked face, and he would send Andrea another slew of text messages and calls—all of them going unanswered.

His dreams took the chaos of his outrage and paranoia and turned them into gnashing nightmares that woke him abruptly. In one, the Suburban's headlights burned into the back of Andrea's Porsche as Rich followed her through Beverly Hills's midnight streets. In another, Rich was snapping pictures of her suicide and posting them online for the world to see. For the world to see what Chris had *made* her do.

In yet another dream, Chris saw Tray Mansfield. Though Chris's dreams were often haunted by the specter of the dead kid, this one was different, as it involved Rich, who was spreading like a virus into every dark cranny of Chris's fevered mind. At first, Chris, hovering like some unseen ghost, saw the kid on some nameless Californian beach. Tray was standing by a dinghy that was pointed toward the choppy waters, the dark, desolate skies matching the look on the kid's face. His hair was the color of ash, his sunken-in eyes pondering the eternity of ocean. Then Chris *was* Tray somehow, on a sinking wooden dinghy he'd gouged a hole in with a thick combat knife, and there were anchors tied to his legs and dark, salty water was slowly filling the boat. Eventually, the icy water swallowed the dinghy whole, and Chris—in Tray's skin—was being dragged down into the endless, deeper, darker waters. He heard Rich's voice. "Tell everyone what you've done, or I'll make sure you end up nothing."

Chris was startled awake from that one, soaked in cool sweat, swearing he could still feel the bitter, salty chill of Pacific Ocean waters.

At around seven a.m., sunlight trying to spill in through the curtains, Chris heard over the bright sounds of birds chirping in the trees the squeak of the front gate opening. He jolted up out of bed. He peeked out the window and watched Andrea's red Porsche pulling in, the gate closing behind her. Behind her, a movie star in sweats jogged past, her hair tied back into a bobbing ponytail and wearing a gray sweatshirt with slowly spreading sweat stains.

Chris released the curtain, sat back on the bed, waited. He heard the Porsche's engine die, the front door opening and closing, then slow footsteps up the marble staircase. She stopped when she reached the bedroom door, waited a few seconds, then opened it.

He was sitting on the edge of the bed when she entered. She crossed the room about halfway and stood in a ray of morning sun that beamed in through a partially open curtain. He could tell she had been crying all night by the reddened, sleepless eyes, the mouth downturned. Her brow kept furrowing.

"Where were you? I've been worried all night about you. I didn't know where you were or if you were okay." He didn't bother to mention Ryan, the graveyard shift security guard, approaching Chris and asking if everything was all right, which Chris had told him everything was. What could Ryan do? The guy wasn't paid to follow Andrea.

"I was at a motel," she said, her voice small and hurt.

"A motel? What if Rich found you? The guy's crazy, 'Drea! What if he hurt you?"

Doubt flickered across her face.

Chris, who had been sitting on the edge of the bed, stood up. He slowly approached her, wanting to wrap his arms around her, press her small, pretty face to his chest, tell her everything was going to be okay.

But she shook her head at him, pain in her eyes, stopping him in his tracks. He stood there in the middle of the room, the hardwood cool beneath his feet.

"I thought you loved me."

"I do!"

"I don't believe you!"

"What, 'cause I'm not ready to have a kid with you you're gonna hate me?" He felt relief saying the words he'd been waiting all night to say.

But he softened seeing her trembling lip. He reached out and touched her glum face.

She allowed his touch for a moment, shutting her eyes and trying to absorb the warmth of his knuckles against her cheek. Then she shook him away, rejecting him once again.

"You'll never be ready," she said.

"What?"

"For a kid. I was thinking about it all night. You'll never have a kid with me or make an album with me. You're *using* me." Her eyes, now burning with fury, caught the two shelves of Grammys that sat polished, waiting to be admired.

"What're you talking about—"

His protests came late.

With two backhanded swipes, her knuckles pinging against the small phonograph statues, Andrea smacked most of his Grammys off the shelves. The awards struck the hardwood with a dull *clink! clink! clink!* Chris tried closing the few steps' distance between them, but Andrea snatched the few Grammys left standing on the shelves and flung them like gunfire. The first one hit his chest with a biting sting, then it clanked onto the floor.

She shot two more at him, screaming, "Liar, liar!"

The second one bounced off him. The third zipped past his right ear.

He snatched her wrists. "Stop, stop! Why're you doing this?"

She tore herself away, then stormed into the center of the room. Chris watched her hands carefully, but they only went up to cover her flustered face.

"You gonna pick those up?" Chris said bitterly, nodding at the fallen awards.

Her features were a mix of shame and anger. She looked away as Chris kneeled to the floor.

"That's what I thought," he said, picking one of the Grammys off the floor and cradling it. "What right do you have?" he added, picking another of the miniature golden phonographs off the ground, checking it for damage. "Demanding I have a kid!"

The words were coming out hot and felt good. He'd been dying to tell her that, too.

He looked at her. Her hair wild and uncombed and glowing in the morning light, she had her fist pressed to her mouth, catching sobs. She hung her head, as if mourning the children she'd never have.

Chris felt a twinge of guilt, looked away. He picked up another of the fallen Grammys.

They had a press conference in less than two hours. Chris needed to think about that. They needed to get ready.

"Chris?"

Chris peered up. Her grin was sharp as a sickle. Flames burned in her cheeks. Threats hung in her eyes. Her fist was coiled at her side. She was squeezing it so hard her whole arm was trembling.

"Andrea?" Chris said, unnerved, uncertain.

He thought, *She's gonna start swinging at me.*

Then:

Whack!

To his horror, she struck herself. There was a popping sound when her knuckles smashed into her own nose. He dropped the stupid statues and rushed to Andrea, who was bent over, groaning. Dime-sized droplets of blood dripped onto the floor. Chris snatched her wrists and held them as if in a vise.

"Oh God! Jesus Christ, 'Drea!" he cried, the color draining from his face. "What're you doing? What're you doing?"

He dragged her into the bathroom, trailing drops of blood. He was feeling light-headed and sick to his stomach as he wetted a white towel, sat her on the toilet, and pressed it to her bleeding face. The towel pinkened. Her eyes, filled with betrayal, darted from his as he tried to search them for the source of her pain. Those eyes seemed to say one single accusatory thing. *See what you made me do?*

It wasn't true. What she said about him wasn't true. No, he wasn't using her. What the hell was she talking about?

He tenderly mopped the blood from her face. There was a little yellow bruise at the bridge of her nose, nothing big.

He shook his head at her. Why was this happening? He'd never wanted to hurt Andrea. Now she was hurting herself.

He caught a look on Andrea's face he didn't like. It was a vampiric look. Like she was feeding off his fear.

"Stop that! What're you looking like that for?"

That's when she said, "At the press conference today, you're gonna tell 'em. You're gonna tell 'em this album is a Chris *and* Andrea Flowers album."

CHAPTER TEN

Chris had met Andrea while backstage at a show a couple years earlier. There had always been something sad about her, an aura of insecurity, melancholy. You could see it in her performances. She was stiff and never opened her eyes. She hung her head, and her voice cracked as she sang. Backstage she seemed paranoid, constantly tossing glances over her shoulder, avoiding conversation, and always looking like she was on the verge of tears.

Chris had always wondered why.

It wasn't until that November a few years earlier at a benefit concert for mental health when he found out.

They were both performing. It was before the show began, and Chris was drawn toward the sound of weeping. He found Andrea in her dressing room trying to stifle sobs. There were half a dozen cameramen following Chris around, filming a documentary about him. Chris pushed them away and shut the dressing room door in their faces.

Andrea wiped tears from her eyes and thanked Chris for being there for her. *I have to tell someone,* she said. *I'm going crazy!*

It's okay, Chris said. *I'm here for you. You can tell me anything.*

She smiled gratefully. Then, tears shining like silver pearls in her lashes, she told Chris, *I can't take it anymore. It's this guy I'm with. His name is Rich. He's my husband. We got in a fight last night.*

Andrea showed Chris a text from Rich that read: *You'll be a blip on the radar in ten years from now. Nothing you do is worth it, babe. Have a great show, btw.*

He's making me crazy! Andrea cried, trembling with fury and hurt. *All he does is hurt! He never says anything good about anyone. He's a paparazzi and he hates famous people and I think he hates me too!* Tears rolled down her face. She was starting to hyperventilate. *He loves it when people fail. And now he wants me to fail!*

Andrea started sobbing uncontrollably then. Chris had heard enough anyways.

Call him, he said, furious, chest puffing up protectively.

What?

Call him right now. Tell him you two are through! Look, there's lots of insecure, jealous pieces of shit in this world. You're too talented, you mean too much to too many people, to need to be dealing with this bullshit.

Andrea looked at her phone temptingly.

If you don't leave him, this guy will crush you down and crush you down until you want to kill yourself. 'Cause that's what people who are unhappy like him love to do. You don't need that shit! You need someone who encourages you, who builds you up, not tears you down. Here, lemme see the phone, I'll call the son of a bitch myself.

No, no, Andrea said, nervously scratching her chest. *I'll do it. You're right. It has to stop.*

Andrea did call him. Told him they were through. Chris could hear the little prick's protests crackling through her cell. When Andrea hung up, she seemed relieved, though she was still trembling, having to hold her legs with her slender hands, her fingernails—painted an apple red that evening—digging into her kneecaps.

That was when Rich arrived, somehow slipping through security's fingers and slinking through the backstage labyrinth of halls until he found the dressing room with Andrea's name on it. Chris heard the commotion, an argument, Rich pleading, then yelling. Chris ran to her door at the violence of his tone. Rich, he saw, was short, Chris towering over the smaller man with the hateful, unblinking eyes and dark, curly hair. Chris remembered his anger as he stepped between Andrea and Rich, the cameras trailing him like loyal hounds. Rich was hopped up on cocaine, his eyes almost solid black, his teeth clacking with amphetamine ferocity. Then Rich threw that fateful punch, that tiny, hairy fist stinging Chris in the jaw, drawing a string of blood. Chris swung back, a powerhouse that began with his feet, like he'd learned in boxing, to step into the hit, smashing his fist into the small, resentful face. Rich spun around and fell, letting out a bloodcurdling shriek that seemed out of proportion to the punch when he landed. Chris thought the guy was just being a pussy until Rich turned over and his hand flopped obscenely on the bird-bone wrist, the cameras capturing it all.

Two months later Chris and Andrea were married, Andrea bringing the divorce papers to the hospital where Rich was recovering, his eyes lazy from morphine and his entire right arm bandaged. Then Chris and Andrea went on their honeymoon in London. Chris used to hope, out of spite, that Rich was in agony watching the taped wedding while in the hospital or in physical rehabilitation or wherever the hell he was. Just as long as Rich got to witness how happy Chris and Andrea were together.

But on the drive to the press conference that Thursday morning, Chris's fists clenched tightly around the wheel of his Ferrari, he wished he'd never tried to talk Andrea out of leaving Rich. He wished he'd never met her.

She was wearing a dress that reached mid-thigh, and sparkling high heels. The face that had looked like a crime scene photo had been washed and was now covered with makeup. Chris rubbed his sweaty palms on his blue jeans and on his silk T-shirt as he turned down Cameron Drive, wishing he wasn't even in the same car with her. But people expected them to drive together. He wished he'd called the cops or an ambulance or something while she'd been in the bathroom, slathering makeup on that ugly yellow bruise on the bridge of her nose. He felt dizzy, the outside world a blur of condos and swank high-rise hotels and luxury cars and green-yellow oak trees. Why hadn't he called 911?

He arrived at the three-story complex at the end of the street and pulled around to the back lot and parked in the building's shade. News vans were already parked in the VIP lot even though it was still a little early, sleek-looking reporters being watched carefully and ushered in by bodyguards.

Before they stepped out, Andrea turned to Chris, her features taut. "Try anything cute," she said, "I'll show them these."

She peeled up the dress, revealing darkening bruises on her thigh. Chris felt his heart sink. He caught out the window another handful of reporters slipping into the back entrance and he wanted to scream, to call the attention of their cameras to save him, but she'd already pulled her dress back down over her legs. She gave him an aching look, like this was as painful for her as it was for him.

"When did you . . ." He gestured at her thighs.

"In the bathroom. Before we left." She sounded sad. Desperate. She'd once told him she used to slap herself in the face when Rich made her feel bad.

Chris was horrified, disgusted. What happened to that shy, insecure woman who was weeping in her dressing room? Where had this manipulative monster come from? Or had she been there all along, his head so far into his own game he hadn't noticed any warning signs?

His shock and revulsion curdled into anger, betrayal. "You got this all planned out, huh?"

"I don't want to do this either."

"Then don't."

A few arriving reporters were glancing toward the Ferrari, their eyes lighting up. Andrea looked at them and their cameras like at a lover Chris had chosen over her.

"They're waiting for you," she said.

* * *

It was a venue Chris often used for press conferences. The three-story building loomed over the restaurants and coffee shops at the end of Cameron Drive, morning sunlight warming its red-gray brick façade. It had once been a club and music venue for musicians of a long-gone era and now had been modernized, its hardwood replaced with plush maroon carpeting, with a new stage where two massive flat-screens hung against the wall above it for use in various presentations. There were newly replaced floor-to-ceiling windows. Only a few things remained, like the wood-paneled ceiling, relic of a forgotten year. The ceiling was rather pretty, Chris thought distantly, but he didn't have time to stand around and admire it.

News vans now crowded the back lot and reporters spilled out of them, and latecomers in limos screeched to a halt, some having come directly from LAX. They lugged in camera equipment, flipped through iPhones and iPads.

Billy Boyd, Chris's publicist, was a wizard when it came to the press, the mastermind responsible for the growing crowd of reporters in the cavernous main room now. Billy was a tall, thin, squirrely young man of thirty-three with lightning-fast fingers and long brown hair tied back in a ponytail. Chris didn't get to see Billy much, most of their correspondence taking place over the phone or Skype, but he had always been grateful for his work. Billy knew how to maximize Chris's exposure. Every podcast interview, every talk show booking, anything related to Chris's social media, it was all Billy.

From inside the dressing room, Chris could hear the reporters settling into their press seats. He was in a smaller dressing room extended from the main room, his name on the door. It had once been a men's bathroom where long-forgotten celebrities would take their shits. A row of vanity mirrors lined the far wall. Chris didn't see his usual eager face reflected back, but a pale, wretched mask. Even his personal makeup artist noticed something was off. Jo-Jo, while brushing bronzer onto his cheeks, asked him why he was all jittery this morning. Her eyes, framed in lime-green eyeliner, felt like lasers burning holes into him. Chris told her he was fine, but she glanced down, her hot-pink hair tumbling, nodding at Chris's legs. Chris realized they were jumping. While Jo-Jo brushed more bronzer onto his cheeks and jawline, Chris clamped a slightly trembling hand onto his knee to stop his leg bouncing.

"Sure you're okay? I've never seen you nervous before the cameras like this."

"I'm fine!" He bit his lips seeing her startled reaction in the mirror. He sighed, then said, more softly, "I'm fine."

But he wasn't. He paused at the door on his way out of the dressing room. He kept his sweaty hand on the doorknob for a few seconds, listening to the sound of the restless reporters on the other side of the door. His legs still trembled.

He took a breath, then opened the door.

Cameras flashed like lightning as he crossed the room. He climbed the steps onto the lighted stage, felt a chill in the air. It was like he could feel the ghosts of the acts that used to perform on this stage, those musicians in their pressed suits and wingtips, the big bands playing their brass and woodwind instruments to people now long dead.

He took a seat at a long table on center stage, a microphone beside his nameplate. Red cloth covered the tabletop and hung off the side facing the journalists. He sat alone, as always, at the table. The spotlight felt like an alien sun, burning him. He reached out and slowly pulled the microphone toward him, crackles blasting out of the speakers. He tried to settle into the chair but even its cushioned seat felt hard and uncomfortable. He crossed his legs, uncrossed them, then crossed them again. A hundred reporters stared at him, murmuring, burning with questions.

Jeff was standing offstage to Chris's left. He was standing beside Andrea. He was smiling, oblivious. Andrea stood in shadow, her face blank, staring at Chris with those dead eyes.

The first journalist, a young man with teased blond hair wearing slacks and a dark suit jacket, approached the podium on the main floor. He tapped the microphone. He pressed his lips to speak into it and a loud squeal came out of the speakers, the sound slicing into Chris's ears like fingernails on a chalkboard.

The reporter tried again. "Hello, hello. Hi, Chris."

Chris's throat clicked. Then he replied, "How's it going, man? Thank y'all for coming."

"Chris, you described in your tweet last month that this album was going to be a diary about what happened to you in your twenties, early thirties. Can you elaborate?"

"Yeah, of course." Chris grinned, but his smile felt too large, too many teeth showing. His legs were shaking. "The first track is called 'Under Peer Pressure.'"

There was a flurry of moving hands, the reporters typing this down in their iPhones.

"All the rest of the track names will be revealed on Apple's website later today. But back then I was hanging out with a bad crowd. A lot of the kids will relate to this, and that's what that first song is about. Um, you know, um."

He didn't look, but he sensed heads cocking. He could almost feel Jeff's encouraging smile waning. It felt like this was the first time he'd ever spoken at a press conference, even though he'd done this a thousand times before.

"Uh, yeah, you know. Wanting to fit in. My buddies were using heroin, all my old bandmates from my old group, so I was around it all the time. Starts off as something fun to do. Then seven, eight years later you weigh one-ten and are on the brink of death."

How can I get out of this? How?

A woman swapped places with the other reporter. She had wavy dark hair and was wearing a white button-up shirt.

"Chris, you say your buddies were all using, that heroin was around you all the time. Were there people in your life who were supportive in that you get treatment?"

Chris nodded to Jeff. Jeff waved his hand at the reporters.

"My manager was always there for me, through thick and thin, man. He saved my life."

Jeff smiled pleasantly. But Chris couldn't share in the sweet moment.

He was frozen in his seat. Time seemed to move faster, his pulse climbing along with it. One reporter blended into another, a blur of faces.

"Did any of these people from your past try to get help themselves, or encourage you to get help?"

Each question grew heavier than the last, like a weight was slowly crushing down on his chest.

"No, these people. They weren't good people. We, uh."

Questions started to bleed into each other.

"We all grew up together in South Central, and these people I grew up with. They, uh. They were very negative influences. And that's the conclusion of this album, that you gotta let go of all the negative people in your life if you want to flourish."

"But you were still using heroin after you achieved fame?" a reporter shot back.

"That's what the last third of the album talks about, how the, uh, you know, the past sometimes lingers, how we still cling to all those bad habits. The last track is called 'The Triumphant Ones.'" He could see the reporters leaning forward in attention. "I ain't just talking about me in that one. Because it ain't, you know, just, all about me. You know."

You're fucking up bad.

"We, all of us need to, uh, you know, find the strength to leave behind the destructive parts of ourselves, so . . . The parts that hurt ourselves and the people around us, to be born anew, to be the, uh, you know, the best people we can be."

Before Chris knew it a half hour had passed, and he was facing a wall of confused faces out there.

"Let's just roll the trailer, man," Chris said, then climbed out of the spotlight.

He stood off to the side while those two massive flat-screens onstage lit up. Oddly, he felt better with the lights and cameras off him. It was only Jeff, looking at Chris, who was concerned.

"You okay, man?"

"Hm. Yeah."

"You sure?"

"Yeah. I'm good."

Jeff nodded, pursed his lips, appearing convinced. He remained standing there beside Chris, watching the album trailer.

But his manager's presence couldn't soothe him. He jumped, startled, when he felt a hand clasp his. He could smell his wife's perfume, sickly sweet, like a poison in the air.

Then she whispered into his ear, so quietly Jeff didn't even turn away from the video, and she gave him a much-too-hard squeeze of his hand. "You still haven't told them."

Chris's throat felt like it was swelling up.

Andrea wiped his forehead. "You're sweating."

Chris tried to ignore her, hating her, staring blankly at the album trailer.

It had been pieced together over a single weekend. The opening shot was Chris on the treadmill. The next shot was Chris drinking a kale and apple smoothie. These opening shots illustrated the newfound healthy lifestyle he practiced obsessively. Then there were interview shots of him discussing the album, mixed with shots in the studio with many famous artists, all of them long sober or recently sober, everyone in a celebratory mood as they sang about sobriety on the eighteen-track album. Then it showed the backup ensembles, Andrea included. Chris watched this portion apprehensively because she seemed such a small part in retrospect, a single brick in a massive wall. And now she was demanding the spotlight, demanding recognition for hard work she hadn't done.

I wish I'd never helped her that day.

The video ended, and the release date scrolled, fat white text against a black backdrop that read: *Forever Sober*—October 19.

The reporters ate it up, scribbled, cameras devoured it, the big date finally revealed.

Chris walked across that stage again and sat alone in the spotlight. Reporters started approaching the floor microphone again. Chris's armpits were soaked. Jeff was giving him looks curious and concerned.

"Chris, will there be a new tour?" a reporter asked.

Chris wiped his forehead. "Mhm, yeah. I'll be starting a world tour in January."

"Chris?"

"Chris?"

"Chris?"

The reporters' mouths moved, but suddenly he could no longer hear them. His ears buzzed. The cavernous room was spinning. And then he glimpsed Andrea in the wings and he blurted out the heavy words in three short sentences.

"There's something I have to say, things are, uh, gonna be different this time. This album is a Chris *and* Andrea Flowers album. We're a duo now."

A moment of silence, the kind of silence just before the guillotine dropped.

Chris felt like he'd made the biggest mistake of his life. At the same time, he knew he'd just saved his ass, at least until the next fresh hell descended on him.

CHAPTER ELEVEN

Faces twitched. Heads cocked. Chris was speaking into the mic again, sweat gluing his shirt to his back, droning on, trying not to listen to himself. The camera eyes, once so anodyne, had turned suddenly alien, like they wanted to devour him. His brain was foggy, and the room kept spinning. Somehow, he stumbled on.

"My wife and I have been talking about it. She's my future. We'll be performing more together."

Jeff's face emerged from stage left and loomed larger and larger as he rapidly approached. He was smiling painfully, trying to hide his shock, as he swiped the microphone out of Chris's trembling, sweaty fingers.

A volley of questions came like fireballs and some just as dangerous.

"Chris, will you two be performing together tomorrow night?"

"Chris, when did you decide this?"

"Chris, why are you doing this?"

"Chris, are you tired of the limelight?"

Out of that spinning blur of a room, Chris heard Jeff's voice, could hear the prickle of irritation in it, saying, "That's all for now. Thank you all for coming. Been a long few weeks for Chris. No, no more questions for now."

Chris had always felt like he could sit in press conferences forever, answering their questions, soaking up the camera's gaze, but Jeff was shutting it down now, and Chris didn't want to stop him.

They—Chris, Jeff, and Andrea—retreated from the lingering, chattering journalists. A handful were circling around Andrea like buzzards. But Chris took her hand, an imitation of a loving gesture, gave the reporters a final smile and wave, then hurried to the Ferrari. Jeff told Chris, all gnashing, bleached teeth, that they needed to talk, and to meet him at the studio. Alone.

As Chris left, the news vans and town cars were already screeching away, and a cleanup crew came out of the woodwork to disassemble the press conference setup.

Chris and Andrea didn't say a word to each other on the drive back to the mansion. Chris caught his face in the rearview mirror, his cheeks pale, his eyes wide in shock. Reality felt surreal. The outside world was nothing but a swirl of light and shadow. He hoped that this was all just a nightmare and that he'd soon wake up. He could almost hear the journalists on their laptops, that almost reptilian clicking, spreading his lies to the world.

Then he caught a glimpse of Andrea's hand resting on her lap, looking lonely. Why did he want to reach out and hold her hand, despite everything?

He arrived at the mansion, parked in front of it.

"I'll take the Porsche to the studio later," Andrea said coldly, without looking at him, then stepped out and started walking toward the carved oaken front doors.

Chris rolled down the window. "Andrea!" he cried, almost desperately.

Andrea stopped, turned around, glared at him with those bitter jade eyes.

"We don't need to do this. I'll change. I swear it! What do you want me to do?"

She looked away, considering it. There was a flicker in her eyes, the old Andrea, the one who'd once looked at him with such adoration, the one who'd thought him so generous and kind and *unlike* Rich. Then she squeezed her eyes shut, her face pained, at war with herself. Finally, she looked at him and her tears faded, and her face had hardened into that new steadfast, determined, and very hard façade.

"No, you won't change, Chris. I have to do this."

Then she turned around, and the mansion swallowed her.

* * *

On the way to Studio One, Chris's phone started lighting up with notifications. He didn't check them, just let the phone buzz and buzz and buzz in his pocket. He didn't want to think of the news feeds, breaking the news. Chris's publicist, Billy, would've been the first to have seen the break, Billy ever vigilant, his small hazel eyes constantly glued to computer screens, dreading a scandal. What was happening wasn't a scandal but somehow felt worse. So much worse.

Chris came to a squealing halt into Studio One's sweltering parking lot, parking beside Jeff's Mercedes. Chris stepped out into the waterfall of constant traffic sounds on Sunset, the smell of hot metal and exhaust and death. Chris knew he was being watched, having a sixth sense for such things, and turned and caught a paparazzo snapping pictures of him from behind a dumpster. Another one clicked away from inside an Escalade parked across the street at the curb.

Rich was probably skulking about somewhere nearby.

Chris hadn't thought of Rich since he'd seen him snooping around on Oak Street the night before and now it all came tumbling back.

I know what you did. Five years ago. I promise you I'll make you confess.

Rich's words mixing with his Andrea troubles felt like a flaming whip was lashing his back, making him want to move, move, move.

But, as far as everyone else was concerned, nothing was *wrong*.

Chris relaxed his taut facial features for the cameras, entered the studio slowly, coolly.

Jeff was waiting in the recording area. He was looking intently at the golden records decorating the wood-paneled walls when Chris came in. Jeff was still wearing the slacks he'd had on at the press conference, and his white button-up shirt had a fist-sized sweat stain on the chest and more dark stains under the armpits. He sucked his vape pen urgently, standing in a thinning blue cloud of pseudo smoke.

"Were you followed?"

"Yeah, just a few of the paparazzi guys. Nothing to worry about."

"Nothing to worry about?" Jeff said, smiling oddly. He took a long hit off his vape pen, then stepped through the cloud, smoke curling out of his nostrils. He approached Chris. "So, what's going through your head, exactly? When did you decide this? Did she put you up to it?"

Jeff snarled. "Billy keeps trying to call me, wondering what the hell's going on. He's having to change all the merch to have both your and her name on it. He's having to change everything on the virtual website." Jeff's words were building to a crescendo, his voice rising. He asked once again, "What's going through that head of yours, Chris?"

Chris's cheeks flared, embarrassed for how helpless he felt. He had never felt so off-kilter, so out of whack. "I, we talked about it, and I wanted her name on it." *She just wanted a kid, man.*

Jeff narrowed his eyes. "Well, that doesn't make any fucking sense. She's done what, a hundredth of the work you've put into it? You saw the album trailer, look how small a part of this thing she is!"

"I know, but it's . . ." *Were you ever gonna have a family with her?* "It's more than that, Jeff."

"What're you talking about?"

Chris felt lost in the wasteland between his own good intentions, his empathy for her, and his fear of her irrational actions. He saw her hurt jade eyes. Then he saw the bruises like thunderclouds on her skin.

"There's nothing I can do about it, man!" Chris snapped. *Maybe you did hurt her.*

"So, you just like splitting Grammys down the middle, that it? Sharing the spotlight?"

"No, it's just, we don't even know if it's gonna be a Grammy winner anyways." Chris regretted it as soon as it came out, that and everything else he'd said to this friend who'd known him for so many years, saved his life more than once. Worse, he saw it on Jeff's face, the betrayal at such blatant lies.

Jeff looked at Chris as if he were a particularly obnoxious stranger. "Okay, who am I talking to? Is Chris Flowers available? Because I'd really like to speak to Chris-fucking-Flowers!"

"I'm . . ." Chris's face flushed and he fumbled for words, wondering where his confidence and control had gone.

"Chris!"

"Yeah, it's me."

Jeff took a hit off his vape pen, took a step closer to Chris, looked straight into Chris's eyes. "Do you remember fifteen years ago? Your old crew? Remember what you did? You left them, your friends, your wife. You left them for me. You left them to go on to become one of the most famous musicians in the world, and now you want to share the spotlight with her, with this woman you don't even really know. You want to put her name on an album she's barely had anything to do with? Are you trying to do like a Bradley Cooper, Lady Gaga type thing, or what? Help me understand, Chris." Jeff put a hand on Chris's shoulder, gave him a squeeze and a gentle jostle, as if trying to shake the answers out of Chris.

"Look, Jeff, I just, I need to go right now. I'm meeting with Ray. I just, I need to go to the gym, lift some weights, clear my head. I'll tell you later, all right?" Chris wasn't sure if he could keep that promise.

Chris was heading for the exit when Jeff said something Chris didn't catch.

He turned around, faced Jeff. "What?"

"I said it's something I'm afraid of."

"What is?"

"You and your pal Ray. You want to end up like him, or what?"

Chris sensed the deeper, biting implications in Jeff's words. All he could say was, "I'll be here around noon, bro. I'll figure it out."

CHAPTER TWELVE

The gym was called Beverly Hills Health and Wellness, and it was located right off Rodeo Drive. Chris was parked beside Ray's black Dodge Charger. It was a beauty, a 1968 model, restored, and looking brand new. Ray had been texting Chris for the last half hour, wondering where he was, saying that he would be in the weightlifting room waiting for him. Chris had texted him a short while ago that he was almost there. Now that Chris was there, he wasn't quite ready to enter. He was wearing his aviator sunglasses, the sun reflecting off them, and staring at his phone. He had succumbed to the temptation after all, scrolling obsessively through the news feeds, through his social media, reading what the world had to say about him, to him. He checked the virtual website, a computer-animated Chris Flowers playing shopkeeper (Chris had even done voice recordings for the website). Billy had specifically created the website, of course, to promote the upcoming album soon after the name of the album had been revealed in June. Chris noticed Billy had already gone through and updated everything. It was strange and gut-wrenching to see *her* name next to his. Chris and Andrea Flowers T-shirts, Chris and Andrea Flowers mugs, hats. On the Apple website, where you could preorder the tracks, it was now Chris and Andrea Flowers.

Chris *and* Andrea Flowers.

His eyes were wide behind his sunglasses, his flesh feeling clammy. He was still trying to get over the shock of it all. He wasn't, however, surprised to see the overwhelmingly positive response to this breaking news. It didn't make him feel any better.

He rested his head on the steering wheel, devastated.

Then his phone started to ring, startling him. His thoughts scattered, then returned darker.

The caller ID was staring at him. He didn't know the number. It wasn't from anyone in his contacts.

"Chris Flowers."

A moment of silence. Then that voice, the demon voice. "You hung up on me."

Chris stayed silent.

"Don't worry. I'm not offended. It's only gonna make it worse for you. I have all the time in the world."

It was Rich. Calling from a different number now. Same disembodied intonation.

Chris tried to parry his fear with anger, giving the steering wheel a hard squeeze. "Why're you doing this to me?"

Eerie silence.

"What do you want?"

"I told you what I want, Chris."

Chris was trapped, wanting to hang up, yet compelled to hear what came next. He realized he was holding his breath.

"I want you to tell everyone what you did."

Chris's heart hammered against his chest.

How does he know? How the fuck could he possibly know? Just play it dumb. Like Jeff said, if Rich had proof, you'd already be fucked.

"I don't know what you're talking about." Chris's eyes were wide as half-dollars and darting left, right, left, right, searching for Rich's black Suburban.

"You know exactly what I'm talking about."

"Stop calling me!"

He was about to hang up, but then that devil's voice crackled, and said something that stopped Chris. "What'd you just say?"

"Andre Childs told me everything."

Chris had heard right the first time. That name reached its nightmarish hand from out of the swamp of his memory. He wanted to disappear in that moment, to just melt away into the soft leather of the car seat. He glanced at the gym's entrance and saw some famous movie star entering through the sunlit doorways. Chris wanted to follow, wanted to hide inside.

"Your old dealer," Rich said.

"I don't know who you're talking about, man."

"See, what I did was knock his ass out. Then I brought him home with me and when he woke up he spilled everything. And I couldn't believe it at first. But the way he was screaming. He wasn't lying."

The color drained out of Chris's face. He didn't move, didn't speak, didn't breathe.

"He's been dead in my basement since yesterday. Still need to get rid of him. I honestly couldn't believe it." There was something sad in the way Rich said this that Chris couldn't understand. "*The great Chris Flowers* capable of such a thing."

Sarcasm. Rich was toying with him, that was it. Chris could hear the smile in the voice. Rich was relishing Chris's discomfort.

A bead of sweat ran down Chris's face. His frightened eyes picked through traffic. "Where are you?" he said, voice barely above a whisper.

"Don't worry about it."

Chris glanced over his shoulders and out the back window at a passing car, catching a glimpse of an anonymous face, but it was just a stranger—a movie star face behind the windshield, face slick with sweat after a morning workout, pulling out of a parking space and leaving. Chris, once again, peered out both windows and down the aisles of cars. He saw a few black cars, a black Audi on the other side of Ray's Charger, a black Rolls-Royce, a black Jaguar—but no Suburban.

Chris's face suddenly lit up, thinking about the picture he'd taken last night, the picture of Rich's license plate number.

"I'm gonna call the cops, asshole."

"They won't find me."

Chris's smug grin wilted at the confidence in the demon voice.

"I want you to leave me alone!" he cried, hating the panic in his voice. "Just leave me the fuck alone! Hear me?" Chris took a few deep breaths to smooth out his shaky voice.

"I'm nowhere near you," Rich said, sounding relaxed, unrushed.

A chill jolted up Chris's spine hearing the triumphant, infernal cackle on the other end.

Then a rustling sound, the sound of the phone moving.

Another voice, a second one, unaltered by a voice changer. "Chris! Chris!"

The panic in the voice stirred dark places in Chris's soul. "Hello?" Chris was frozen, waiting.

"It's Daryl. It's me, man."

Then the voice faded.

Daryl?

The scared voice, distant and tinny now, said, "Please. Stop. Untie me! Let me go!"

The sound of the voice being stifled, the voice muffled now and protesting through something.

Then the first voice returned, the dark and hateful and huskily distorted voice. "I thought about taking Andrea at first."

Chris felt his blood turn to ice and words died on his tongue. That desperate voice, that other voice, he knew that voice, he thought, his dread growing.

Daryl? Daryl Walker? Can't be!

"But I knew taking her would be almost impossible, the cameras on you two all the time. Anyways, you might like that. Me taking her away. I saw the news this morning. Man, that's some kind of shit going down between you two. You probably want her gone now, huh?"

Chris felt those words pierce him like a blade. It was like Rich was reading his mind.

But Chris said, "No, no. That ain't true!"

"And your old friend Daryl was so easy to find online. I found articles about your old band and bandmates. Chris and the Luminaries." The demon voice chuckled darkly, mockingly. "I looked Daryl up. Saw he was working at a Guitar Center in South Central. I followed him home after he got off work. When he saw Andre, I told him that's what was going to happen to him. That it was up to you."

He's bullshitting me. That's it. That's all this is. Bullshit!

"If you don't confess to what you did, Daryl dies. And don't bring the police into this either. This is between you and me. If you get cops involved, I'll slit Daryl's throat. I swear to God I will."

Chris wiped sweat from his face, trying to inject himself with confidence. "Listen to me—"

Click! The line went dead.

Chris slowly took the phone away from his ear. He stared at the phone number once again, now able to take a full breath. His mouth watered, and he bit his lip, squeezed his eyes shut, feeling like he was going to puke.

But he didn't.

He held it back, took a few more breaths.

He stepped out into the boiling sunshine, and the first thing he wanted to do was block that number like he had the first. His thumb hovered over the Block button, but he hesitated. He wasn't yet sure how or why, but he thought maybe he might need it at some point.

For now, he buried his phone deep in his pocket, like some dark, deadly secret. He felt woozy suddenly, having to lean back against the Ferrari's hot metal for support.

There's no end, he thought despairingly.

With that phone call, his greatest fears were coming alive, like something he'd thought dead and long buried had come back to life to plague him.

But he wouldn't think about it.

Couldn't think about it.

He was moving, taking steps toward the gym's entrance. It felt good to move.

CHAPTER THIRTEEN

Beverly Hills Health and Wellness was one of the best gyms in the state—probably even the country. People asked Chris, with all the money he had, why didn't he just expand his gym room at the mansion, have a personal trainer come to him? They asked him why he paid four hundred bucks a month to have to drive out of his way to work out. Chris would always shake his head and tell them it wasn't about the money. Chris enjoyed the company. He enjoyed meeting up with Ray every week. Beverly Hills Health and Wellness was his *spot* and had been for years.

He walked to his personal locker and slipped into some boxing trunks and a silk fitness shirt that shimmered under the bright gym fluorescents. He found Ray in the weightlifting room, the old man lifting dumbbells—those big black arms beefy with muscle.

Chris grinned warmly at his old friend. Ray's gray hair was dark with sweat, and a sweat stain was slowly spreading and darkening the back of his white jersey.

Ray turned and greeted Chris with a soft grin, his brown face frosted with a fuzzy gray mustache. "I've been waiting."

"I know, I know. Just had some stuff to deal with, man."

Ray was at the height of his glory when Chris was in his late twenties. Ray had been in his forties then and was playing his eclectic R & B and soul and pop-rock sound to sold-out shows. Before he was a household name, Chris had been one of the many faceless in the massive sea of people who adored Ray. When Chris was twenty-six and had put out his first solo debut, Jeff was able to wrangle a meeting between the two of them at the infamous Whisky a Go-Go, where legendary acts like The Doors, Mötley Crüe, and Guns N' Roses had performed. The memory burned like one of the brightest stars in Chris's mind. People shoved past *him* to get to Ray, and Ray would sign autographs, sipping beer as he chatted with worshipful fans.

Chris wasn't sure why he was thinking about it now, but Ray had once told Chris a story about that night. *I don't know about that guy, Jeff,* Ray had said. Ray's manager and Jeff were getting drunk as Chris and Ray gossiped about the business. When Chris had gone to piss out the four pints he'd just drank, Ray overheard the managers talking about the young singer/songwriter's rising stardom. *You sure,* Ray overheard his manager asking Jeff, *this kid won't just fizzle out like some of these other youngsters?* Then Jeff apparently said, *Bro, the kid's wrapped around my finger. This kid's gonna take me to the top! Just wait and see!*

Ray hadn't brought up that night since, and Chris didn't care for him to. Maybe because he didn't want to believe that Jeff had said those things, even though Ray was one of the most honest men Chris had ever known.

Watching the old man doing leg extensions and military presses, Chris felt a sadness come over him. It was a sadness he felt every week when he and Ray got together, though Chris could never figure it out. It was watching the way his old idol would suffer and sweat, watching the way some people only gave him a transitory glance of recognition while most didn't know who the hell this old dude was. Now people shoved past Ray to ask Chris for autographs.

Chris spent a half hour lifting weights with Ray, warming up. With every rep he felt the outside world getting further away.

That was good.

Gazing around the club, he felt insulated, surrounded by movie stars in corners working out with their personal trainers, or pop stars on high-tech interactive bikes working on their cardio. In another room was a giant swimming pool, the sharp scent of chlorine wafting in every time the door was opened. There was a giant sundeck, and there was even a miniature golf course in another room where the movie producers and movie moguls liked to play their Putt-Putt.

Later, Chris and Ray went for a few rounds in the boxing ring.

Chris's strikes were electric with the pressure steaming inside of him. He danced easily around the lumbering heavyweight Ray, took little bites with left jabs, then stepped into his solid right hooks. He easily deflected the big old man's hard yet sluggish swings.

Chris won.

He always won.

After a few hard rounds, Chris and Ray left the ring and sat on a bench in the corner of the gym. Chris sipped cold bottled water. He looked at his now ungloved fists and saw they were *still* trembling, tension somehow returning, fear of what was outside these walls creeping back in. That phone call. He couldn't shake it.

Ray sipped some bottled water, his steady eyes studying Chris. "Something wrong, kid?"

"No," Chris said, promptly. *Yes. How does Rich know about Andre? That Andre was my dealer? How could he possibly know that?*

"Chris, come on," Ray persisted, his once elegant voice now damaged by years of beer drinking.

Chris felt the old man trying to peer down into the well of his soul but found himself not wanting to let him in on anything. Not like he used to. He just shook his head, brushing off the questions. "Nothing, man."

Rich is bullshitting you. Has to be.

Chris picked at the gloves that dangled around his neck, and he tapped his fingers on the water bottle.

"Kid?" Chris was always *kid*, even at forty years old. "Usually I can't get you to shut up. You always talk to me."

Then what Jeff had said earlier at the studio started worming its way through Chris's brain. About *ending up* like Ray.

"I said nothing." Chris regretted how harsh he sounded.

But Ray patiently backed off, raising a hand up. "Okay." He was quiet a moment longer, then his face brightened. "I saw that stuff about you and your wife in the news this morning. Everyone's talking about it. Congrats, man. You two going duet—"

"Bitch," Chris said not trying to hide his disdain.

The brightness dimmed on Ray's face. "Kid, that's your wife. I thought y'all were happy together?"

Chris tightened his mouth, feeling bad for saying it, but he hadn't wanted to be reminded of that. "I thought we were, too. But she's trying to ruin me, man."

Ray gave Chris a prickly, skeptical look. "Because you two a duo, now you think she's trying to ruin you?"

Chris dabbed fresh, nervous sweat from his forehead with his towel.

"Kid, no one's trying to ruin you."

Chris snorted, then sipped his water.

What could the old man do anyway? Maybe Jeff's right. Ray hasn't done much for years now. And now he's trying to what? Mentor me?

Chris eyeballed the exit with an increasing desire to leave. He looked at the wall clock. 11:29. "About time for me to go—"

"You know, I used to think the same shit."

Chris remained seated. "What shit?"

"Same shit as you."

Chris doubted that very much, his thoughts returning to Daryl's voice on the phone. *That couldn't be Daryl. Couldn't be. Rich just has a buddy or something and they're probably laughing their asses off at me. Rich wants to scare me into confessing. To snare me like a rabbit in a trap!*

"It ain't just her. There's other people too who want to fuck me up."

"My ex-wife," Ray said rubbing tenderly the ghost of a wedding ring on his old, brown finger. "She wanted me to settle down. Stop touring."

Chris clenched a fist, feeling a jolt of impatience. He'd heard all this before.

Ray looked up, pondering, his eyes heavy with regret. "She was a good chick, man. But she wanted me to stop touring, and she wanted me to have kids. And 'scuse me if I already told you all this."

"Nah, you're good." *Get it over with.*

"But I kept thinking, 'Man, she wants me to stop touring. She wants me to have kids.' Shit, I thought she was sabotaging me."

Chris looked at Ray.

"Sabotaging me so that I'd end up an old forgotten nothing, man."

Chris said nothing.

Ray sucked his teeth repentantly. "Turns out that's bound to happen anyway. And I realized that I was just being an asshole then. She wanted a family, and wanted me to stop acting like such an egotistical prick all the time. And now I wish I would've stayed with her. But all those eyes on me, man. All those lights and cameras! I wanted that. But if I could go back, man. I'd choose her."

Pity curdled into frustration.

You're lucky you're still making enough from royalties to afford coming here, old man!

Chris was singed from the heat of his own thought. He hung his head, regretfully, as if he'd actually spoken the words to Ray. He unconsciously glanced at the wall clock again, checking the time. He turned to Ray.

"Honestly, man, I think I should get going."

Whack!

The entrance doors smacked open. Chris's attention was drawn to the boisterous group entering the gym, the posse orbiting a young man with hair dyed so bright blond it was almost white. Chris recognized who it was immediately.

Ray peered across the gym, drawn to the muscled young man shoving his buddies around. "I seen him somewhere before."

"That's Bailey Carter."

Chris had never seen him here before. The young pop star and his buddies, wearing tank tops and Bermuda shorts, were giddy, glancing around at this new place like they were going to kick it in the ass. Chris was unable to deny how much Bailey looked like Chris had when he himself first walked through those doors.

"He a musician, ain't he?"

Chris nodded. "Pop star. He's been sweeping the Grammys past couple years."

A memory returned to Chris, unwanted. It was March, three years ago—the last Grammys Chris attended before going on his hiatus to work on *Forever Sober*. The host that year was a singer who'd been prominent in the sixties and seventies. The host stood at the podium, his voice echoing off the walls of Staples Center, the air buzzing in anticipation of the moment. *And the Grammy Award for Best Album of the Year goes to . . .*

Chris's heart galloped as the whole thing came back to him like some bad dream.

One of the cronies pointed. Bailey's famous bright blue eyes shot across the gym at Chris. Then Bailey grinned devilishly, nodding in greeting.

Chris had been sitting at a table with Jeff, the cameras on Chris's face. Chris had been grinning like he was the sun and everyone else revolved around him.

The host looked up and into the cameras. *Bailey Carter!*

The kid had won Best Album of the Year, beating Chris's album, *Forever Golden*. The kid was just nineteen then, had hot-pink hair that year, and he was wearing a purple suit. He fist-bumped friends and hugged family. As he was prying himself from the embraces of proud family and friends, away from drinks he wasn't even old enough to be drinking, Chris jumped up, cursing the young man, yanked himself from Jeff's gentle grasp, and stormed down the aisle, drawing perplexed gazes as he climbed up onto the stage. His wingtip shoes twinkled like stars as he crossed the stage of honor and stood in front of the has-been host, dominating the microphone in front of all those unblinking eyes. There was a hushed silence at first, then confused chattering started to ripple among the glittering crowd.

"Come on, you all know I'm the greatest!" Chris's words echoed throughout Staples Center, like he was howling at the gods who betrayed him. "You all know I had the greatest album of the year and the greatest pop song of the year! You all know it! So why're you doing this?"

He was quickly ushered from the stage, his head shaking and his fists clenched. Then he'd stormed back down the aisle as Bailey Carter sauntered up, uncrossing his arms, then accepting the phonograph-shaped hunk of gold. The gold that belonged to Chris. The look Bailey had given him that day always stuck with Chris: it was the look of a child who'd just been punched in the face by his father. Disgust and confusion turned into a smoldering anger as Bailey approached the microphone. "Thank you, Mr. Flowers," Bailey said, dripping sarcasm, before making his speech.

"Is he trying to ruin your career, too?" Ray's voice cut through the memory.

"What, old man?" Chris shot back, not liking the sarcasm in Ray's voice.

Ray was chuckling, shaking his head. Then his eyes wandered, as if he were lost in the past. He smiled sagely. "I know I was never a hundred-time Grammy winner like you or nothing, but I made a pretty penny once, and I used to be seen everywhere."

Chris snickered. "You ain't nowhere to be found, old man." Chris meant it as a joke. It didn't sound like one.

Ray didn't seem to mind though, shrugging it off. "It's fine. I know where I stand, kid. Every time we get together, we have these same talks." Ray tapped a finger on Chris's sweat-glossed head.

"The hell're you talking about?" Chris said, smiling, but an edge was in his voice.

"Hey, superstar!"

Chris was drawn to Bailey's shout, the voice piercing, vengeful.

"I'm talking to you!"

Yeah, I hear you, asshole. Start acting tough after your balls drop.

"You still want those Grammys, superstar?" Bailey taunted.

Chris cracked his knuckles, was about to spring up from the bench when Ray's warm, reassuring hand descended on his shoulder.

"Come on, kid, don't. He's just being a punk. Just leave it."

"I'll fight you for those Grammys, superstar!" Bailey continued. "How about it? A round in the ring! You win, you can have the fuckers!"

"Just go on, kid. Just get up, and walk out that door. Forget it. It ain't worth it."

"Come on, superstar! Come get me!"

Chris shot up onto his feet, and Bailey's full, young lips curled into a smug grin. Chris, boxing gloves dangling like a threat around his neck, started marching toward Bailey. He could feel Ray's eyes on his back, his own glowering as he marched toward the young megastar.

Bailey's taunts had attracted attention. A few movie stars had stopped punching bags and set down dumbbells to catch the action. Two movie producers buried their white golf-gloved hands in their pockets, faces eager. A country music star paused her sit-ups, sat straight up, waiting. A few other celebrities who'd just gotten out of the pool, towels around their necks, hair damp, were pointing at Chris and Bailey. Chris was also aware of the gym's cameras, watching from above.

Chris stopped about halfway to Bailey.

You wanna fight the kid you tried to steal Grammys from?

Chris's fury cooled as he glanced at all the cell phones turned to film him and up at the cameras hanging from the ceiling.

You got enough on your plate without having a scandal for Billy to clean up.

He was moving again, but he didn't stop. He didn't look at Bailey. He headed straight for the exit.

Chris could hear Bailey's cronies making "bock! bock!" chicken sounds, and Bailey's mocking words chased after him. "Yeah, that's right, pussy! Keep walking!"

The front doors shut behind him, muffling the taunts.

Chris imagined Ray sighing with relief and sipping cold water.

Chris just stood near the entrance for a while, listening to the chuckles of Bailey and his buddies petering out. He almost went back inside to go knock some sense into that cocky piece of shit.

There's enough going on already.

He took a breath, then started heading toward the Ferrari.

But as Chris was crossing the parking lot, his sneakers clapping on the baking asphalt, his phone started ringing again.

CHAPTER FOURTEEN
2008

Chris heard voices and felt pain singing in his head. Out of the darkness, he saw a bright light and thought maybe he was in the fabled tunnel of the dead. Then shadowed heads passed over the light like angels. The dark heads emerged as people in white masks. Chris felt the coldness of reality. He saw rolling fluorescents overhead, heard frantic voices and shouted orders, felt tubes like fingers being shoved down his throat. Heads swarmed the light of the small tunnel he was trapped in. The masked people had hard, determined brows, their concerned eyes blinking down at him.

Then the darkness came back.

He didn't know how long he was in the darkness again, but when he awoke, he saw a face emerging. A long nose wrinkling and runny, cheeks on fire, tears running from dark eyes and down hazelnut skin. Pink glossy lips trembling with worry, sad brown eyes flashing from panic to disappointment. She shook her head at him as his eyes slowly focused on her. His wife.

"Maria," he said.

"You son of a bitch," she cried. She raised her hand, and he thought she was going to slap him across the face. But it was just to cover her mouth and stifle a sob.

Manny, who'd been sitting in a plastic chair in the corner, stood up and approached, hands folded together, looking like a scolded child. But Maria grumbled something at her brother, and he shied away, sat back down.

"Do I have to call the rehab again, Manny?"

"I'll do it. I'm gonna quit this time."

With reality's creeping return, Chris felt a horrid, escalating sickness. It felt like the worst flu ever. His tongue and throat felt thick, almost like he was being strangled from the inside. A wave of nausea crashed into him, the room spinning, his eyes and mouth watering. Maria helped him puke a ghoulish yellow waterfall into a fat silver pot that was on the floor and already caked with vomit. Maria dabbed the vomit from his lips with a cool, damp hand towel, the towel lightly browned with vomit already. Chris didn't know how long she had been standing there, wiping vomit from his face. He couldn't even remember puking what was already in the pot.

He looked at her face, at the bags under her eyes. She was clearly exhausted with worry. Shame flared his cheeks red.

Manny approached Chris again, tears glistening in his eyes, his long dark hair in a ponytail, and he kissed Chris's forehead.

The last thing Chris remembered was feeling something warm wrap around his hand—Maria's short fingers weaving themselves around his.

Maria was speaking, but her voice was getting further and further away. "Chris? Chris? You have to stop! You have to stop."

She pressed his hand against her bulging, pregnant belly.

"I will," Chris said.

He felt the baby kicking, and it brought a smile to his face.

He held her hand, shut his eyes.

Darkness took him again. All was oblivion for a while.

When he woke up next he was no longer holding her hand. He could only feel cool, empty air. His eyes peeled open and he found himself in that same hospital room, only it was empty. He realized he must be in the ER.

As reality slowly returned, so did the intense nausea. He leaned over and puked mostly bile into the now-clean silver pot. The floor was scuffed with long black streaks that needed buffing, evidence of the thousands of patients rolled through here on gurneys. Chris shut his eyes to stop the world from spinning, could hear the murmurs of doctors, an occasional laugh, the beeps of monitors, the soft footsteps of nurses.

A pair of footsteps grew closer, prompting Chris to peel open his gluey eyes again, expecting a nurse. But it wasn't.

A familiar face approached.

"Back from the dead." Daryl Walker materialized out of the fog of Chris's dope sickness. His black skin was a shade darker than Chris's. His hands were in the pockets of his silver basketball trunks. He was wearing a band shirt, the words *The Last Luminaries* written across it.

"Dumbass," Daryl said bitterly as he dragged a chair over to Chris's bedside.

Chris propped himself up, making the IV pole rattle, peering woozily through his gold-dyed dreads. It felt like millions of needles were stabbing into his body, and his skin kept flashing hot, cold, hot, cold.

"You've been here all night."

"What time is it?"

"Seven a.m. Doctor said you can leave in a couple hours if you're feeling up to it."

"Where's Manny and Maria?"

"Sleeping in the lobby. I was coming to check on you."

Memories started bubbling up in Chris's mind. He remembered Momma sitting at the table playing Scrabble, the game they'd been playing for three days, and he remembered the front door opening and seeing Mrs. Williams walking toward him.

"Oh shit!"

"What?" Daryl said.

"Momma! I was supposed to go back and . . ."

"Chris, Chris. It's cool, man. We already talked to Mrs. Williams."

"You did?" Chris said, releasing his grip on the hospital bedsheets.

"Mrs. Williams stayed with her."

"Do they know?" *Know that I overdosed on heroin?* was Chris's next question, but he didn't finish his sentence. He was sure Mrs. Williams knew, the looks she had been giving him, the way she was always asking how he was doing. And if Momma found out?

Momma has Alzheimer's, so it won't matter anyways.

Chris squeezed his eyes shut against that biting thought.

"We just said you were sick," Daryl said with a reassuring grin. "I was sorry to hear about your momma, man."

Chris tried to take comfort in his good friend's words, but that last thought was trying to unhinge his mind. His poor, poor Momma.

But not just his Momma. He saw the dark circles beneath Daryl's eyes. He had to look away as he asked, "Were you here all night too?"

Daryl nodded. "It's all good, bro."

Chris was squeezing the sweat-soaked hospital bedsheets again, tears running down his face. "I just—I—I fucking hate myself!" *I don't deserve any of these people. I deserve to fucking be alone!*

Overwhelmed, he sobbed into his hands.

"Hey, hey, bro." Daryl leaned in and gave Chris a long, comforting hug. "I'm here for you."

Daryl smelled like bitter hospital lobby coffee and hair product. Daryl drove to his older sister's in Mid City every Tuesday for a haircut. She owned a beauty salon and barber shop, and she gave him discounts. His hair was immaculate, nearly shaved down at the sides with short dark curls on the top. He also had a quarter inch of dark beard he trimmed meticulously. He was twenty-five and still lived with his mom and dad in Hyde Park, his bedroom and the family bathroom kept as precisely ordered and organized as he kept his face, hair, and attire. Ever since Chris could remember, his oldest and best friend had been like this. Daryl Walker didn't drink or even smoke cigarettes. No surprise that his bass playing was as cool and controlled as he kept the rest of his life.

As Chris hugged his dear friend, crying into the man's shoulder, he couldn't help thinking about the worry he must have caused these people—his family.

"I'm so sorry, man," Chris said.

Daryl peeled away from the hug, gave Chris a comforting pat on the shoulder. "Hey, I know what'll cheer you up!" A smile brightened Daryl's face and Chris saw a secret sunshine that was glowing in Daryl's cheeks, ready to burst forth and be revealed. "I have some good news, man."

Chris wiped tears with the bedsheets, then nodded, encouraging Daryl to continue, wanting good news, *needing* good news.

"The guy you emailed from that bar, El Lugar? He got back to us. He wants us to play there."

It took a moment to sink in, and Chris didn't know if he even believed it at first. El Lugar was a bar in Hollywood. It wasn't a stadium, but it was in *Hollywood.* They'd never played in Hollywood before.

Daryl was smiling and nodding, reacting to the cheerfully startled look on Chris's face.

"They want us to play, bro!"

A smile spread on Chris's face, his heart pounding, excitement tingling him all the way down into his bones. He felt as giddy as a little kid. "Oh man!"

"Bro, it's gonna be killer! You're gonna slay them!"

Chris smiled, humbled, then patted Daryl's shoulder reassuringly. "*We're* gonna play a killer show, man."

Daryl stayed with him for a long time, and the conversation grew lighter. For a while.

Then Daryl's face grew serious again, something heavy on his mind. His eyes glittered with tears, and he said, "You can't do this anymore, man. The dope. You could have died."

"I know, bro. I won't anymore."

"You have to promise."

"I promise, bro."

"You could have *left* us, man." Daryl's voice cracked.

"I won't leave you."

"Promise, man."

"I promise I won't ever leave you, bro."

Daryl sighed, looking relieved. He and Chris hugged again, holding each other for a long time.

CHAPTER FIFTEEN
JULY 2023

Chris let his phone ring, walking faster. When he got to his car and climbed in, he checked it. It *wasn't* the same number that had called him just before he'd entered the gym. He hung his head and sighed, relieved. The number didn't leave a voicemail.

He was checking his messages, scrolling down, when he came upon something that drew his attention.

There was a text, the number Rich had called him from, sent at 10:45, just as Chris had passed through the gym's front doors on his way in. There was an attachment to the message. Chris's thumb hovered over it.

Then, like a saving grace, a text from Jeff popped up. Chris took a breath, a bead of sweat rolling down his face, then he clicked on Jeff's message, ignoring Rich's.

Where R U?

On my way.

Chris started the car and was about to pull out, was about to head to Studio One where he'd have to face the morning's fallout, where he'd have to face his wife, when his phone started ringing again. It was the number that had just tried calling him. Chris once again let the call ring itself out. The person trying to call him didn't leave a voicemail, but did send him an ungrammatical text.

Chris its Wally Chlds. Plz anser.

Wally Childs. Andre Childs's little brother. Why was he calling?

Chris called back furiously. "What're you doing, man? What're you calling me for? How the fuck did you get my number?"

"Listen, man!" Wally cried, then gave a trembling sigh. "Can you meet me?"

At the same time, Chris's phone buzzed, another text from Jeff:

Okay, C U soon.

"I can't, man. I'm busy! What's this shit about? You don't just go calling me out of the blue. Christ, like what the fuck do I want with you?"

"Please," Wally said, sounding urgent.

Something in Wally's fearful, earnest voice rattled Chris, and he remembered how Rich bragged he'd learned Chris's secret. From Andre.

Chris sighed, trembled. "Shit, man. Okay. Where do you wanna meet?"

* * *

Chris had to dodge a few paparazzi on his way to San Vicente Boulevard. He made a few sharp lefts, then a few sharp rights until his rearview mirror was finally clear of the pursuing cars. He was in traffic heading south on San Vicente, buried in the never-ending river of glinting steel, heading toward Mid City. He didn't know how the thought came up. Perhaps it was the dream he'd had the night before where he had turned into Tray sinking to the bottom of the ocean, or perhaps it was Rich's phone call still haunting him, but he was thinking of Tray Mansfield. As Chris moved at a snail's pace in the slow-moving traffic, his mind returned to that day five years ago.

Chris thought the kid had died right there in his lap, because the kid's terrified, agonized eyes staring up at him had slowly shut, blood trickling out his ears and nose and out the corner of his mouth. An ambulance backed up, and the ambulance technicians, like angels in white, came pouring out. Chris helped them scoop the mangled kid from the pavement and into the back of the ambulance. They rushed him off to the hospital. Tubes were jammed down Tray's nose and throat, and the world held its breath, waiting for those brilliant blue eyes to open once again.

Those eyes *would* open again.

Tray woke up out of his coma three weeks later. Chris had always wondered how the kid had survived, a miracle. The world waited for him to speak, and it was months before he could even do that. The world waited for his arms and hands to heal, so that they could pick up a guitar once again and spread beautiful music to the whole world. His arms and hands did heal, but something was wrong. The doctors said it was TBI, or traumatic brain injury. That devastating accident had stolen something from Tray, obliterated some part of his mind that, it seemed, he would never get back. Tray would watch videos of himself with a wistful look in his eye, as if wondering where his gift had gone. He would plunk hopelessly on his guitar. Then he'd weep, a distraught and shrill sobbing, his tears splashing on the mahogany guitar body, the kid's muse gone.

Chris had wanted to die hearing that sound.

And thinking about it now made him want to die all over again.

So he cut the thoughts off, even shaking his head as if that might rattle them out. He hadn't thought about this in so long. He wouldn't now.

He had other matters to attend to. Had to get some answers from Wally.

He got off the exit, driving until he reached Fifth Street in Mid City. Mid-City was five miles or so from Beverly Hills, though it felt a world away. It was a little too close to South Central for comfort. The deeper he'd ventured into south LA, the more the city transformed. Lamborghinis and Rolls-Royces were replaced by generic dented sedans. The streets were dirtier, used syringes dropped on the sidewalk. They had agreed to meet in an empty parking lot where an outlet mall, since abandoned, used to be. Wally said over the phone it was a place he did drop-offs, where he and his buyers could meet and exchange. Chris told him hell no at first, figuring it must be a hot zone for cops. But Wally insisted no, that was why they went there, because it was reasonably quiet. And indeed it was quiet. Empty, except for the black Oldsmobile Wally said he'd be driving. Chris parked behind a graffitied dumpster, his Ferrari now hidden, wishing he'd brought a different car, thinking more and more that this meeting was a bad idea.

Chris locked his car, then headed toward the empty parking lot's lonesome Oldsmobile, Wally's familiar face framed in the driver's side window. Chris's eyes darted, searching for any pair of peering eyes, for someone who might recognize him and perhaps snap a ruinous picture of him returning to his old haunts and the old, dirty laundry of his past.

Wally's hair was longer since Chris last saw him. He had long, curly dark hair almost like an Afro. His nervous dark eyes jumped as Chris approached, then he gave a small acknowledging smile. The dented car door opened, and Wally stepped out into the defaced and trash-strewn parking lot. Chris hadn't seen or heard from Wally in five years. Five years and the guy called out of the blue. What did he want? How'd he get Chris's number?

He was a short man with stubby arms and legs. He was dressed head to toe in black, even in the scorching heat: black T-shirt and black jersey shorts. He stood behind the open car door, like he was hiding behind it, his paranoid eyes darting about in their sockets. He was holding a half-empty forty of Pabst.

Chris approached, shooting looks over his shoulder, making sure no one was watching him. Rich would love to catch this; this was his kind of shot. Chris glanced down the streets. He didn't spot that black Suburban. Not yet, at least.

But what had Rich said? Something about the cops.

They won't find me. I'm nowhere near you.

So where the hell was Rich?

"Thanks for coming, brother." Wally's breath was sour with stale beer.

"I ain't your brother," Chris said tightly. "What're you calling me for? How'd you get my number, man?"

Wally scratched his face. "Well, Andre had this little black notebook that he's had for years. Kept all his contacts in it. I searched it on the off chance that your number was still there. Wasn't thinking I was even gonna reach you. But I did."

Shit.

"Look, man, Andre's gone."

"What do you mean he's gone?" *Shoulda got a different number, like Jeff said. The fucking arrogance!*

"He's not at home. No one can get a hold of him."

"What're you talking about?" Chris's attention drifted suddenly to the sound of a car cruising by on lonely Fifth Street, a black van that filled Chris with fleeting dread.

Fuck! That's him! That's him—

But it wasn't. The black VW cruised down Fifth, coughing exhaust. Chris tried to swallow but his throat was sand.

You need to cool it.

His cell phone buzzed and drew his attention away. A text from Jeff: *What the hell? Where R U?*

Chris was seized with the urgency to leave this place, his legs trembling, his feet shuffling on the hot asphalt.

He typed back to Jeff: *Be there soon.*

Wally tapped nervously on the forty, took another trembling drink. "Look, I ain't told no one about—you know. I was just scared for my brother."

Chris glanced toward the sound of another car driving by—an oblivious dented blue Mazda cruising down Fifth.

"We was at a friend's Tuesday night after 'Dre got out of prison," Wally continued. "We was celebrating, you know. Passing a fifth around, a couple blunts. Andre left later on. It was real late, after midnight at least. Said he was gonna go grab some of his coke from the house. We don't live more than a few blocks away from our buddy's, so he just hoofed it. But the rest of us, we—" Two white-pink apples flared in Wally's cheeks. "We just passed out, man. And when we woke up he wasn't there. So I knew that he must've just crashed when he got there, back at our place, I mean. I figured he must've forgot about the coke. But when I got home yesterday morning, Andre wasn't there."

Chris shrugged. "So what? He could be anywhere."

But Chris felt a sudden, unexpected chill. That hated voice returned to him, Rich's voice, dark with threats. *He's been dead in my basement since yesterday. Still need to get rid of him.*

"Nah, man," Wally said, certain. "He's gone. He ain't answering his phone either! He always does!" Wally paused, set his forty on the hood of the Oldsmobile, and pawed out a cigarette. Fingers trembling, he offered a Marlboro to Chris.

"He could be anywhere," Chris said again, weakly, waving the offered cigarette away.

Wally lit his Marlboro and sucked on it with twitching fingers, then shoved the red pack back into his pocket.

The sound of a slowing vehicle. Chris's eyes jumped to see a cop car slowing down on Fifth, the cop staring at them behind sunshades. Chris turned away, trying to hide his face.

Wally hid the forty behind his back.

Chris wasn't looking, but he could still hear the cop car idling. Then the cop, appearing to lose interest or his suspicions assuaged, continued his patrol down the street, running his eyes over the homeless tents sprouting red and green on the curbside as he cruised off into the boiling sun.

Chris felt his phone buzzing, Jeff urgently texting him.

"What do you want from me, Wally?"

"Did something spill? On your end? Do you know anything? I mean, what if a crazy fan of, you know, that kid's, what if he wanted to kill my brother? Was just waiting for the day he got out of prison. You know? I just wanna be sure."

Chris checked his buzzing phone.

Jeff again: *Where the hell R U?! Album to finish!*

Chris's face grew stormy. He was suddenly sick to his stomach. Was it possible?

What if Rich has been keeping up with Andre's case? What if he tailed Andre from prison?

"Chris?" Wally said, lips trembling over his nicotine-stained teeth.

Chris tried to untangle his thoughts, shook his head. "No, I don't know anything. What, you think he was abducted or something?"

"I don't know. Maybe. I'm just worried. He's my brother, man." Wally smoked less than half his cigarette before smashing it out under his black sneaker, then worked on downing the forty, trying to bolster calm fear with it. "I know you done right by us." Wally smiled, grateful, fearful.

Chris recalled Andre's dream, something the guy had been talking about since Chris had started buying from him in his twenties. It was Andre's goal to be able to make enough money so that he and his brother could get out of South LA, to leave this life of selling heroin with his brother on the streets.

"We were gonna be set. But he just got out of the slammer, and then he's just settling back in . . ."

"What do you want me to do?" Chris suddenly cried, his voice tinged with panic.

Wally was staring at him, alarmed.

"Maybe he got arrested or something, Wally. Driving around even though his license was suspended."

Wally shook his head. "He wasn't driving. We walked to our buddy's place. I told you that. I told you our buddy only lived a few blocks from us anyways."

Chris's cell was ringing with calls from Jeff. Chris fidgeted, looked at the time on his phone. Almost one.

"This was your idea," Wally suddenly said. Maybe the booze was giving him some added courage, but there was some heat in his voice. He eyeballed Chris suspiciously.

"Your brother knew what he was getting into."

"He spent five years in prison for you, man!"

"And he was paid well for it. He was probably ecstatic coming home to all those numbers in his bank account."

"But five years, man."

"Your brother was willing to do even more!" Chris said pointing his finger at Wally. "And not for me. For you, man."

Wally's eyes darted away.

"Think if he'd gotten involuntary manslaughter," Chris continued. "That's seven years right there. Or second-degree murder, Wally! Ever think about that? Fifteen to life!"

"But you told 'Dre, you said, 'Nah, man, we'll make it look like an accident, I'll get you the best lawyers money can buy.' Told him they wouldn't give him fifteen to life!" Wally said.

"And they didn't."

Fear and tears were swimming in Wally's eyes. Chris looked away shamefully, his words feeling cold, unsympathetic. But Chris wanted—*needed*—to get out of there.

"He got off good. And he was a good boy in prison, got some Good Time, Work Time."

Wally's face creased, perplexed, saddened.

Jeff was trying to call again. Chris didn't answer.

Wally, seeing Chris on his phone, pulled out his own cell. He seemed desperate. "I'll try him again." He sounded doubtful, like hope was curling up and dying inside him.

Chris watched Wally stabbing thumbs at his phone. He slowly looked at his own phone, thinking about that number that called him on Wednesday morning. The number he'd hung up on. Hadn't it been familiar to him, even if only distantly, at the time? After wiring that massive lump of money to Andre's bank account, Chris had once and for all deleted both the Childs brothers' contacts from his phone. He told them to do likewise. Maybe they both had. But, of course, Wally had rediscovered Chris's number in Andre's little black phone notebook.

He looked at Wally on his phone, his legs feeling rubbery.

He didn't want to know.

Don't, just leave.

But now he had to.

"Lemme see."

Wally muttered, "Shit! Still not in service!" He ran a hand through his curly hair.

"Lemme see his number, man."

Wally shoved his phone in Chris's face, looking at Chris with frail hope.

He just stared at the number. He didn't speak, didn't blink, just stared.

That cell had called Chris Wednesday morning when he was in the car with Andrea. The number he'd hung up on.

Which meant . . . what? It meant Rich had Andre's cell phone.

Wally noticed the sudden change in Chris's mood. "What, what is it, man?"

Chris shook his head, his mouth open but no words coming out.

Chris's cell was ringing. Jeff again.

"Look, man," Chris said, taking a full step away from Wally. "I gotta go. Lemme know if something turns up." This sounded cold to Chris, but he had to go. He had to.

Wally nodded, polishing off his liquid courage. Then he climbed back into his Oldsmobile and sped away.

When Chris got back to his car and buckled himself in, he pulled up the number Rich had called from two days before under Recent Calls.

There it was.

The same number he'd just been staring at on Wally's phone.

Andre's number.

Chris's thumb hovered over the call button with trepidation. But he forced himself to press it and put the phone to his ear. Even though Wally had already tried, and in front of him, Chris had to hear it for himself.

"The person you're trying to reach is disconnected or no longer in service," said the robotic voice. "Please check the number and try again."

Still under Recent Calls, Chris tried calling the second number Rich had called from.

"The person you are trying to reach is disconnected or no longer in service. Please check the number and try again."

Chris took the phone away from his ear and stared into space, his face darkening. He just sat there for a moment until another buzz from his phone snapped him out of it. Another urgent text from Jeff.

Get ur ass here now!

CHAPTER SIXTEEN

Chris parked beside Andrea's red Porsche. During his drive on San Vicente Boulevard, heading back north, he kept seeing in his mind a little white house.

But Chris pushed the image out of his mind.

He didn't say anything to Jeff about what had happened when he entered the cool, air-conditioned studio and was subjected to Jeff's volcanic tirade.

"It's two o'clock, man! We've been waiting!" Jeff paused, catching the spooked look on Chris's face. He sucked his vape pen, then asked, "You sick or something?"

"No, no."

"Sure?" The blotchy red in Jeff's face was fading a little. "You look like you're about to barf, man."

"I'm good," Chris said. "Let's just do this."

Jeff's brow furrowed, unconvinced. But he didn't press. He only took another hit off his vape pen, the cool, sweet smoke curling out of his nostrils. "All right, man. Whatever you say."

Monte and Frankel were sitting in their usual spots at the sound mixer.

Andrea, now changed out of her lavender dress and into dark jeans and a plain white T-shirt, was in the recording booth, chugging water from her tin flask, prepping her voice.

He was moving, moving. Chris paced frantically throughout that final recording session, from one end of the studio to the other. He felt like he was trying to outrun a demon. One of the demons was, in fact, there with him. And she worked smoothly—surprisingly smoothly compared to yesterday—through her recordings. Chris had been preparing himself, ears perked, body clenched tight and waiting, for his wife to call him into the recording booth to tell him it was *their* album now after all. Maybe they should start from square one and duet the entire thing? He was waiting for her to say she wanted to do lead vocals of her own, waiting for her to demand Monte and Frankel make her previously recorded tracks more prominent, almost matching the volume of Chris's lead vocal tracks.

She didn't do any of that, though she still seemed genuinely pleased. Bitterly pleased somehow.

The other demon was a small, white house on Leonard Street in South LA that he kept seeing in his mind. He would be staring over the hefty shoulders of Monte and Frankel into the recording booth, Andrea singing harmonies on tracks twelve and seventeen, the last two she needed to finish today, and he'd see that house.

He was your best friend.
Does he still live there?

But he kept pacing, kept trying to shake off the thoughts that just wouldn't let him go.

Monte and Frankel occasionally shot concerned glances over their wide shoulders as Chris paced the small studio space. Jeff would peer warily through a constant haze of bluish smoke. Andrea gave him worried looks too, but Chris saw through her Halloween mask of concern hiding, barely, the devilish twinkle in her eyes.

It was a far cry from the final recording sessions of Chris's previous albums. Final recording sessions were a joyous time. A time of celebration. Both Chris and Jeff were usually dancing around the studio at this time. Jeff would dance himself into a coughing fit, and Chris would be bubbling with laughter. Everyone was usually all smiles, the studio brimming with an ecstatic, positive energy.

Now Chris paced, fidgeted, his face twitching, then he'd pace some more.

Rich has Andre's phone.

By the session's last hour, Chris was sweating even though the studio was air-conditioned, his chest and underarms and the back of his neck wet.

Jeff grimaced behind a hazy curtain of vape smoke, occasionally popping antacids.

Monte and Frankel just looked sad and bored, elbows on the sound mixer and faces propped in their cupped hands.

It felt like a funeral rather than a final, celebratory recording session. In a way it was a funeral, only it was his solo career in the coffin.

Andrea was the only one who seemed sincerely happy. Though her happiness befuddled Chris. The finished product of the album hadn't *changed*, not even a little. It was maddening picturing both their names on the front of the album, the album essentially the same. Why? Why didn't she go further? She had already ruined Chris's life enough, why not rub salt in the wound?

"I think it's cause for celebration," Andrea said, pretending to sound oblivious to the puzzlement and frustration prickling beneath the stony faces around her.

Chris watched as she went to the mini fridge in the corner and pulled out a bottle of champagne and some glasses she'd apparently brought herself. Jeff gave Chris a look as she poured glasses. She handed one each to Monte and Frankel, knowing full well they wouldn't refuse a little bubbly after the four-hour session. Jeff shook his head, a bitter refusal, at an offered glass. Then Andrea offered the glass she'd just offered Jeff to Chris. Chris crossed his arms and shook his head, not just in refusal of the drink, but in disgust at her. In outrage. She shrugged and began sipping the glass herself.

While the three polished off the bottle, Jeff found a corner of the studio to escape into his cell phone, hardly looking at anyone else those last fifteen minutes or so that everyone was at the studio.

Chris glanced at Andrea, watching the way she schmoozed with Monte and Frankel. It was just like she always talked to them, only it wasn't. There was an artificial quality to her now, her grins and her words as fake as plastic.

This fakeness continued at home when Andrea called her personal chef, Amy, to cook some stroganoff. Chris was in his gym room, lifting weights in front of his recording camera, and every few minutes he would hear a burst of laughter like buckshot coming from the kitchen. Andrea and Amy always laughed a lot when they were together, but Andrea's laugh sounded synthetic now, like nails being driven into Chris's ears. No amount of push-ups, sit-ups, or chin-ups would make it go away. Yet he ignored the muscle aches and cramps from the workout with Ray earlier, and he slipped on his boxing gloves and punched the punching bag.

Whack! Whack! Whack! His gloved fist sunk into the punching bag. He was trying to punch away the image of that little white house on Leonard.

The earplugs only made it worse. He'd put them in to block out Andrea's shrill, phony laughter, but he felt even more isolated in his skull.

Whack! Whack!

And that house kept coming back. Other images came too. He saw Andrea hitting herself, blood and tears. He saw Marianne popping her pills.

Whack! Whack! Whack!

Then he saw the pair of headlights and the sound of a car breaking bones and he felt that warm pool of blood spreading beneath him, and he saw Tray Mansfield's eyes blinking helplessly up at him. He saw the doctors trying to explain to a furious, inconsolable Marianne Mansfield as they showed her MRIs of her son's brain—explaining, in scientific terms, how the light of her son's genius had been stolen from him after that accident. Tray Mansfield, head wrapped in bandages, crying tears of frustration as he tried to remember how to play his guitar, as he tried to remember how to write beautiful songs.

These images he couldn't seem to push from his mind, guilt and shame slowly devouring his soul. *Whack! Whack!*

The sun sank behind the hills and shadows clotted and stars glittered the night sky. A gentle, ominous breeze, still warm with sunshine residue, whispered through the palm trees.

Drenched in sweat, Chris pulled off his gloves, stopped the video recording. It wasn't helping. Odd. It always helped.

Wearing a pair of gym shorts and a towel wrapped around his neck, wiping his face with it occasionally when fresh dots of sweat appeared, he slowly approached the kitchen, where he heard the sound of running water. Amy must've left already, as he no longer heard her voice. But he could smell the beef stroganoff in the air.

Andrea's back was turned to him. She was rinsing her dinner plate. She turned off the water, set her plate on the dish rack to dry.

Chris stopped at the threshold of the kitchen feeling like a dark, heavy coat had been draped over his shoulders. He felt that tangle of bitter emotion in his mind, shame and guilt.

But he had to do something.

He scratched his burning, sweaty face, then grabbed a corner of the towel hanging around his neck and dabbed the sweat off.

Andrea still had her back turned to him, but she knew that he was standing there. She didn't acknowledge him.

Pop!

The sound of the popping champagne cork startled Chris. Andrea poured herself a fresh glass of bubbly.

"'Drea?"

She didn't turn around. Didn't speak.

He pushed away the images of her blood and tears, her pain. The images of the bruises on the tanned skin of her thighs flashed in his mind like a warning.

Then a new thought came to him, and he pulled his phone out of his shorts pocket, turned it on. He opened a video.

"You know, I was thinking about our honeymoon to London."

He pressed Play and peered at the screen, watching the two of them strolling down Carnaby Street in London. Chris, in the video, was holding the cell phone in selfie mode and their faces were bright, and Andrea seemed genuinely happy, her arms wrapped around Chris's waist, and she was smooching his neck. Pedestrians in the video glanced over their shoulders once, then again with a double take, then they'd cry out Chris's name and then it was like Chris was a magnet dragging along all his London fans in a long tail. He had a massive following in the United Kingdom.

The sound of their—Chris's and Andrea's—voices mingling happily together in that video had grabbed Andrea's attention. She was facing him now, holding her glass of champagne. She and Monte and Frankel had finished off that one bottle back at the studio and now she was working on this one alone. The fresh bottle stood waiting like a comfort on the counter. Her eyes were slightly pink, a little bloodshot. That fake grin was gone, her lips downturned, her face sagging with dejection.

Chris was torn between pity and his own anger at her.

"I was thinking we could go on another trip." He looked at her bright and genuinely happy smile in the video. He wanted that again. "Remember how much fun we had?"

She narrowed her eyes at the sound of the pedestrians yelling out Chris's name. But she looked like she was considering it, like she was mulling it over in her mind. "Go where?"

"We could go back to London. We could go to Japan. Brazil."

To his surprise, a chuckle escaped her. "What?"

She pursed her lips, shook her head. It looked like she was doing everything in her power to not explode in rage. "Nothing."

Chris just realized he'd inadvertently listed off places where, like in the UK, he had massive followings. Was that what she was laughing at? What was so funny to her about that?

"Okay, where would you like to go?"

She crumpled her lips, mocking deep thought.

"Would you quit it?"

That Halloween mask was back on, that cruel twinkle back in her eyes. She was hiding her sadness, her dejection, from him.

"What am I doing wrong?"

"You know what you're doing."

"No, I'm thinking about where I want to go," she said, then drained her glass. As she was refilling it, she said, "Tennessee."

"Tennessee?"

He knew what was waiting for her there, old friends, family, her hometown. But for a vacation? Anywhere else would have been preferable.

Yet Andrea was nodding determinedly.

"Why?"

Her plastic mask faded for a moment, and she glanced around. Though Chris couldn't read her expression, he noticed the sadness had returned. But she kept trying to bury it under that sometimes stoic, sometimes angry face.

"Because it's so *loud* here."

"Loud?"

She nodded, sipping bubbly. "Mmm. You know, I hate Rich with a passion," she added, brow sharpening, a thousand painful memories passing in the flicker of a second. "But he said something I've been thinking a lot about."

"I'd take what he says with a grain of salt, babe."

She put a finger to her lips and shushed Chris. Something about the gesture incensed him.

"He said how you could die choking on the fumes of people's egos here. All these celebrities crawling all over each other. 'Look at me. Look at me!' Just how pathetic so many of these people are." She grinned cunningly, took another sip.

Chris realized it must've been a jab at him, however clean the blade that sliced. He wanted to snatch the drink from her hands, wanted to slap that cute, smug look right off her face.

"He was right about that. *Definitely* was about that. That's why I think not a trip, but a complete change of scenery is in order." There was a sly look in her eyes.

Chris's face twitched as it hit him. "You want to move."

She glanced around the room again, and this time her mask faded for a longer period and he could read her unhappiness. Everything around her was expendable, the look said. There was a weightiness to her aura now. Even desperation.

"There's a place just outside my hometown. Three hundred acres. An old farmhouse for sale." She took a step closer.

Chris realized she'd already been scouting, apparently.

"It's a beautiful place. And the people in the town are wonderful. They're *real*."

"Real, huh?"

Chris wondered how *real* these people were. What did that even mean? He wondered how these people actually compared to her childhood illusions, her soft memories of them.

"Yes," she said sharply. "We could get horses. I had one when I was a little girl. Chickens. Goats."

"You want us," Chris said, pointing his finger from her to him for clarification. "To leave this." He gestured to the magnificent mansion surrounding them. "To just drop everything and leave Beverly Hills. What about our careers? Our music?" There was an edge to his voice now.

The look on her face told him everything. The look on her face said *Yes*. He noticed pink flaming her cheeks, her eyes a little more bloodshot, and he wanted once again to snatch her drink and put her to bed. But there was an earnestness about her, an urgency, that was beyond mere drunken ramblings. She really had thought long and hard about this.

"You're serious."

Her mask was gone, her face pure and grave. Chris's mind flashed to the images again, her punching herself, her tears, her pain.

All she wanted was to have a family with you. To make music with you.

He looked away, couldn't stand looking at her for another painful moment, and dabbed fresh sweat from his face with the towel around his neck.

He took a moment, considered what she was saying. He could almost hear the barnyard animals and feel the sweet, hot air. He imagined them both wearing cowboy hats for some reason, and the thought brought a brief, amused smile to his face. He thought about living in some rambling, old farmhouse. A big two-story place. He thought about making trips to the town's small, local grocery store.

Then he saw himself standing in the vast and barren three-hundred-acre field with the sun shining down on him. No paparazzi. No Rich. No Wally. No Andre. No Marianne. No cameras. No spotlights. No anyone.

The last thoughts turned his face pale, made him feel sick to his stomach.

He faced Andrea again, questions burning in his eyes. She stared at him, waiting.

Then she said something, but she'd spoken so quietly he'd missed it. "What?"

"Please," she said. Her plastic mask was completely gone now, just a raw desperation, woe, even hope in her emerald eyes. She looked at him like this was their last chance.

Then a sudden feeling of betrayal struck Chris like a sucker punch. Because he remembered her at the banquet, her chilliness when Marianne was talking about Chris's new album. He thought about that dinner he and Andrea and Andrea's mother, Carly, had shared last month, remembered Andrea rolling her eyes when Carly was talking about Chris's album. He could see it clearly now, like the rose-tinted glasses had been lifted from his eyes. His wife, sweet, humble little Andrea, was no better than bitter, insecure people everywhere. Chris generally ignored the haters. Haters who were critical of successful people like him, those who were envious because they wanted what Chris had but knew they'd never have it. He hadn't realized, until now, that he was married to a hater.

"You jealous bitch."

Andrea's mouth dropped. "What'd you say?"

"You just can't stand it, can you? You can't stand my success. You hate living in my shadow, huh? You *want* me to fail! That's why you're doing all this shit with the album. It's why you want me to move to fucking Tennessee with you. You wanna sabotage me!"

Andrea shook her head. She looked baffled. "Is that what you think? You really think I care about that bullshit?"

"What do you want me to think?"

Andrea drained her glass, her face stony again. She was done explaining to him. She snatched the champagne bottle from off the counter, and as she poured herself another glass she said, "Last chance, Chris."

It was a threat. And Chris felt his heart hammering. But he steadied himself and felt a small but glorious smile appear on his face. "Fuck you." He leaned in as he said it, feeling powerful.

Her eyes widened. She was stunned. Her red fingernails clicked threateningly on the champagne bottle.

Then, in a rage, she threw it at him.

He ducked, and the bottle shattered on the hardwood floor behind him, scattering glass shards and booze.

Andrea charged at him. "I hate you! I hate you!" she screamed, punching him.

Any remaining love between them withered and died.

Chris snatched her flinging wrists. "Bitch!" he cried.

Then, in the blink of an eye, she was on the floor. He had shoved her, hard. She gazed up at him, her face mottled like a child's after a fit, tears streaming down her freckled cheeks, those big green eyes flashing with betrayal.

She was trying to stand back up.

Chris, remorsefully, tried to grab her by her hands and help her back up.

She smacked his hands away. "Fuck off!"

She shoved past him and stormed toward the front door. But she stopped, hand resting on the doorknob, like she had forgotten something.

Then she whipped around. Her face was a red sun of fury. Her smile was humorless, full of malice. "I'm gonna ruin you, Chris Flowers!"

Then she exited, slamming shut the massive oaken door behind her and rattling the mansion's bones. Chris heard the sound of her Porsche screaming off into the evening. He stood there for a moment, stunned. His flesh was crawling, his head buzzing. He realized his whole body was trembling.

    He looked at the mess on the floor, then took the towel from around his neck and cleaned up the shattered champagne bottle. The towel had his golden initials embroidered into it, and the white towel turned the color of urine as he swabbed up the booze.

    When he was finished, he sent a text to Jeff.

CHAPTER SEVENTEEN
2008

Chris and his group were playing at a bar called Mike's. Out the windows you could see the streaming headlights of evening traffic on Hollywood Boulevard. The skyscrapers of downtown were silhouettes against the orange sky, night getting thicker, shadows starting to gather. The bar wasn't enormous, wasn't a stadium, but it had two large rooms. The far room was the bar and had tables and flat-screen TVs showing a football game on mute, the announcers' commentary in subtitles. The band stage was set up in the other, larger room, a restaurant setting with tables and booths and waiters and waitresses passing in and out.

Chris peered through the hot spotlight, could see into the bar area where the shapes of a few hunched figures were moping over beers, picking at baskets of fries or buffalo wings. Most of the people in the bar that night were pressed against the stage, forty or so faces like happy blooming flowers around Chris's feet. They'd played at empty bars all throughout South Central. They'd played to hunched shapes who stared into beers, guzzled them like dinner, then left without even glancing at the band playing in the corner. Every time Chris entered an establishment like that, his heart sunk. It was a feeling of utter despair and humiliation playing only to a bartender who was more interested in the TV, or playing to Maria—ever present at every show, always giving Chris a thumbs-up even when she was the only one there. Sometimes a nice couple would come in, cross the dark, empty bar, and sip their beers and bob their heads politely to their music. This was somehow most embarrassing of all; he'd rather play to no one.

Chris was playing hot tonight. He could feel his love for music, could feel its healing powers leap like electric demons out of him, jumping into the ears of the crowd. He peered through the spotlight, spotted Maria standing in the back under the bathroom sign. She said she hadn't been feeling good, but said she wouldn't miss Chris's show for anything. She glanced at the crowd of forty, then gave Chris two thumbs-up, and beamed a bright, toothy smile at him.

It had been two months since they played at El Lugar. The bar's manager gave it to Chris straight. "Anyone can play someone else's songs. You guys have been together, what, four years, and you say you haven't gotten any traction? It's because you guys are a cover band. Playing covers of Otis Redding and Prince and Genesis, that's all well and good, but you guys need to start writing your own music if you want to get anywhere. You say you don't have a lot of originals, but the ones I heard on your guys' band page, they're something special, I think."

They were on their last song, an original. Chris strummed his guitar, a chord progression he'd written all on his own, and sang lyrics that came straight from his heart. Most of the songs on their set list that night were originals, with a few covers thrown in for added spice. After what El Lugar's manager told them, Chris had been struck with inspiration, writing a flurry of originals. He realized for four years he'd been nothing but an imitator. He'd always known he wanted to play music, had always known music had healing power, had always known the soul of an artist was burning within him.

He realized he'd been afraid to really try to write something on his own. Manny and Daryl weren't songwriters, didn't have the ambition to write music on their own, so it was left up to Chris. He'd spent too many years envious of the talent of those who'd written the great songs he covered, and too insecure to write music of his own.

Not anymore.

He strummed the final chord of the night, Daryl slapping the last bass notes, Manny rapping out the final beats of the drums, and Chris held his head high as the music faded, as the applause swallowed the silence, supremely confident in the recent music he'd written, in the show they'd just played. He kept his eyes shut, drinking in the applause and the cheers like he was standing under a warm, golden ray of light.

Yet Chris's feet were glued to that stage, and he was still staring at the audience even as they scattered from the floor to the bar in the next room to get a few beers in them before the next band came on. Chris supposed even if these were his fans that they could like other bands too—you didn't have to *just* like the Beatles or *just* like the Temptations. You could like them both.

Then a slew of people started pouring in through the front entrance, people who hadn't watched Chris perform, who were *only* there for the next band. There were at least a hundred people in the bar now, and Chris was done playing. But he still couldn't move.

"Hey, Chris?"

Chris finally turned around, his back to the microphone and spotlight.

Daryl looked exhausted and more ruffled than usual. His beard had grown longer, and his hair wasn't cut. Had he stopped going to his sister's as much? His T-shirt was soaked with sweat, and bags hung under his eyes. His eyes were also a little bloodshot.

Chris had been surprised that Daryl started drinking. Three empty pint glasses, froth at the bottom, were standing beside Daryl's bass amp. Was the stress of juggling his day job and the band finally taking its toll?

We're all juggling band and day jobs, Chris thought bitterly.

"You okay, bro?"

"Yeah," Chris said.

"Show's over, man."

I don't even shoot up at band practice anymore. I at least wait till I get home to do that. "I know. Man, can you do your drinking when you get home?"

Daryl's face twitched. "What?"

"You're getting sloppy, man. In your playing."

Daryl's look of confusion turned into annoyance. "Man, why you gotta get on my case? You've been doing that a lot."

"Because I care about the group! Because . . ." Chris stopped, took a breath, realized his shouts were drawing looks of concern from a few people sitting at their booths and eating thick cheeseburgers.

He sighed. "I'm sorry, bro. I'm tired, too. I know it. We all are."

Chris helped carry gear to the van in the back lot, bumping past the headlining act who were setting up their amps and drum set.

It was a dry, warm September night, still early enough that the moon was a hazy, ill-defined blur through the smog.

Chris stuffed in his guitar amp, the last of their gear, then clicked shut the door. He glanced toward the glowing rear entrance where the next band was hauling in their guitars and amps. The sound of the chattering, anticipating crowd—*including my fans!*—spilled out.

"I'm gonna stay for a bit," Chris said without looking at Daryl or Manny. "Watch the next act." Chris chewed his lower lip; it was the last thing he wanted to do.

"Did you notice my sister's been in the bathroom the entire time we've been hauling shit out?" Manny's voice was prickly.

Chris faced Manny, his long brown hair in a ponytail, his face filled with color, looking healthier. He was managing to stay off the needle. He scratched his scraggly mustache, shot Chris daggers.

"Yeah, she's been in the bathroom the entire show, bro," Chris bit back.

"You realize she's about to burst. Sicker than a dog."

Chris's face was burning. "Yeah." *I ain't stupid, asshole.*

"You gonna stick around? Not take her home?"

Chris looked at Daryl, ignoring Manny.

Daryl's eyes were fixed on the streaming lights of Hollywood Boulevard, his face creased with discomfort. *He's still pissed off. I told him I was sorry. If he wants to be an asshole, then fuck him.*

"After work, band practice tomorrow."

He and Daryl bumped fists. Chris offered his fist to Manny to bump.

Manny didn't bump back. He just turned around, climbed into the driver's side of the van, and the van growled to life. It was like Manny had turned into the van itself, this big metal creature, snarling at Chris. Exhaust spewed into the warm, dry air.

"Man, he's been acting weird lately," Daryl said. "Do you know what's up?"

Chris shrugged, then lied. "I'm not sure, man."

Daryl nodded, then climbed into the passenger's seat of the van and Manny screeched out of the back lot.

Chris returned to the bar.

He searched for Maria. Several people stopped him as he crossed the room, complimenting him on the killer show, their beer breath wafting in his face. Chris unclenched his fists, his thoughts less thorny.

Manny can be pissed at me all he wants. But he's lucky to be in this band. Daryl, too. I write all the songs. Where would those two end up if it weren't for me?

Chris spotted Maria coming out of the bathroom, wiping her mouth and then crunching on some mints. Her bobbing belly looked about to burst under her loose T-shirt with the band's name on it. The dark circles beneath her eyes stood out on her ashen flesh. However, she smiled anyway, no matter how sick she felt, when her eyes met his.

As she approached, Chris stared at her belly.

You're going to be a father. And soon. Anytime now.

The thought sent a flood of excitement and uncertainty shooting through him, as it did every time he *really* considered it. Was he ready? Would he be able to support a child? It hadn't been planned, having a kid, though a family with Chris had been a dream of Maria's. When Chris first found out she was pregnant—and saw how overjoyed she was about it—some of his excitement had been feigned, for her, really. He had hoped to be truly well established in his musical career first, wanting to support his family solely from writing and playing music, had wanted to have achieved that dream first. But after El Lugar and after tonight's show he felt himself growing confident again, felt that he would be able to juggle raising a child and still pursuing his dreams of becoming a successful musician.

"They loved you!" Maria said, then wrapped her arms around him.

Chris's smile faded when he looked at the hundred or so people pressed up against the stage, their attention intensely focused on the band up there now doing sound checks. "Check! Check! Check one!

Check one, two!" More people trickled from the bar area sipping cold bottles of beer, then merged into the massive pulsating crowd.

"Wanna stick around and see the headliners?" Chris asked.

Maria promptly shook her head.

"I wanna stick around. Mingle a little."

Maria looked at him like he'd gone crazy. "You wanna *mingle?*" Her voice was edged with impatience.

"With my fans?"

"With your fans? But they're watching the next band?"

"Look, I don't . . ." Chris bit his tongue, studied his wife's gray and waxy face and her dark, sunken eyes. He sighed and brushed back some of the sweaty strands of dark hair clinging to her forehead. "I'm sorry. I know you ain't feeling good, babe." He sighed, nodded. "Okay. Let's go home."

On their way back to their apartment at Hoagland Heights, they drove through a McDonald's.

Later, Maria passed out in front of the TV, the coffee table littered with burger wrappers and French fry containers.

While she snored, Chris was in the bathroom sitting on the closed lid of the toilet using his McDonald's straw to snort heroin off his knuckle. It was a fine white powder; Andre had told Chris it was pure, so he could just snort it straight up.

You promised Maria.

The dope felt like snorting cinders, his nostrils stinging. But soon the hard edges of reality began to soften.

It's just for sleep. Maria doesn't need to find out. She doesn't need any more stress.

Chris flushed, even though he didn't use the toilet. He stuffed the baggie of dope in his little hidey spot under the sink, then left the bathroom. His legs felt rubbery as he crossed the living room toward the couch where his wife snoozed. The dope would help him cross the lonely bridge to sleep. It was his least favorite part of the day, the time when you're in bed alone with your thoughts and trying to get to sleep.

He curled up on the couch with Maria, creeping in and spooning her quietly so as not to wake her.

At some point, the sound of the TV getting further and further away, Chris drifted off.

His respite didn't last long.

It was maybe an hour later when Chris was woken by Maria's cries of pain.

"Chris! Oh God, Chris!"

"What, babe? What is it?" Cold reality washed over him, her panicked shouts piercing through his hazy, dope-clouded brain.

"The baby's coming!"

CHAPTER EIGHTEEN
JULY 2023

Jeff called almost immediately after the message had been sent. It felt good to step outside. The house seemed to be expanding, seemed to be growing all around him, swallowing him whole, so he sat on the top step of the stone stairs that led down to the gravel driveway. Chris answered the call, put the phone to his ear.

"It's really done?" Jeff's voice sounded almost giddy.

"Yeah, it's over. I just kicked her ass out of the house."

Chris caught the skid marks, dark, angry scars left by the Porsche's tires as Andrea sped out of there. But even more so, he caught the fear in his voice.

"Thank Christ." Jeff sighed. "The people are gonna get whiplash when they find out she's not on the album."

Chris was trying to focus on what Jeff was saying, but his eyes drifted to the edges of his estate, to those thick outer shadows. A warm breeze whispered ominously through the palm trees and shrubbery.

Jeff was saying other things now, joyous things, sounding like—hallelujah!—he'd found Jesus or something, but Chris couldn't share his manager's excitement and enthusiasm. He just sat there under the warm blue moon and stared at shadows. The night-shift guard was still walking the property, but Chris no longer felt safe. Was Rich out there? Following Andrea, maybe? Was what Rich said on the phone earlier that morning true? What would Andrea do?

Then Jeff's voice rose out of the bubbling dark morass of Chris's worries and fears.

"Chris? Chris, you still there?"

"Yeah, I'm here, man."

"So, was it?"

"Was it what?" Chris had missed the question.

"Was it ugly?"

Jeff must have meant the breakup scene, to which Chris said, "Yep." Chris also realized that now that Andrea was gone, he could tell Jeff what'd happened. He felt Jeff needed to know, to understand Chris's bizarre behavior earlier that day. And so Chris told him. He told Jeff everything.

When he was done, Jeff said, "Ah, I see. Makes sense why you were acting all fucked up, man. Christ, I always knew that bitch was crazy."

Chris stared out into the dark, crickets chirping, dogs barking in the distance. He shivered in the warm evening air, wondering what tomorrow would bring. But something else was gnawing at him. When she'd turned around wearing that ferocious, determined grin and said: *I'm gonna ruin you, Chris Flowers!*

"She said she was gonna fuck me over, Jeff."

Jeff didn't have an immediate response. Chris could almost hear his manager's thoughts as he ran through the possibilities of what *that* might mean. Then he could hear the *bubbly* sound of Jeff sucking on his vape pen.

"Well," Jeff finally said, "you can always, you know, hire someone."

It was meant as a joke, but it only sounded like half a joke.

Chris was ashamed to picture it so clearly. A hired gun pointing a silenced pistol at Andrea's temple and firing.

He shook the thought from his head. "Hey, man, why would you even *think* something like that?"

"It's not like it hasn't been done before."

Chris knew what Jeff was getting at, and Chris wanted to pretend he hadn't even thought it.

A sudden unexpected chill was in the air now, though it was nothing the breeze had carried—it was an *inner* chill.

Chris suddenly regretted answering Jeff's call.

And why did you ever tell Jeff about that business five years ago?

Because Chris could trust Jeff—after all they'd been through together.

"Well, shit, man, I'm just glad it's over. And we'll just see."

Jeff was talking about tomorrow.

What will happen tomorrow? Chris thought.

He stared off into the shadows, a lost gaze, and he saw it again. That house. That white house on Leonard Street. The one he'd been to a thousand times.

He was your best friend, man.

"Chris? Hello?"

"Yeah."

"Jesus Christ, man. Snap out of it."

Chris bobbed his head, wanting to break free from his grim thoughts. "I know, I know."

"It's done. And things . . ." Jeff paused and sighed uncertainly.

Chris could hear it in Jeff's voice, Jeff trying to convince himself.

"Things will go back to normal. All right, man?"

"All right," Chris said, voice trembling.

"Hey, I'm here for you. All right? I'm not going anywhere."

A small smile appeared on Chris's face, and he tried to take consolation in his manager's words, though he couldn't. They said goodbye, then Chris hung up.

* * *

He returned to the gym room. He could still smell the sweat, sour and pungent, from his earlier workout. Now there wouldn't be any interruptions. He was reminded of that when he walked through the silent and eerily empty house.

He turned on his cell phone camera, set it up on its tripod, pressed Record, then turned on the ring light using its remote. He examined himself a moment in his selfie camera mode, pressed a button on the ring light remote to bring it up. He went to work sliding the weights onto the bench press bar, remembering when he was thirty-one, thirty-two maybe, and Ray had said he'd started hitting up this place, this gym, in Beverly Hills that, as Ray put it, "you could definitely afford now, kid." Ray was the one who'd introduced Chris to Beverly Hills Health and Wellness.

Chris put a hundred and ninety-five pounds' worth of iron on the bench bar. He regarded this with a troubled look, his mind skimming back over those early memories. After Chris got sober, he'd worked himself up to pressing two-fifty, two-sixty pounds. Of course, he'd been hitting the weights almost every day back then as compared to his routine two or three days a week now. Ray said he'd once been able to press over three hundred pounds himself during his younger, slimmer years, that he just wasn't working himself as hard as he used to. Still, the old guy had been pressing one-sixty today, and that probably wasn't even his max.

Chris felt a fierce determination suddenly grip him and he added more iron rings to the press bar. Two hundred and ten. Two hundred and twenty-five. Two-fifty. Two-sixty. He felt his blood drumming desperately, urgently in his veins.

Do you wanna end up like Ray?

With two hundred and sixty pounds of weight ready to be lifted, Chris took a seat on the black, foam-padded bench, could already feel a sweat breaking out on his forehead before even lifting the thing.

Then he regarded the camera that was still recording him, and he suddenly felt words rising up in his throat. He would be posting this video to his social media. This was going to be a video meant to address the fans. So he looked into the camera's eye with the respect and dignity as if all his fans were standing right there before him.

"Hey, everyone," he said. "Chris Flowers here. The reason I'm talking to you all here today is 'cause there's been another change in plans with the album that I think you should know about." He shifted on the bench, suddenly feeling uncomfortable for some reason. Then he continued. "Well, you see, me and my wife had plans to surprise you all with us doing a duet album. It didn't start that way. See, I felt sorry for her. You all know the critics didn't take too kindly to her most recent solo album." He pursed his lips, made a solemn face, like a sad face at a funeral. "I wanted to give her a boost. You know, put her name on the album, make her feel good. But then I changed my mind right quick." He gave the camera a sly wink and grin. "Because you all were expecting a Chris Flowers album and have been for the past three years. And I wasn't gonna cheat you all on that. I love y'all."

He beamed a grin into the camera, held it, held it for far too long, until it was almost cartoonish. Words died on his tongue. A shame-filled red spread across his face and forehead and down his neck. He was feeling disgusting somehow, like he'd caught himself red-handed doing something terrible. But what? He made videos for his fans all the time. But it wasn't that.

You're lying. About Andrea. You're lying to your fans.

The thought soured his stomach.

The camera was still staring at him, and Chris found himself frozen, at a loss for words. He looked away from the camera, submitting, unable to hold its eye contact.

Images of the day's events haunted him when he shut his eyes.

Chris lay back and was glaring challengingly up at the mass of iron suspended above his head. He told himself not to worry about the video. He could edit that last part out later. Then he took a deep breath and gripped the cool bar. He shivered slightly in nervousness: it'd been years since he even tried lifting two-sixty. But then he pictured himself ten, fifteen years from now, but looking and behaving just like Ray, a defeated, *forgotten* old man. He ignored his anxieties and hesitations and lifted the damned thing.

He immediately wondered if he was going to regret his rash action. It took all his might just to heave the bar over the metal lips that held it in place. It felt like a car was on top of him, slowly crushing him down, slowly breaking bones. But to his surprise he was able to hold the weight up off his chest. He kept his arms extended straight out, dreading bringing that weight down only to lift it back up again. It took everything he had to do the first lift, lowering the deadweight dangerously close to his skull. It made him think of an anvil like in one of those Wile E. Coyote cartoons. But he managed it, then pushed through a second lift, then a third, a pained, agonizing expression on his face. He ignored his howling muscles—muscles already well-tested from his previous workouts today. But he wasn't going to stop, not until he did ten. No, fifteen, he decided.

In the middle of number six he felt something like a mosquito in his ear. Like flies on his face. But it was nothing external. It was something going on *inside* him. Inside his own mind.

He tried to focus on the searing pain in his muscles, the fire in his forearms, trying to ignore the gnawing images of what he'd lost. Like Andrea's beloved Taylor acoustic-electric, looking somehow tragic sitting up there in their bedroom, un-played, abandoned.

He did a seventh, then to his surprise and pleasure an eighth rep.

He thought of all the women in the world who would watch him lift two-sixty.

He could have any woman in the world, he realized.

Any woman.

Then Rich reappeared, that mosquito-in-the-ear feeling returning. He saw Rich's grinning, bearded face, heard that baleful, altered voice, remembered Rich's threats.

He has Andre's phone.

He was on number ten, the bar kissing his chest, and now he was trying to heave the weight back up into the air to do five more. But the weight seemed to have grown exponentially. The hands of gravity began shoving the bar back toward Chris's chest. His arms trembled. His muscles felt like they were on fire.

You're crazy if you don't change your number, Jeff had said.

No need, man. Everything went perfect. Ain't nothing to worry about.

It's Daryl! It's me, man. Please. Stop. Untie me! Let me go!

Chris still tried to push the thoughts away, tried to focus on his self-induced pain. His arms now felt like toothpicks trying to hold up concrete blocks. Sweat pooled in his eyes, which widened in terror as he realized he couldn't get the bar back up to its perch, and there was no one to call out to. No one was coming to save him.

Then the bar was squarely on his neck where it met his chest, strangling him. He was gasping for air, trying to lift this impossible weight. The world grew dark for a moment, the ceiling lights seeming to dim. With a last effort he managed to slide off the side of the bench and out from under the bar, which he just managed to ease down on the bench seat. Chris landed on the bright blue matted floor. He was choking, clawing at his burning throat, his crushed windpipe trying to take in oxygen. He was on his hands and knees, and he coughed and hacked phlegm onto the mat until he was able to take in precious little sips of air.

Sweat-drenched, mouth a gaping hole gasping for air, he looked up and stared into the camera that was still recording him. He snatched the cell phone off its tripod, then erased the video, but not because of the incident at the end.

You lied to them.

He decided not to tell the world about Andrea or the album. Not now. That could wait.

He lifted the bar—the bar that had almost killed him—back up onto the metal lips, then sat on the bench seat. Hot sweat dripped off his brow. He realized he could lift weights all night and punch his punching bag or take a plane across the world, but nothing would banish those images from his head. Sleep would be impossible. Rich was in his mind again.

That white house on Leonard Street.

Then a single word rose to Chris's lips, the word heavy with regret, weary with panic. "Daryl."

* * *

If anyone had asked Chris even a week earlier if he ever would return to South Central, he would've insisted the idea was batshit crazy. There was no reason to return. He didn't play shows there. He had no family or friends there, at least not anymore. That place he had shucked off like the dead skin of an old life best left forgotten.

And yet return he did. He felt he had no choice but to go, to go back to that place, and found himself in his Ferrari, nodding goodbye to his night security guard, who just gave him a dubious look, then nodded back.

He drove under a moon full and bright, at first somehow reassuring as he looked up at it. When Chris reached the end of his quiet street, he stopped, hesitating, trying to convince himself to turn around, to just go back home. What was he doing?

But he couldn't go back.

He wasn't yet sure why. Unfinished business?

Daryl was your best friend since high school, man!

So he had to go.

As he neared the lights of town, he realized it wouldn't be wise to drive his Ferrari into South Central. His worried eyes jumping to the rearview mirror, he started making turns, heading toward his massive car compound on East Murray Street.

* * *

His Ferrari purred past the sign that read *Chris Flowers Automotive: Car Collection and Social Club—Membership Only.* He drove past the members' parking lot, punched in the code, and entered through the main gate. He drove past the massive outdoor racetrack. As Chris drove by, he took a moment to relish memories of sitting behind the wheel of one of his dozens of flashy cars, under a thick race-car helmet, zipping around the corners of the racetrack, the place packed during one of the club's weekend extravaganzas. He remembered the applause like a fine rain. The people, all their eyes on him. Thinking about it made him feel tingly all over.

But he shook his head, snapping out of it. He was here alone, nothing going on, no event, no reality TV show being filmed, just him and an empty lot.

He entered the garage, parked in an empty spot surrounded by sports and muscle cars, stepped out, and scanned the collection. A wave of bitter anger struck him, and he cursed Rich in his head—Rich, the cause of all of this; Rich, the reason why he was skulking around now.

He approached his old beige 1972 Chevy El Camino with the black stripe running down the hood.

He tapped nostalgically on the car's cool roof, remembering back to the days he used to drive this thing. "You'll do fine."

But it ain't fine, he thought, his face crinkling, resentful. *Nothing about this is fine! This ain't like me, cruising around in my old El Camino, hiding, like a coward!*

Chris sighed, resigned, reminding himself he couldn't drive that damn loud Ferrari around South Central.

That's like wearing a Hawaiian shirt at a funeral.

The garage opened its steel mouth again, and Chris pulled the beige Chevy El Camino out into the night.

He drove the old boy around the corner, its heavy vibrations sending old memories through his fingers.

The lights of the city rolled off the car's unassuming, workaday lines. It wasn't a car that made heads turn. It wasn't like the Ferrari.

Look at me, sneaking around like some nobody.

Still, he peered into the rearview mirror, saw no suspicious black Suburban following him. No one else was pointing him out and drawing attention to him either. And he could have that, at least for the time being.

He was surprised he hadn't seen Rich. When had he last seen him? The night before?

Chris kept the radio off as he crept deeper into south LA. He didn't want to hear news about himself or anything. He just wanted the silence for a bit. But with the silence came thoughts of Rich that trickled into his skull. As he cruised in his Camino deeper and deeper into the city, the landscape transforming around him, skyscrapers rising and looming like dark figures above him, he started thinking about things Andrea had said about Rich.

Chris supposed he was trying to get a handle on this man.

Andrea met Rich after she moved to LA from Nashville. They were both going to California Institute of the Arts, she for music and Rich for English. He wanted to be a novelist. Andrea met him in an English composition course she was taking to give her songwriting skills a boost. She had fallen madly in love with the small dark-haired and dark-eyed man who dressed in all black and sat in the back row. She said she'd been smitten by the young poet. He was very romantic back then, she said.

That was crazy to Chris, that this evil little man had ever been romantic.

Andrea and Rich married the year Rich published his first book. His book failed miserably. And it crushed him. He'd been working on that book since his freshman year, three years of his life down the toilet. Three years.

It made Chris think about the three long, hard years he'd been working on his own project.

Andrea said Rich got really depressed and that she tried to help pull him out of it. She encouraged him to get work in journalism or in the movies while she focused on her music career. He could get started on another book.

Didn't happen that way, Andrea had said on their honeymoon. She took a sip of red wine and explained, *He was in line at the supermarket when he saw a tabloid showing this unflattering picture of some actor or musician or something. That was the moment he decided to pursue a career as a paparazzi guy. It was so painful, seeing someone who was so full of dreams turn into this bitter, destructive creature.*

A creature now trying to ruin Chris.

Chris checked the rearview mirror again as soon as he passed under the I-10 overpass and into South Central. It was still clear.

What seemed like hundreds of liquor store signs glowed in the shadows. Church steeples stabbed the starry sky. Chris drove past endless bus stops and saw the formless shapes of homeless people sleeping on many of the bus stop benches. He saw an old, bearded man talking to himself on the dirty sidewalk. He saw parked cars and shady figures shooting paranoid glances his way. It brought Chris back to his younger years, and he recalled how unnerving it was to walk these streets at night by yourself.

He found and turned onto Leonard Street. Chained dogs barked at him from behind fences. He passed a few beater cars abandoned on the curbs, some guy wearing a black hoodie peering in through one of the car's windows. A middle-aged woman with her hair up in a messy bun smoked a cigarette on her front porch, absentmindedly watching the inconspicuous El Camino cruising by. Stray cats flashed across the street, Chris nearly hitting one.

He pulled up to a small house on the corner of the street.

Daryl's old house.

Chris parked on the curb beside another car, a dented blue Volkswagen. Daryl's? Maybe his mother's or father's? Did Daryl still live with them?

Chris stepped out of the car. The air smelled like cigarette smoke, fried food, and car exhaust. He searched the windows of the house for signs of life, but the curtains were drawn, the house only glaring back ominously. He locked his car door, then approached the sagging chain-link fence that cordoned off a tiny square of yard overgrown with weeds.

What the hell am I doing here?

If you don't confess to what you did, Daryl dies. Get cops involved, I'll slit Daryl's throat.

The front door, heck, the whole house, needed a fresh coat of paint. Chris remembered the house had been better taken care of back when he was still living in the neighborhood. The walls had been a bright white and not so weathered, the front yard a neat patch of green and not the weed-choked patch of dirt strewn with beer cans.

Chris knocked on the door, but no one answered.

He quickly glanced behind him, hearing a car's rumbling approach; a low-riding gray Chevy with the speakers blaring bone-rattling gangster rap at earsplitting volume cruised slowly by then disappeared around the corner.

Chris knocked again, glanced left and right, then behind him again. No one there, no one on his ass, just the bright calling of mockingbirds in the gnarled oaks lining the street.

He knocked on the door again. "Daryl?"

He knocked yet again, hoping, but then was deflated when only silence returned. "Daryl, it's Chris."

Chris glanced behind him as he tried the knob, and to his pleasant surprise it turned, the door opening without resistance.

"Daryl?" Chris said as he entered the house and shut the door behind him, muffling the sound of barking dogs.

His armpits ran with sweat, which also rolled down his back as he entered the living area of the house, his feet crunching over junk food wrappers and pizza boxes.

He was your best friend. We used to play guitar here and watch movies.

Every surface was covered with empty beer or soda cans, mostly beer. Cigarette butts and ash littered the grimy countertops. A few cockroaches crawled across *Guitar World* magazines. It looked like death itself had passed through this place and left in its wake rot and shadows. A few weak lamps were on, lighting up corners of the small living room. A battered acoustic guitar lay propped in the corner.

Chris was surprised at the filth of the house, and at the number of empty beer cans lying around—an alcoholic's wasteland. It was a stark contrast to Daryl's early years, when he had disapproved of alcohol and cigarettes, spending hours cleaning his parents' house, and also maintaining his well-groomed appearance.

Chris's wandering eyes caught the tattered couch. Was it the same one that'd been here when Chris and Daryl were teenagers?

We used to sit there, eyes bright with big dreams, cracking jokes, playing guitar together, writing amateurish songs.

Chris hung his head in sadness, then looked away, the painful memories cutting into him.

On the far wall he noticed two urns side by side on a shelf. He approached. Framed photographs sat beside the bronze urns, and the kind, craggy faces of Daryl's parents stared back at him. When had they died? How long had Daryl been left alone here, alone with the ghosts of his dead parents?

"Daryl!" Chris said, an edge in his voice now.

He checked the empty kitchen area. Nothing but towers of unpaid bills on the countertops surrounded by more crushed beer cans.

"You here, man?"

The house felt smaller than Chris had remembered. In his growing panic, it felt like the walls were closing in around him.

He searched the bathroom and then the two bedrooms, his dread growing. He knew he was getting desperate when he searched under beds and in closets.

The house spat him out into the backyard. He wiped his sweaty forehead with the back of his trembling hand. His attention was drawn across the yard and over a rusty chain-link fence to the sound of a TV blaring out the open slide door of the neighboring house. He started walking toward the fence, saw shadows stirring behind a glowing window. He stood at the edge of the yard in shadows, his hand curled over the fence, about to call out to whoever it was. To ask if they'd seen Daryl.

You want somebody to see you now? Here?

A giant rottweiler's brown and black face appeared in the open doorway and the dog started growling, its hackles going up.

Chris slowly backed away.

The dog started barking, and a voice roused from inside said, "Whatcha barking at, huh?"

Chris turned and hurried back into the house before anyone could spot him. He stood in the living room of that silent and empty and filthy house. His eyes darted, swearing he saw movement, something creeping, skulking about in the corner. On closer inspection he realized it was just a rat picking through the garbage, making little squeaky sounds.

Chris shuddered, tried to ignore the rat.

Your old friend Daryl was easy to find. Just a quick online search. Working at a Guitar Center.

Chris suddenly pictured Daryl on the couch in his Guitar Center uniform, having just got off work and picked up a case of beer on the way home. Chris pictured the fading light of dusk trying to pierce the closed curtains, and Daryl smoking a cigarette and sipping his fifth or sixth beer, glancing occasionally at the shrine of his parents on the far wall, at the bronze urns that gleamed dully in the lamplight, at the pictures.

Rich warned you. He warned you. But you didn't listen. Rich has Andre's phone.

Daryl was forty, same age as Chris. How long had Daryl been here alone in this house, drinking away the years, middle-aged and working at Guitar Center? Chris could feel the dark despair in the air. Then the vision turned evil when Chris pictured the front door creaking open on its rusty hinges, and a dark lone figure standing in the light.

You didn't listen, and now Daryl is gone. Rich has Daryl's phone. Did Rich follow Daryl home from work at Guitar Center?

What was Chris doing here? What, did he think Daryl would be here and that he was going to just stop on by and catch up with his old friend? And even if Daryl was here, would he have even allowed Chris into his house?

Then Chris remembered something. Something he had forgotten about. He pulled his cell phone out of his pocket, remembering the message Rich had sent, the message with the attachment.

You didn't forget about it! You've been avoiding it completely!

He opened the message, hands trembling.

What popped up stole his breath.

He realized he wasn't at this house because he assumed Daryl might still be here. No, Chris was here because he *needed* to be here, *needed* to see the empty house for himself.

He was staring at a picture of a black man tied to a chair under a bare yellow bulb. The man's eyes were jaundiced, his puffy cheeks spiderwebbed with burst blood vessels. A beer belly hung over a pair of wispy legs in silky black shorts. He had a head of thick black hair with wisps of middle-aged gray in there and a full, scraggly beard. A red bandanna was tied around his mouth. Daryl stared back with terrified, pleading eyes, hands tied behind his back.

There was a simple caption. *NO POLICE. BETWEEN YOU AND ME.*

CHAPTER NINETEEN

He felt drunk all of a sudden, the El Camino's steering wheel with a mind of its own. It took Chris all his effort just to try to keep the Camino moving in a straight line down the street. He hated himself for not calling the police. He almost had, but hesitated at the last second, just as he hesitated calling the police after Andrea had struck herself. He was shackled by his fears. What if he did call the cops, and what if there was a massive investigation that hit the news? And then what if Rich—wherever he was, watching the news—made good on his threat of killing Daryl in cold blood?

Chris could see his new destination in his mind and found himself on Diamond Street.

Yeah, man, Andre had said when Chris had made that fateful call five years ago. *I'm living on Diamond Street now, got in trouble with some gangbangers, man. So me and Wally are here now. Haven't heard from you in years, though I'm hearing all about you, man. Ain't you clean now?*

I am. Been clean a year, man. I ain't calling about drugs.

Chris could see Andre and Wally's house now, getting closer.

Rich's words filled Chris's skull: *He's been dead in my basement since yesterday. Still need to get rid of him.*

Then Chris's mind started exploding with questions, questions he'd been trying to drown out all day, questions that now filled his mind.

Was it really true? If Rich had been following the case, it would have been a simple thing to determine Andre's prison release date. Then to follow Andre home from California State Prison, keep watch on him. Then keep tabs on him until, as Wally had told him, he went to "go grab some of his coke from the house," in the wee hours of Wednesday morning, when Rich had waylaid him.

But Rich was in front of my house Tuesday night! What was that? A taunt? A warning?

Chris had no way of knowing.

He gripped the steering wheel fiercely, guilt like a red-hot poker going straight through his heart, the fires of shame making his face hot with tears. In frustration, he punched his dashboard like it was a punching bag until his fist was stinging. He was only a few houses away, and he suddenly wanted to stop, to turn around.

But when he thought about Wally's face earlier that day, how worried he was about his big brother . . .

You need to tell Wally. He deserves to know.

He would avoid talking to Wally over the phone. Instead, Chris opted to drive by their house on Diamond, seeing if the lights were on. Maybe Wally was home.

As Chris slowed down in front of the house at the end of Diamond, he was rehearsing how he would reveal the news to Wally. "Wally, bro, your brother, he's—Um, Wally. I'm so sorry, man. But I think Andre's—"

The words died on his tongue seeing the house's dark windows.

But there was something else.

Chris squinted through shadows, couldn't quite make it out.

He turned off his car, got out, and locked it, then inched timidly toward the home's dark windows. His nervous footsteps sounded on the cracked sidewalk, his eyes darting down both ends of the empty street. The warm breeze carried the sounds of barking dogs and the muffled voices of a man and woman fighting inside one of the neighboring houses.

Do Not Cross police tape was draped around the house and across the front door. Chris gulped, felt a chill down his spine, took a step back, shaking his head. The police tape validated the seriousness of his situation.

He muttered to himself, his voice sounding weak and far away, "Shit. Rich, you goddamned psycho. What've you done?"

It was time to go. He'd looked long enough.

He couldn't be seen—

The flashing, throbbing red and blue lights of a police car bathed him in their eerie light.

Chris thought about running, wishing he'd never even come.

He cautiously approached the driver's side, which opened, a young, dark-haired officer stepping out. He stopped a few feet short of Chris and looked Chris up and down. The officer's name tag read: *Vasquez*. He rested his hands on his belt, near his holstered pistol, his clean-shaven early-thirties face cautious.

"Officer Eddie," he introduced himself, puffing out his chest, putting some power in his voice. "Noticed your car scoping out this place. Looked like you were checking out the property."

Eddie's face softened, and he paused, smiling slightly. He tilted his head, curious. "Don't I know you from somewhere?" Then the officer's face brightened. "I do know you. Aren't you that famous singer?"

Chris smiled, relieved, shoulders relaxing. "Yeah, that's me, man."

Eddie took his hand away from his belt, offered a handshake.

Discomfort melting between them, Chris pumped the hand.

Then Eddie glanced around the street, a street far from beautiful Beverly Hills. "The hell *you* doin' *here*?"

Chris released Eddie's thick, warm hand, shuddered. That slender candle flame of pride that had flickered to life at Eddie's recognition of him wavered, almost going out. "I used to live around here." Chris glanced at the dead-looking house behind him, warm summer evening breeze playing with the police tape. The house had probably already been picked clean by investigators, Chris figured. "What happened?" he asked, voice cool, not sure if he even wanted to know.

Eddie shook his head, regretfully. "Can't talk about it, man."

The deathly words returned with new urgency: *This is between you and me. If you get cops involved, I'll slit Daryl's throat. I swear to God I will.*

"Can I get a picture with you?" Eddie was grinning warmly, already pawing out his cell phone. "My little girl won't believe me otherwise."

Chris felt his face heat up. Strange. He'd taken thousands of selfies with thousands of fans. This was the first time ever he *didn't* want to.

Eddie caught Chris's hesitation. "Please, man. She loves you, and I don't see her that much. Only on weekends." Officer Eddie's face drooped with sadness, and his Adam's apple bobbed, swallowing a growing lump in his throat. "I wanted to take her to your show tomorrow night, but it was sold out."

Chris sighed, relenting, and pointed at the officer's cruiser. "In front of the car, man."

Chris stepped next to Eddie, a bright smile on the officer's face, the police cruiser behind them and dirty Diamond Street hidden by its bulk. Hidden. No one needed to see Chris here.

"She hasn't yet been to one of your shows," Eddie continued, clicking the camera mode on his phone. "My daughter. That's like her dream. To meet you." Eddie raised the camera in selfie mode, smiling like he struck gold, giddy at the thought of showing the picture to his daughter.

Chris's feigned grin was twitching, nervous. He couldn't understand why taking a picture with Eddie didn't feel good—didn't feel *right*. It'd always felt good and right. But his eyes were so wide, so loud with concern and fear, when the flash went off.

"You look scared to death, man." Eddie laughed.

Chris sucked his teeth, brimming with frustration.

His nerves sparked watching helplessly as Eddie was jabbing thumbs at his phone.

"Are you like posting that or anything?"

The cell phone glowed warmly in Eddie's grinning, satisfied face. Tapping on his phone, he said, "Yeah, for sure. I appreciate it." His lips pursed sadly. "You have no idea."

Terror was eating through Chris's heart. He wanted to snatch the phone out of Eddie's hands.

"My daughter will freak."

"Cool, cool. But would you mind waiting on that, man? On posting it."

If you get cops involved, I'll slit Daryl's throat.

Eddie stopped pecking at the phone, looked up at Chris.

"Trying to keep a low profile here."

Eddie nodded, eyes narrowed, skeptical. But he obliged.

Chris sighed through his nose, relieved, seeing Eddie turning off his phone then shoving it back into his pocket.

Eddie put his hands back on his belt, looked at Chris nervously. "So what *are* you doing here?"

Chris took another look around, the street quiet and empty. No unwanted attention. No one watching him, that Chris could tell at least.

A grin flickered on Chris's face, a spark of confidence.

"Look, here's the truth, man. I'm looking for a friend of mine. I think he's in trouble. I've been getting harassed. A man named Rich Howard. He's been calling me, making threats. Look, I don't know what happened *here*," Chris added, gesturing at the house behind him. "But Rich Howard is involved, I can tell you that. *Rich Howard.*"

There doesn't have to be a big investigation, Chris thought.

Eddie shook his head, tapped his fingers on his belt. "You'd have to come down to the precinct and swear out a complaint. Even then, we'd have to get a separate warrant to go there again, dig deeper. Unless there's proof."

"Fuck the warrant. Is he dead? Is the dude dead? Andre Childs?"

Chris was sure of it, and his mind was suddenly bombarded with thoughts of Andre's cold, blue corpse.

Bleeding in my basement. Dead now. Need to get rid of him.

But Eddie wasn't going to tell him what happened there. Eddie stared at Chris, his eyes growing more skeptical with every passing moment.

"Stop looking at me like that, man. Look, I used to know the dude." Chris wondered distantly, and with a touch of pain, if Wally knew. Did Wally find out what happened here? "He used to be my dealer. But all that shit was a long time ago, man. So your daughter don't have to be disappointed in me or nothing."

"I hope not, man." Eddie's face grew stormy. "I quit drinking 'cause of you."

The truth and earnestness in the words shocked Chris for a moment, then he felt their sadness.

"It broke me and the old lady up. I don't blame her. It was all me. But my daughter showed me your music and told me about your story, how you beat your addiction, how you're writing an entire album about that." The skepticism on Eddie's face was replaced with a fleeting dreaminess. "Was almost like an odyssey. Like you were like, I don't know, some kind of warrior or something. And I saw your updates online about the album, and I thought that if Chris Flowers has got this, well, then I got this. Let me get my shit together too. And I haven't had a drink in over a year now." Eddie's eyes were dewy and confessional.

"Look, I appreciate you telling me, and I'm sorry about you and the old lady. And I'm sure your daughter is very proud of you."

That one seemed to hit Eddie's nerves. The officer shuffled his feet.

"But I'm trying to tell you," Chris said, trying to keep panic out of his voice. "Rich Howard, man. He . . ."

Wants me to confess.

"He's trying to get back at me because he was in love with my wife and because I kicked his ass. And he's—"

Trying to ruin me.

"He said he was going to hurt a friend of mine." Chris stopped abruptly.

"Do you have any proof of that, Chris, uh, Mr. Flowers?"

Chris showed him the picture. The one of Daryl. Chris had to glance away when pulling it up. He raised it up, the cell phone glowing on Eddie's face.

Chris was surprised, outraged, when Eddie just bobbed his head hopelessly. The officer seemed unmoved by it.

"Do you think this is a joke, man?"

A pair of headlights crept by, and Chris promptly took the phone out of the cop's face, let it hang at his side a moment, hiding it. Unwanted light rolled over Chris. Chris looked away, hiding his face. His heart started racing when the car stopped, headlights burning on

Eddie's back, casting the officer's massive dark shadow over Chris. Strangely, Chris felt better in the shadow, out of the evil light.

Eddie, in silhouette, turned to look. Another cop cruiser. Eddie waved the other cop away confidently.

Chris was finally able to take a full breath once the cruiser drove off, continuing its patrol down the street.

In the following silence Eddie looked at Chris again, a strange look, and any hope Chris felt drained away.

Chris shoved the picture into Eddie's face again. "My friend's out there somewhere!" Chris said, pointing into the darkness. "I don't know where he is. Come on, look at this!" Chris took a step closer.

Eddie cocked his head, gave Chris a nervous look. "I'm looking."

"Please, man!"

"Look, Chris. Like I said, this is something you should take to the authorities—"

"But you *are* the authorities." Chris insisted, his voice too loud for that time and place. He took a deep breath to calm himself down. "You should've heard the guy," Chris explained, a little calmer. "He's crazy. I think he's been calling me on other people's phones. First Andre's, then Daryl's. I think he's been destroying the phones after, so he can't get tracked or something. I tried calling them. But they're not in service no more. Rich destroyed them. He told me not to get anyone involved. No cops."

"You're talking to me."

Why was Chris telling Eddie?

I'll slit Daryl's throat.

"Please. All I want is to make sure no one else gets hurt," Chris said, feebly. "My friend is missing, and I know Rich has him. And if we get Rich?"

Eddie shook his head, cutting Chris off. "I'm sorry, Mr. Flowers." He gave the picture of Daryl a final confused, cynical look. "I'm just a beat cop. Take the picture to the station. If you really believe your friend is in danger, then, like I said, the best thing you could do for him is get the police involved and start an investigation."

This is between you and me. If you get cops involved.

Eddie turned around, heading toward his cruiser.

"Wait!" Chris cried, voice jumping with desperation. He put his phone back in his pocket.

Eddie turned back around, faced Chris again, curiosity sparking through his disillusionment. He tapped his polished black shoe impatiently.

"Look, man!" Chris pointed at his own face. "Do I look like I'm back on drugs? Back here looking to score? I know that's what you're thinking."

Eddie didn't say anything.

"I know it sounds crazy what I'm saying, but . . ." He quieted himself, his eyes dropping to Eddie's badge as an idea began growing confidently in his mind. He weighed the risks.

If you get cops involved—

But Eddie was only one cop.

The plan seemed to come to life when he remembered the picture on his cell phone, not of Daryl, but of Rich's license plate, the number he'd written down the night before then photographed for the security people. He showed that picture to Eddie.

"That's the dude's license plate number. If you can just find him and arrest his ass—"

"Look, man—"

"I can get you into the show tomorrow night." The words slid easily out of Chris's mouth.

Eddie blinked, stunned.

Chris just held up the license plate picture, like bait.

"I'm telling the truth. He's going to hurt an old friend of mine if I—*we*—don't stop him."

Eddie became rigid and cold again. "You trying to bribe an officer?"

"And tell you what else I'll do to sweeten the deal. Backstage passes for you and your daughter. Not just Friday night. But for the rest of your lives! How's that sound?"

Eddie's eyes sparkled a little.

Chris grinned pleasantly, seeing the toughness in Eddie's façade slowly melting.

Still, Eddie was wrestling with doubt. Chris considered ways of erasing that doubt completely. Then he thought about Rich planting the little baggie of cocaine on his windshield. Andrea said Rich had been pulled over once before when they were still together, and he'd been arrested on the spot high as a kite on coke and carrying it in the vehicle with him. It was something real, something tangible he could give to Eddie.

"You pull him over," Chris said, self-assured. "This guy's a cokehead. Been in trouble with it before. You *will* find it in his car. Pull him over for that. And call me. That's all you have to do."

Rich will have nowhere and no one to run to after I get my hands on him.

Chris could almost hear temptation clashing with duty in the officer's tough mind. Chris was still holding the picture of Rich's license plate number up for Eddie, and it glowed on the officer's tormented face. Eddie swung his head around, as if searching for that other officer who had cruised by moments earlier.

"Come on, man. Backstage passes for you and your daughter. *For life!* I think your daughter will be impressed with a daddy who somehow made it so she could meet her hero."

Eddie, looking ashamed, hung his head, contemplating. He fidgeted, cleared his throat, scraped his tongue over his teeth.

CHAPTER TWENTY

Chris was racing down South Grand Avenue, grinning triumphantly in the moonlight, nearing the interstate, when his phone rang. He pawed the glowing rectangle out of his pocket, looked at the number, and frowned with recognition. It was Wally.

After Chris left Diamond Street, he considered texting Wally or giving him a call, asking him if he was all right and where he was staying. But Chris decided against it.

He pursed his lips, nostrils flaring in frustration, face red hot, the call making him feather the brake, the galloping Camino slowing. Chris checked the rearview mirror randomly—no one tailing him still—the phone in his hand ringing like doomsday bells.

With trepidation, expecting the worst, Chris answered.

"Hello?"

"It's Wally, man."

Chris first felt relief at the sound of Wally's voice and not that demon voice as he cruised past old houses.

He had been fueled by fresh confidence after winning Eddie over. It felt like South Central's streets had given him a guardian. Or a hunter. If Rich went out to prowl those streets, Eddie would be there.

But that confidence was threatened, and a chill slithered up Chris's spine when he heard choked sobs coming out of his cell.

"Can you come meet me again?" Wally said, the words desperate. "By Fifth. 'Member? Where we was at earlier today? We can meet there."

Chris realized the man was hammered. He could almost smell the boozy breath coming out of his phone. He pitied Wally, knew the man had seen something horrible, but Chris didn't want to think about that. He tapped the accelerator like he was trying to stamp those thoughts down. He just wanted to get home.

"Can't you come?" Wally said, drunken voice trembling with a sadness that clawed at Chris. "I need to talk to you, man."

Chris stamped on the brake again, passing a house where a family was having a barbeque—the man at the grill stood silhouetted against the back porch light, family around a picnic table behind him, and the man looked up, his face orange in the glow of the barbeque, and stared at Chris as he cruised by. He hid his famous face, looking away, burying it in shadow. The Camino's headlights revealed a road sign, beyond it the ramp that curved up to the restlessly buzzing interstate I-110, and Chris slowed to a stop. All he had to do was get onto that ramp and take that to the Santa Monica Freeway, and he'd be on his way home.

Even though he was far from it, Chris said, "I'm at home." He rubbed his heavy eyes, sitting helplessly in his idling Camino.

Then Wally said, "Please."

Chris could tell Wally was trying to muffle his sobs over the phone.

Chris sighed, staring at the sign, headlights glowing on it. He pictured in his mind the two brothers, Andre and Wally, together, arms wrapped lovingly around each other's shoulder.

Someday, man, I wanna make so much money so Wally and me can be free from all this shit, Andre once said.

He'd also once confided to Chris: *Sometimes I think about maybe robbing a bunch of banks, stashing the money far away someplace. Even if I had to spend my life in prison, it'd be nice to at least see my little brother out, you know, of this life.*

This is all my fault.

It was a disturbing thought, a thought that had been eating him ever since he'd left Daryl's old place. Yet it was a thought he swore he'd banished after Eddie said the words: *Okay, man. I'll do what I can.*

Chris stared at the interstate sign in front of him, realized maybe he had been trying to run away, run away back to his mansion where he could hide.

"Okay, man," Chris said. "I'll be there." He wished different words had come out.

* * *

With growing dread, Chris drove at a gloomy pace down Fifth, out of South Central and then into Mid City, until he finally reached that lonesome graffiti-splashed parking lot where he'd met Wally earlier that day. The place was spookier without sunshine.

The Oldsmobile sat in shadow, Chris's approaching headlights illuminating Wally's sullen face hunkered behind the steering wheel. Wally raised shining eyes into Chris's blinding headlights, then Chris switched off the ignition. Wally was smoking a cigarette, his face glowing a dull, deep orange whenever he took a drag. The cigarette smoke floated in the pale moonlight. Chris waited in the car a moment, a suspicious feeling in his gut. Wally just sat there, not moving.

Chris stepped outside, a couple of the parking lot's orange streetlights flickering.

Bottles clinked as Wally moved, opening his car door, mumbling incoherently, something about where was Chris's Ferrari, why was Chris driving that old El Camino? Then there was the hollow clink of an empty fifth of Johnnie Walker cracking on the pavement. Wally turned, flicked the last of his cigarette, and it sparked on the asphalt.

Then, to Chris's surprise, he pulled out a handgun, a small, shiny Beretta, and pointed it at Chris. The silver gun gleamed in the streetlight.

Chris froze mid-stride, hands raised. "Whoa, shit, man." He couldn't believe it; it felt like the air had been sucked from his lungs, his heart racing. "Wally?"

Wally's face was mottled in rage, eyes rheumy from whiskey, dangerous with accusation, the pistol trembling uncertainly in his drunken hands. "Your fault, Chris!"

Chris trembled, feeling sorry—*feeling stupid!*—he'd come. "My fault?"

"Man, I found him!" Tears glistened in Wally's eyes, and his voice was strained with hysteria. "Someone dumped him in the yard. Like he was garbage."

Chris was repulsed by the thought. An image flashed in his mind: Rich snorting a line of coke, pulling up to that house on Diamond

Street, then kicking Andre's corpse out the passenger side door, the body slapping the hot ground. Chris shook his head in revulsion.

"His throat was cut, man!"

Chris kept his hands raised, fear freezing him solid.

"And it's your fault!"

"No, man," Chris said, shaking his head, his words trembling with terror. "It ain't. It ain't my fault. I swear it."

Chris shut his eyes against the accusatory thoughts that filled his mind.

Would Andre still be alive if he hadn't hung up on Rich yesterday morning?

Chris couldn't tell Wally that. Wally might kill him.

Wally teetered closer, extending his gun-wielding arm out as if wanting to jam that pistol down Chris's throat. Chris winced regretfully under the pistol's cold black eye. It looked like Wally was about to squeeze the trigger, his finger teasing it, and Chris flinched, waiting for the blinding white flash and the pain that would inevitably follow.

"Wally, come on." Chris' voice cracking at the strain. "I have a life. I have people who care about me. A wife, man."

"Shut up!" Wally shouted, his voice echoing down the streets.

"Wally, please, man. Why didn't you call me?"

Wally's chin trembled, and he squeezed his eyes shut as if against returning to painful memories. "I found him, man. And after I called the police . . ." Wally gulped, his face ugly with sorrow. "I went out and got more wasted."

"Wally . . ."

"Then I went to a buddy's, and he gave me a gun to protect myself 'cuz our forty-five's missing! But then I thought I could use this one to put a cap in your ass, too."

Chris flinched. Did Rich have a gun now?

"Wally, listen."

"I loved him, man," Wally said, his voice softer and thick with tears.

"I know you did, man." Chris took a deep breath of the muggy evening air, trying to steady his voice with reason. "Just listen to me, please. You're slammed right now, and . . ."

"Fuck you!" Wally was suddenly raging again. "The whole thing was your idea. That's why he dead."

I was looking through some old notebooks, Chris had told Andre over the phone five years ago. *Have an idea for a new album maybe. Found your number that I'd written down years ago, if you can believe it. Hey, remember when you were talking about wanting to get out of the city with Wally? You still want that?*

"It's not what you think. It's a man named Rich Howard." Maybe it was that dangerous hunk of silver in his face that drew out the wretched truth. Maybe it was because Chris felt the man deserved the truth.

"Who the fuck's Rich Howard, man?"

"He, Rich, found out about—" Chris glanced around, seeking rogue cameras or recording devices or other listening ears. Even though there was no one around, he lowered his voice to a near-whisper. "Tray Mansfield. About *that* business." Chris shook his head, still baffled by it himself. "Somehow Rich found out. I think he killed 'Dre to get at me, man. Because he hates me. I kicked his ass. And he's obsessed with my wife." *Who's now fair game.*

Wally started shaking, as if a furious tremor had started in his bones. Chris felt a moment's relief when the gun wandered away from him, then tensed up again, seeing Wally's face transform, his eyes suddenly vengeful, murderous, darting in their sockets, seeking his brother's killer.

"I got someone on it," Chris said gently, but it was like trying to douse a bonfire with a single bucket of water.

"You told me you didn't know shit!"

"Wally, listen up."

"Who you got on it? Since when?"

"I heard about it on the news," Chris said quickly, trying to fill the hole he was digging himself into. "About 'Dre. I was broken up about it, man. And so I didn't call you or nothing. I'm sorry." Chris even tried to force out tears. He felt disgusted with himself.

Wally was quiet a moment, pondering.

The sound of distant sirens was in the air.

"You hire someone to do a job?" Wally finally asked, his voice still hot with outrage, but appearing as though he bought it.

Chris nodded. "Look, I don't know how this Rich dude found out about, you know, that business five years ago, but I'm going to find out. I promise you that." Then Chris added, hoping it might get him out of his present situation, "I hired the guy, to avenge your brother's death . . ."

"Fuck that!" Wally suddenly snarled, cutting Chris off.

Chris stiffened again, Wally taking a hard step closer.

"I want to get him," Wally cried desperately, slurring his words. "Where's he live?"

"I don't know where the dude lives. I already talked to my guy about this."

After Eddie said, rather ruefully, *Okay, man. I'll see what I can do,* they exchanged numbers and Chris, while they were still standing there, texted Eddie that picture of Rich's license plate. Eddie turned pale, looking ever more uncomfortable, shifting from foot to foot, the longer they talked.

"Rich is a paparazzi guy. Means he takes pictures of celebrities. But this guy in particular, Wally, he tries to ruin people like me by taking scandalous pictures. He's gotten in a lot of trouble in the past. Probably uses motels and different names." Chris took a breath, trying to inflate his voice with self-assurance, trying to calm this raging creature in front of him. "Man, I already told you my guy's on it."

"I'll do it. You don't have to pay me. You take me with you and when he shows up, I'll shoot him dead."

Chris considered this fleetingly, feeling repulsed at the thought of driving around with Wally. What if they were seen together?

Then Chris pictured Wally shadowing Chris in one of his cars while Chris cruised around like bait to draw Rich out.

"No." And he remained stony and unswerving when Wally shoved the gun closer to Chris's face.

"What?"

Chris stared into the pistol's empty black eye, the barrel inches from his face, smelling the cold, greasy gunmetal. Then he said, genuinely sincere if also cautious, "I don't want to drag you into this."

"I already am because of you."

"*You* called me, man," Chris said, trying to keep his voice steady. "And the answer is still no." Chris just wouldn't be able to stand it if something terrible happened to Wally. But at the same time he pictured Wally in a prison jumpsuit taking the stand then pointing a guilty finger at Chris for a plea bargain. "Wally," he said gently, "you ain't thinking right."

"*I'm* gonna kill him. Not no one else."

"You need to sleep this off, man," Chris said, his voice cracking in fear as the gun waved in and out of his peripheral vision.

His fear deepened when Wally's eyes shone strangely, narrowing in accusation. "You used him." Wally howled, tears running down his face. "My brother."

"I *helped* him," Chris reminded him gently. "Helped! Look, I remembered from years ago Andre talking about wanting to make enough money to get the hell out of here so you and him didn't have to sell dope no more. I had the money. Remember, Wally? Remember the plan? We made it look like an accident, right? So your brother wouldn't spend the rest of his life in jail, so's the two of you could leave this shithole together. Right?"

Why you wanna do this, man? Andre once asked Chris.

Don't worry about that. Just do your part.

Wally glared at Chris for what felt like forever, waving the barrel in his face. Then, to Chris's relief, the violence seemed to ebb away, and Wally's trembling, wrathful face relaxed.

Chris dared to move a half step closer to Wally, who took a full step away, raising the gun. "Stop! Stay back!"

"I wanted to help. I swear it. Your brother had been my dealer in my early years and my *friend*." The word was empty, untrue, on Chris's tongue. "*That's* the reason."

Wally looked away, the rage gone from his eyes. Chris was hopeful.

Maybe some lucidity was getting through the booze cloud.

Wally's shoulders sagged, like he was sinking into some inner hell. He sighed, lowered the gun. Tragic, bitter tears streamed down his sorrowful face.

Chris took another half step forward. "Wally, give me the gun, man. You don't need no gun in your current state."

Wally leapt back in furious defense, pointing the gun at Chris, prompting Chris to shoot his hands up again.

"'Dre was all I had left," Wally said, his drunken voice pathetic and soft. Despair deepened in his face as he took a step back, then another, to come to rest leaning against the frame of his car.

Chris saw the anguish creeping into Wally's eyes. Wally was getting further and further away, making irrational decisions, whiskey-influenced decisions, decisions better left to a sober mind. Chris could feel the other man's hopelessness, like a heavy, black, all-devouring cloud. Wally hung his head, then looked up into the city's hazy summer sky, as if perhaps pondering heaven and hell, pondering where his brother might be now. And contemplating maybe, could it be possible to join him?

"Wally, just give me the gun, man."

Wally looked at Chris. An eerie smile appeared on Wally's tearstained face, and he stared at the gun in his hand, sighing deeply as if in resolve.

"Wally!"

Chris was momentarily blinded by the gunshot, then picked at his buzzing ears, his heart in his throat.

Wally was grinning, pleased in death, through the waterfall of blood gushing out his nose as his back slid down the car's doorframe and he came to rest on the ground, eyes staring sightlessly upward.

Chris couldn't think for a moment. He approached Wally's dead body, feeling dizzy and sick, unable to process what he was seeing. Wally's dead body. His dead body. A man who was *alive* only seconds ago.

"Oh God."

Tears filled Chris's eyes as he stared down in horror at the corpse at his feet. Wally had stuck the barrel into his mouth. The back of his head was blown wide open. Pieces of skull and brain were painted on the asphalt.

Chris fought the urge to puke. Hand still clasped over his mouth, he said, barely above a whisper, "You coward." Then, filled with horror and disbelief, he cried, "Oh God! You chickenshit coward!"

Chris, startled, whipped around at the sound of people muttering, shadows stirring, a few homeless guys climbing out of their tents to see what'd happened. Chris was breathing fast and hollow, hyperventilating, and the sounds of distant sirens spooked him into a speedy retreat. He hurried to the Camino, turned the ignition, and got the hell out of there.

* * *

Chris parked the El Camino in its space back at the car club, then climbed into his Ferrari. That was when it started to hit him. He'd driven the whole way there with his eyes wide open, stunned, not even thinking about what had happened. Then when he was behind the wheel of his Ferrari he stared into space, a hollow feeling in his chest, and he started breathing heavily. It felt like he'd ran a thousand miles, he was so out of breath. He started thinking about Wally's face, the way Wally was smiling up into the dim starlight, smiling like he was happy, like he'd found a way out of his despair. Like he'd found a way, though Chris could hardly bear the thought, to be with his brother.

Chris opened the car door, leaned out, and puked until tears were running down his face. He wouldn't bother cleaning up the puddle of vomit. He just shut the door, leaned back, and wiped his mouth with his shirttail.

Chris wanted desperately to convince himself that it wasn't his fault, that Wally killing himself wasn't somehow his fault.

Why did Chris feel like he should have stayed there with him? Why did he feel like such an asshole for leaving him there like that, leaving him there for the cops to clean up?

What could you have done for him? He's dead!

He pounded his head against his steering wheel, hard, thudding hits that rattled his skull.

Your fault!
Your fault!
All your fault!

Then he remembered something and glanced up tearfully at the cameras in the corners of the garage, little fancy white protrusions with red blinking lights. One was pointed right at him. He sat back against the leather car seat, pulling himself out of its view so it wouldn't catch his disgraceful blotchy-red face. So it wouldn't catch the degrading tears rolling down his cheeks.

You used him. My brother. You used him.
Chris shook his head slowly.
No, no. I didn't use Andre, he tried reminding himself.
But Chris remained unconvinced.

When the tears stopped, he turned the ignition, and the Ferrari growled to life and purred.

He spent the drive home, tears drying, his brain throbbing, trying to convince himself that he wasn't at fault. But he'd be staring into the taillights of a car in front of him as he cruised down La Cienega Boulevard and he'd see Eddie in his mind again, the officer throwing glances over his burly shoulder, searching for that other cruiser. Eddie's face was white, shocked with himself, yet determined to please his estranged daughter. Chris's whole body was shaking as he considered the arrogance and impulsivity and desperation of his decision to bribe Officer Eddie. As arrogant as deciding not to change his number. *Nah, Jeff, it went off without a hitch. There's no need to be paranoid.*

It ain't true! I didn't use Andre! Oh God, Wally.

Chris parked in his empty garage, wiped the residue of his tears, gave his reflection in the rearview mirror a single disgusted, shame-filled glance, then got out.

He entered the eerie emptiness of the mansion trying to steel himself with positive affirmations, trying to keep his thoughts from wandering dark alleys.

Rich's days are numbered. Maybe eventually I can get a whole bunch of hired cops behind this?

* * *

Officer Eddie had kept scratching at his clean-shaven face with one hand as he checked his cell phone with the other after receiving Chris's text. He kept shuffling his feet, kept fidgeting, as Chris explained to him, "I ain't expecting you to catch him tomorrow. So you don't have to worry about it, you and your little girl still got the tickets no matter what." Eddie tried to smile at the mention of his daughter, but the smile faded from his pallid face just as quickly as it had come, the man unable to take consolation in Chris's words as the enormity of his fall overwhelmed him.

* * *

Eddie told Chris not to have high expectations for this business—that's how Eddie referred to it, eyes zipping left and right, *this business*—to be resolved in a day or a week. Or even longer. Eddie said he had a large, labyrinthine beat but that he would cruise every street searching for the car whose license plate Chris had texted him.

Chris had showed Eddie the picture of Daryl again, though Chris couldn't bring himself to look at it. It felt like a cancer on his phone. But he'd made sure to tell Eddie, "You're telling me it might take a while to find him, and I get that, man." Chris had choked up at that point, still feeling utterly helpless. "Just please hurry, man. Rich's stomping grounds is Beverly Hills. Do you know anyone there who could help us?" Eddie's face didn't betray much, and all he said was that he'd see what he could do. Finally, with a look of curiosity, Eddie asked, "What does this guy want from you?"

* * *

Chris peeled off his clothes in the bedroom, trying not to look at Andrea's derelict guitar still leaning up against the far wall. He made his way to the shower, feeling slothful, like he was carrying the burden of an extra thousand pounds.

The shower felt baptismal, rinsing off the grime of the day, though the hot stream of water wouldn't wash away the memories of the last few days. They spread and blackened like a stain inside him. Dark thoughts crept into bed with him and tangled like tentacles around his heart, and he tossed and turned, sleepless hours ticking by.

CHAPTER TWENTY-ONE
2008

Maria gasped in the passenger seat as Chris rushed her down the late evening streets. He squeezed her hand the entire time, the streetlights rolling over his excited and panicked face. Relief washed over him as he pulled up to that glowing EMERGENCY sign. He helped her inside, sweat rolling down his face. She moaned and struggled with each step, and he shouted encouragements and squeezed her hand as tight as he could without hurting her. He called out for help, and she was swooped up by a flock of nurses and carried off on a gurney into the delivery room. His heart pounded with fear and excitement as he rushed alongside the rolling gurney, never letting go of her hand. The doctors squawked at each other, leaning over Maria's sweating, agonized face.

In the delivery room her legs splayed open and a gloved and masked doctor knelt, encouraging Maria to "Push! Push!"

"I'm trying," she cried out.

Chris stood beside her, holding her hand. "I'm right here," he kept telling her. "I'm right here, baby."

"It hurts!" she cried. "It *hurts*!"

"Deep breaths," the doctor said.

Maria tried a slow breath in and out, then another one, in and out. But then she shook her head rapidly, her breathing speeding up again. Chris's cheeks burned, wanting her pain to stop. He told her to do what the doctor said, told her to take slow, deep breaths. He rubbed her hand tenderly, trying to remain calm even though adrenaline was making his heart bang in his chest. His panic and exhilaration had helped to burn off the last residue of the dope cloud, the bump he had at home earlier that evening.

"Here it comes! I can see the head!" the doctor said.

Chris felt a grin spreading on his face, and he gave Maria's hand a hopeful squeeze.

"Give me another big push, Maria!" the doctor cried.

Maria breathed, breathed, bit her lips, then yowled in agony at the effort. Chris squeezed her hand really hard and firm, tears in his eyes.

"I'm here, baby," he whispered to her. "You got this."

Chris wasn't sure how long he stood in there with her, but eventually Maria stopped screaming and started breathing slower, until her face relaxed with relief.

The doctor cried out, "There he is!"

Chris kissed Maria's hand, relief washing over him. "Good job, babe!" He smoothed away the sweaty strands of hair clinging to her forehead. "You did good, babe. I'm so proud of you."

He looked at the doctor, wanting to get a look at the baby, wondering when he'd get to cut the umbilical cord. The father cutting the umbilical was a ritual Chris had heard about, though he sometimes worked himself up thinking about it. Would it hurt the baby? Would it hurt Maria?

None of that mattered because it wouldn't be Chris cutting the umbilical cord that day.

It all started when the doctor's eyes suddenly changed and he called out for his assistant.

"What? What is it?" Maria said, alarm creeping into her exhausted voice.

The doctor said nothing. He cut the cord himself, took the baby into another room.

Chris felt a chill running down his back. He couldn't even breathe for a moment, his heart seeming to skip a few beats. He finally managed some words, crying out after the exiting nurses, "What's happening?" Chris and Maria were left alone in the room for a few minutes, both fearing the worst.

Chris wanted to go into the room where the doctor was, but he was tethered to Maria's hand, and he wasn't about to let her go. His heart went *bam! bam! bam!* like a hot red fist against his rib cage. He thought about his little hidey-hole under the bathroom sink at home where he hid his baggie of dope. He would give anything to sneak some into a bathroom stall where he could do another bump, a little something to bring down his gut-wrenching anxiety.

"What's wrong with my baby?" Maria cried into the empty room.

Chris didn't have an answer for her. He stared at the door on the opposite end of the room, waiting for the doctor to return. He wrapped his arm around Maria's shoulders and hugged her, felt her breathing against his body—her breaths fast and shaky.

It seemed like an eternity, but finally the doctor returned. He stared at Chris and Maria, shaking his head. "I'm sorry," he said calmly.

Chris felt his stomach knot and his mouth watered, about to puke.

"What? What happened?" Maria cried, her voice rising unnaturally high.

The masked doctor approached, his sky-blue eyes brimming with tears. He shook his head tragically. "We can't find a heartbeat, Mrs. Flowers."

Maria didn't say anything for a moment, but Chris felt her squeeze his hand so tight that it was hurting him.

"Let me see!"

"Mrs. Flowers—"

"Let me see!" she yelled.

The doctor turned to his assistant, a masked woman, dark hair in a ponytail. He nodded at her. She left the room and returned with a small bundle in her arms. She passed it to the doctor.

The life was sucked from Chris's face when the doctor held the bundle out to Maria. Maria's mouth hung open, words catching in her throat, her face paper white. The doctor revealed the tiny baby's face, eyes cloudy with death, the lipless mouth slightly open, the baby's little hands curled up. Chris's eyes filled with tears as all the dreams he had for this child vanished before his eyes. Maria whimpered as the baby was taken away from her again, the doctor's assistant carrying him out of the room.

Chris stood there with Maria for the longest time, tears sliding warmly down his face.

"My baby. My baby." Maria sobbed, her voice echoing down the white hospital hallways.

Chris wrapped his arms around her, and they cried together for a long time.

FRIDAY, JULY 18, 2023
CHAPTER TWENTY-TWO

Chris's ringing cell phone stirred him from a fevered sleep. He sat up, rubbed the dark moons under his eyes, picked up the ringing phone from off the mahogany nightstand, and stared at it—eyes widening with alarm.

Jeff.

Chris threw blankets off his sweat-soured body, feeling a ping of urgency seeing the time on his cell, 8:44 a.m. glimmers of sunshine trying to peek through his shut curtains.

A sudden dread gripped him seeing the upswell of texts and notifications, but he ignored those for the time being to answer Jeff's call. "Hello."

"Get your ass to the studio, Chris," Jeff said, immediately cutting Chris off, voice sharp and nervous. "This is fucking serious. I just got done talking to Billy, and he's gonna be here on Skype. He's pissy right now, but has good reason to be."

Chris tried to keep Jeff's panic at bay. "Calm down, Jeff. And tell me what's going on?"

"Did you hear me? Get your ass here now!"

"On my way," Chris said, jolted off the bed by Jeff's shouted words.

He hung up, tossed the phone on his bed. He didn't even bother to shower, though he needed one, just jumped into the first thing he grabbed—a silk training shirt and some shorts. He quickly splashed some icy water on his face in the bathroom sink to wake himself, though the panic in Jeff's voice had already done that. His phone was lighting up like a Christmas tree, and Chris snatched it up from off the bed and just stared at it for a second, too afraid to look through his texts and social media notifications. He knew, just *knew* it had something to do with Andrea.

Her threats loomed over him like a dark cloud as he raced down his marble staircase and outside into his Ferrari.

I'm gonna ruin you, Chris Flowers!

Chris didn't even bother turning the radio on, paralyzed with anxiety, just kept his trembling hands on the steering wheel, focused on driving, while his ignored phone buzzed and buzzed incessantly in his pocket. He would know everything when he got there.

He came to a screeching halt when he reached the studio and jumped out of his Ferrari into the early morning heat. He trotted across the parking lot, past Jeff's silver Mercedes glinting in the climbing sun, and crashed into the studio, bursting through the doors to the recording area, wiping his sweaty face with the back of his hand.

Jeff, his face etched with worry, stopped his pacing and turned to face Chris. He nervously bunched up the sleeves of his button-up shirt, then took a puff from his vape pen with twitching fingers. Pale blue smoke swirled under the warm ceiling lights.

Billy's face was framed in a silver laptop, his young, keen hazel eyes narrowed to agitated slits. He tucked a strand of auburn hair back into the bun behind his cocky little ears. Chris was waiting for the little dude's thin, almost lipless mouth to open, for that whiny voice to jump out and into his ears.

But it was Jeff who spoke first. "Did you hear anything?" He walked through his own thundercloud of smoke, his face down in his cell phone, the screen glowing on his fretful features. He was tapping on his cell, but Chris didn't know who he might be texting. "Anything at all on the way here? On the radio?"

Chris shook his head. "I figured I'd wait till I got here. What's the problem?"

"She's all over the news."

Chris was speechless, a sinking feeling in his gut.

Then Jeff raised his cell phone. He hadn't been texting anyone, he'd been pulling up a video. It was a live video. KTLA 5 Morning News. Chris had been to that news studio at least a dozen times himself to discuss his life and career with the hosts. Chris recognized the two pristinely groomed newscasters, Scott Sanders and Ellie Grier, sitting behind the polished oak table and looking solemnly at their guest.

Chris was standing frozen a good three paces from the screen.

Jeff closed the distance when Chris wouldn't and raised the screen to Chris's horrified face.

Chris shuddered when the camera closed in on a close-up shot of Andrea. She was wearing a mournful, silky-black halter top and a black and white striped skirt. Gnarly fist-sized bruises darkened her sleeveless arms. Her face was red and puffy. Her eyes were black craters.

"Oh God," Chris said, his voice sounding small and pathetic.

She really did it.

Chris's horror became outrage, and he glared at his sniffling wife as she wiped tears from her blackened eyes. He could almost feel it, the accusations of millions and millions of watching people shocked to their cores.

Ellie Grier introduced Andrea, then she pursed her lips, folded her hands on the desk, and said, "We're honored to have you here to talk to us about the things that have been happening behind the scenes."

Scott Sanders nodded in agreement. He was in his late fifties, his hair unnaturally dark and shiny, sculpted as perfectly as the hedges on Chris's Hill Street. He looked sagely to the studio audience with his sad brown eyes. "We get so caught up in the image, we don't always know what's happening in the background." Scott gestured to Andrea. "Which seems to be the case here."

Chris bunched his fist, knuckles cracking.

"Andrea, can you tell me . . ." Ellie Grier paused, gesturing to the cameras, the entire world watching unblinkingly. "Can you tell *everyone* what's been going on?"

The newscasters waited patiently while Andrea, sucking back tears, was trying to gather herself.

"Take your time," Scott Sanders added tenderly, then looked down and smoothed a wrinkle out of his dark suit jacket.

Andrea chewed on her split lips, her bruised nose wrinkling as she choked back sobs. Chris imagined the people watching, the entire world, faces tearstained as they waited for the next shocking revelation.

Then Andrea seemed to settle herself and faced the world. She turned to her hosts like they were priests, wiped stray tears, and said, her voice cracked and confessional, "It's been going on since we got married in January." The studio lighting was warm and forgiving on her damaged face, the cameras exalting her courage. "Last night I told him I can't be silent any longer..."

Shut up, Chris thought bitterly, his heart ready to spring from his chest.

"I told him I can't let him beat on me anymore. 'I can't be married to you anymore,' I said to him. 'It's over!'"

Shut up! Shut up! Shut up!

Chris imagined whoops of approval from the tear-stricken audiences watching all over the world.

"Good for you!" Ellie Grier said, wiping a stray tear from her own eye.

Andrea gave Ellie an appreciative smile. Then her face darkened.

"But Chris said I *couldn't* leave. Said I *had* to finish the album. I said no." Her face twisted into a tragic mask, her lips trembled, and she held a coiled fist to her mouth as if trying to keep the shrieks of terror and pain inside. "And he *raped* me."

A gasp of horror and outrage from the newscasters, and, Chris imagined, those watching this shattering betrayal. He wanted to stop her, to reach into the screen and duct-tape her mouth shut.

"That's horrible!" Scott said, looking at Andrea with equal parts regret and fury on his face. "That monster."

Monster. Monster. Monster.

Chris felt the word ripple out across the world, felt himself turn evil in the gaze of the fans who had idolized him. He shook his head, aghast, his face ghostly white with sickness, mouth watering. He doubled over, hands on his knees, sucking in deep breaths.

"But it's over now," Chris heard Andrea say. "Thank God it's over."

"Okay!" Chris said. "I've seen enough!" He straightened himself back up, pushing on his kneecaps, feeling light-headed.

Jeff stopped the video, put his cell back into his pocket, then took a hit from his vape pen.

"You get how serious this is?" Billy shrieked tinnily from inside the laptop.

Chris did. He knew the world was going to butcher him alive.

He looked at Jeff, desperately. "Oh come on!" Suddenly his cell phone felt like a sewer in his pocket, brimming with foul things. "The bitch is lying! And you know it, Jeff."

"Your show's been canceled tonight," Jeff said regretfully.

It was a shotgun blast to the chest, and Chris's breath left him.

"You have rape and abuse allegations against you now," Billy said, his tiny laptop eyes boring into Chris.

"I didn't touch a hair on her head!" Chris cried, flashing teeth, hating the doubt in Billy's voice. He looked at Billy. "You're my publicist, man. You're supposed to be able to deal with this scandal shit."

"Putting up pictures of you giving the homeless guys at the park clothes and food won't get you out of this one," Billy said.

"It's not just the Hollywood Amphitheater," Jeff chimed in, glancing from Billy to Chris.

Chris could already feel it coming, and he gulped, bracing for the words like a freezing-cold wave.

Jeff sucked on his vape pen, exhaled. "The rest of the tour, too."

That shook Chris to the bone. Jeff checked a notification on his cell, and Chris wondered if that wasn't yet another venue canceling another Chris Flowers show.

Chris shook his head, stunned. "Can't be. That album, three years we spent on it." Chris looked at Jeff, searching frantically for a solution in his manager's face, feeling a sudden chill realizing he wouldn't be up on that stage tonight. "All those people, they've been waiting."

Billy kept staring at Chris, distrustfully.

It rubbed Chris the wrong way. "Billy, I didn't touch Andrea," he cried. He took a breath, trying to calm himself. "Swear it. We have to stop this. Please, just get something going. Get me some press coverage."

"Billy's already been working on it," Jeff said, a glint of hope in his eyes that relieved Chris.

Chris could hear the lightning-quick sound of Billy's savvy fingers going *click click click!* Billy's magic fingers had always been able to summon press conferences, able to conjure a thousand cameras and a thousand journalists instantaneously. Chris had done impromptu press conferences before, but never under such circumstances.

"He's setting up a meeting with the reporters," Jeff said. Then, with a hopeful grin, he added, "At the old club building again. Like yesterday."

Billy suddenly stopped typing, then glanced between Jeff and Chris. "They should start arriving in about twenty minutes," he said, his tinny laptop voice crackling with tension.

Relief washed over Chris, like a glass of cool, refreshing water after a long workout. "Thank you, man."

Billy stared at Chris gravely, doubts darkening his face. "It's a start. Next we can set up a live lie detector test."

"Yes!" Chris said, and smiled—the smile like sunshine on his face.

Ring! Ring! Ring!

Chris, filled with new, subtle confidence, checked his phone to see who was calling.

He faintly recognized the number. Where had he seen this number before? Could it possibly be *him*?

Jeff nodded. "Answer the damned thing already."

Chris turned away from Jeff and Billy, hearing Jeff's voice like a calming salve trying to pacify.

Chris answered the call. "Hello."

There was silence a moment. Then a voice came on. A voice Chris remembered well. "Baby?"

Chris turned from Jeff and Billy to hide his face. A single word got lodged in his throat and came out of his mouth almost a whisper. "Momma?"

"I miss you, baby. I ain't seen you in so long."

She obviously didn't remember him visiting her on her birthday two nights ago. He wondered how she remembered his number—let alone how she even remembered him.

"I miss you too, Momma."

He could almost hear the press stampeding their way to the old historic club on Cameron Drive. Soon they would be swarming that cavernous main room, just as they had the day before, all those cameras rolling.

"Why don't you come see me no more? I don't see no one." Her voice wavered, sounding heartbroken.

Chris pinched the bridge of his nose with his thumb and forefinger, hating himself thinking about all the times she'd probably called during brief moments of lucidity like this, and he'd ignored the calls.

"Momma?"

"Baby, I'm scared. I woke up this morning. Thought we was home, and you was in your crib." Her voice cracked and thickened with tears.

Suddenly, Chris's lips trembled, and he was wiping tears from his eyes. He realized the two sharply whispering voices behind him had stopped talking, trying to listen in, so Chris took a few more steps away from them, out of earshot.

He thought about the breaking news, the lies about him, spreading, viral. "Momma?" How do you tell your mother you didn't abuse your wife?

But he didn't say it. It didn't sound like she knew anything about what was going on. Then he wondered if Annie Hart knew. If the other nurses knew.

"What, baby?"

Heart pounding, Chris felt himself coming to a decision.

"Baby, please. Help me. Please."

He was surprised at the words that came out of his mouth. "I'm coming, Momma." It was crazy to him how his momma's voice got to him.

A distant memory bubbled up. It must have been fourteen, fifteen years ago. He was at his momma's house and she was trying to make a peanut butter and jelly sandwich for him, but she couldn't remember how. But he remembered walking toward her, wanting to help her, and it was how he felt now. It seemed crazy to him that in the midst of what was going on he still didn't care if Annie Hart or the other nurses had heard the news—*the lies!*—or not, and he didn't care if they arrested him when he arrived. He just needed to go.

"You're coming?"

Chris checked the time. 9:14. He considered how long it would take for him to get there in light traffic. "I'll be there in thirty, forty minutes. Okay?" he added softly.

"Oh, my baby boy."

Chris hung up. He shoved the cell back in his pocket, then turned and braved the two sets of stunned eyes blinking at him.

He gestured to the exit, tears fading. "I gotta go."

"Go where?" Billy said, his voice prickly.

"Don't worry about it. I just gotta go!"

"What about the media?" Jeff cried, wrapping an arm around himself like his gut had gone sour.

"I'm sticking my neck out here for you," Billy hissed, his laptop voice sizzling. "I'm putting my career on the line for you, my reputation, my credibility! You think these journalists will take me seriously again if you don't show and they think I'm just jerking them around?"

"Look," Chris said, taking a desperate step forward, locking eyes with his publicist. "I swear to God I want to be here for this, more than anything." Chris was shaking as he said this. "But it's my momma. She wants to see me."

Billy pursed his lips, nodding, looking deeply insulted.

Chris tried to backtrack, was starting to say something, but it was too late—any remaining bridge of trust between Chris and Billy turned to cinders before Chris's very eyes.

"Fuck it." Billy pressed a button on his end, and his Skype box went dark. Gone. The open laptop just a blank, empty face.

"Shit!" Jeff cried.

He approached the laptop, as if he might be able to somehow summon Billy's face back to the dead screen. Chris could feel the tension thickening in the air as Jeff slammed shut the laptop. It was loud enough Chris thought he might've broken it. Chris sighed, the realization of what just happened sinking in.

Then Jeff turned around, his wrinkled face turning ruddy with rising anger. He approached Chris, stood face-to-face with him, took a long, angry pull from his vape pen, then blew it intentionally in Chris's face.

Chris was stunned, waving the warm, sweet smoke away. "What the fuck, man!"

The smoke cleared, revealing Jeff's waxy face, dark with disappointment. "Your momma."

Chris's momentary anger at Jeff's adolescent gesture faded, and he sighed. He was suddenly feeling truly sorry for having to leave Jeff like this. But the press conference could wait. Momma was more important.

"She needs me," Chris said.

He was turning around and about to head toward the exit when he felt something, like a sharp hook, dig into his right shoulder and force him to turn back around. Jeff's meaty fingers crunched into Chris's shoulder blade with a strength fed by fury, and Chris winced at the sharp pain. Jeff furrowed his frosty brow and shook his head back and forth perplexedly, breathing warm nicotine breath into Chris's face.

"You're gonna blow your whole career, *our* careers..."

"Let go of me, man!" Chris yelled, then with a jerk he pulled himself free.

Jeff's face twitched, appalled with Chris. "What's happened to you?"

"I'm sorry, Jeff," Chris said sincerely.

A tear fell, and he wiped it quick, then turned and fled.

"Chris! Chris! *Chris!*"

The studio doors shut behind him, cutting off his manager's devastated howls.

* * *

The world turned into a merry-go-round the second he stepped out the door. The sun blinded him, and it felt like trying to run underwater as he walked across the baking black asphalt to his Ferrari. He thought about that brick building at the end of Cameron Drive, thought about the impromptu press conference, thought that this time his tongue wouldn't be chained by Andrea's threats; he'd be able to say what he really felt. But as he fired up the car's ignition and as the car growled to life, he saw his momma, saw himself at thirty years old, and heard the old fires of irritation burning in his voice as he told his momma, *I make money, big money now. You can move anywhere you want!* But she would shake her head, embarrassed, saying she didn't need to move anywhere fancy. There had been more streaks of gray in her hair then, and the stress wrinkles had deepened, the crow's-feet etched around her eyes, eyes that had been growing increasingly fearful and confused, a near constant scared and perplexed look about her.

Chris ignored the paparazzi cars tailing him as he cruised down Sunset. Sweat covered his face, and he kept wiping his forehead with the back of his hand. He didn't turn on the radio or check his phone at stoplights, knowing full well that both would only spew hatred at him.

Faces turned ugly as Chris was reaching the interstate. It felt like everyone in Beverly Hills at that moment was looking at him, gawks turning into glares. Some flipped up sunshades for a better look, and others leered and flashed nasty looks in the morning sunlight. These were faces that only yesterday Chris would've turned to and shined his famous teeth in a proud greeting grin. It suddenly felt like an oven under Chris's silk jersey T-shirt and not even the A/C was helping. He started feathering the throttle, picking up speed. Wanting to gallop away. He was near the on-ramp to get onto the interstate to head to Santa Monica. He didn't make it.

The lights of the police car in his rearview mirror made his heart almost stop. Those red and blue lights flashed threateningly. Chris hadn't run a red light, hadn't been speeding, at least he didn't think he'd been going too fast. Chris pulled to the curb and sat in his idling car, the on-ramp onto the interstate a quarter mile away.

He pulled his registration from the glove compartment and set it on his lap, getting it ready for the cop, a black man wearing big aviator shades. The cop glanced up, down, up, down. Chris assumed the guy was on his computer looking up Chris's license plate. He hadn't been pulled over since he was a teenager, and he remembered the cop then had taken what seemed like a long time before stepping out of his cruiser and approaching the driver's side window. But this felt like an eternity. Chris checked his phone: 9:36. He could feel time slipping away, and as his impatience mounted, he had to resist the reckless temptation of slamming on the gas pedal and zipping away.

Chris checked his phone again. Almost ten minutes had passed. He peered into his rearview mirror again and swore he saw a grin flicker on the cop's face.

Finally, the cop stepped out. He was a hulking man with thick arms and wide shoulders. He looked like he was in his late thirties with the beginning flecks of gray in his sideburns. He lumbered to Chris's window; Chris pressed a button and the window buzzed down. Chris had to squint when he looked at the cop, sunshine spilling over the cop's hefty shoulders. A name tag read: *King*.

"What's the problem, Officer?" Chris said, gently as he could, through gritted teeth.

"License and registration, sir." King's voice was thick, husky, chilly.

Chris passed the items into King's big, dark hand, and King started poring over them while standing there, his back to the sunlight, traffic droning by.

Suddenly there was the sound of a car horn blaring intermittently, like someone was pissed off and pounding on it. Chris saw the flash of the car, sun glinting off its chrome, a face staring at him.

Chris shifted in the leather seat.

He asked King once again, his voice pricklier this time, "What's the problem?"

King was silent, eyes still hidden behind the aviators, Chris staring at his own sour face in the two tiny round mirrors. King just kept stonily flipping through the registration papers. A few more cars started honking. Was it Chris they were honking at?

Finally, King said, "You ran a red light back there. At the last intersection."

Chris furrowed his brow, wondering if in his panic he had indeed ran a stoplight. But he found himself shaking his head, remembering, swearing he'd passed through green lights exclusively.

"That's bullshit," Chris said.

King lowered the registration papers from his face, and Chris could feel those icy eyes boring into him from behind the sunshades.

Then someone screamed from a passing car, "Fuck you, Chris Flowers!" Chris glimpsed a face mottled in rage.

Officer King didn't seem fazed by it, never flinching, just kept staring at Chris, those sunglasses making it look like he had giant, hateful silver eyes.

There was more abuse shouted from the street, more colorful profanity, scorching words of contempt bursting from car windows.

Someone cried out, "Rapist!" followed by the *ping!* of something hitting Chris's car, bouncing off it. Chris saw a penny roll into the middle of the street, slow down, and spin dully before settling by the double yellow road lines; someone had flicked their dirty, measly change at him. Chris glowered at the cop, who was still reading the registration papers. He wondered at first if King truly hadn't noticed until he saw that twitch at the corner of King's mouth, an echo of the smirk Chris had seen earlier when the cop had lingered in his cruiser.

"You ain't gonna do nothing about that?" Chris said, flipping his chin up, gesturing toward the street as more people blasted their horns and cursed Chris out their windows. It was a vile river of contempt.

"About what?" King asked glibly, the ghost of a smirk on his face.

"Real cute."

King lowered the registration papers. "What was that?"

A car slowed, and someone shouted, "Yeah! Arrest his fucking ass."

It was like the whole world had King's back. Each howl of abuse or shout of encouragement for King to arrest Chris's ass felt like a blade slicing into him deeper and deeper.

King was trying to shrink Chris with a withering stare behind those shades, and Chris was struck once again by King's vaguely insectile look, an insect trying to bully a god.

"Do you know who I am? Huh? Do you know who you're talking to?"

Chris realized this was the line he'd been prepared to say to Annie Hart or any of the nurses if they wouldn't allow him to see his momma. What right did they have? What right did Officer King have?

King took off his sunglasses, revealing not the furious eyes Chris was expecting, but dark, sunken eyes, eyes filled with hurt. "You're a lying chickenshit," King finally said. "I just didn't think you were like that, man. But you are. You think you're special, man? You're just like the scum I deal with every day."

Something about King's words cut deeper than the curses from the street.

"You gonna teach me a lesson, big man?"

"I am right now," King said and grinned smugly. The grin said: *Got places to go, superstar? Not while I got you here, you don't!*

Chris grinned right back, looked at the cop like he was made of cellophane. Saw through to another unhappy person—bitter, jealous, insecure—trying to take it all out on someone more successful. Chris was sick of that shit. Shitty job, shitty life, that was the officer's own damn fault.

"Look at you!" he taunted, fury in control of his tongue. "You miserable piece of shit! You hate your life, huh?"

"Watch it, buddy."

"You wanna kill yourself, I'll bet. You think you can hurt me? I'm gonna live forever! My music will be played for eternity!"

When Chris was done King just looked at him funny, that smirk back on his face, pitying him.

Chris didn't even realize he was chewing on his lips, the echo of his fearful, almost desperate tirade in his head, the words ugly, and he felt somehow embarrassed. He scratched his reddening face.

"Keep telling yourself that, buddy."

Chris sighed heavily, pinched his eyes, wondering how long he would be trapped there on the side of the street, when his phone started ringing its welcoming distraction. However, Chris felt his stomach flip-flop and suddenly got the image in his head that it was *him*.

Rich.

Calling to taunt Chris some more. Or worse, calling to tell Chris that Daryl was dead.

Chris didn't care what King would say and answered the phone. To Chris's surprise, King didn't protest, just rubbed the dust from his aviators with his thumb and put them back on.

"Mr. Flowers. It's Sergeant Bradford."

Chris saw Bradford in his mind, a stocky man with graying hair and a mustache and tired eyes, sitting in his office at the station on Murphy Street, an office he knew from a previous, innocuous encounter the morning after he'd clocked Rich.

"Mr. Bradford. What can I do for you?" Chris's voice was still prickly. He was staring out the windshield at the traffic shrinking into shimmering mirages in the distance, ignoring Officer King as if the dude didn't even exist.

Bradford sighed, as if whatever he had to say was difficult and baffling even for him. "Wondering if you could come to the station."

Chris wiped his forehead.

"Chris?"

"Yeah, am I under arrest?"

"No, no," Bradford reassured him thinly. "Just some questions."

Chris shut his eyes tight, wrestling with the fact that his momma would have to wait a little longer.

Then he gave Officer King a cursory, spiteful glance. "I can't because one of your true blues won't let me."

"What true blue?"

"Officer King. Says I ran a red light I never ran, and now he won't let me go anywhere."

Chris saw King's twitching lips out of the corner of his eye.

"He's grinning at me right now."

"Is it Ollie?" Bradford asked.

"Are you Ollie?" Chris asked, getting no reply. "He won't answer, but I'm guessing yeah."

"Put him on."

Chris passed King the phone, and the cop glanced down at it, then stared at Chris for a moment.

"Your boss," Chris reminded him.

Ollie King took his time answering the phone. Chris could hear the crackle of Bradford's voice speaking into Ollie's ear, Ollie King glancing around saying, "Mmm. Yeah. Yes, sir."

Then Ollie handed the phone back to Chris, and Chris told Bradford he'd be at the station shortly, as he was about ten minutes from Murphy Street.

King held on to Chris's license and registration for a long time as he was passing it back to Chris, both men looking down at the tug-of-war until Chris yanked his papers out of King's thick fingers.

King glared at Chris from the side of the road as Chris drove off.

CHAPTER TWENTY-THREE

The paparazzi had always been there. Always been his shadow. They had been waiting for Chris in November after the incident at the mental health benefit concert at the Glasgow Theater when Chris punched Rich in the face. Chris had arrived to answer some questions regarding that particular episode, and he'd stepped out into the warm November sun, its light a radiant, colossal spotlight that kissed his face and made his cream silk shirt shine. He had even worn a tie that day, a bright red one to go with a matching pair of running sneakers. There had been the sounds of cameras' motor drives clicking away, and Chris had turned to see one of the paparazzi guys poking a fancy massive black camera out from behind the oak on the emerald lawn in front of the police station. Another was in the bushes, rustling, poking that long, extended camera eye out and snapping pictures. Two more were by a white Land Rover parked up the police station's driveway. Chris, as always, slyly glanced away as if he'd never even seen them, then headed into the police station.

They were waiting for him today, too, only now Chris's armpits were soaked and he was trembling when he stepped out of his car. They stirred in those same spots, behind the oak, in the bushes, behind the open doors of a Mercedes parked up the street. And this time Chris turned away from them not out of a feigned unawareness but out of a sickness in his gut, out of shame. The sunlight was a toxic fiend, and the paparazzi had turned from friends into enemies. He searched in vain for Rich, though Rich wasn't amongst them. Where Rich might be and what he might be doing only made Chris feel sicker, more ashamed, more helpless. His soul was a shivering autumn leaf in a violent gale.

Inside the station, as he made his way across the carpeted main room toward Sergeant Bradford's office, he received stares. Officers and detectives in their dark uniforms frowned, shook their heads, then turned away. A detective sitting at her desk glanced over her mound of paperwork and held Chris's stare, and he could still feel her eyes boring into his back as he entered a hallway. More glares and strange, disappointed looks behind office windows, officers and detectives glancing up from important phone calls to sneer at him.

Chris felt a wash of relief as he approached the glass door with the words *Detective Sergeant Bradford* in big, dark letters across it. He wanted to jump into that office like it was a foxhole, to escape the crossfire of the hateful stares of betrayal he was receiving. He knocked, knuckles tapping the warm glass, and Bradford glanced up from a sea of paperwork. Bradford looked tired in his clean, dark uniform, but also pleased to see Chris. Those puffy eyes embedded in rings of darkness, like pits of insomnia, lit up suddenly and a smile flickered at the corner of Bradford's mustached mouth. Bradford waved for Chris to come in, and Chris entered. The office smelled like men's cologne, bitter coffee, and long, hard hours.

Bradford gave his mountain of paperwork a look as if to say, *I'll get back to you.* Then he stood up, offered Chris a meaty hand.

"Chris."

Chris shook the offered hand. "Sergeant."

Bradford scratched his gray mustache, pursed his lips.

Then he nodded at the door. "Let's take a walk."

Chris was led down two more halls to an interviewing room. Chris had been questioned in here before, only now he wasn't wearing that cream-colored silk shirt, red tie, and red sneakers. He wasn't brimming with confidence like he had been when Bradford had asked him easy, dismissive questions about the incident at the show. They had even laughed about it, Chris and Bradford, Bradford asking how it felt to belt that little shit Rich Howard in the face. Best feeling in the world, Chris had told him.

Chris took a seat at the table in the middle of the room. The chair had no foam padding, hard and ugly. The fluorescents above buzzed.

Bradford didn't sit just yet, first asking Chris, "Want some coffee?"

Chris's body was tingling with exhaustion from the past several nights of bad sleep and he couldn't deny he was tired, so he nodded.

Bradford turned, put his hand on the doorknob, paused, then glanced over his shoulder.

Voice lowered, he asked, "How do you like it?"

Chris could almost hear the criticisms Bradford was trying to avoid: *Why're you being nice to him? Who cares how the wifebeater and rapist likes his coffee!*

"Black's fine, man."

Bradford nodded, left.

Then Chris was alone, his mind steeped in darkening thoughts. It felt like the room was getting smaller. Chris, realizing the trouble he was in, buried his face in his hands. Should he just keep his mouth shut, call a lawyer?

Bradford returned with two Styrofoam cups of coffee, sat them down on the table, and slid Chris's over to him. Chris thanked him, took a sip. It was hot and strong and bitter, and it took some of the edge off.

Bradford settled into his chair on the opposite side of the table, sipped his coffee.

They said nothing for a moment.

Bradford broke the ice. "Andrea reported what happened earlier this morning, before she went on the news. Said she wanted to go viral with her story before I gave you a call and asked questions."

Chris sneered, bobbed his head bitterly. *Of course. She wanted me to see that video.*

"Chris." Bradford leaned forward, chair squeaking. "Tell me the truth, man."

"I didn't touch her. I loved the girl. Thought I did, at least."

Bradford leaned back, nodding, believing Chris.

It was at least a candlelight of warmth in all this darkness.

"Andrea has a history of not choosing the best dude to be with. You know?"

Chris could almost hear Rich's protesting voice, arguing with a detective in this very room at some point, being questioned about his harassment of celebrities.

"But when I heard her saying all this shit about you, I thought, Chris? Nah, can't be! Not the guy who gives all that money to charities. Like that one, what is it?"

"The Tray Mansfield Foundation for Young Artists."

"Bingo," Bradford said with the snap of his fingers. "I've seen pictures of you on the internet giving boxes of clothes and food to homeless people, all out of the goodness of your heart, man. You've given money to charities, the homeless, cancer research. Hell, you've spoken at women's marches, man."

Chris's eyes hung down. He caught his reflection in the black mirror of his coffee.

"I thought she had to be wrong. It just didn't fit. I mean, I figured you wouldn't hurt a fly, man."

Chris finally looked up, locked eyes with Bradford, tried to keep dark truths out of his face. He just smiled, nodded a little, then said, "Right. I wouldn't."

Bradford nodded sympathetically. Then his warm smile withered.

"Not everyone thinks so though." Bradford glanced over his shoulder, and Chris remembered the gauntlet of sneers and sour glares he'd had to trudge through in the police station's office space. He realized it was just the smallest reflection of what the entire world was thinking about him. "Still, not everyone is sure about Andrea, either." Bradford stared at him for a moment before continuing. "There's always two sides to a story. There're those like me who don't believe the great Chris Flowers would be capable of doing something as horrible as that."

"Yeah," Chris said, gave his Styrofoam cup a little squeeze. "But no one's gonna believe sweet little Andrea did that shit to herself."

Bradford sipped his coffee, a few drops staining his thick gray mustache, and took that in. Then he said, "People put you on a pedestal, Chris. The great Chris Flowers."

Chris flinched. He cleared his throat, then said, "A lot of people have already made their judgements, it seems. They need someone to tear down, to make their pathetic lives feel better. Like that stupid fucking cop of yours. Ollie King. You need to fire that asshole, Bradford. Women were being raped while he was wasting time taking his bullshit out on me."

Bradford's forehead wrinkled as he gave Chris an odd look of disappointment.

Chris sighed. "Sorry."

Bradford waved it away. "I'll talk to King. Don't worry about that. But you are—were like a hero to him."

"Oh come on, man."

"You helped me too. Don't know if you realize that."

This drew Chris's attention. He noticed a touch of melancholy in the sergeant's tired face.

Bradford scratched his mustache. A little redness started flaring in his pallid cheeks.

"I have a son. Jake. He's twenty-one. Just turned. We just had his birthday. The only one of our three who's still at home." He pursed his lips, nodded as he was telling, and Chris listened patiently. "He was nineteen when he got in a car wreck. He was drunk. Being stupid. He needs help eating and shitting. We have to wipe the poor kid's ass for him." Bradford wiped a silent tear with his knuckles. "He loved music. Wanted to go to music school. Become a musician. And you were his absolute favorite. His biggest influence. Even now when me or my wife put on your music he gets this big smile on his face and his eyes, they just light up and it's like there he is, you know? There's my big man."

Chris glanced away, sadness burning in his chest, as the sergeant wiped another stray tear.

"You make him happy, man," Bradford said. "I thank you for that. I want you to be able to keep making music, to keep playing shows, making people happy. But this is a tough situation, man. You do realize that?"

Chris pinched his eyes, nodded. "Yeah, man. I get it."

Bradford polished off his coffee and explained to Chris that he would need to return to this room, most likely many times, talking to detectives, telling his side of the story, having to be recorded, taking lie detector tests.

"Would you mind sticking around?" Bradford asked, standing up. "I'm gonna grab one of my detectives. We'll bring in a tape recorder, ask more detailed questions."

Shit. "Sure."

Chris was left all alone again.

He sighed, took a breath. The air felt thick. He peered into his empty Styrofoam cup, wanting more coffee even though he could feel his heart thumping away in his chest. He felt a dim self-assurance thinking about the lie detector test Bradford mentioned.

Answer truthfully, you'll come out on top.

However, this fiasco would probably go on for a long time. Perhaps years of jumping through legal hoops. Courtroom battles with his soon-to-be ex-wife. The worst part was that his entire career, his entire *life,* would have to be put on hold. It was just like Jeff had said, his show tonight at the Hollywood Amphitheater was cancelled.

Chris crushed his Styrofoam cup in his clenched fist.

His world tour next year cancelled.

His album.

Dear God, his album would have to be pushed back. Probably for years.

At least until this shitstorm blows over.

Silence swelled as Chris waited. Dark thoughts crowded his mind. He thought about his momma again. He wondered if she was still expecting him. If she even remembered she had called. The thought made Chris want to smash one of the windowless walls around him.

But he was stuck here. And he didn't know how long it would be before he would get to see her again.

She's tried calling you. But you don't answer, Annie Hart had said. *You haven't been here in a year.*

Chris was already exhausted pondering the ugly years ahead, the years of pain and cruelty he'd have to endure from people who'd once loved him.

While these thoughts gathered, he felt a sudden shadow on him. He glanced up, thinking Bradford was back. The door had a long, skinny plexiglass viewing window and a detective with slick dark hair had stopped a moment to peer in. To Chris's surprise, the man had a smile on his hard, bearded face.

The hell you grinning at? Chris thought.

Was he gawking, like Chris was a sideshow freak or a zoo animal?

The man left only to be replaced by another detective, a man with a swoop of blond hair who gave Chris a thumbs-up.

Chris glared back, resisting the urge to give the man the finger.

Then that detective left, and the door opened and Bradford entered with a smile on his face. He looked relieved about something. Chris's chest tingled with anxiety, with anticipation.

"What?"

"You're a lucky man," Bradford said, smiling.

"Why?"

"Check your phone."

CHAPTER TWENTY-FOUR
2008

Nearly two hundred people were staring at Chris up on that stage, their faces like sunflowers staring up at the sun. Their applause felt like bathing in molten sunshine. Chris had just strummed the final chord of the last song of their set. He smiled and thanked the audience and, while squinting through the spotlight, spotted the man in the back with the long, gray, slicked-back hair and burning blue eyes. The man was staring at Chris, intently, eagerly. Chris thought he recognized the face from a previous show, but he didn't think much else of it at that time. He was too focused. His favorite part, the warmth and love he'd just radiated out into the audience, was rebounding back to him, Chris's original tunes embedded deep into their minds. He took this precious moment to relish in his favorite sounds: the cheering, the sound of hands coming together, the sound of the joy he'd just brought to them. He and his songs wouldn't soon be forgotten.

That warmth from the standing ovation remained in his chest as he and his band made trips hauling guitars and drums and amps out to the van parked in a pool of orange streetlight in the back lot. They were the headlining act that night, the name *Chris and the Luminaries* blazing in large black letters on the marquee in front of the club, with a couple other little brother bands in smaller script beneath their name. Chris had only recently decided on the name change. Manny especially didn't agree with it, telling him, "It ain't all about you, man!" Chris countered with, "I book the shows, I write the songs, I *am* the band!"

It was late and, being the headliners, they were last to play, so they weren't bumping amps with another group as they lugged their gear down those narrow backstage halls and into the van. It was a warm LA December night at a club called Swag. It was a nice, clean club on the Sunset Strip, though it wasn't the Sayers Club or the Hollywood Bowl.

Chris had recurring dreams about playing in such places, spotlight as bright as the sun, gazing out over the sea of people, his original music rippling out like a lovely, glowing wave and touching every single one of them.

Then he saw Manny, scowling as he lugged the bass drum toward the van, and was reminded of Manny's little stunt. Manny had seemed to grudgingly accept the name change and even allowed Chris to paint it in gold letters over the bass drum's face, for all to see when they played. But Manny had, at some point before the show, painted over the golden words, replacing them with the original band name. Chris had been mortified, and to assuage some of the perplexed looks from the audience, some of whom were glancing from the bass drum's face to posters that clearly stated it was *Chris and the Luminaries* playing, tried to stand in front of the bass drum, trying to block out Manny as much as possible. How would they get into the big leagues with a drummer who was sabotaging the band?

But before Chris even had a chance to confront Manny, he was approached by a familiar face.

He was putting his guitar, nestled into its hard case, in the back of the van, between his guitar amp and Daryl's bass amp, when a voice coming from behind him said, "Excuse me?"

It took Chris a moment, but he soon recognized it was the man with the slicked-back gray hair, that eager look still smoldering in his blue eyes. The man was halfway through a cigarette. He was wearing a dark suit jacket, slacks, no tie, and gleaming black dress shoes.

Manny was already in the van, sulking in the passenger seat, but the man had caught both Daryl's and Maria's attention. Daryl had just put his bass guitar into the back of the van and cracked a can of Miller. Maria, out of her stretchy pregnancy pants and looking so small, and somehow sad, without her bulging belly, had just set some cables into the back of the van, the last of the gear, and shut the door.

"Can I help you?" Chris said.

The man took a drag off his cigarette, the smoke orange in the streetlight, and said with his slightly raspy voice, "I was wondering if we could talk."

"Sure. Wanna talk to us now, here, or—"

"No, I mean, I wanna talk to *you*."

Chris felt a jolt of excitement run through him. He had to suppress a flattered grin. Chris said yes, and they agreed to meet at a table near the bar in the club. With that, the gray-haired man smiled, flicked his cigarette, then disappeared into the club's glowing back entrance.

Neither Maria nor Daryl shared in Chris's excitement, and his ecstatic grin wilted. Chris said he'd only be a few minutes, but Maria said she'd just ride with the boys. Daryl just sipped his beer, wouldn't meet Chris's eyes. What, were they all still mad at him? It was true, wasn't it? Chris was the band, worked the hardest, was the reason people went to their shows. Manny and Daryl did little else. Chris, however, did regret calling them deadweight at their last practice. He thought maybe that was over the line.

When Chris went in to give Maria a peck on the lips, she turned her head and smiled painfully as his lips landed instead on her cheek. He didn't pay it much mind; his blood quickened with excitement at meeting this enigmatic and important-looking man.

As Chris watched the van speed off to join the lights of the Sunset Strip, he felt a stab of irritation. Who did they think they were?

But his frustrations were quickly soothed inside the club. The crowd of about two hundred had dwindled down to about fifty who had remained to drink into the wee hours, some stopping Chris to shake his hand or raise their glass to him, to tell him what a killer show he'd put on. That he—Chris—had put on. Not the band. Him.

Chris took his time on his way over to the bar, making sure to acknowledge everyone who acknowledged him. He found himself momentarily distracted by a pair of women who said, "Hi, Chris," in unison and started gushing to him. He drank in their curvaceous bodies, felt himself growing hard. Over their shoulders, he saw the gray-haired man sitting at a round table by the bar, sipping a beer. The man noticed Chris but didn't appear irritated at the intrusions. In fact, he seemed genuinely delighted at Chris's mingling. Chris apologized to the man anyway when he finally reached the table, then shook his hand.

The man introduced himself as Jeff Bentley, a music manager who was on the lookout for an upcoming artist, and he was about to change Chris's life forever.

CHAPTER TWENTY-FIVE
JULY 2023

In November, many months before his current predicament, on a day that was warm and gray, Chris had walked out of this same police station with a smile on his face. The paparazzi guys were still there, of course, but Chris had kept grinning pretty, not just for their benefit, but because he had come up with a plan he was pleased about. Rich Howard, in an arm cast in the hospital, was being harassed by detectives while Andrea was free—separated from Rich. While sitting in his car outside the police station, Chris had pulled up the number she'd given him and called her, asked her if she wanted to go to dinner with him that evening. He could almost hear the smile in her voice when she said yes.

Now, eight months later, Chris wore the same triumphant grin on his face when he exited this police station.

That grin remained on his face on the drive to the historic club building. His ego was like an inflated balloon on the verge of exploding as he drove through the building's back lot, where he'd been only the day before. But there was still a shadow cast over his excitement, ever since he'd checked his cell phone like the relieved Sergeant Bradford had gleefully told him to do.

Chris approached Jeff, who was standing in the bright sun wearing a pair of shades and still wearing his white T-shirt and shorts from earlier at the studio. He was leaned back against his Mercedes, talking on his cell phone.

Chris had tried calling Jeff the second he'd stepped out of the police station, the station's closing doors muffling the sound of applauding detectives, whistling and clapping in celebration for Chris. Jeff's line had been busy. Then Chris'd received a brisk text from Jeff telling Chris he was on the phone and to meet him at the old historic club building.

The sun dazzled Jeff's razor-cut white hair and made his fat gold rings sparkle. As Chris approached Jeff, he noticed commotion near the building's back entrance. People in gray jumpsuits were busy sweeping the lot. The droning sound of a vacuum came from inside, that big plush carpet being cleaned spotless by one of those giant wide-area vacuums. They were getting it ready for the press conference.

When Chris's shadow fell on Jeff, Jeff turned, gave Chris a big smile, his bleached teeth shining in the midmorning sunshine, then he raised a "one moment" finger and continued to talk into his phone.

"Yeah, I know. It's unreal."

A warm breeze stirred the fronds of the palm trees and carried the sounds of traffic coming from Cameron Drive. The air smelled of car exhaust and the faint kelp scent of the sea.

"Thank you so much. All right, bye."

Jeff hung up, turned to Chris, grabbed his shoulders, gave them an apologetic rub.

"Can you believe it?"

"No," Chris said.

And he truly couldn't.

When he saw what the news feeds were saying, he'd realized those detectives peering in at him through that skinny viewing window weren't jeering him or mocking him. They were encouraging him; their beaming faces suddenly made sense.

Andrea had posted a video on her social media, sometime soon after she'd gone on KTLA 5 with her story. Both Chris and Bradford had watched it together.

In the video she was sitting behind the wheel of her Porsche, holding the camera in selfie mode. It looked, judging by her surroundings—other shiny cars and the bright overhead fluorescents—like she was in a massive multistory garage, and Chris had wondered if she was still at KTLA 5. It was difficult to read the expression on her face, only that she was upset, her lips pursed tight and her eyes darting. She looked startled. Stunned. Her cheeks were fish-gray.

Then her bloodshot jade eyes fixed onto the camera's eye and she was staring at the entire world.

"Hi, everyone. This is hard for me to put into words."

Chris had turned the video up to hear it better. A few other detectives had entered the interview room and gathered around Chris to watch.

Andrea's brow creased; her cheeks flared. She chewed on her lips.

Chris had been on the edge of that hard, uncomfortable seat.

"All that stuff I said. All this." She pointed at the bruises on her face. Then she shook her head, squeezed her eyes shut. "None of it was true."

Chris had been stunned, his eyes opening wide, wanting to rewind the video and hear it again.

It was out.

The truth was out.

She kept her eyes squeezed shut, too embarrassed to hold eye contact, even with a cell phone camera.

Chris felt an earthquake in his bones, his confusion turning into outrage.

Why was she doing this?

She had been so determined.

I'm gonna ruin you, Chris Flowers!

So why would she change her mind like this?

Chris had felt the rest of the world's growing irritation reflected in the souring faces of the detectives there at the station, in the popping of their knuckles, in the bite of their perplexed murmurs while the video played.

"What the...?"

"Is she trying to piss people off?" someone else uttered, and Bradford shushed him.

"I lied to you," Andrea continued. "All of you." There were traces of despair and frustration in her voice then.

The video ended after a mere thirty-two seconds, Andrea's last words, "I'm leaving. I'm sorry."

Thirty-two seconds.

Thirty-two seconds and Chris's life had changed.

He'd felt the way a fish must feel after being reeled to the surface and out of the water, gawked at and handled by a fisherman, gasping, on the brink of death, before finally being released unwanted back into the water.

Chris had heard in the cheers of the detectives around him, felt in the gentle pats on the back from Bradford, the relief in his fans all over the world. He could feel their anxiety, as well as his own, like a weight being lifted from their chests, able to breathe again. Bradford would be able to go home to his son, Jake, and would be able to explain that Chris wasn't a *monster*. Chris was as good as he'd ever been.

Chris's mouth still stung from how wide his smile had grown, but he'd also felt the beginnings of a deeper confusion that troubled him on his way to Cameron Drive and to the historic building where he was now standing in the hot breeze with Jeff.

Did she change her mind on impulse? Chris wondered. *Was she feeling guilty?*

Chris shook his head. "It doesn't make sense."

Jeff waved it off. "It don't need to."

Chris wanted to believe that. He wanted to be as completely immersed in the relief and euphoria as Jeff was, as Chris's fans were.

But there was still that shadow. Chris thought he saw something, a dark cloud of fear somewhere beneath Andrea's face as she was confessing.

"Something ain't right about it."

Jeff's face clouded with offense. Chris could see his own unenthusiastic face reflected in his manager's sunglasses.

"Your—our—asses have been spared. And you're questioning it?"

"I'm just saying..."

"Do you know who I just got off the phone with? The people running the Hollywood Amphitheater. They said this is the first time they've ever cancelled a superstar then called to get him back on."

A smile flickered at the corner of Chris's mouth. He had to admit he was happy about that. He was already preparing a little speech of gratitude to all the fans who'd had to endure all the craziness. He even had a hot little joke ready, apologizing for the whiplash they'd probably experienced trying to keep up with all the hectic news the past few days. He could already hear their relieved laughter, a pleasant tingle in his ears.

But then Andrea's words returned like a gunshot: *I'm gonna ruin you.*

"You should've heard her last night, man. It don't make sense."

But Jeff was already raising his hands, cutting Chris off. "I don't want to hear it, Chris."

The cell in Jeff's pocket chirped. Chris figured, like the Amphitheater, it was another stadium calling to tell Jeff that Chris Flowers wasn't cancelled. Chris was being green-lighted again. Chris was surprised at himself for his own lack of enthusiasm. His world tour for next year was back on; he would still get to play the big show tonight. His album wouldn't have to be pushed back for years.

But he thought about Andrea's video, thought about the fear he swore he'd noticed in her face.

Could Rich be involved in all this?

As Jeff checked his cell phone messages, he said, "If it's such a big deal to you, ask her yourself." He sounded apathetic. Snide.

But Chris didn't think it was such a bad idea.

Though he would keep his mouth shut about Rich.

Jeff won't hear it.

Jeff put his phone back in his pocket, then gestured to the janitors sweeping and vacuuming near the rear entrance. "We're having that conference still." It sounded more like a demand than a request. "I was able to calm Billy down," he added with a sly grin. "The press keeps buzzing. The conference is in a half hour."

Chris glanced at the rear entrance with longing, with relief imagining himself alone at that table and the cameras hungry for his every word.

And this time his words would not be twisted by Andrea and her threats. This time he wouldn't be played like a puppet.

I miss you, baby. I ain't seen you in so long.

Chris felt a lump forming in his throat.

Why don't you come see me no more? I don't see no one.

Was Momma still waiting for his arrival? Had she forgotten?

If she's already forgotten, then you don't have to feel obligated to—

Chris pushed that repulsive thought from his mind completely.

"What is it?" Jeff said, already defensive, almost angry.

"No. We can do all that shit later. Tomorrow. We can do it sometime tomorrow."

"What?" Jeff said again, a little harder, flabbergasted.

"I promised my momma I'd visit her."

"Your momma?"

"Call it off. We can *always* do this kind of shit, man. I gotta go."

It was then Jeff did something strange, something Chris wouldn't understand until later.

Jeff yanked off his sunglasses, took a step forward, his irate Botoxed face inches from Chris's, his breath sweet and hot with nicotine. His eyes were icy blue orbs searching Chris's face. Jeff was searching for something. Something on Chris's face.

Chris stiffened with discomfort at the inspection. "What?"

Jeff pursed his lips, shook his head. "Nothing."

CHAPTER TWENTY-SIX

There'd never been secrets between Chris and Jeff. Jeff caught on quickly to Chris's addiction. Chris had been determined to finally get clean, but it would be nearly a decade of recovery and relapse before Chris was finally able to overcome that piece of his old life that clung relentlessly to him. Jeff got Chris into high-end drying out facilities where Chris would spend many months at a time. It took eight stints in rehab, until, at thirty-four years of age, Chris finally kicked it completely. During one of his drying out phases Jeff, out of a kind of camaraderie to express his trust after their years of friendship, had confided to Chris he'd started smoking heavily ever since the day he found his big brother in bed, his face blue with yellow frothy foam caked around his purple lips. Jeff had been twenty-two, his brother thirty, and they had been living in an apartment together. The suicide note told how failing his American Idol audition for the sixth time sent him spiraling into an endless despair, and so one night he decided to take an entire bottle of Prozac. Jeff's brother had worked his way up to eighty milligram daily doses and had taken an entire bottle of thirty the day he picked up his fresh prescription at the pharmacy.

Jeff was visiting Chris at the luxurious McCarthy facility right there in Beverly Hills and they were sitting on a bench outside. Jeff had wrapped his arm around a pale, withdrawing Chris, and said, "I loved my brother," wiping a tear from his eye. "He was so talented, man. Why couldn't he have just stuck it out? He just needed to believe in himself more." He'd been gazing up into the clear, blue sky, as if asking God. It was the only time Jeff had ever talked about it. A devastating event in Jeff's life, and he had confessed that to Chris. A few days later, he'd checked himself into a private psychiatric institution for a week.

But at that moment of confession sitting on that bench next to Chris, Jeff had pulled out his pack of cigarettes and vowed if Chris could stick out staying off dope then he'd stick it out with him and would stop smoking. Jeff never did quite kick the habit but had definitely cut back then had switched to vaping which Chris argued wasn't a healthier option. To which Jeff would say that he wasn't ingesting as much nicotine and that was what counted. Under the stress of the last few days' events, however, it seemed like Jeff's old insatiable nicotine craving had been reawakened. Jeff now puffed near constantly on that vape pen and was going through those nicotine cartridges like crazy.

It used to be like that between Jeff and Chris. And while driving to Santa Monica, Chris wondered what had happened. It felt like something had gone wrong during the past few days, like something between them was deteriorating.

Chris did, however, send that text Jeff suggested to Andrea:

Why? was all he wrote.

She hadn't texted back. Probably wouldn't.

Chris was cruising up that long, snaking driveway on the bluff under the perfect blue sky heading toward the fancy nursing home when his phone chirped, a text notification. He feathered the brake, felt excitement prickle his blood as he checked his phone.

It was Ray.

We still getting together today, buddy?

Ray meant at the gym. There would be plenty of time before the show tonight, and even though Chris felt a little sore from over-exerting two hundred and sixty pounds the night before—*stupid*—he texted back.

Yes. Be a little later. Few things to take care of.

Ray texted back a Thumbs Up emoji.

Then Chris, who was still idling in the middle of that quiet tree-lined street, started to drive again.

***

The lady at the main desk, a middle-aged woman wearing black horn-rimmed glasses and with a black ponytail, gave him a funny look as she logged Chris into the guest list, her computer monitor glowing on her mistrustful face.

He received similar strange looks from the unit manager, Annie Hart herself, as he was walking down the hall heading toward his momma's room. She brushed her blonde bangs out of her face, rubbed her exhausted, sunken eyes—looked like she might be pulling a double shift—and gave him looks bordering on the rude. Looks of confusion. Skepticism. She must have seen the news too.

He ignored them all as he reached the end of the floral-patterned hall. He took a breath then entered his momma's room. He left the door as it was, open a crack, then approached his momma who was sitting in a blue armchair facing her window with its grand view of the ocean. Her back was to him, and she was just staring eerily and silently out the window.

"Momma?" Chris said, though she must not have heard him. She didn't turn around or acknowledge him.

Looking out the window, he saw the sun making the water sparkle like diamonds. A few gulls wheeled and squawked. A few ships crawled along the horizon so distant as to appear like grains of rice.

When Chris reached her chair he could see in her lap her favorite picture, the one of her holding an infant Chris. Her wrinkled hands were wrapped loosely around it, like she'd forgotten it was even there.

"Momma?"

She was startled, whipped her head to look at him.

"Sorry. Didn't mean to scare you," he said with a smile.

Cloudy eyes blinked back at him. He tucked her wiry, gray hair tenderly behind her ear, and she wrinkled her forehead, not recognizing him.

"It's me, Momma."

"Who're you? What're you doing in my house?" There was a flare of that old sass in her voice.

Chris reached out and grabbed her hand, but she resisted, was trying to yank her hand away from his.

"It's me, Momma. It's me. It's okay. I'm here. You called me."

She tried resisting, and Chris was afraid she would explode like she did sometimes. Her eyes would turn into bright spooky lanterns. She'd speak gibberish, would cry out for *help! help!*

But she didn't explode or get aggressive. She just looked at him, perplexed. "What?"

"You did, Momma. You *remembered*. Then you called me. It's me." He pointed at the picture. Momma was smiling in the picture. Infant Chris had been tickled into a toothless smile too. "It's me. Your boy, Momma."

She stared at the picture for a moment, trembling.

Then something happened.

Chris wouldn't call it a moment of lucidity, not like how she had seemed lucid when she called him earlier. He'd been told by doctors, and had experienced it with his momma, that people with Alzheimer's do at times have hours, even days of lucidity. But what happened here was more what Chris could only discern as some nightmarish place between lucidity and dementia.

She started sobbing, moaning half words, tears falling onto the picture.

"Momma." Chris hugged her, held her for a long time.

As he was holding her, he heard the door squeak and glanced up to see Annie Hart's tired, ruddy face peering in. They locked eyes. Annie's mouth was slightly open, about to speak. But she didn't. It seemed like a little bit of that mistrust in her face had thawed. Then she was gone.

The next time Annie poked her head in was to announce lunch. Chris had turned the TV, on and he and Momma were watching some old sitcom together. Momma wasn't completely lucid, and Chris had to constantly remind her he was her son and that this wasn't her house back in South Central.

She needed help walking, Chris taking her by the arm and guiding her down the halls to the fancy lunchroom with the glossy hardwood floor. The elderly residents sat at round tables. The chefs could be heard in the kitchen, shouted orders, clanking pots and pans, while the residents sat, mostly silent, in the elegant room awaiting their favorite meals. Waiters and waitresses, dressed in smart black-and-white uniforms, emerged from the kitchen carrying out everything from hamburgers to sandwiches, lasagna, soups, salads. They had it all.

Chris and his momma chose a table at the outer edge of the restaurant. Old big band music of a bygone era played gently over the speakers. A smile spread across Chris's face when he watched his momma raise her hands up into the air, moving to the music. Chris wondered if she was reliving memories of when she would crank up music in their old house on Campbell Street and dance. If she was, then at least they were happy memories. And she did seem happy now, so it made him happy. "Yeah! Go, Momma! Go, Momma!"

Nurses, hovering nearby, smiled at Chris.

The nurse aides fed some of the residents who needed help eating. Some didn't need help.

An older aide offered to help, spotting Momma struggling with a bite, but Chris said, "I got it."

His momma tried again, raising a spoonful of homestyle mac and cheese—one of her favorites—to her mouth, but her hands shook so badly the food just plopped back down onto the plate. Chris encouraged her to try to eat by herself, reminded chillingly of years earlier how he'd encouraged her to play word games like Scrabble. When she dropped some food onto her lap, Chris started feeding her bites. He felt like a father feeding a child, raising bites, telling her to open up.

"It's okay, Momma," Chris said, noticing her embarrassment and frustration, her face twitching, her cheeks burning red.

He raised bite after bite until she was full, then helped her polish off her favorite drink, a tall glass of bubbly Coke with a straw. He raised the glass and straw to her lips. "Drink up, Momma."

After lunch Chris guided her out to the sundeck overlooking the ocean. The air was warm and salty, and the sun beamed down hard from high-noon above them. A few of the other residents had found their way out there, too, sitting in the shade in lounge chairs under umbrellas. Chris and his momma were standing by the railing. Nurses and aides stood guard, watchful, making sure none of the residents fell over the side and into the bushes and rocks ten or so feet below.

Something had been eating at Chris. He knew Annie Hart had been keeping an eye on him, the squat woman in blue scrubs who always in the periphery from the moment he'd walked through the door. But it wasn't that. It was what Annie said a couple nights ago when he visited Momma on her birthday: *Why can't you at least visit her more often? I see people almost as famous as you coming in every day. Busy as you. They make time.*

Chris hung his head, the sun punishing on his face.

Why don't you come see me no more?

Chris turned to his momma who was glancing around looking disoriented, her eyes milky, her brow furrowing.

"Momma?"

"Am I at my house?"

"No, Momma."

She's tried calling you. But you don't answer.

I miss you, baby. I ain't seen you in so long.

He gently grabbed her shoulders so they were facing each other.

"Momma, I need to tell you how sorry I am. I'm sorry I've been such a shitty son."

She was quiet a moment, then suddenly she said, "It's okay, baby."

He swore there was a flicker of lucidity in her eyes, her voice warm and certain and forgiving.

"I love you," he said, his throat thick with tears.

"I love you. I don't know who you are, but I love you."

They were back to staring out over the ocean, Momma saying once again how beautiful a day it was.

"Yes, it is, Momma. Yes, it is."

Then Chris received a text.

Andrea.

His heart started pounding as he opened it.

LAX parking lot. Half hour.

He didn't know if she meant she'd give him half an hour to talk or to be there in half an hour, but he assumed it was the latter.

He put his phone in his pocket, turned to his momma. "I gotta go, but I'll be here tomorrow. And the day after that. And the day after that. And the day after that. I promise." He gave her a kiss on her forehead.

"Bye, baby."

"Bye, Momma."

Then Chris headed for the exit.

He passed Annie Hart on the way out. That mistrustful, perplexed look on her face had melted completely. She even smiled and nodded at him.

CHAPTER TWENTY-SEVEN

On the way to Los Angeles International Airport, Chris couldn't stop thinking about his and Andrea's first dinner together. He wore a suit and she wore a beautiful shimmering dress and big dangling sparkling earrings. They had steaks and salad and key lime pie at a fancy fine dining place called Bradshaw's. He remembered the way her cheeks blushed when he wiped some key lime pie from her chin, then he'd broken her up with a joke and she grew comfortable again. He remembered the way she looked at him over a glass of champagne, her eyes smoldering with hope and excitement and even awe—awe that the great Chris Flowers had chosen her out of all the other women in the world to go out with.

But her eyes were much different when he found her that day at the airport.

Zipping texts back and forth she guided him to her location smack dab in the middle of a thousand other cars. Luckily, a nearby car pulled out and Chris filled its spot temporarily and then stepped out and walked a few cars down to Andrea's bright red Porsche. Airliners droned on the distant runways and traffic control towers blinked red as all kinds of jets growled across the sky. A boiling early afternoon breeze smelling of diesel stirred garbage over the roadways.

Chris approached the passenger's side of Andrea's Porsche and instinctively tried the door handle, hoping he'd be able to climb in for a few minutes and talk, but the door was locked. Andrea wasn't even looking at him. She was wearing big sunglasses and simple, drab clothes, jeans and a t-shirt, and was staring out the windshield. Still without looking at him she pressed a button, and the passenger's side window rolled down, the seat, he saw, already occupied by a small suitcase.

She finally peeled off her sunshades and looked him square in the eye, a look that was far different than she had at their first dinner together. The bruises hadn't gone anywhere, her face still covered with them, eyes two dark craters. Chris thought he should feel angry at her, thought he even had the *right* to feel angry at her. But then that dinner came back to him, not the dinner itself, but what happened immediately after.

"I have a flight to catch, so I don't want this to take long."

Before asking about her video, he glanced down at her suitcase, then back up at her. "Where're you going?"

"You know where."

He remembered what she had talked about the night before. "Tennessee," he said, nodding.

"I wouldn't have done it, you know."

He knew she meant the video, the confession. "Then why did you?"

Her eyes darted, and her face burned red. She shook her head. "Wasn't my idea."

"What're you talking about?"

She pulled out her cell phone, dinked around on it, pulling something up.

Then she held her phone in front of Chris's face.

What he saw stunned him.

It was a picture of Andrea standing in front of a mirror, her face a bloody mess. She slid her thumb, revealing other pictures showing her in mid-action, raising a coiled fist to the air and making a clenched face, bracing for pain, pounding on her arms and thighs, appearing oblivious that the pictures were even being taken. The camera shots were at a slanting angle, like an intruder had to peer around the corner and in through the open bathroom to capture the devastating images reflected in the bathroom mirror. Then Chris knew.

There *had* been an intruder. And there was only one person it could be.

"Rich."

Andrea put her phone away, winced and touched her swollen cheeks. Then she broke eye contact with Chris, stared out the windshield again.

"He followed you."

Andrea nodded. "Yup." There was a tinge of regret in her voice. Regret for Rich having followed her.

"Where'd you go?"

"A motel. Same one I was staying when I took off two nights ago. Some cheap two-star place on Beverly Boulevard."

"Where'd you stay?"

"Why do you care?"

"Just curious."

Andrea was quiet a moment. Then finally said, "It's a place called The Drifter if you must know. Not some place a man of your tastes would appreciate. But the manager kept his mouth shut. Staff were barely present. It was *anonymous*." She said this with a smile, like the word itself was a breath of fresh air. "It was perfect, or at least I thought."

"You didn't see him follow you?"

Andrea looked away, shook her head. "He might've jimmied the lock on my room somehow. I was drunk, maybe I forgot to latch the door. I'm thinking he climbed in through the window though, took his pictures then slinked out."

Chris had to suppress elation from his face, wanting even to applaud the little bastard.

"He texted me this morning," Andrea said. "Just after I got off KTLA. Bastard was obviously watching, too. Told me if I didn't confess to what I did, he was going to release the pictures."

Chris felt a chill hearing that word.

Confess.

His forehead wrinkled in profound confusion. Then he got it.

Rich is trying to ruin me, not her.

"It doesn't make sense," Chris said, mostly to himself.

Was it a warning?

Andrea, snatching her suitcase, answered bitterly, "Of course it makes sense."

No it doesn't. Not at all.

"Bastard was just waiting to see what I'd do, then he sent me the pictures."

Andrea stepped out into the sun, put her massive sunshades back on hiding her face behind them. She shot Chris a vile look.

"You know what? I'm actually glad all this happened. I'm so sick of dealing with this shit."

Chris remembered bitterly after their first date at the restaurant, full of steak and salad and pie, then noticing paparazzi guys hidden behind trees and cars. He remembered turning away from them, once again slyly pretending they weren't there, and facing Andrea and locking eyes with her. She had looked like she was about to burst with anticipation. Then he leaned in and kissed her, long and sweet.

"Andrea...."

"We'll set it up later how you can send my shit to me," she said, ignoring him, glancing worriedly and idly at her cell phone.

"Don't go."

She glanced at him slowly.

"We can work something out. Please. I can help you. We'll fix it. You're too talented—"

"Chris."

"I'm serious! I really mean it this time!"

She smirked. "Sure you do."

He felt like he was falling, pity swelling his heart.

"I'm sorry, Andrea. For *everything*." His voice was genuine, warm, sincere.

She stared at him, and Chris swore he saw the glint of a tear behind her sunglasses. Then a sly grin broke across her face.

"There's room for you on the plane." There was weak, vain hope in her voice.

Chris had been wondering why she'd told him all of this. But then he thought perhaps she had been holding out hope that he might still go with her, that it was possible even after everything that had happened that they could pick up the pieces and start a new life in an old, rambling farmhouse in Tennessee.

But Chris said nothing.

"That's what I thought," she said resentfully, a catch in her throat.

Then she turned around, abandoning the Porsche like the rest of her life and stormed off toward the airport terminal and out of Chris's life forever.

CHAPTER TWENTY-EIGHT

Chris was cruising the streets of Beverly Hills, Rodeo Drive, Hollywood Boulevard, Sunset, hopeful eyes glued to the rearview mirror. He was driving right out in the open, using the Ferrari like bait, hoping. He even drove past the The Drifter where Andrea said she'd stayed twice, hoping to draw Rich out.

While driving down Melrose Avenue he snapped his eyes to the rearview mirror, noticing a dark vehicle approaching, the hair on the back of his neck standing up. He pulled to the curb and waited. It was indeed a black Suburban. It crept in traffic, slowly approaching.

It passed by. Chris sighed. Different license plate.

That was the third black Suburban he'd seen in the last half hour, and Rich was nowhere to be found. Heat flushed Chris's face, and he hung his head on the steering wheel, burning with frustration.

Then his phone beeped. A text. He checked it, feeling a mixture of hope and terror.

It was Eddie. *Meet me at Albert. West Adams. I-10 overpass.*

Albert Street was in the West Adams neighborhood in South Central. The street ran beneath the I-10 overpass that acted as a kind of dividing line separating South Central from downtown. Chris had to ditch a few paparazzi guys on the way as he passed through Mid-City to get to Albert. They were mere miles from Fifth by the empty parking lot where Wally killed himself.

Chris was pleased to see Albert Street was quiet. Eddie's cruiser was parked at the curb. Chris parked behind a dented Subaru on the opposite side of the street, stepped out. The I-10 overpass stretched across the sky and Chris could hear the steady hum of the traffic overhead as he crossed Albert and approached Eddie's cruiser. Looking at Eddie's face, Chris noticed something seemed to be wrong. Eddie just sat there, his eyes drawn down. The driver's side window was still rolled up and Chris had to knock on it to get Eddie's attention. Eddie was startled, like he'd been pulled out of a deep, gloomy daydream. The window buzzed down and revealed Eddie's grim face. Eddie looked pale, sick, his eyes dark underneath.

"Hey, man," Chris said, curious, cautious.

Chris saw in the dim cruiser Eddie had pictures plastered everywhere, showing Eddie himself in civilian clothes with a young girl. Chris assumed the girl must be Eddie's daughter. The pictures showed her at varying ages, and in each one Eddie looked proudly and lovingly at her, a stark contrast to the ashen face now.

"I got drunk last night," was the first thing he said.

Chris was stunned, and dark feelings welled up. He felt suddenly thrust into the role of priest, listening to the officer's sinful confession.

"I thought you quit."

"I thought I did too."

Chris didn't know what to say, so he didn't say anything, only felt the sun baking the back of his head, the windless smoggy air as he breathed shallowly. A sudden guilt started chewing away at him, made him scratch at his face and at his bare arms sticking out of his silk jersey shirt.

Chris's nervously wandering eyes caught the pictures of Eddie and his daughter again. "What about your daughter, man? Come on, you don't want to let her down."

Eddie just chuckled in his throat, looking regretfully at the pictures.

Chris tapped his foot anxiously, worried Eddie might be bailing out, that he couldn't handle the guilt. Eddie's eyes dropped down again, and Chris realized the officer was staring at his own badge gleaming in the sunlight. Eddie's gaze was fixated on it.

"What about your daughter at the show tonight?" Chris said, tone light, trying to lift Eddie out of his gloom.

To Chris's surprise, Eddie snapped Chris a look, the officer's face going from disgust to betrayal to self-loathing.

He shook his head. "She calls me this morning in tears, hearing all that stuff about you."

Chris looked at the picture of the Hispanic girl with the dark hair and the innocent, bright smile and those hopeful eyes. Chris even noticed in one she was wearing a Chris Flowers t-shirt—the most famous one of him in sunglasses, howling passionately into the microphone. He felt horrible for a moment picturing a sweet little girl, a fan who looked up to him, seeing all that stuff that Andrea had accused him of and realizing her role model was actually a *monster*.

"I was bailing out at that point."

"But it wasn't true," Chris reminded him, cutting him off, heat in his voice.

"I know. My daughter called me back." Eddie's face bunched up. "She loves you."

The dark hand of the past clutched Chris, and for some reason he heard Marianne Mansfield's voice talking about her son's love for Chris, and he saw the boy's loving face.

Chris recalled the suicide note written in Tray's elegant hand: *I am nothing now. I am nothing.*

Eddie sulked silently a moment, sipped from an ancient coffee mug.

That word struck Chris again, like lightning out of thin air.

Rich's distorted voice, growling: *Confess.*

Confess.

Chris turned his head at the sound of a car approaching only to see a blue Toyota appearing from around the corner and then disappearing down Albert. A jolt of panic lit up Chris's eyes.

"Look, man," he said to Eddie, trying to keep his cool, "I know you ain't feeling so good about all of this. But it's for something good. I have an old friend somewhere out there. I ain't even sure he's alive," Chris added, feeling his throat tightening, feeling helpless.

That evil word shook him to his core again:

Confess!

Confess!

"But I know how much it would mean to you to reconnect with your daughter—"

"I'm not bailing," Eddie cut him off.

Chris let out an audible sigh of relief.

"I did something bad."

"I know. You got drunk—"

"Not that." Eddie looked out the windshield down Albert Street. "This is where my jurisdiction ends," he said, as if pointing out a gateway he couldn't cross. "I had a buddy in rehab. He now works at a department in Beverly Hills. He's not doing so well now. Got into cocaine a little while back. But it just made me think. You said you wanted a guy in Beverly Hills?"

Chris nodded. *As many guys as I can get.*

"And you said this guy who's stalking you is into cocaine? If there's someone who could sniff it out, it's my guy."

Chris was suddenly uncertain at his bald assertion that Rich was still using, still traveling in coke circles. Therefore, he would definitely be carrying. But what if he wasn't?

Still, Rich had been in Beverly Hills, and as recent as last night.

"You already talked to your guy?" Chris asked, scratching his chest.

Eddie nodded, rubbed the dark circles under his eyes, groaned something about these double shifts killing him.

He rubbed his face and said through the cracks in his fingers, "He wants a cut."

"Just money?"

"Just money," Eddie said gloomily, removing his hands from his face and staring blankly ahead.

Chris thought about the endless numbers in his bank account, bobbed his head confidently. "That's not a problem. How much does he...wait." Chris paused, a worried thought flashing in his mind. "Wait, did you tell him who I am?"

Eddie shook his head, the genuineness in his face relieving Chris.

"He has some debts to pay. My buddy. And he was asking for twenty-five."

"Grand?" *Pocket change.* "How about a quarter mil. Each."

Chris smiled at the corner of his mouth, searching Eddie's face for enthusiasm—his grin drooping unable to find any. Eddie did appear shocked by Chris's offer, but joyless, as if the money meant nothing to him.

"I can wire you the money, and you two can divvy it up, you know, however you want."

"No, no," Eddie said, to Chris's stunned surprise, his palms out as if he were pushing the money away.

"What?"

"I don't want your money." The look of both betrayal and self-disgust on Eddie's face unsettled Chris. "Twenty-five. No more. Some old buddy I am," Eddie added with sarcasm. "I was the guy's sponsor, you know."

Eddie turned on the ignition, ran his hand through his black hair. Chris noticed the officer's hair was dewed with sweat. Eddie told Chris he couldn't wait to get home, that he was getting off early tonight, couldn't wait to see the look on his daughter's face when he would surprise her about having front row tickets to the stage and backstage passes. But there was still that look on Eddie's face, in his pinched features, his flaring nostrils, his tightened lips, that signaled that he felt he didn't deserve it, any of it. The last thing he said before driving off was, "I'll call if something turns up. And I'll see you tonight at the show."

***

Chris cruised casually down nearly every street in Beverly Hills, once again exhibiting his bright banana-yellow Ferrari out there like casting a glimmering hook into rushing waters, hoping to draw out that skulking black Suburban. He was burning through tank after tank of gas as he cruised down Mulholland Drive and Beverly Drive, Coldwater Canyon Avenue, Pico Boulevard and Wilshire Boulevard, peering down every alley and doublechecking the license plates of every black Chevy he saw in traffic or parked on the curb.

While refilling his car he checked a new message from Ray:
Hey, kid, ain't got all day.

Chris realized how much he wanted to be at the gym, squeezing the gas trigger and feeling the icy rush of fuel as it reached the handle, while holding his cell phone with his other trembling hand. An hour so far and no luck finding Rich's Suburban.

Chris texted eagerly back: *Almost done.*

He put his phone back into his pocket, then peered into traffic, searching for a black spec in that silver river, waiting until the gas trigger clicked off with a full tank.

Back in traffic he tapped the wheel impatiently, waiting to spot Rich's Suburban. When he did find it, he would stick to it like glue and make a quick call to Eddie, who would send his guy, and that would be that. That was how it was going to work.

But Chris was quickly realizing Rich, or his Suburban, anyway, wasn't anywhere to be found. He cruised Rodeo Drive, Doheny Drive, Pico Boulevard, Wilshire Boulevard, then Pico yet again. And again. He went in circles. Sweat from exhaustion rolled down his face. His face burned, flushed with growing anger, his eyes scanning the streets and jumping into the rearview mirror, begging for the black Suburban to come creeping out of the woodwork. Another half hour passed and still nothing. And he was getting a swarm of texts from Ray. Stuck in traffic on Wilshire, he slammed his fists against the dashboard, boiling with a weary frustration. He texted Ray back telling the old guy he was on his way. He took another hopeless glance around him, but Rich was simply nowhere to be found.

He took a left onto Mulholland Drive, which was about fifteen minutes from the gym. He was anxious to be within its walls, yet self-disgust dripped like icy water droplets into him, shocking his soul.

Daryl is out there somewhere, and you want to go boxing?

Chris strangled the steering wheel, wondering what else he was supposed to do.

Confess!

The word poisoned his mind.

He turned onto a quiet, lonely street named Stretton to try and beat traffic on his way to the gym. Chris noticed a homeless man out the passenger's side window, holding a cardboard sign that read: *I have been replaced*—the words written in a desperate scrawl. Chris stopped the car, rolled down the window. He gave the man all the money in his wallet, several hundred bucks, and wished him luck.

The sidewalks were deserted, and no paparazzi captured his philanthropic deed to then splash it out on social media, there wasn't even a traffic light camera to record it.

CHAPTER TWENTY-NINE

With every curl, every pushup, every pullup, Chris felt that dark cloud of dread inside him shrinking. Yet he kept his phone close. Bench pressing, or at the pullup bar, it never left his pocket. He would eagerly check it after a rep, sweat rolling down his face and onto his cell phone screen, waiting for Eddie's number to pop up. Famous faces, gleaming with perspiration, approached, armpits soaked, hair hot and damp, tearing Chris's attention away from his cell. It seemed everyone wanted to talk to him about what'd happened that bizarre morning. It was mostly musicians who Chris had worked with or performed with who approached him. They danced around the obvious questions, asking about it, but most of all just wanted to express their relief that none of the accusations had been true. Then they'd return to their muscled personal trainers or their exercise bikes, and Chris would return to his workout— checking his phone some more.

Ray, while doing a biceps curl, his frosty gray mustache wriggling with the effort, sweat running into his eyes, tried nudging Chris to bare his soul. "You all right, kid? Been a crazy morning for you."

Chris shrugged it off.

Before he and Ray went for a round of boxing, Chris checked his phone once again, his face flushed with impatience. Still nothing from Eddie. He knew this was something that would take time, possibly days or weeks or even months. But it was killing him thinking about this going on any longer. He wanted Rich caught right *now*. He growled in his throat, set his phone down.

He yanked on his scarred boxing gloves, jumped into the ring with Ray. They started with a few friendly rounds of jabs and hooks, nothing too serious. By the third round something like a switch had been flipped, his fists began to fly with reckless abandon. He started hammering into Ray. It started with an image that popped up in Chris's head. While Chris's feet danced around the lumbering old man, he imagined that *he* was Ray, a forgotten old man whose life and work no one remembered anymore. He remembered Jeff's words.

You might just end up like him.

No! Things became blurry as Chris's stress and worries boiled over. His fists turned nasty, his jabs devious, biting in Ray's gut. His face. A gut shot made Ray guffaw, and Chris gave the old man's gasping face a brutal right hook.

The next thing Chris knew he was staring down at Ray who was beaten to a pulp, his nose gushing scarlet onto the blue mat, bruises darkening on his face, flesh ruddy and swelling. Ray gave Chris a confused, sad look. Chris's raised fists slowly sank to his sides, and his shoulders sagged. He glanced around and noticed heads turning, movie stars and musicians shooting looks of disapproval. A sudden pity tormented Chris, and he kneeled and helped the old man to his feet.

Later, they were sitting at a corner bench, and Chris was staring sadly into his old friend's battered face. There was dried blood in Ray's mustache. Ray pressed an icepack to his mashed nose.

"I'm sorry, man," Chris said for the fourth or fifth time.

"It's fine," Ray said, his words biting, annoyed.

"I didn't mean to go that hard."

Ray shot Chris a doubtful look with one blood-filled eye. Then he took a breath, a sage sigh. "I used to be the same way. When I was a younger man and full of myself."

There was something patronizing in Ray's words that Chris didn't like. Not at all.

"Just saying," Ray said, a little gentler, having caught the fiery look in Chris's eyes. "You remind me so much of me when I was younger."

You might just end up like him.

"I'm nothing like you." Chris regretted it as soon as it came out. But he couldn't stand that thought, him getting older, washed-up, fading away from the limelight. Rich once included Raymond Jones in an article he wrote about ten washed-up celebrities still trying to cling to their fame. But while Ray sometimes played his hits to less than spectacular crowds, Chris never got the impression Ray was clinging to his fame. Rather, he seemed to have accepted his fate with a stoicism and a humility—something Chris didn't understand either. *Your career is going down the tubes, and you don't care?*

Ray was silent a moment, though he didn't seem offended by what Chris had said. His blood-filled eye slid over to Chris, and was filled with pity. He looked like he was about to burst with the things he wanted—needed—to say to his younger friend.

But the only thing Chris felt he needed to listen to was what Jeff had said.

The gym's front doors smacked open.

Bailey Carter strutted in, again, people kissing his ass on their way out. Bailey brushed past them, ignoring them, his eyes darting, searching.

One of Bailey's cronies, clinging to the superstar like a remora clinging to a young shark, pointed to Chris. "There he is, man."

Chris and Bailey locked eyes. Chris filled his chest with air, puffing himself up like a quail, and noticed Bailey was doing the same thing.

"Been looking for you, *rapist*," Bailey's tiny grin was sharp and bright.

Chris hands curled into hard.

Then Ray's wrinkled hand landed on his fist.

"Come on, kid. Forget the little shit."

Chris yanked his hand away as Bailey kept flinging taunts at Chris, the insults arousing chuckles from the cronies. "Come on, you old rapist. Haven't you heard? You're out. I'm in. You're nothing but old news, you old fuck. You fucking rapist. Rapist!"

Chris stood up, unable to stand it any longer. He was about to charge Bailey when Ray said something that stopped him. "He's not wrong, kid."

Chris whipped back around. "The fuck you say, old man?"

Ray stood up, removing the icepack from his face, and approached Chris. Chris had to bite back pity seeing the swollen eye, the smashed nose and split lips and purple cheeks.

I ain't ending up like you, old man.

"Look, kid, I know I ain't as much an influence on you as I used to be when I was younger. I know I ain't as important as I used to be. No one lasts forever. You're full of yourself, kid, and you think you're immortal. But you ain't, trust me on that." He flipped his chin up at Bailey. "He ain't either, though he thinks so too."

"I'm talking to you, Flowers," Bailey cried, unable to hear Ray from across the gym, his shouts boring into Chris's ears.

Ray placed his hand on Chris's shoulder. "Kid, you're smarter than this. But you got an ego the size of Texas. Let it go, man."

Chris knew the old man's words were meant to be humbling, but Chris wasn't humbled. Far from it.

He shoved Ray's hand away, jabbed a finger into his barrel chest. "You have no idea what you're talking about, old man. You gave up. You started drinking and stopped writing. Maybe you stopped drinking again but you also haven't written a single tune in a decade. You were a god. But now look at you. And now you're trying to give Chris Flowers life lessons? I'm gonna be studied. I'll be remembered *forever.*"

The beginnings of a crowd had gathered. People had stopped punching their bags and had stopped their machines to check out the ruckus. Chris felt a warm glowing sensation in his chest feeling eyes blinking at him. He felt better and better as more and more people turned away from their workouts to focus on him.

Ray's battered face withered, and he sighed. "In one ear and right out the other, that's the way it always is with you, kid. I was *exactly the same.*"

Chris turned away, started marching toward Bailey Carter, Bailey's grin widening with beckoning.

"Goddammit, kid!" Ray shouted after him.

The desperation in Ray's voice stopped Chris in his tracks. He spun around, faced the old man.

Ray's lips trembled with fury. "Your ego is suffocating, man!" He nodded resolutely. "I'm done with it. I'm *sick* of it! And if you fight him, *we're* done, Chris. You hear me? We're done."

The gym hushed—even Bailey for the moment—all eyes on Chris and old Raymond Jones. Seeing the hurt in Ray's shiny swollen eyes, Chris knew Ray meant what he said.

But maybe that wouldn't be such a bad option.

What was Chris doing hanging around the old guy anyways? Did he really need Ray in his life? As far as Chris was concerned Ray was *dead weight*. Ray had once meant something to people, but not anymore.

You might just end up like him.

No, I won't.

Hearing the taunting chortles from Bailey Carter behind him reignited not just an anger, but a contempt, a hatred he'd been harboring toward this kid for years. Ever since Bailey beat him at the Grammys and stolen away *his* awards, he had hated the little shit with a deadly passion. Every time he heard about the kid in the news or heard one of his newest hit songs, it felt like Chris was being robbed all over again. He realized he hated all the young, upcoming artists in the music industry.

Chris had made his decision, and he wasn't going to pass up a chance to crush Bailey Carter's vocal cords.

He shook his head at sad, old Ray, then said, "Get fucked, old man."

He turned his back on Ray, could feel the old man's disappointed gaze burn into his back.

Chris approached the grinning young man, glared defiantly as he stood face to face with him. Bailey wasn't large, maybe five-five and one-forty, but up-close Chris realized Bailey was all muscle. The arms were long but brawny. The legs were stubby but thick. Chris knew, hidden under that white tank top, was a rippling sixpack. While the top of the kid's bleach-blond head only reached Chris's chin, Bailey was pure twenty-two-year-old stallion.

Chris ignored the sounds behind him, Ray packing up his gloves and padded boxing helmet, then his feet stomping the floor as he lumbered off. Chris only caught a glimpse of Ray's back as he left, the entrance doors slamming shut and the sunshine swallowing the old man.

But Chris bit back his regrets, focused on the young man, his nostrils twitching when he caught a strong whiff of the kid's hair chemicals.

Bailey uncrossed his arms, his knotty young fists crackling and popping. The cronies chuckled around their god. Chris had to bite back his own self-doubt, noticing Bailey's eyes were bloodshot and pupils dilated, the eye almost swallowed completely by black. The kid was on something. Coke? Meth? Chris wasn't certain and could only picture Bailey and his buds snorting white lines of something in their Mustangs or Jags before entering the gym.

"I passed that parking lot five fucking times today. Seeing if you'd be here."

"Here I am."

Bailey glanced back at his cronies. "This old asshole thinks he's gonna fight me."

Chris grinned savagely at Bailey's giggling friends. "Do they do anything or are they just decorations? Like you're a little Christmas tree or something."

The cronies crossed their arms, glared at him with confrontational eyes. One of them stepped out of the rest of the group, balling his fist, and took a step toward Chris.

Bailey raised a hand, pressed it to the young man's chest, said, "Be patient, be patient."

His face was hard and beet red and he was snorting, chest puffed up, but he obeyed Bailey and took a step back, joining the rest of the group. Flustered, he ran his hand through his mop of hair, shaved at the sides and impeccably groomed on the top. Chris noticed almost all of Bailey's cronies wore their hair and even dressed like Bailey Carter himself. The air around these guys was sickly-sweet with men's cologne and hairspray.

Then, bitterly, Bailey said, "You tried to take my Grammys. You call me a talentless little prick. The things you've said about me over the past couple years online, man. I used to think you were all right, man. I even used to *look up* to you. But a lot of us are getting sick of your shit. Then on top of it all you're a *rapist—*"

"Fuck you, you little shit!"

"And now you think you can take *me* in a fight?" Bailey clicked his tongue against his teeth, made hissing sounds like a snake, then he shook his head mockingly.

A round of chuckles and chortles and snorting from the cronies. They sounded like hyenas.

Bailey sized Chris up, then said, "I've been waiting for this day for a long time." He grinned, then added, "I'm gonna destroy a dinosaur."

Chris took a step closer, now maybe an inch from Bailey's face. But the kid didn't step down. Bailey stood his ground defiantly, cracked his knuckles, the *pop! pop!* sounds like warnings. Chris took another look at the young man with the knotty fists and the long ropy arms made of iron, and strangely he felt his body shudder. It felt like anxiety. It felt like a lack of confidence. For a moment, panic gripped him, his feet shuffled. He wanted to bolt. His muscles and bones were trying to tell him something, whispering in his ears, warning him about his impending doom. But he ignored that feeling. Because a small crowd had gathered around at a safe distance. Bailey's cronies glanced at each other with masculine delight. Many of them already had their cell phones out, recording them.

Chris sneered. "You think you can replace me? You're a spoiled brat who never had to work a day in your life. No, Mommy and Daddy in Beverly Hills could give you anything you ever wanted. It's a big fucking mistake on your part if you want to fight me."

Bailey stood there for several heartbeats longer, clicking his teeth. Then he swung around, demanding his gloves, which one of the cronies had been holding them for him. The cronies gathered around Bailey as he yanked his gloves on, giving him pats and gentle urging punches on the shoulder. "Kick his ass, man," Chris heard. "Kill the motherfucker."

Bailey was already in the ring, jumping up and down, while Chris was pulling his second glove on.

The cronies whooped as more people flocked around the ring.

Chris felt his pounding heart, felt mounting panic and anxiety again, but he shook it off and climbed through the ropes.

He stood at one corner and shadowboxed for a few seconds. Then when he felt he was ready he smacked his gloves together warningly, the gloves stained with old Ray's sweat and blood, and turned to face Bailey.

Bailey took few more sharp jabs at the open air, then met Chris at the center of the ring. "You're going to get fucked up, old man," Bailey said with a leer.

One of Bailey's posse climbed through the ropes to count them off.

Chris fixed his eyes on Bailey.

I wish you'd just die, kid.

"I'm never being replaced," Chris muttered to himself. "Ain't no one replacing me."

"Fight!" the young man yelled, then fled the ring and joined the crowd.

Chris raised his fists, guarding his face. He and Bailey mirrored each other, glaring over raised boxing gloves.

The ring was theirs. Time slowed down. Clocks stopped. Cell phone cameras recorded them.

Bailey moved with the sleek confidence of a jungle cat. He circled Chris on fast feet, shoulders rolling. Dilated eyes fluttering, Bailey took his first swing, going for the face. But Chris ducked to the left and the right hook whistled past his ear.

Chris took his first couple swings, a few left jabs and a right hook that hit Bailey's abdomen. Bailey grunted painfully, took a step away from Chris to shake it off. Chris's sudden burst of confidence was short-lived as Bailey charged, backing him up against the ropes, Chris trying to block the flurry of fists. The rubber ring ropes chewed into Chris's back as he leaned back away from Bailey's ferocity, blocking harsh left and right hooks.

A hard right struck Chris's gut, knocking the wind out of him, the bolt of pain jolting his body, his eyes blooming open with agony. He managed to give Bailey a desperate shove, sending him staggering into the center of the ring, shook it off, and settled back into his hunched fighting stance.

Chris felt a flash of humiliation as he glanced left and right, noticing the cameras recording his winded and gasping face. Every breath was like fire.

Bailey, reinvigorated at the sight of Chris's weakened condition, charged again. Chris, sweat dripping, sidestepped the lunge, and gathered himself at the center of the ring.

Bailey howled a war cry, pushed himself away from the ropes, then rushed after Chris, unleashing a burst of hard punches. Chris blocked, answered back with jabs, then tried to swing firm right hooks, aiming for Bailey's throat. His goal was to break the kid's windpipes.

Wham! Chris stunned Bailey with a stiff left to the face, then *whack!* a savage right hit—*bull's eye!*—to the esophagus. Bailey staggered back, reaching for his precious wounded vocal cords, and Chris grinned, delighted, feeling a surge of new confidence. Chris ignored the jeers and boos coming from the people gathered around the ring.

Chris's focus shifted for a split second hearing the crowd chanting, "Bailey! Bailey! Bailey!"

Ain't no one replacing me. No one.

Bam! Bailey's fist broke Chris's block, and he saw shooting stars, thoughts scattering. He shook off the disorientation.

I won't be forgotten. Ain't no one replacing me.

Then *whack!* Another fist clocked Chris square in the face. Chris almost fell but managed to stand his ground. He felt a red river of blood running from his nose, blood droplets falling silent and spotting the blue matt and soaking into his boxing trunks.

Ain't no one replacing me!

Momma. Momma.

He saw her eyes again, those cloudy eyes, staring sightlessly at him.

You can't forget me, Momma! Don't forget me—

Whack! Another fist struck the right side of Chris's face, this one getting him in the ear. Chris pressed his gloved hand instinctively up to his searing, ringing ear, and that's when the fists whizzed through the air, taking bites out of him, Chris grunting and groaning and seeing flashes of white and red. He fell to his knees. But didn't go down.

He rose back up to his feet in stubborn defiance. A defiance that was ultimately in vain. Bailey's fists struck like wrecking balls, aiming mostly for the throat and the face. Chris's neck was swelling, and it felt like a tire was hanging around it. It became difficult to see through his puffy eyes, but he felt his knees hit the floor, then felt his buzzing head slam into the blue mat. He knew then that he was lying face down in his own blood and that he wouldn't be able to get back up, not for a while at least. He felt claustrophobic all the sudden, his swelling tongue cutting off his oxygen. He just focused on his breathing, taking in tiny swallows of precious air. But it was hard to breathe through the blood bubbling out of his nose and mouth. The ring looked like a crime scene.

He couldn't hear anything at first, the ringing in his head too piercing and loud. But slowly, like forms appearing out of fog, the cheers of the crowd emerged.

"Bailey! Bailey! Bailey!"

Chris's right eye was completely swollen over, but he could still see a little bit out of his left eye. He saw Bailey's thick muscled legs jumping up and down in a celebratory dance. Then Chris's eyeball slid up toward the ceiling and saw the kid raising his bloodstained gloves into the burning fluorescent lights Bailey was grinning like he was the next big thing.

Maybe he was.

And the hungry cameras ate him up.

Chris lay defeated, tears spilling from his lesser-swollen left eye and running into his pooling blood.

He heard Bailey shouting something about his own greatness, his legend.

No one helped Chris up. He managed to rise to his feet by himself, receiving unsympathetic stares from everyone there as he dragged himself half dead toward the exit.

CHAPTER THIRTY

Chris was sitting in the now bloodstained seat of his Ferrari, still parked outside the gym, using the rearview mirror to dab dried blood from his ruined face. The swelling had gotten worse over the past twenty minutes he'd been sitting there mopping up the blood. He'd finally gotten the nosebleed to stop but could taste blood in the back of his throat. Looking into the rearview mirror, he turned his purple, swollen face to the left, to the right, his face growing more unrecognizable by the minute. He didn't even look like himself. It was like he was wearing a grotesque Halloween mask.

Why were they cheering for Bailey? Was it because they'd watched Chris beat the living shit out of Ray?

Chris bunched up and lobbed the bloodstained towel into the backseat, regretting his stupid decision to fight the kid.

It was nearing 4:30 and the sun was blazing down. Chris stayed in the car in the gym parking lot. While it was a temporary refuge, he knew there was no hiding. That footage was already viral, already spreading: *Chris gets his ass kicked by Bailey Carter.* He was expecting a phone call any minute from Jeff. He knew what Jeff would say, and Chris was well aware he was performing tonight. He gave his neck a gentle rub. It felt like golf balls were lodged in his throat. And when he sipped from a bottle of water it was more than painful. Would he even be able to sing tonight?

The thought terrified him, though he knew he would have to force himself onto that stage no matter what. He had to be there. People had been waiting months to watch him play at the Hollywood Amphitheater. He couldn't let them down. He wouldn't subject his fans to more disappointment.

But he didn't have much time to ponder it anyway. While racking his brain with ways to soothe his throat—saltwater gargle, *lots* of pain relievers, honey and tea—not wanting to give his fans a less than stellar show, his phone started ringing.

He checked it, fully expecting it to be Jeff, but it wasn't. Chris was even able to grin through his agony seeing it was Eddie's number.

He answered promptly. "Hello." The word came out more like a croak, like he swallowed glass and was trying to talk.

Eddie waited a moment before answering. "H—hello?" He sounded uncertain.

Chris guessed Eddie hadn't seen the video yet.

Chris cleared his throat, then said, "It's me. Got in a fight. Punched in the throat."

"Shit." There was a buzz to Eddie's voice—the sound of good news waiting to be revealed. Then he said three words that made Chris forget for a blissful moment about his aches and pains: "We got him."

* * *

Chris turned onto Franklin Street, where Eddie said to meet his buddy. It was about ten minutes from the gym. It was a quiet, tree-lined street close to Chris's neighborhood right on the outskirts of the hustle and bustle of the city, and it made Chris wonder what Rich was doing there. How had Rich managed to get himself caught so easily? Was he just driving out in the open? It seemed to go against everything that malevolent voice had threatened the day before, all that stuff about not being anywhere near Chris, about not being caught by the police.

Chris took a deep breath, released his tight grip on the steering wheel, trying to be grateful that Rich had even been caught at all. And so quickly.

The road curved and then straightened out again, and as Chris was cruising—doing about twenty around the corner—he spotted the police cruiser about a quarter mile down the secluded straight stretch of road.

He came to a cautious stop, put the car in reverse, and backed up until he was out of sight, around the corner. He wouldn't take any chances, didn't want to draw any unnecessary attention toward the cruiser.

He took a slow deep breath, then stepped out. First, he checked down the curving street behind him. Nothing but sidewalk, an empty BMW and a few other cars, though it didn't look like any paparazzi had tailed him. He walked around the corner of the street. His heart was pounding harder, his head ached, his wounded ears rang, and his face stung where the kid's gloves had scraped the skin. The sunlight pouring through the leaves of the oak and fig trees burned his swollen eyes, and, when he came around the corner, he had to squint through the hot rays to see it. The black Suburban was parked off the right side of the road in front of the cruiser. The closer Chris got to it and those flashing red and blue lights, the more he couldn't believe it. A tiny, delighted grin tugged at his mouth.

Chris approached a tall skinny bald cop who was standing near the passenger's side door of the black Suburban. The cop appeared to be poring over registration papers. He glanced up at Chris's approaching footsteps. Chris read the nametag: Vincent.

Chris suddenly recalled the cop who had come to Marianne's when Chris had called about the baggie of cocaine on his windshield. Chris remembered those bony arms and those spidery hands, remembered when Vincent had removed his sunshades and revealed those troubled, bloodshot eyes. Vincent's eyes were hidden behind those same sunglasses now. This was Eddie's guy, Eddie's buddy, the guy Eddie had sponsored while both cops were trying to clean up their lives.

Vincent cocked his sun-kissed bald head, giving Chris a strange curious look.

"I know I look like shit," Chris said, getting it out of the way.

Vincent nodded, then glanced away from a passing car. Chris kept his back turned to it. He hoped whoever was in the car wouldn't recognize him. Vincent certainly hadn't, or wouldn't he have said something? Still, the grumbling engine made his heart skip a beat. Then the sound of the car faded around the corner and was gone. Vincent looked at Chris again.

But Chris's attention was drawn to the cruiser, having noticed in his peripheral vision something moving in there. Through the tinted windshield—all the cruiser's windows were tinted—something was moving in the backseat.

Rich.

Chris could see the outline of Rich's head, just a shadowy figure. But Chris could feel Rich's eyes on him.

"Eddie said you pulled him over?"

"Don't say his name," Vincent snapped, glancing around the empty sidewalk cautiously.

"He said you pulled him over for running a red light?"

"I spotted him on Rodeo and tailed him a good five minutes. I think he got spooked and was trying to lose me. He ran the red light before he turned onto this street." Vincent glanced over his shoulders, then lowered his voice as he said, "I was told what I might find if I searched the car. Exactly what I found. Five grams worth. A gram of crack cocaine too. Guy was blazed on it. Mouthy son of a bitch." Vincent scratched his shoulders and clicked his teeth. "Do what you need to quick," he added impatiently, glancing around again. "I don't want to be out in the open long."

Chris nodded, couldn't agree with Officer Vincent more, then turned around and started walking toward the police cruiser. He thought about Daryl as he stepped closer and closer, thought about how Daryl had been innocent in all of this and hadn't been expecting what happened to him. Where was he? Was he still alive? Chris, refortified in his fury, bunched his bruised fist, the pain somehow bucking him up.

He could see through the windshield that Rich was on the left side, so Chris entered on the right side. There weren't internal handles on the rear doors, so Chris just gave the rear window's vertical metal bars a yank and the door clicked shut. Now he was locked in the cool tinted dark with Rich.

Chris had forgotten how small the guy was. Rich's head barely touched the backseat's headrest. He was maybe five-three. Maybe one-thirty. Tiny. Smaller than Bailey Carter, though without Bailey's muscle. He had short, skeletal arms sticking out of a simple black shirt, arms behind his back, and Chris assumed the handcuffs were clamped extra tight around the guy's twiggy wrists. A pair of stonewashed jeans hid a pair of stubby, skinny legs. His shoes looked like kid's shoes.

Chris was baffled.

This was the guy who'd been giving him nightmares? *This* was the murderer who'd been tormenting him?

He seemed thinner since Chris had beat his ass back in November, though Chris knew it was probably the cocaine bingeing. Rich's hawkish nose wriggled, the nostrils crusted with cocaine residue. His eyes were red and sunken, his cheeks pale and gaunt, his hair dark and greasy and wild. He had sores on his face, and he needed a shower.

Chris noticed Rich narrowing his eyes, bitterly, at first not recognizing Chris. "Is that..."

Then his face relaxed, a grin surfaced out of that dark neatly-trimmed beard.

He chuckled savagely, looking very pleased with himself. "What the fuck happened to you?" Rich seemed to find the sight of Chris hilarious.

Rich apparently hadn't found out about the fight yet either, probably had been too busy trying to ditch Officer Vincent.

But that didn't matter right now.

"You sick fuck," he muttered painfully, his voice still very tender.

Rich nodded. "I get it. You set this up."

"Got you now, you bastard."

It's Daryl. It's me, man. Please. Stop. Untie me! Let me go!

"Where is he, Rich?"

Rich grinned. "What the fuck are you talking about—"

Whack!

The punch was like a snakebite. Square in the nose. Rich was startled by it, took him a moment to realize what'd happened, his face flushing bright red. The pain caught up, and Rich let out a yelp. A slow dark trail of blood ran from his nose and he made a melodramatic gagging sound like he was choking on his own blood. He shifted, his shoulders moving back and forth, the handcuffs rattling with resistance. He used his shoulder to wipe the blood. Chris smiled, feeling delicious satisfaction.

Rich looked at Chris, sniffled. "Why're you beating on me?" Then his voice took on a mocking tone as he said, "You got no one to look at you—"

Whack!

Chris cut him off with another punch, this time striking Rich's right eye.

"Fuck!" Rich yelled.

"And no one to save your ass," Chris reminded him.

Now it seemed to be dawning on Rich exactly how much trouble he was in. He looked at Chris, fear mixing into the hatred in his eyes. He started breathing faster. In an act of desperation he tried to yell for help at the top of his lungs, but Chris clutched him by his long greasy hair, yanked his head back—his pleas curdling into a cry of pain—then he smashed Rich's face against the car door. His cry for help went unheard, though Vincent was glancing around nervously, pretending to be poring over Rich's documents.

"No one's coming to save you," Chris said.

Rich spat a wad of blood into Chris's face. Chris felt something harder, a tooth or a piece of a tooth, hitting his cheek.

He snatched Rich by his tiny shoulders.

"This is illegal!" Rich cried helplessly. His breath was foul. "I'm gonna sue both your asses. You and that shit-for-brains cop out there!"

"He has your blow, man."

"Fuck you!"

"And he's gonna arrest your ass unless you tell me where Daryl is."

"I don't know what you're talking about, man! I don't—"

Wham!

A gut shot. The rest of Rich's sentence died. He was trying to curl up, looking almost childlike, against the pain. The handcuffs rattled as he struggled against their resistance. Then he leaned his forehead against the back of the driver's seat, cursing Chris between gasps for air.

Chris was trying to hurry for Vincent, desperation trickling in, wondering if this ill-considered approach, beating the answer out of him, would work. Chris noticed Vincent was getting impatient. The cop was now opening and closing the black Suburban's doors. Making noise. Maybe Rich's cries of pain were a little louder than Chris thought?

Chris snatched Rich by the shoulders again, turned him so he was facing Chris—their faces inches from each other. Rich was clearly scared, his eyes wide, and he breathing heavily on Chris. Chris noticed a lot of Rich's teeth were rotten, probably from smoking crack cocaine.

"You killed Andre."

"What?"

"And you're hiding Daryl somewhere! You told me! You with your little voice changer thing, man!"

Rich's eye was already swelling, almost shut. And What Chris saw in the other eye, besides terror, baffled him. It was confusion. In fact, Rich was looking at Chris like Chris was the crazy one here.

"I've never called you in my life!"

Chris shoved Rich. Rich's back slammed against the car door, and he made a hiccup-like sound.

"If you don't talk, man, you're going to prison for a long time. They see you bloody like this and, well, that's 'cause maybe Vincent had no choice. Maybe he was defending himself. That's more shit on your plate. See any cameras here?" Chris added, gesturing to the quiet and camera-less street around them. "Besides, you think anyone's gonna believe your ass? No one even cares about you."

Chris thought about all Rich had done, all the pain Rich had caused him. He also couldn't help but feeling sorry for Andrea and all that she suffered at the hands of this man, even though she'd tried screwing Chris over. Rich was an apocalypse, turning all he touched to ruins.

Though time was burning Chris felt a cruel smile on his face, about to boil over with all that he ever wanted to say to Rich and others like him.

"Andrea told me everything about you. How you couldn't cut it as an artist. You know how many people like you are out there in the world, man? You want it so bad. You want what I got, and you got shit. You're nothing, man. You're an insect."

It felt good letting that poison out. Rich needed to hear it.

But Rich wasn't listening.

He even yawned.

Chris knew the guy was trying to get under his skin. It was working, anger flaring in his gut. Rich then looked at Chris, blood running into his beard and from his sharp little chin, a self-satisfied grin on his face. Chris had to fight the urge to beat the guy to an unconscious pulp.

Then Rich bobbed his head, feigning interest. "You done?"

"Nah," Chris said, balling his fist. "I ain't done."

"Well, it doesn't matter anyways. Because I got what I wanted. And if I could've had it both ways I would've."

"What're you talking about?"

Rich licked blood from his lower lip. Then he leaned forward, as if about to reveal a secret. "Do you know how much I could've made from those pictures? Huh? You should thank me."

It took Chris a second, but then he understood what Rich meant about having it both ways. If Rich could've ruined both Andrea and Chris then he would have.

Chris was confused. What was Rich doing? Where was he going with this?

"Stupid bitch shouldn't have left. We had ten years together."

There was the sound of a shutting door that momentarily drew Chris's attention out the windshield. Officer Vincent had returned Rich's registration papers to the Suburban, and he was now pacing, arms crossed. Chris was almost out of time. And still hadn't gotten anywhere with Rich. He felt jolted with sudden panic.

"Chris, I really don't care about you. See, for me, I deal with self-absorbed asshole celebrities every week. Don't get me wrong, I fucking *love* my job. But what I really wanted was to see the look on the bitch's face after I texted her those pictures." Rich let out a dark chuckle, and his eyes gleamed delightfully as if he was reliving the moment. "I was on my way to the bar to celebrate when that stupid fucking cop pulled me over."

Chris' heart was pounding twice as fast now, and he'd broken out in cold sweat.

"Man, I had a pretty good buzz going. You really know how to ruin a good time. Hey!"

Desperate, Chris snatched Rich by his curly hair and started yanking upward as hard as he could, like he was trying to jerk the guy's head right off his body. He glared hard into Rich's pained, shrieking, lying face, wanting to bust it open.

"Last chance. Where's Daryl?"

"So let me get this straight," Rich said, trying to bury his trembling voice by keeping up his self-assured charade. "You think you're being blackmailed or something—"

Whack!

Chris socked him hard in the face again, while still holding him up by his hair, mashing the nose into a bloody stump.

"Shit!" Rich cried. "Is this about the shit I put on your car? I was just having some fun. I do it all the time—"

Chris cocked his fist back, ready to spring it again, and Rich's eyes suddenly glazed over with genuine fear. He scrunched his face up, brow narrowing, mouth pursed, eyes squeezed shut, bracing himself.

"Where's Daryl?"

"I don't fucking know—"

Whack!

"Where is he?"

"I don't—"

Whack!

Chris popped him in the mouth again. Teeth cracked, blood ran.

"Tell me now!"

"I don't know—"

Whack!

Whack!

Whack!

Chris couldn't stop, his mind clouded with rage, and by the end of it he felt like he was watching his right arm from a distance, repeating that movement like a jackhammer. With a jerk Rich managed to break from Chris's grasp and was trying to curl himself into a ball on the cruiser's back seat. Chris didn't care what body part he was hitting anymore, just as long as he was hitting something. His knuckles clicked on skull and smashed into face, arms, thigh, and crunched into ribs. It felt almost sickening how much Chris was actually enjoying it, enjoying the hurt he was causing someone who'd caused so much hurt. Though something eventually pulled Chris out of that red cloud. It was a sound coming from Rich, quiet at first. Chris lowered his bloody fist, startled by the whimpering coming out of the man, who recoiled, curled up in a ball against the car door, Rich trying to push himself as far from Chris as he could. Rich's whimpers were broken up by those unexpected sounds. All the rage built up for this man evaporated as Chris listened to the whimpers swell into sobs and wails.

"P-please stop! No more! P-p-please...."

It was the sound of a man nearly insane with pain, and it was then Chris saw—really saw—what he'd done. Rich was bleeding from his ears now as well as his nose and mouth. Both eyeballs were swollen shut, though tears managed to leak out, and snot mixing into the blood. Chris noticed bits of rotten teeth on the car seat between them, and also a few pieces of broken teeth were on Chris's lap too.

Chris was confused by the pity he felt. This was the man who'd been trying to ruin everything. Yet somehow Chris couldn't help but feel bad for what he'd just done, and it was getting excruciatingly painful listening to the nearly-hysterical sobbing and protests of innocence. Chris could almost believe the man was innocent in that moment. Almost.

That was when the door on Chris's side opened.

"I don't know what's going on," Vincent had started to say as he opened the door, "but I think—"

Then his words stopped, and his mouth dropped open, his expression shifting from horror to outrage at what he saw. "What the fuck, man!"

Chris was still wrestling with a growing pity when he climbed out of the cruiser, feeling sick. Chris couldn't stand to be in there another second anyway, those sobs starting to really get to him.

He shut the car door and told Vincent, "Just get him to a hospital, man."

"Oh, just fucking great! What am I supposed to say?"

"Say what you want. He got in a fight over coke, whatever."

Chris looked away from Vincent's beet-red face, looked at the tinted passenger's side cruiser window but only saw his own mangled reflection. He could hear, just barely though, the muffled sounds of Rich's whimpers. Now he not only felt pity, but a returning anxiety. The relief he'd been filled with on arriving, on seeing that black Suburban pulled over, had vanished. Now something felt wrong. Very, very wrong. He glanced at the Suburban. He'd made a mistake, only he wasn't quite sure what.

Officer Vincent clawed nervously at his shoulder blades, his face turning a maroon color, waiting with a growing impatience for Chris to say something.

But Chris had the sudden urge to flee, to just get back to his Ferrari. He took a step backward.

"I gotta go, man. I'm sorry,"

Chris turned around and was a few steps down that sidewalk when Vincent shouted, "Hey!"

Chris stopped, faced Vincent.

"What about my money?"

Chris remembered wiring the twenty-five grand to Eddie's bank account before heading here to Franklin Street, and told Vincent, "I sent it to Eddie, man. You're supposed to talk to him."

Then Chris turned away, and this time he didn't stop as he made his way down that long stretch and to his car hidden around the corner. Rising above the mockingbirds and the fiery breeze stirring the oak leaves and the sounds of dogs barking in the distance, Chris heard Vincent call out, voice dripping sarcasm, "Thanks a lot!"

* * *

Chris climbed into the Ferrari, shut the door, and sat for a moment around the corner, paralyzed. He noticed when he glanced down that his gnarled fist, had gone from bruised and slightly swollen to now looking twisted and arthritic, fingers crooked. There were gashes, some deep, across his knuckles. The skin was shredded and dangling, carved up by Rich's teeth. Then he felt the pain as the adrenaline left his system, waves of it in his wrist and in his kinked fingers. He wondered if he'd broken any bones in his hand, worried if he would even be able to use this fist again. He wrapped his fist up in the blood-soaked towel from the backseat, and found himself nervously checking his phone with his left hand. He knew he'd be swamped with calls and texts from Jeff:

What happened?!
I watched the fight! The video is viral!
Where R U?!

Chris, ignoring another incoming call from Jeff, realized there'd been another reason he was checking his phone. Only he didn't want to believe that reason. And that reason was he was checking to see if he'd received any more texts or calls from who?

He couldn't get the sound of Rich's sobbing out of his mind, how real, how genuinely confused the man sounded. Could it be?

No, Chris had to push that returning, intrusive thought out of his mind, and he poked two fingers out of his towel wrap. It was agony trying to start the car, his twisted fingers struggling to get a grip on the keys. Jolts of pain shot up his arm as he turned the ignition. He managed to start it, painfully, but didn't pull out just yet. He wasn't sure where he should even go. Daryl was still out there somewhere, and he'd gotten nothing out of Rich.

And what if there was nothing to even get out of Rich?

Chris was terribly thirsty, and so he grabbed a bottle of water from the console and sipped on it, trying to cool his raw throat. His hands were trembling around the water bottle. He tried to convince himself that it was just his nerves, that it had been a hell of a couple of days, and the stress of it all was starting to take its toll. He struggled getting the bottle cap back on, the cap falling and landing in his lap a couple times, his hands were shaking so badly.

Chris was shaking his head, not wanting to believe the thought that was growing like an evil flower in his mind.

But what if Vincent's cruiser was carrying away the wrong guy?

Chris jerked his head off the leather headrest, the sudden movement sending pain through his injured hand as he unconsciously clenched it. He hadn't fallen asleep, but more drifted off into his thoughts, finding himself in an ugly place. He was thinking about Tray's funeral now. There it was, clear in his mind. He pictured that bright, sunny day at Hollywood Forever Cemetery. He saw Marianne Mansfield all in black, tears cutting through her eyeshadow and streaming like ink down her face. Tears running down his own face. He remembered approaching the open casket and peering in. The plush coffin with its velvet walls was filled with flowers of all kinds and colors. Chris had been holding a rose that he dropped into the coffin on top of the mountain of flowers. In the suicide note Tray had written that he didn't want his body to be found, that he was planning to take a dinghy and an anchor and sink himself once out to sea. Search parties hadn't turned up a body, despite the weeks of searching. Tray was presumed dead.

Two years. Two years the kid tried to hold on, his guitar in the corner slowly gathering dust, rubbing his skull as if he could wish the genius that had abandoned him back into it.

The impact of the car had stolen his brilliance, his light, leaving the kid a husk. An empty shell.

Chris looked up, then glanced down the street. A cobalt-blue Jaguar appeared around the corner, whatever celebrity inside hidden behind tinted windows. But the Jaguar didn't pay Chris any mind, just cruised by. Chris watched in the rearview mirror as it disappeared around the corner behind him.

The Jaguar had startled him still, and it was because he was still on edge, still on alert. With Rich being taken to the hospital and then in all probability to jail where he'd be off the streets, out of Chris's life, he should feel elation. But still something was knotting Chris's stomach.

For some reason, the streets felt dangerous. *Still* felt dangerous. Like whatever had been menacing Chris was still out there.

But he couldn't allow himself to believe the alternative.

Not possible! The only way that could happen is if the dead returned to life. And that doesn't happen.

When Chris brought the water bottle up to his lips for a drink, water sloshing out, his hands shaking so violently.

That's when he saw her in his mind, felt her in his memory.

Maria.

"Oh no," he said, nearly whispering it to himself.

And that was when, despite the agony in his mangled right hand, he slammed his car into drive and sped off down the street.

CHAPTER THIRTY-ONE

Chris had the urgent desire to go back to Santa Monica. Back to the nursing home. But he kept going, realizing that his momma was safe there. No one could get to her. He crossed the threshold into officer Eddie's jurisdiction, back into South Central where Chris believed the real danger lay.

Where Andre had died.

Where Daryl had gone missing.

A new terror gripped him as his Ferrari zipped down the trash-strewn streets of this poor neighborhood. He didn't have time to take in the sights of his old stomping grounds by daylight, the glowing red lights of liquor stores flaring by and the sun flashing behind the steeples of the churches. With the tunnel vision of obsessive focus, he only caught people turning their heads out of the corner of his eye—homeless people in ragged clothes panhandling on the street corners, someone standing beside a sidewalk table selling fake jewelry, clothing, DVDs. He glimpsed people smoking cigarettes on their front porches or on the balconies of their apartments, all shooting strange and awed looks at the Ferrari screeching by. It seemed like everyone in all of South Central was looking at him, but Chris didn't care. He remembered Maria had worked at the Barney's Burgers on Sebastian Street in his old neighborhood of Hyde Park, and that was all he could think about.

He came to a squealing halt in front of the old Barney's Burgers, thinking *still there, thank God,* and parked in the shade under the big sign that showed "Barney the Pig" holding up a tray with a burger, fries, and drink. Chris rushed inside. The air was warm and heavy with the scent of fried food. He was getting baffled looks from people eating fat, greasy burgers at their tables—a few pausing midbite, just blinking at Chris. That's when he realized how crazy this was.

Searching the employees in their light blue uniforms, who were staring back in bewilderment at Chris, he looked for her. Just as quickly he realized with a sinking heart how miniscule the chances were that she still worked there.

Still, he waited at the counter while one of the employees was getting the manager for him. The manager came out from a back office and approached Chris. She was a short woman who looked be in her mid-thirties with curly red hair tied back in a ponytail. At first she was giving him the stunned look that the customers were giving him, then she shut her gaping mouth, tried to smile, and asked him who he was and how she could help him.

Chris started to say something but froze midsentence. The manager had just asked what his name was, and he was dumbfounded. He realized the looks he was getting from the customers and from the employees and from the manager herself, it wasn't because they recognized him. In fact, they *didn't* recognize him. Chris, over the course of his career, sometimes liked to just drop in on the ordinary people in ordinary restaurants or in ordinary coffee shops or clothing stores, and the looks people gave him were similar. But Chris had been in such a rush that he'd forgotten his injuries, what he must looked like, bruised, disheveled, dried blood on his nose. Like a crazy person. Some looked worried even, anxious, tightening their grips around their thick hamburgers.

But that no longer mattered. Briskly, he asked the manager if Maria Martinez still worked here, but all he got was confused eyes and shaking heads.

"Maria Martinez," he repeated.

She only shook her head again, glancing from him to the exit like she wanted him to leave.

Back in his Ferrari, Chris was on the internet on his cell phone. Jeff was trying to call for the fiftieth time, but Chris ignored it as he Googled Maria Martinez. He didn't even find a Facebook account for her. He also considered that her last name could be different now if she'd remarried.

No luck on the internet, Chris then found himself at their old apartment in Hoagland Heights but, as Chris figured, she'd long since moved out. The middle-aged black couple now living in their old apartment said they didn't know anything about any Maria Martinez.

When Chris climbed back into the Ferrari, still ignoring his endlessly ringing phone, he was struck with despair, rested his throbbing head against the steering wheel.

He suddenly remembered Maria's brother, Manny, lived nearby. Manny had lived in that little yellow house on Clancy Street, Chris recalled. They had all lived close by one another in this neighborhood. It was funny how vividly it all came back, though as the memories returned so did pain, pain Chris had been trying to avoid for the better part of twenty years. Something particularly regretful was how Manny had grown to hate Chris ever since that day he'd searched Manny's phone to find Andre Childs's phone number. Chris had remembered that slip the day he'd OD'd at Manny's house, when Manny had inadvertently divulged the name 'Dre while on the phone buying the dope. Chris went through Manny's phone when Manny wasn't looking, found the contact 'Dre, and that was how Chris met Andre Childs. Chris then told Andre that Manny *gave* Chris the number. "I can't believe you," Manny had screamed when he'd found out. "You're a selfish piece of shit, and you only care about yourself!"

Maybe Manny was right. Something else that bothered Chris was that Manny never told Maria about this incident—it was like Manny, in some weird way, still at least honored Chris, even though he hated him.

What would Manny think of him now if he just dropped in after fifteen years? Chris didn't think Manny would just offer up his sister's number out of the goodness of his heart. Chris had abandoned Maria, just up and left her with his first taste of success.

Still, Chris put the car into gear and started making his way to Clancy Street, knowing he had no other choice. He only hoped Manny still lived there.

As he drove, his phone—that he'd set on the passenger's seat—rang and rang, the sound like nails being driven into his head. He checked it and wasn't surprised to see Jeff calling for the hundredth time. It was already 6:00 p.m., and Chris hadn't spoken to Jeff since that morning. He suddenly felt bad for the guy, like a worried brother he hadn't checked in with. He pictured Jeff at his luxury apartment back in Beverly Hills, probably already dressed and ready for the show, pacing back and forth through thunderclouds of vape smoke.

Chris decided to finally answer, to put Jeff's mind at ease. "Hey. It's me—"

"Why the fuck haven't you been answering me, man?!"

"I know. I'm sorry."

Jeff was quiet while Chris cruised down Cherry Street, nearing Clancy. He passed small houses with tiny dirty yards where children glanced up from their toys, eyes sparkling, mouths dropping, dazzled by the sight of Chris's Ferrari—the kind of car they'd only ever seen on TV. Chris had been just like those kids once upon a time.

"You sound like shit," Jeff finally said, sounding disappointed.

Chris hated the sound his voice was making too, grotesque, almost croaking. "I know, I know."

"Do you know what time it is?"

Chris paused. What exactly had been his plan, and how would he explain it to Jeff? He had to warn Maria, even if she wanted never to see him or hear from him again. He had to warn her of the potential—and highly probable—danger she might be in. Though how would he explain to Jeff that he believed Tray Mansfield had somehow faked a suicide, had somehow stayed out of the public eye for the past three years, had learned about what'd happened from Andre, and was now threatening Chris with phone calls and murdering people from Chris's past? Chris almost didn't tell Jeff; it sounded crazy even to him.

"Jeff," Chris said, remembering when Jeff had talked about his brother who'd committed suicide, considered how Jeff had been there through the years of Chris's addiction. Jeff had always had Chris's back. Chris took a breath, then said it, "I think Tray Mansfield's alive, man. I think he's been calling me."

Jeff was silent as Chris was driving down Clancy Street, nearing Manny's house.

Then Jeff started chuckling, which turned into hysterical cackling. Chris didn't blame him.

"Jeff, I'm serious! I think he's going after my ex-wife. Maria."

"You mean from fifteen years ago?"

"Yeah, man!"

Jeff stopped laughing. There was the familiar bubbly sound of Jeff smoking his vape pen. But Jeff remained silent.

Manny's house suddenly came into view, and Chris found himself muttering out loud, filled with a quiet elation, "There it is."

"There what is?!" Jeff said, fuming.

Chris didn't answer right away, which only prompted more barking. "Chris? Chris!"

Chris was too focused on parking. He parked about fifty feet down the street from Manny's house, not wanting Manny to look out the window by chance and spot the Ferrari—this big luxurious car like a middle finger straight out of Chris's rich and famous life. Too late for a car swap now.

Chris's eyes lit up seeing a van parked at the curb in front of the house. The words: *Luis's Heating & Air-conditioning* were written in big, bold, black letters across the side of the van. Manny's dad's company. Manny must still be working for him. Unless someone else who lived at the same house worked for the same company. Chris found that unlikely.

Jeff was still squawking in Chris's ear. "Chris? There what is? Where the fuck are you?"

Chris was humiliated to admit it to Jeff, but he did. "South Central." He glanced up and down the street, endless houses all bunched claustrophobically close together and beater cars parked or on cinderblocks in the yard. Chris felt eyes peering out windows at him, but he didn't care anymore.

Then Jeff snorted. "I knew it."

Chris didn't understand what it was Jeff knew or thought he knew, though Jeff sounded self-assured. "Know what?"

"You're using again."

Chris was stunned at first.

He recalled earlier that morning when Jeff turned into a bloodhound, stepping up real close to Chris and staring deeply into his eyes. Jeff must've been trying to sniff out drugs, searching Chris's eyes for dilation, checking to see if they were bloodshot. Jeff was assuming Chris was back in South Central because he was back on the needle.

But Chris reminded him, "I don't have to be in South Central for that. There's drugs in Beverly Hills too."

"Maybe you aren't in South Central."

"Shit, do I have to send you a picture, man?"

"Look," Jeff said, his voice suddenly softening. "I understand you've been under a lot of pressure lately. But this? Going back on the needle again ain't the answer."

"Jeff, you ain't listening!" Chris cried, feeling further away from Jeff than he'd ever felt before.

Jeff was starting to sound teary as he explained, "Chris, I watched you go from one-eighty to a hundred and ten pounds. And you were just, you were out of your mind, man."

"Jeff—"

"Puking. Shitting your pants. I'm not going through that again. I just can't do it." Jeff sighed. "If you want to destroy yourself, you're on your own this time."

Chris knew Jeff wasn't going to listen. But he didn't quite expect Jeff to say what he did next.

"So I'm giving you a choice right now. If you don't get your ass back here, right this fucking minute, we're done. I'll find someone else."

"Are you serious?" Chris felt like he'd been stabbed.

"I'm sorry to have to do this. But it's out of love."

Chris squirmed in his seat, even considered it as he touched the gearstick temptingly, feeling the dark stain of guilt spreading with every sniffle on Jeff's end.

But when Chris looked at Manny's house, he knew nothing was going to stop him from finding Maria.

"I'm staying."

"So that's how it is, Chris? After all these years—"

Chris turned off the phone, cutting Jeff off, squeezed it in his hand, then tossed it in his lap. He punched the passenger seat next to him, boiling over with frustration, then stepped out of the car and shoved his cell phone into his pocket.

He walked up the street, up the driveway, trembling as he passed Manny's van. The house glared at him, somehow hostile and unwelcoming. His sneakers slapped down the stone walkway leading to the front door. As he passed the barbeque, the only thing in the yard, Chris heard what he thought was someone fighting coming from inside Manny's house, then realized it was a couple's bitter words coming from one of the neighboring houses.

Heart pounding, Chris paused at the front door. He shut his eyes against his prickling anxiety, took a leap of faith, then knocked.

When no one answered, Chris knocked again, a little louder. Then he waited.

"Please answer, man," he whispered to himself.

Finally, there was the soft, padded *thump! thump! thump!* of footsteps on carpet. The footsteps stopped when they reached the door, and Chris could hear breathing coming from the other side.

Then a voice growled harshly, "I said just leave me alone right now, Victor!"

Victor?

It took Chris a second to gather up the courage to say, "Manny? Is that you, man? It's me, Chris. Chris Flowers."

There was a long silence. Chris could almost feel the anger growing in that silence, as if the door itself was about to burst into flames.

Then the voice on the other side growled, "The fuck do *you* want?!" It was a resentful voice, icy and bitter.

"I need to talk to you, man. It's important. Just a couple minutes."

Then he heard a deadbolt sliding open, the door unlocking. It was cracked open just wide enough for a familiar face to fit through. Manny's deep brown face was gaunt, his cheeks sickeningly pale. He looked like a shriveled mummy compared to the last time Chris had seen him. He tugged agitatedly on the half-dollar gauges in his ears, his bloodshot brown eyes filled with a momentary confusion.

"The fuck happened to you?" With a dark smile, Manny added, "You look like shit."

Chris almost said the same thing back, but instead hung his head, looked away from this refugee of a life he'd abandoned long ago. Chris felt so ashamed he couldn't even speak. He was expecting Manny to shut the door on his face, tell him to fuck off, but Manny didn't. He turned away, left the door hanging open, and Chris followed the invitation.

Manny was shaking his head, his graying ponytail bobbing, grinning, and he muttered to himself, "This oughta be good." When he glanced over his shoulder his wicked grin faded, his eyes paranoid. "Shut it and lock it behind you."

Manny meant the front door. Chris wondered if it was because of this Victor Manny had mentioned before, but didn't say anything about it, just shut the door and clicked the bolt in place.

He followed Manny into the living room, past a pile of work uniforms folded neatly on a wooden chair. Manny approached the coffee table, digging a half-inch roach out of an ashtray, tucking a few silvery strands of hair back behind his ears. He lit the roach and took a long drag. Chris got the impression that Manny had just got back from work and wanted to relax. The pungent smell of marijuana quickly spread making Chris feel nauseous.

Chris's eyes narrowed sadly as he studied his old friend. Manny was wearing an extra-large black shirt that looked like a tent trying to hide his skeletal body. His skinny arms, once lean and muscled from his years of drumming, made his hands seem cartoonishly big. His legs were like twigs poking out of cargo shorts.

"I didn't think you'd still be here." Although Chris was relieved that Manny still was there, he wasn't sure why he'd brought it up, only that it sounded friendly, and he was trying to think of a way to gently get Maria's number.

But Manny wasn't having it. He glared through the weed fog. "Where the fuck else would I need to be, huh? Not all of us get to live in mansions." While Chris was fumbling for what to say next, Manny looked him up and down, that wicked grin of his twitching. "So what happened to you?" There wasn't an ounce of concern in his voice.

"Uh, a fight."

"And I take it you lost."

"Yeah."

Manny smiled delighted, then said, "Good."

Chris sighed. There was no other way to do this, so he'd just have to jump into it. "Manny, I know you hate me."

Manny snorted. "That's an understatement, bro." He took another drag from the roach and started blowing the smoke at Chris, like he was spraying a can of Raid at a fly.

"I just need to talk to Maria."

Manny's lips parted over his yellow teeth, grinning at Chris absurdly. "You're serious?"

It felt like asking someone for a favor after sticking a blade in their back.

Manny chuckled, puffed on the roach, muttered, "That's never gonna happen."

"Please, man! I tried looking her up, but she ain't nowhere to be found. I tried our old apartments, and I even tried at the place she used to work."

"She don't want to be found. Especially not by you."

"She's in danger, man!"

"Nice try, asshole." He tapped ash.

Sitting beside the ashtray on the coffee table and surrounded by a small army of empty Miller beer cans, Chris spotted Manny's cell phone and he felt his pulse quicken.

Chris wouldn't bother trying to explain to Manny his whole Tray Mansfield theory. Time was short, and Chris didn't think telling it would convince Manny anyways. And while he was feeling more desperate by the minute, he was trying to keep himself from sounding desperate or demanding. "Just let me call her. Or you call her."

"She tried to kill herself."

Chris froze, couldn't breathe. His skin crawled. "What? When?"

But Manny wouldn't answer, watching almost in cold pleasure as the pain creep into Chris's face. And, indeed, Chris was in pain as he conjured a hundred horrific scenes in his head. But he bit back his tears, glanced at Manny's cell phone on the coffee table again.

"I need Maria's number. And I'll take it if I have to." Chris was surprised at the words coming out, his desperation boiling over, his voice edged with danger now. His muscles and bones still ached, and probably would for a while, after that beating. He felt so exhausted already he could just pass out right then. He wasn't sure he'd be able to leave here with that phone unscathed.

"You wanna do that?" Manny threatened, balling his fist, knuckles popping.

He took another hit off the roach, just a nub pinched between his smoke-stained thumb and forefinger. Manny spotted something, something hidden behind the beer cans, as he was mashing the roach out in the ashtray. He glanced at Chris, caught Chris's eyes on his cell phone, grabbed and shoved it into the front pocket of his cargo shorts.

While Manny reached down to grab whatever it was he'd been looking at, Chris was suddenly assaulted by images of Maria's ashen face and her pregnant belly bobbing through the crowds of the shows they used to play together. But those images vanished as Manny held up the black pouch he'd grabbed from the coffee table. His eyes glittered, and a cold grin spread across his face as he walked over to Chris, cradling the pouch in his hand. Chris knew what was inside, eyeing it with dread, an evil buried long ago returning to haunt him.

If it had been a boy they were going to name him Louis (after Louis Armstrong) and if a girl they would've named her Bessie (after Bessie Smith). As Manny unzipped the black pouch, Chris couldn't help but be bombarded by those images again, couldn't help but feel he'd had a hand in Louis's premature death—all the added stress he'd put on Maria, all the hurt he'd caused, how cruel he'd been to her and Manny and Daryl, his heroin addiction, then leaving her on top of it all. As he watched Manny reaching into the pouch, Chris wondered if he wasn't getting what had been coming to him.

"You want Maria's number, you'll have to earn it," Manny said deliciously, pulling out the paraphernalia—fresh needles, a bent flame-darkened spoon, a lighter and lastly a tightly wrapped baggie of what looked like black tar heroin.

The dope winked temptingly at Chris, like an old and dark lover who wanted him back. An old and dark lover Chris wanted nothing to do with.

He took a step back, shaking his head, afraid. "The fuck you doing, man?"

Manny's grin widened. "Man, I ain't bullshitting you!"

"Go on. You're the big, clean, sober popstar."

"I can't do that shit no more."

"Then you get nothing."

"Someone's going to kill your sister, Manny."

Manny chuckled. "I knew you wouldn't be able to do it."

Manny was right. Chris wouldn't. Couldn't.

Manny smirked. "Gotta protect that image, huh The big sober popstar image."

"Manny, please—"

"Do it."

Chris considered trying to wrestle Manny down to the floor and digging out the phone and making a run for it. But his aching bones and tender muscles screamed at him in protest, telling Chris he'd collapse before even making it to the bolted door.

***

Minutes later, Chris found himself sitting on the couch. He was surprised that it was even the same couch, as if he'd stepped through a time warp in which nothing had changed in fifteen years, shoulders slumped in defeat, tying the tourniquet around his upper right arm.

The underbelly of his forearm was clean and smooth, the old track marks long healed. A healthy blue vein started to bulge in his tingling arm.

Chris heard the flick of the lighter, Manny sitting to Chris's right, two flames in his eyes as the black tar burned down to a sour-smelling, bubbling bronze liquid. Manny was grinning triumphantly. His cell phone was a rectangular bulge tucked in the pocket of his cargo shorts.

Appearing satisfied, Manny set the lighter on the coffee table, put a cotton ball into the tar until the cotton, soaking it up, turned brown. Then he touched a fresh needle's nose into the cotton ball and Chris watched as the needle drank its fill.

"It's clean, right?" Chris asked, suddenly paranoid. "The dope? The needle?"

Manny nodded. "Brand new. Don't fucking worry about it." The words icy and vengeful.

Manny handed Chris the gorged syringe, and Chris took it but didn't shoot it. He just stared at it a moment, gripped with fear. It was like holding the grim reaper's hand. He tried to pass it back to Manny. "That's too much. You trying to kill me, man? You know I've been off the shit!"

Manny's cold, sweating hand was shaking with impatience. "Take it. I won't give you shit if you don't."

Chris stared at the needle helplessly, then looked at Manny's cell phone taunting him from inside Manny's pocket. Chris took the needle with trembling hands. The initial shock of this whole situation had worn off, and Chris realized what he was doing, realized the tourniquet tied around his bicep and the blood flow being cut off, the needle like it was filled to bursting in his fingers.

"Man, come on," Chris pleaded.

"Go on, shoot it."

Manny held the lighter flame under the spoon, cooking his shot of dope. The smell was thick and gut-wrenching, butane and the slightly vinegary smell of cooked black tar.

Manny turned his tourniquet-strangled arm up like a dead fish going belly up. He kept flicking at his scarred, red-flared arm trying to prod up any vein. Chris noticed a trail of neglected yellow abscesses, lumpy mounds of infected flesh running up and down the twiglike arms.

Manny glanced at Chris. "The fuck are you waiting for? You're going first! I need to watch and make sure the big, clean, and sober superstar gets his fix!" Manny's lips curled ghoulishly over his yellow teeth.

Chris sighed, filled with dread, too exhausted and hurt to try and protest. His hands shook violently as he held the needle tip to his arm, and he had to take a few deep breaths to steady himself. The needle sniffed his flesh, the tip just grazing the surface of skin. Manny's eyes devoured this with delight. Chris took a final deep breath, the needle finding its spot then entering his vein. Chris squeezed his eyes shut, clenching against the burning sting. He pressed the plunger, felt the tar vomiting itself into his blood. The unpleasant sting immediately began to fade. It suddenly felt like there was liquid sunshine in his veins. A warmth had started in his chest, his heartbeat slowing, his muscles feeling like hot rubber. Then the pain started fading. In his face, in his throat, in his bones, the aching emanating from the fist bruises that covered his body, all of that hurt going went away.

"Press it all the way, motherfucker!"

Chris found that he couldn't, his fingers too numb. He also found he didn't care when Manny assisted. The needle, with a little help from Manny, had now emptied itself completely into Chris's bloodstream.

Manny unsnapped Chris's tourniquet for him, because Chris couldn't do it himself, didn't even care if it was left tied on or not.

Chris felt like he was buried in warm sand, like he was radiating a heavenly glow.

Then the *rush!*

The black tar stampeded through his body, a numbing dreaminess coming over him. and his head lolling back unintentionally. A grin spread like warm butter across his face.

But his grin faded fast when a maw of darkness began to devour consciousness, his blood turning green on the flood of heroin. He shot at Manny helplessly, already slouching, feeling like he was sinking deeper into the couch, further and further away from reality. He felt distant panic, but couldn't cry out for help.

Light was fading. Chris tried to keep his eyes open but couldn't. Then everything went dark.

CHAPTER THIRTY-TWO
2008

Chris couldn't stop staring at the business card. He sat on the edge of his bed, glancing from Jeff Bentley's phone number on the card to pictures that covered the walls. The pictures were interspersed with posters of Chris's musical idols. Wedged between Prince or Otis Redding or The Beatles or Raymond Jones were pictures of Chris and Manny and Daryl from over the years. There was one taken by Maria at Roscoe's House of Chicken and Waffles catching Chris midbite and Manny and Daryl chewing and smiling at the camera. Another pictured them at Watt's Towers at sundown. His favorite, also taken by Maria, was the night they played at El Lugar. It had been their first "big" show—though the place had had about only twenty people in there that night. But Manny and Daryl were both smiling, both so happy in the picture. Chris appeared to be too focused to smile, his mouth wide open belting out the chorus of one of his originals, his eyes squeezed tight in intense concentration, the yellow spotlight warm on his face.

Chris turned his cell phone on and dialed the number on the card. He'd been rolling Jeff's offer over in his mind the entire weekend. Chris surprised himself when he'd initially rejected the offer while they were talking over beers Friday night at the club. Jeff had asked if Chris had a manager, just him, not the band ? Chris said, he didn't. Jeff told Chris that he could get him into the really big clubs, into the stadiums, the only catch was that Jeff wasn't going to manage the band. Just Chris.

"Jeff Bentley."

"It's Chris Flowers." Chris hesitated a moment, like he was about to jump off a cliff. Then said, "I'm in."

"That's great! I'm glad to hear it! So you quit?"

Chris gave the pictures a sad look. "I'm working up to it."

"Well, get that over with, and we'll meet up let's say... Tomorrow's Monday. Let's just do tomorrow at my place. We'll sort out your new life."

Chris looked at the pictures of Manny and Daryl yet again, couldn't speak.

"Chris?"

"Yeah." Chris snapped out of it.

"Sound good?"

"Yeah, yeah, sounds good."

After hanging up, Chris sat there on the edge of the bed for a while, head buried in his hands.

Then Chris heard the apartment's front door opening. Maria was home. She worked the Sunday through Thursday shift, so today was technically her Monday.

Chris forced himself up onto his wobbly legs and headed down the hall toward the kitchenette. He was both tingling with excitement and feeling sick to his stomach.

Maria's uniform was speckled with grease, her eyes heavy from staring at flipping burgers all day. She set a few greasy burger bags on the counter. On the front of the bags was a dopey picture of a smiling yellow pig and the Barney's Burgers logo.

"Chris?" she called out, thinking he was in another room.

Chris took a breath, mustering up his courage, and appeared from around the corner.

"Maria?"

She handed him one of the burger bags, a small devilish grin on her face. "Yeah."

The burger bag was still warm and smelled delicious. "I need to say something."

"Eat first," she said, her grin widening, excited. "I made this one special for you."

"Oh," he said playfully, smiled, reached into the burger sack. He felt the hard edge of something that felt like it didn't belong. He pulled it out. A brochure. It read: Sally's B&B. The front of the brochure showed a two-story cottage under perfect blue sky, white picket fence, red and yellow and blue wildflowers, golden beach. Instantly, Chris felt heat in his cheeks. "Oh wow," he said.

Maria's hands were clasped together. She blushed, giggling with excitement.

"Bed and breakfast." Chris said.

"Yeah!" Maria pressed up against him. She took the brochure. "I've been saving up. Work's been great about letting me bring home burgers!"

Chris smiled, near tears, overwhelmed. A part of him wanted to let it all out, all that stuff that'd had him buzzing ever since Friday night at the club with Jeff. He wanted to insist on paying for the B&B since he would, like Jeff had said, be making more money than he knew what to do with. But he kept his lips sealed. Besides, she seemed proud that she'd saved up herself and surprised him, and Chris didn't want to ruin it for her. His heart melting, he wrapped an arm around her, brushed her dark wavy hair away and kissed her forehead.

He sniffed at her hair. "You smell like French fries, babe."

She gave his ass a frisky pinch.

Then he furrowed his brow, curious. "You shouldn't have."

"Yeah, we'll be there a whole week!" she said, pointing at the brochure. "Right on the coast. Just us."

Chris kissed her.

Then she looked at him. "What'd you want to tell me?"

Chris looked at the brochure, felt horrible all of a sudden.

He smiled, shook his head, and said, "Nothing. Nothing important."

She looked suddenly sad.

"Hey? You okay?"

She shrugged. "Yeah." Then she hid behind a broken smile.

It had been two months since the baby had died. Maria told the doctor, tearfully, that she'd noticed a decrease in the baby's movements a day or two before she gave birth but didn't think it was anything to worry about. The doctor went on to tell her Louis died of an undiagnosed placental abruption, where the placenta detaches from the uterine wall before delivery, depriving the child of oxygen and nutrients.

Maria barely talked to anyone for weeks after. And there were times she still woke up crying in the middle of the night, and Chris would hold her until she went back to sleep.

But something told Chris whatever was bothering Maria now wasn't about Louis.

"Okay." She pointed at the brochure again, her face trying to brighten back up. "We'll have to get up early tomorrow."

"Early tomorrow?"

"Yeah."

"A whole week?"

"Yeah."

"Starting tomorrow?"

"Yeah?" Concern tinged her voice.

But if Chris was at the B&B with Maria then he would miss tomorrow's meeting with Jeff.

"What?" Maria asked, noticing the thoughts flickering across his face.

"Nothing. But what about your work?"

"I took the rest of the week off. My boss already knows."

Chris's jaw locked, heart pounding. She had *already* taken the week off. He'd rather die than break her heart.

Maybe he could call Jeff back, ask to change days? Maybe they could meet next week or something?

But Chris couldn't swallow that thought either. How would he look then? Like a flake. Jeff told Chris he'd just finished up with some useless flake, and that's exactly how Chris would look, too. Jeff wouldn't take someone like that seriously, someone who didn't prioritize their life's work.

Plus this was more important than some trip to a B&B, wasn't it? If anything, he and Maria could always take another trip like that. Hell, they could take trips like that every month once Chris became a star. And he wouldn't always have *that* opportunity.

"You don't want to go?" she said sadly, like she read his mind, seeing the apprehension in his narrowing eyes.

"No, I do," Chris said, shaking his head, his heart breaking. He bit his lips, looked at the burger bag, tried to smile. "Let's eat, babe. I'm starving."

They plunked down on the couch as was their nightly ritual, and Maria laid out their hamburgers and French fries and ketchup packets on the coffee table. As they ate, Maria talked about her day. Chris was trying to avoid the subject of Jeff, his meeting the next day. But then he realized, nodding at Maria as she told him about some asshole customer, that he'd have to tell her. And it would have to be tonight. He had to tell her he couldn't go with her tomorrow, no matter how much it broke his heart.

Chris held off telling her long after they ate. Stuffed with burgers and fries, they lounged on the couch, watching some movie made in Mexico with subtitles (one Maria really liked). But Chris couldn't focus on it. He held onto Maria, his arm around her shoulder, her head leaned tenderly against his chest. She reacted to the movie, laughing, then she would tilt her head up at him, and he would pretend to react with her, laughing at the appropriate parts. Then he would stare off into space again.

About halfway through the movie, out of the blue, he told her. "I quit the band." He took a breath, held it, unable to breathe.

Maria tilted her head up at him. "What're you talking about?"

"Manny and Daryl. Our band. I quit."

She shook her head, flabbergasted. "What? Why?"

"Look, I ain't obligated to play with them forever."

"But it's gonna kill them. They idolize you. I don't get it. And you've been working them both to death doing all these shows. You should've seen them on the drive back Friday night. I had to drive them, they were so tired. Then you just up and quit?"

Chris turned off the TV, looked her square in the face. "I have this opportunity. You know that man who came up to me after the show?"

Maria shrugged, nodded.

"He's a manager, a big time manager, and he's looking for someone to represent. He said I had *star quality*." Chris's smile withered seeing the look on Maria's face.

"They're like family to you, Chris. With all that you've been through together you're going to just dump them, like they're nothing?"

Chris said nothing.

"Have you told them?"

"Not yet."

Maria's face darkened.

"They're holding me back." Chris realized he was parroting what Jeff had told him the night before, what Chris had already felt deep down inside. "I don't need a band. The people don't come to see Daryl and your brother anyways."

Maria's eyes sharpened, her face reddening.

Chris paused, trying to find softer words. He tried on a smile, reached out and touched her shoulder.

"This'll be good for us. I'm going to put Momma in a good place. I'll be able to support us. Don't you see that?"

Maria brushed his hand away. "What's wrong with you?"

"What do you mean?"

"I mean the thousand shows a week. The way you've been treating Manny and Daryl. Manny was talking to me last night. Says you treat them like shit all the time. At shows. At practice. You're their hero, Chris. You have no idea how much you mean to them. To me." Tears welled in her eyes.

Chris had to look away, her gaze too painful to hold. He tried thinking about meeting with Jeff Bentley tomorrow. He tried thinking about his and Maria's new life together.

Chris *had* to be there.

"I know you've been through a lot," Maria said, scooting in closer, voice cracking. "With your momma. With Louis." She swallowed, sucked in her lips.

Chris's face blanched, and he tried to banish thoughts of that deathly white hospital, of the shriveled dead child.

He thought about meeting with Jeff tomorrow.

"And I know you're doping again."

Chris was stunned, but he still tried to cover up the shock on his face. "What?"

"I found your stash," Maria said firmly. "Under the bathroom sink. Don't lie to me."

Chris said nothing. He looked away.

"You promised me. You promised me you would stop. You almost died. You think being a big star is going to help fix you? It's going to make it harder for you."

Chris wiped his eyes. "You don't know what you're talking about."

"I don't want you to end up dead because of all this pressure you're putting on yourself. That's why I wanted us to go to the B&B." She grabbed his hand like she was trying to stop a train wreck. "Let's just go. I'll pay for an extra night. We just get up and go right *now*."

Chris looked at her for a long time. He considered leaving with her right then.

He wanted to.

But he didn't. He pulled his hands away from hers.

"I can't go."

"What?"

"To the B&B. I need to stay. I've got work to do. I'm meeting that guy Jeff Bentley tomorrow."

Maria could only stare at him a moment, mouth hanging open, astonished. Then she said, "You don't want to go with me?" Her voice sounded small, sad.

Chris hardened himself.

I'll make sure you will be remembered, Jeff had said.

"Stop looking at me like that, Maria! Stop trying to hold me back!"

Maria scooted away from him, stared at him, shocked. Then she stiffened with anger, shook her head, snorted. "Fine, Chris. Go. Be the big star."

"Maria, your brother and Daryl are no good. They're *nothing* without me."

"Shut up!"

"So you're gonna flip burgers the rest of your life? Huh, gonna be happy doing that?"

Tears rolled down her face.

"Maria." Chris suddenly felt sick at what he'd said. Hated himself for saying it. "I'm sorry."

"I'm glad he died."

Hurt slowly crept into Chris, his face waxy, his palms clammy. "What'd you say?"

She didn't answer, looked frozen by her own words. However, she didn't take it back, just glared at him, trembling with fury.

Chris shook his head at her, unable to believe she would say such a thing, unable to believe they had both said such things to each other. Then he wiped tears from his eyes, a flash of anger giving him the boost he needed, then he grabbed his electric guitar, and he stormed out the front door leaving her there in tears.

CHAPTER THIRTY-THREE
JULY, 2023

Chris's eyes peeled open, and he felt himself climbing out of darkness. The world was spinning around him like a dark carousal. He couldn't remember anything at first, and he wasn't sure where he was. Then slowly, as reality returned, the strange house became familiar again. He was in Manny's house.

He was lying face down on the gray carpet next to the coffee table. The carpet stunk and was covered with ancient brown beer stains. He shakily pushed himself up and got as far as to his hands and knees when he was gripped by sickness. His whole body trembled as the wave of nausea struck him and he puked, spattering a mostly yellowy bile onto the carpet. The sickness he felt was relentless. Everything ached and he had a vicious pounding migraine. Every inch of his skin felt scorching hot. The first thing he wanted to do was curl up on that carpet and sleep for a couple days, just sleep until the sickness passed. Still on hands and knees, he hung his head on folded arms, like a man praying desperately for his torment to end. And he *was* praying, a nearly silent murmur, pleading to any listening god for mercy. "Please, make it stop. Make it stop."

It didn't stop. Not for a little while. He puked twice more, the last time just dry heaving. When he finally found enough strength to peer up from his little hell on the floor, he saw an empty couch in front of him. He couldn't remember why he was even there, on that floor, in this place, for a moment. It was like some beast had devoured part of his memory and left just a gaping black hole. But then it slowly came back to him and his heaving, panicked breaths slowed. Manny had been sitting there. With him.

"Manny?" he called out. "Shit."

Chris groaned as he pulled himself up onto rubbery legs. He almost stumbled but used the couch to hold himself steady. His searching eyes spotted a clock on the wall and he had to squint through blurry vision, like he was drunk, to be able to read it. His eyes widened seeing it was 7:26 p.m. Something was coming back to him.

He had a show. He remembered it started at nine. Still, he couldn't remember when he'd gotten here or how long he'd been passed out.

While stumbling across the room, using the wall to keep himself propped up, his hand brushed over a small round vanity mirror that drew his attention. He had to squint, his eyes extra-sensitive to the living room ceiling light reflected in the mirror, to get a good look at himself. The swelling hadn't gone down. He still looked like he'd been stung by a thousand bees, cheeks, brow and lips all tender and pink and puffy. He also noticed a grayish-yellow crust around his mouth, a dried river of blood that'd run from his nose.

I OD'd.

He breathed painfully, making little snorting sounds through his nose, but also realized there was a great relief in his deep, heavy breaths. He probably should be dead.

He didn't question it further. He just counted his blessings, then stepped away from the mirror and lumbered across the room, still using his hand to prop himself up against the wall. The entire world was fuzzy and dreamlike, and he realized he was still very high when he had to fight the unrelenting urge to just take a seat, let the world solve its own problems, to fall asleep for a few hours.

His tingling legs wanted to stop right there, wanted to buckle beneath him. He stopped for a second, shaking off the sensation that a weighted blanket was draped over him, trying to force him down onto the ground. He took a few deep breaths, trying to stop the spinning of the room around him.

He forced himself to move, left foot, right foot, left foot, right foot. He lugged his way into the kitchen area, but didn't see Manny. When Chris saw the kitchen faucet and saw beautiful, perfect drip-drops of water plunking from it, he rushed over to the sink, zombielike, hands clamped to the grimy counter, pulling himself toward the water. It was all he could think about, nothing else, something to quench his hellish thirst, and he grabbed the first glass he found, a dirty one from the sink, didn't even bother to wash it. He filled it to the brim then guzzled it down in one go. It was like the waters of heaven. He filled a second glass and drank that, feeling himself getting a little stronger, feeling his whirling mind slowing down, the pounding in his temples becoming less violent. He drank a third glass, all that his belly could take, feeling like he was about to burst, then set the glass on the counter, gently scrubbed and washed the blood and crusted foam from his face, then left the kitchen.

The water tamped down his sickness, at least temporarily, enough to where he didn't have to cling to the walls as he headed down a hallway. His feet clinked over empty beer cans and wine bottles that'd been left strewn on the floor as he made his way toward a room at the far end of the hall. The room's door glared back with a dark energy. Nothing good was behind that door, Chris thought, as he slowly approached, his shadow creeping along the wall. He put his hand on the cold knob, took a breath, then opened it.

Manny lay on the bed, arms and legs flopped out, head lulled back. Chris approached the bed, stiffening in repulsion, wanting to flee. Manny's face was blue and swollen. His eyes, once so bright, were now pale and milky with death, staring sightlessly up at the ceiling. Chris gazed, horrified, at his old friend. His puffy eyes bulged. The hairs on his arms and on the back of his neck stood up on end.

"Oh God."

An empty needle stuck out of Manny's purple arm. The veins looked like black roots of death. The bluish corpse was grinning.

"Goddammit, Manny."

Chris felt like he was in hell. So much else had been his fault. Sometimes it felt like everything he touched turned to ash. Was this his fault too?

Chris wanted to collapse in that moment, the hopelessness unbearable. Distantly, he wondered if he had stayed with Maria, if he had gone with her to that B&B fifteen years ago, would any of this have happened? Would things have been any different?

It was the thought of Maria that pulled him out of his hopelessness, and his eyes were drawn to a familiar rectangular bulge in the pocket of Manny's cargo shorts. The tears stopped flowing, yet Chris hesitated, revolted at the idea of digging into his dead friend's pocket. But he was reminded that the sun was setting, time slipping away, and Maria might be dead by tomorrow.

He ignored his repulsions and reached into the jeans, pulling out Manny's cell. Chris kneeled among the dirty needles and empty beer cans, turned the phone on. All hope drained from his face seeing the phone's battery at only one percent. Then the phone darkened and the screen read: Phone shutting down.

"No, no!"

The phone's dead face stared back at him.

"Fuck!"

He glanced along the walls, spotted the outlet beside the bed, phone charger plugged in.

But before Chris could plug the phone in, there came a *bam! bam! bam!* from somewhere in the house. Frozen, he threw a glance over his shoulder. The sound had come from back down the hall and across the living room. The front door. Someone was knocking on the front door.

With shaking hands, he plugged the charger into the phone, the charging battery symbol popping up.

"Shit."

Three more knocks came—*Bam! Bam! Bam!*—followed by a gravelly, muffled voice that cried, "Manny, I know you're there! Please, babe. It's Victor!"

Chris, not moving a muscle, phone still in hand, could hear the front door clicking against the bolt. The sound brought a small relief, the locked door buying Chris a little more time. But how would he get out of here?

"You OD'ing on me again, asshole?" Victor cried harshly.

There was a moment of silence, thick, heavy. The doorknob turned, again held shut by the bolt.

"Goddammit!" yelled the voice.

Then a flurry of fist-pounding on the door. *Bam! Bam! Bam! Bam!*

Chris tried to turn on the phone again, but the battery still needed a moment longer.

"Come on," Chris said, trying to urge it on, sweat rolling into his eyes, his chest a buzzing hive of panic.

"Honey, are you all right in there?"

When no answer came for Victor, he gave the front door a few more desperate and frustrated pounds, then shouted, "Fine! I'm calling the cops. They can drag your ass to the fucking hospital again."

Silence.

Chris's whole body trembling, he tried the phone again and to his relief it turned on. The phone's background picture popped up, a picture of Manny with his arms wrapped lovingly around a dumpy, balding man wearing a Costco employee t-shirt. Chris assumed this must be Victor. Chris had to shake off the sadness trying to grip him and quickly searched through Manny's contacts. He scrolled down until he reached the M section and there it was, Maria's number.

His attention was briefly drawn to a clicking sound coming from somewhere in the house. The kitchen maybe? Chris remembered the tiny house having only one door (there was no backyard, so no backdoor was necessary), but it had several windows large enough for a man to fit through.

Chris had to hurry. He pulled out his phone and, a phone in each hand, typed with his thumb Maria's number into the contacts of his phone. He was trembling, and it felt like an eternity, but he finally got Maria's number saved into his contacts. Then, fast as he could, he put his phone back in his pocket and the other back into the corpse's pocket.

He gave Manny a final, grave look, wanting to say something, some parting thoughts even.

But he couldn't.

He had to move.

He left the room, crept down the hallway, being careful to avoid the empty beer cans and wine bottles. His worst fears were confirmed when he slowly peeked around the corner and into the kitchen. The same man in the picture on Manny's phone, same Costco t-shirt and horseshoe of dark hair around his balding head, was standing at the kitchen window framed over the kitchen sink. *Click! Click!* The sliding window slammed against its bolted lock as Victor, face flushed red, struggled to force it open.

With the front door unattended and Victor preoccupied on the opposite side of the house, Chris crouched and scurried to make his escape. He quietly unbolted the door, turned the knob with a soft click, then peered his head out. He looked left, right. It was clear, the only sound distant barking dogs and loud rap coming from the open window of one of the neighboring houses. The sky was turning rosy with the coming dusk. The sun was sinking in the sky, casting long, hot orange rays of dying light.

Chris took his chance, quietly shut the door behind him, then started tiptoeing down the walkway toward the house's rusted yard gate.

Yes, yes! Home free—

"Hey, asshole!"

The shout stopped Chris in his tracks halfway across the yard.

He turned to see a red moon-shaped face growing and growing as Victor was getting closer. Chris tried to run for it, but didn't realize how sick he still was, how woozy and loopy, and his legs got confused and tangled themselves and he tripped, landing hard on the cement pathway. The dull pain of scraped elbows and kneecaps smoldered through his dying dope cloud. He tried to get up, to scramble to his feet, then felt a pair of hands helping him up with a violent yank.

The man said, "I called the cops."

Victor was a short, powerful man and had thick arms and meaty hands that dug into Chris's biceps. In Chris's weakened state, Victor easily maintained his grip. The man was breathing exasperated breaths through his open mouth, and Chris saw crooked teeth as yellow as corn. Chris caught the spark of jealousy when he glanced into Victor's brown eyes.

"Who the fuck are you?"

Chris tried to avert his face, saying nothing.

"What the fuck are you doing here?!" Victor shouted, his face turning a shade redder. Spittle bubbled at the corner of his mouth, and he dug his fingers deeper into Chris's biceps.

Chris winced against the pain. Cold sweat ran down his clammy flesh.

This is it. Fucked. Won't be able to warn Maria.

He could hear siren wails in the distance, drawing closer. It jolted him with panic. He tried to yank himself free, but didn't have the strength to pry himself loose from Victor's clutches.

"Who the fuck are you? Where the fuck is Manny?" Victor's beady, resentful eyes bored into Chris's face.

Then Victor tilted his head, a flicker of recognition. Chris hung his head, trying to bury his face in shadow.

He's gonna recognize me! He can't! Not now.

"What were you doing in there? Is he in there?" Victor gestured to the house behind him.

"Yeah, he's in there. I'm a friend. Get off me." Chris tried to shove himself free.

"Where have I seen you? How long you know Manny?! I swear I've seen your face before." Victor was squinting, trying to make the mangled ruin of Chris's face into something he recognized.

Chris gave Victor another shove, but Victor dug in deeper.

"Say something, you fuck. Tell me who you are." Victor's eyes narrowed. "I've seen you. I know I have."

Chris shook his head, then said something he thought he'd never say. "No, I'm I'm no one. Just leave me the fuck alone."

Chris finally managed a burst of strength and gave Victor a shove that broke Chris free and knocked Victor to his ass in the low hot sun. Chris ran, not looking back to see if Victor was chasing. He shuffled in a sick dance down the sidewalk, then across the street toward a few hooligans checking out his Ferrari. They scattered on Chris's arrival, and Chris hopped in, hoping Victor wouldn't remember his face enough to help the cops. Looking out the windshield he didn't see Victor, who likely had gone inside the house.

Chris shook off thoughts of Victor discovering Manny's blue corpse, shook off thoughts of Victor in a hot bright police interrogation room, a police artist across from him.

The sirens were closer, louder.

Chris slammed the Ferrari into drive and sped out of there.

CHAPTER THIRTY-FOUR

Chris found he couldn't leave South Central, or at least didn't want to. Not until he heard from Maria. He tucked himself into a back alley, still feeling trembly and paranoid after that encounter with Manny and Victor, and he sat in the alley's shadow, brick walls on both sides rising up and squeezing the sky into a reddening dusky stripe above. He pulled up Maria's number on his phone. It seemed to glare back at him, mixing with his dope sickness. His mouth watered, and he suddenly felt like he was going to puke. He rolled down the window, stuck his head out into the hot evening air, and gagged, the sound of his retches echoing grotesquely off the old brick alley walls. Mostly bile came out, sticking to his car door, and he wiped it from his chin. He didn't understand where his sudden compassion for Maria or Daryl or Manny had come from. When was the last time Chris had even thought, or cared, about these people? Maybe Andrea was right. When was the last time he ever really thought about anyone other than himself?

Chris took a brief, precious moment, stared straight ahead, engine idling and headlights illuminating dark figures walked by, their heads turned, eyeballing the Ferrari.

Chris pressed the green call icon, and he started shaking, his whole body, as the phone purred in his ear. It rang and rang, and Chris stared into the little patch of street ahead. Cars passed. Chris stiffened in the leather seat when a police cruiser passed, thinking about Manny and Victor, wondering if Victor had figured out who he was, wondering if the cops were already on the hunt for him.

There was a momentary pause as the call went to voice mail, and Maria's voice came on the phone, triggering in Chris equal measures of hope and terror. "Hi, you've reached Maria. Please leave your name and number, and I'll get back to you soon as I can."

The sound of her voice chilled Chris, the icy hand of the past creeping down his spine. He wanted to bang his head against a wall, wanted to shout out how sorry he was. How sorry he was for just leaving her, abandoning her, all those years ago. Chris panicked, pressed the red end call icon before the *beep!* went off.

Leave a message! Or send her a text! he thought frantically.

But he wanted to hear her voice, to hear that she was all right from her own lips. And he needed to say he was sorry.

He tried calling again, muttering to himself, "Please be okay."

He got the voicemail again. And again. And again. But she wasn't answering. He would have to send a text, like a message in a bottle, and hope it would reach her.

He was in the middle of a text, trembling fingers typing urgent words, when his phone started ringing. His heart almost stopped. It was Maria calling him back. He answered, his stomach muscles tightening, fear and guilt mixing into one writhing creature in his ribcage. What if it wasn't her but that voice?

"I see you've been trying to call about fifty fucking times. Who is this?"

She sounded furious, but something else smoldered in her voice. Panic? Sadness?

Chris gulped painfully. *Say something.*

"Maria, listen to me. I think you're in danger. Get somewhere safe."

"Who is this?! And how do you know my name?!"

Chris hesitated.

"Whatever."

"No, wait. I'm here. It's me."

"Who's me?"

"It's *me*. Chris."

She went quiet.

Chris spoke into the awkward void of silence. "I got into a boxing fight and got punched in the throat. So that's why my voice might sound—"

Click!

"Hello. Hello! Maria!"

She was gone. Everything he wanted to say to her died in his chest. He tried calling again. It rang a couple times, then went to voicemail, like she'd been maybe considering answering, then rejecting his call. He tried again, and this time it went straight to voicemail. He told her to get someplace safe, that she was in danger, his words panicked and leaping rapidly from his tongue. He also sent her a text for good measure, repeating and reinforcing his voicemail: *U R in danger. Get somewhere safe.*

He set the phone on the passenger's seat, hoping it would light up with a call, or at least hoping Maria would get his hectic messages.

But she won't understand, will she? She wouldn't see the danger coming. It's just her asshole ex-husband calling out of the blue, fifteen years too late, telling her someone's after her.

He squeezed his eyes shut, wishing he could go back, wishing he would've taken that trip to the B&B with her. He couldn't blame her for hanging up on him. Chris had left her all alone after she'd lost a baby. Left her all alone when she needed him most.

A wave of sickness crashed into him. It felt like his blood was coagulating in his veins, his skin suddenly burning hot. He leaned out the car window and gagged on bile. He wiped his chin, stomach acids burning the back of his throat. Then he sat awhile. He checked his phone hopelessly. It was almost 8 p.m. Chris felt creeping panic with every second ticking by, the cooling twilight air around him growing darker, wanting to slam the car into gear and hurry to the show, to that colossal stage and those bright spotlights.

His eyes sparkled with hunger as he imagined the stage light's warmth on his skin.

***

Chris parked his Ferrari at the back entrance of the Hollywood Amphitheater. The massive concert hall was near Wattles Garden Park, only a few streets from Hollywood Boulevard. Chris had taken the interstate and, in light traffic, was there in a half hour. As he'd cruised the freeway's streaming river of steel and headlights, something kept telling him to turn around. To go back to South Central. But he kept going, got off the interstate, and drove until he saw the endless sea of parking lots and parked cars, and bouncers keeping the rivers of human beings in check. The lines stretched and curved around the parking lot, thousands of people waiting anxiously to get in. Chris had to show his face to a confused security guy, who just shook his head and winced, gesturing at the superstar's ruined face, and Chris was able to enter the back lot.

He parked in the employee section, in a space that was marked specifically for Chris Flowers, but he didn't get out right away. His window was rolled down, and he could hear the anxious chatter of the waiting concertgoers, a dull cacophony that made Chris's heart buzz with growing excitement. He could smell cigarette smoke wafting from the endless lines of people, could smell jasmine and the sea. But then there it was again, that feeling that had hounded him on the interstate. He'd checked the mirrors the whole way, waiting to hear the wailing of sirens, waiting to feel those flashing blue and red lights against his skin. He'd even been expecting cop cruisers waiting for him here, where they'd take him to be part of a line up with Victor behind the mirror-glass pointing at Chris, crying out, "That's the guy I saw at my house." But none of this had happened. It relieved Chris, and he took a deep breath, looked at the massive structure of the Hollywood Amphitheater against the purple sky.

What if Tray was already on his way to her? Or what if he was with her now?

He still couldn't believe what he was thinking that Tray Mansfield hadn't killed himself, that the kid had faked his suicide and was out there somewhere.

Chris checked his cell phone again, but there was nothing from Maria, and hope died within him. He rested his head in utter defeat against the steering wheel and let the sound of the chattering crowds in the vast parking lots soothe him. He pictured that stage, imagined a janitor buffing it, making it shine. And he imagined the light technicians tinkering with the spotlights and floodlights. He wanted to bask in it, in those lights and in the cheers of his loving fans, like a sunfish, to destroy the dark noise between his ears. He needed it now more, the limelight more than ever.

He stepped out of his car and headed inside.

* * *

Chris felt much better in fresh clothes, his dirty t-shirt and gym shorts balled in the corner of the dressing room. He looked at himself in the vanity mirror. He still looked like a train wreck, but a train wreck in a white Tom Ford crewneck silk t-shirt and Bermuda shorts. He'd also taken four two-hundred milligram Ibuprofens to try and knock out his roaring headache and to dull the aches in his bruised body.

He dug around in his personal closet, grabbed his Adidas—tall ones that rode high above his ankle which he wore for every show—sat on the red leather couch, slipped into them. He could feel the rumble of the huge crowd through the leather cushions. He checked his phone. 8:45. Almost showtime. But bitter disappointment seeped into him seeing Maria still hadn't gotten back to him.

He closed his eyes, trying just to listen to the vibrations of his fans settling into their places. But his toes started to swelter in his sneakers. He wanted to dash, to return to South Central.

The absurd and bizarre image of Tray Mansfield skulking about, leaving a trail of mayhem, filled Chris's mind.

Daryl. Where are you, man?

Chris crossed his arms, feeling suddenly ill.

That word came back to him.

Confess.

Confess.

Confess.

Someone knocked at the door, and Chris welcomed the intrusion, getting up on shaky legs, walking to the door. He wondered if it was Jo-Jo, his makeup lady, coming in to patch him up before the show.

He opened the door, surprised to see Jeff standing there.

Jeff was decked out in a solid black suit, no tie, and black dress shoes. The dark clothes made his gray hair and pale Botoxed face glow like a lantern. He was giving Chris the same horrified looks the ogling backstage workers and the Amphitheater managers had.

"Shit. I saw the videos, but I didn't realize...." Jeff didn't finish his sentence.

"Shouldn't you be with your new client?"

Jeff waved away the sarcastic remark. His face softened with remorse. "Can I come in?"

Chris didn't move.

Jeff sighed, hanging his head, regretful eyes sliding up. "Please."

Chris's body, stiff with anger, began to relax in his old friend's presence.

Jeff pulled out his vape pen and took a few thick hits off of it, big blue clouds of smoke pluming in his wake.

"Big crowd," Jeff said, trying to melt the frosty air between them.

Chris's dressing room door was open a crack, backstage sounds spilling in, the sounds of 25-thousand fans settling with their food and wine into bench and box and super-seats.

Chris had to force his attention away, eyes lasering in on Jeff. "You said you were going to ditch me, man."

"I did say that, okay?" Jeff took a step closer. "I was worried you might be back on the needle. Just the way you've been acting lately."

That shot of dope was still lingering in Chris's blood, but Chris didn't say anything.

Jeff continued, "And I get it. All this pressure with Andrea and the show and the new album. And that stuff you told me about Rich a few days ago." Jeff put a hand gently on Chris's shoulder. "I don't want to lose you, man. I love you. Let's just put all this behind us."

Chris listened. The sounds of thousands of fans haunted the backstage halls and trickled into the room. Jeff gave Chris's shoulder a comforting squeeze, reassuring Chris of their long future together. Chris thought about the albums he had yet to write.

What're you doing?

The warmth in Chris's face frosted over.

Maria's still out there. Daryl.

"Chris?" Jeff said uneasily, detecting Chris's mood change.

"Nothing."

Jeff removed his hand from Chris's shoulder. His face downcast at the perceived offense. He took a hit off his vape pen, nodding, roses burning in his cheeks. "I know what you're thinking about. What you told me on the phone earlier." Jeff, like reading Chris's mind, continued, "Thinking about your old buddies. About your wife." Jeff's tone was harsh and sarcastic.

Chris didn't like it.

Then Jeff's cruel face emerged from a thinning blue cloud of vape smoke. "Why're you hung up on these nobodies?!"

Chris took a full step away, stepping out of Jeff's toxic nicotine breath. His mouth hung open, words failing him.

His ringing phone spared him having to answer Jeff. He pulled his phone out of his pocket, checked the number, and his heart started racing.

Maria.

"Maria! I'm here!"

The first thing he heard was sniffling, the sound of someone sucking back tears.

"Maria?"

"Jesus fucking Christ," Jeff grumbled to himself, took a fat rip from his vape pen.

Chris turned his back on Jeff and stormed out of the room, leaving Jeff behind him like he was dead snakeskin.

As Chris rushed down the backstage hallway he heard Jeff's shouts withering away behind him. "Chris, I'm sorry, man. Hold on a sec. What about the show? What about the show?"

"Chris?" Maria finally said, the voice small and lost.

Chris burst through some backdoors and into the backlot, feeling better the further he was away from Jeff. He stood under a streetlight with summer bugs swarming the bulb. The air was warm and sweet.

"Maria, you okay?" Chris tensed up, waiting any moment for that other voice to come on.

"It's Manny. He's dead!" Maria fell apart as she was saying it, her words deteriorating into sobs.

The sounds she made nearly brought him to his knees, and he staggered under the harsh light, which brought him back to the ER all those years ago. After they had lost Louis, the kind of moans and cries that'd come out of her.

"Maria—" *I know he's dead,* he wanted to say, but didn't, couldn't. *I was there.*

"I was on the phone with the police when you called." Her words were broken up by hiccups, sniffles.

That other voice, Tray's voice, wasn't there with her. Chris was relieved for that.

"I'm so sorry, Maria."

He found himself desperately wanting to be with her, to sit across from her, look into her eyes, tell her how sorry he was for everything. He'd explain what'd happened over at Manny's. He'd come clean, tell her everything straight to her face.

Maria sniffled, collecting herself. Then she said, "Manny and his boyfriend were found dead. Together."

It felt like his dope sickness returned. The stars started spinning. Chris had to hold himself up against a post.

His attention was momentarily, greedily, drawn to the faint anticipatory murmurs of his fans settling into their seats, a part of him wanting to go back inside. "Can you come?" Maria asked suddenly.

"You want me to come?"

"Yes."

"To come see you?"

"Yes."

"Right now?"

"Uh-huh."

Chris found he couldn't stop his legs, feeling like they were moving him all on their own to his Ferrari. He realized now why he hadn't been swarmed by red and blue lights when he'd first got here. Victor was dead before the cops arrived.

Chris left a trail of burnt rubber as he screeched out of the backlot, the confused security guard turning his head.

Chris tapped on the steering wheel anxiously. "Maria, are you safe?"

"Yes."

"Are you sure? Were you followed or anything like that?"

"I'm fine. I don't understand. All that stuff in your messages."

"Did Daryl know where you live?" Chris knew something was very wrong with the way he'd phrased that question, taking a sharp right then heading up the on-ramp onto the interstate. Then it hit him that he was speaking in past tense, as if Daryl was already dead. "Or did he know where you work?"

"No," she said, then started sobbing.

The sound seared Chris's ear, made him slam harder on the gas pedal, his Ferrari screaming down the interstate. He thought back to the hospital, the agonizing weeks after Louis had died, Maria waking up in the middle of the night screaming, Chris holding her and shushing her back to sleep. He thought about the last night he ever saw her, that night he told her he couldn't go to the B&B with her, the night he left her all alone in that apartment.

"Maria, I'm so sorry. I'm so, so sorry."

"It's okay."

But it wasn't. It wasn't okay, what he'd done.

Then an idea brightened his face. A way to know she was safe, see her, and please his fans. "Hey, do you wanna see a show tonight?"

She hesitated. Chris thought he'd gone too far.

"A show?"

"Yeah, my show."

She was quiet, like she was thinking about it. Then she said, "That'd be nice."

"Okay," Chris said, beaming. "I'm on my way to South Central. Just text me your address, and I'll be there shortly."

After they hung up, Chris shifted in his seat, stared straight ahead of him with steely determination, blinking back tears. The Ferrari shrieked down the interstate, Chris weaving in and out of gaps in traffic, hurrying, hurrying.

CHAPTER THIRTY-FIVE

Chris turned down Grasmere Street, passed abandoned cars with windows smashed out and tires missing. The sky was freckled with hazy stars trying to shine through the city smog. The houses lining the street were crowded together, many of them dark, their occupants settling in for the night. A couple were derelict, plywood covering the windows and *No Trespassing* spray-painted in red across the ancient doors.

Chris reached the small house at the end of the street, the address Maria had texted him. She was living in Jefferson Park now, a couple neighborhoods from where she and Chris had lived fifteen years earlier. He parked beside a dented Pinto he assumed was hers, stepped out into the warm evening air, and looking at the little house, was filled with fleeting sadness. He wondered, briefly, what life would've been like if he'd stayed with her.

He gazed at the glowing windows, waiting for curtains to stir, for a face to peer out and acknowledge his arrival. Nothing.

He approached the front door with growing unease, opened it and stuck his head into the nicotine flavored air.

"Maria?"

"Chris?" The voice was coming from another room. "I'm in here." Her voice.

Chris smiled, relieved, shut the door behind him.

His grin wilted when he stepped around the corner into the living room. He froze.

The tall man with moon-colored flesh was pointing a large black pistol at the back of Maria's head, the barrel buried in her wavy dark hair. She was sitting, rigid with fear, in an old brown recliner, the figure looming behind her.

A single word rose like a curse to Chris's lips. "Tray?"

Tray Mansfield's eyes, once a hopeful bright blue, were now little silvery shards that glittered, sunk back in cave-like sockets. He was skeleton thin, skin hugging his skull too tightly, his cheekbones sharp and prominent. His clothes were dirty, white t-shirt yellow with age, dark stains—blood?—on his jeans. Running across his face, like a giant pink centipede, that unmistakable scar.

"Chris, I'm sorry," Maria said, voice tense with fear, regret. "He followed me home from work."

Tray gestured with the pistol to the empty couch to Chris's left. "Sit down."

Chris raised his hands, slowly sunk into the couch, his heart a jackhammer trying to break through his ribcage. "Easy."

"Shut up!" That once radiant, magnetic voice was now the bark of a hellhound, and it ripped through the air and spiked Chris's blood pressure.

Staring into Tray's skeletal face, Chris noticed storm-colored bruising above the left eye. Tray'd been struck with something. Chris could almost hear Andre's or Daryl's fists crashing into the kid's face, desperately trying to fend off the kidnapper.

"I'm sorry," Maria said again.

Chris looked at her, thought about her phone call, her weeping voice, thought about the traces of terror he'd missed. He realized Daryl must've known where Maria worked, the information probably tortured out of him by Tray, leading the kid right to her. Chris pictured that pistol trained on her all the while they had talked on the phone.

But he reassured her, "It's okay. It ain't your fault."

Maria's belly sagged out of her McDonald's work uniform. Her nametag said she was a manager. Her mouth was cracked with cigarette wrinkles. Her voice was huskier. Premature gray streaked her once raven hair. She was younger than Chris but looked at least a decade older.

Tray carefully dug something out of his pocket. A cell phone. He approached Chris on long stalking spider legs, his sour body odor oppressive, smelling like death. He raised the cell phone up to Chris's face, all the while keeping the gun trained on him. Chris's chest hollowed out. It was a picture of a black man lying on his back, eyes wide open, mouth grimacing. There was a red gash across his throat, blood soaked into the front of his shirt. The man's eyes were cloudy. He was clearly dead.

"Say hi to your old buddy, Daryl," Tray said, his voice less spooky without the voice changer, but no less threatening.

Chris's vision blurred, his eyes filling with tears. His hands coiled into fists. He shifted, leaning forward, ready to spring up and pounce on Tray. But Tray took a full step back, slipping his phone back into his pocket. Must be Tray's personal phone, Chris thought, one he wouldn't risk calling from. Tray raised the pistol, Chris glaring into its cold black eye.

"Don't get brave now," Tray said, returning to his spot behind the recliner.

Chris's stomach lurched when Tray pointed the gun at Maria again.

Tray smirked. "You thought I was someone else, huh?" He was taking an almost childish delight in having fooled Chris. "I tricked you. Just like you tricked me."

Hey, kid. Why ain't you out there mingling?

"You got me," Chris said, his guilt deepening, thinking about putting the wrong man in a hospital.

His attention was drawn to a sniffle, saw shining trails of tears on Maria's cheeks.

"She's got nothing to do with this," Chris said, trying to keep his voice steady. "Kill me if you want."

But nothing Chris was saying pierced Tray's steely, deadly determination. "No one has to get killed. No one *had* to."

That picture of Daryl hooked itself into Chris's mind, a grim burden. Was it true? If he would've confessed that day Tray had first called would Daryl have been spared? Andre? Would Wally still be alive?

Chris felt sick thinking about it.

He gave Maria a broken smile. "It's gonna be okay."

"You think so?" Tray's voice dripped with threat. Then his face brightened, like an ugly yellow moon. His hateful blue eyes zipped eagerly from Chris to Maria. "Why don't you tell her, Chris. Tell her why all this is happening."

You're helping so many people. Remember that, kid. Go on out there and give 'em some love.

"Chickenshit," Tray said when Chris didn't answer. Not a speck of pity in those boiling blue eyes.

Maria glanced from her terrorizer to Chris, her eyes curious.

Chris's mouth hung open, but he couldn't speak, his tongue caught in his throat.

Tray prodded Maria's skull with the gun barrel.

Chris almost leapt up, but thought better.

He shifted on the couch, heat flushing his face. He put a fist over his mouth, didn't want Maria to hear it, didn't want to hear himself say it.

"I tried to have that man standing there killed." Chris looked away after he said it.

Maria just blinked at him, puzzled, sad. "What? I don't—"

"See, Chris? Wasn't so bad, was it?"

But it was. It felt like he'd been poleaxed.

Chris rubbed sweat from his face. When he looked up, he saw Tray's face was contorted in pain.

"You imagine it, what I went through."

It was all coming back. Chris heard Tray's bones snapping after Andre crashed that car into him. He remembered holding Tray's head in his lap, people gathering around him. He looked at the pink scar that ran down the right side of Tray's face.

"I can't imagine."

"No, you can't. And why'd you do it?"

"Tray—"

"I'll tell you why. It's because you were so threatened by me, wasn't it? You tried to have me killed because I was a prodigy who was gonna eclipse your precious limelight. And I knew you wouldn't do it. I knew you wouldn't confess, even when other people's lives were at risk. You care too much about yourself. I realize that about you now. Everything you do, you do for yourself."

"Kid, please. I'm sorry—"

"That foundation you started in my name? Crying for the cameras at my funeral? Even your stupid social media videos. 'Look at me. Look at me.' Everyone look at Chris-fucking-Flowers."

"Kid—"

"You're a goddamn attention-starved phony. And a liar."

Maria met Chris's eyes now, trying hard to hide her disgust. She now looked torn between whose side she was on.

"You think you're *immortal*," Tray continued. "That's your problem. In millions and millions of years you ain't gonna matter, no matter how big and famous you are now."

"I—I—my songs..." *I'm gonna live forever.*

"If you weren't such a self-absorbed asshole, you'd realize that!" Then Tray softened, brow furrowed, tears of betrayal shining in those cold, blue eyes. "I trusted you, man. I loved you," Tray said, voice cracking, the gun shaking unsteadily in his hands.

Chris remembered Tray's fans surrounding him. He could feel their shadows now, deliciously smothering him. He could feel their eyes on him. He could feel once again the weight of Tray's head on his lap, blood pooling, those blue eyes blinking helplessly up at him, and Chris remembered the thoughts that'd run through his mind: *You ain't gonna replace me. No one's gonna replace me.*

The returning memories weighed dark and heavy in his mind, and Chris stared at the floor for a few seconds, thinking, *What've I done?*

Tray, biting back his tears, remained steadfast. He steadied his grip on the pistol, said, "Tell everyone what you've done, and I'll let her go."

Chris locked eyes with Maria.

She shook her head at him and with her eyes said: *Look what you've done! Look what you've done!*

"I tell them, everyone, what happened and you'll let her go."

"That's right."

"You'll just let her go."

Tray nodded.

"How do I know?! How do I know you won't just kill her after?"

"Keep making excuses for yourself, Chris. See what happens." Tray nudged Maria with the gun barrel. "Come on, get up."

Chris stood up when Maria did. "I ain't making excuses!"

Tray held the .45 on Chris.

"*How?*" Chris said, urgency bleeding into his voice. "How will I know?"

Tray kept the .45 on Chris as he led Maria out of the living room. "Where're you taking her?!"

But Chris knew where. His imagination was filled with visions of that dark basement area in Tray's pictures, the single bare bulb and the cold concrete floor and the dried bloodstains.

Tray grabbed a fistful of Maria's hair, a startled noise coming out of her mouth. He held the gun on Chris while guiding Maria toward the front door.

"You have my word," Tray said. Then he said into Maria's ear, "Keys. Phone."

Maria reached a shaking hand into her pocket, pulled out her cell phone and jangling car keys.

Tray carefully guided Maria outside, stuffing her phone into his pocket, then used the car keys to pop open the trunk. "Get your ass in," he said, glancing over his shoulder down the dark empty street.

Chris stood helpless in the yard's stone pathway, flinching every time Tray waved the pistol at him. Chris's eyes darted, heart pounding, hoping for a passing car, for a face to peek out a neighboring window. The next-door houses were dark, oblivious. The street was dead.

With a *clunk!* the trunk door was shut, Maria inside.

Sweat dotted Chris's forehead. He wanted to scream at the top of his lungs. But his attention was drawn to stomping footsteps, Tray approaching, eyes aflame with threat.

Tray stopped a few feet from Chris, looked left, right. Then he leaned in, voice barely above a whisper, and said, "Follow me, or call the cops, or any of that shit, I'll kill her. I swear to God I will."

Chris believed him.

Tray climbed in, started the gurgling Pinto up, then quietly reversed into the street.

Chris stood there, sweating bullets, watching the Pinto's taillights fade into the deepening night, Maria in the trunk.

As soon as the headlights disappeared, Chris's shock wore off, and his immediate reaction was to jump into his Ferrari, fire it up, and jam the gearstick into reverse. But he didn't pull out. The car just sat there, idling. What was he going to do, tail Tray in his Ferrari all the way to his lair and rescue Maria? Was he going to possibly kill Tray if he had to? Chris didn't even realize, at first, that his thoughts started conjuring up future press coverage. He was imagining his face on everyone's TV and cell phone screens, until he felt a sinking feeling in his gut. Tray's words returned to him: *Everything you do, you do for you.* Chris gazed at his ruined face in the rearview mirror, thinking about that.

Chris had heard someone once say there was no such thing as a nice yard in South Central, but Maria's yard was nice, beautiful bright flowers growing in a window box.

CHAPTER THIRTY-SIX

It was already past nine, past showtime, when Chris got onto the interstate and was heading back to the Hollywood Amphitheater. He knew the audience would be fuming with impatience. He ignored his ringing cell phone, calls from the stadium's management and from Jeff, as he cruised down the interstate. It felt like the longest drive of his life, his mind throbbing with worry for Maria, and still rattled from the face-to-face with Tray.

Tray had said, "You imagine it." To put himself in Tray's shoes. And as Chris looked out into the city's lights, empathy bled into his anxiety. Chris tried to imagine the horror of what it must be like waking up one morning and being unable to write music, the thing that gave him purpose. He imagined it driving him to near suicide, sitting on a dinghy with an anchor tied to his ankles, considering letting himself sink down into the nothingness of the icy black waters of the Pacific Ocean. Pain tore through his heart, and he tightened fists around the steering wheel, imagining Tray's fury. He imagined trading suicide for the fires of revenge, returning from his suicidal paddle with renewed purpose, soul corrupt with hate.

South Central faded into darkness behind him. Driving as fast as he could he zipped through Beverly Hills and West Hollywood, then a few streets north until he got to Wattles Garden Park. But even when he arrived, cruising past that same confused security guard, finding his designated parking space again, he didn't get out of the car for maybe ten heartbeats. It was like his hands had melted into the steering wheel, not wanting to go into that giant, looming stadium, not wanting to go up onto that stage. It was the first time he never wanted to go up on any stage.

He got out of his car and hurried inside.

Jo-Jo, tucking her pink-dyed hair behind her ear, eyes blinking with concern, followed him down a long backstage hall insisting that she patch up his face with makeup. But Chris shrugged her off, told her he was fine, kept walking. Perplexed faces floated past him. It felt like everything turned into slow-motion. He found himself thinking about Tray again on his way to the stage.

Tray had returned from that suicidal paddle. Three years. Three years Tray had waited, keeping up with Andre's case in the news, waiting only to find out that the person who truly wronged him was someone he'd once idolized, someone he'd once loved.

Chris walked down a long hall of shadow, heart pounding the closer he got to the anxious, chattering crowd. For some reason images of his momma flashed across his mind.

He arrived at the threshold where backstage met the mainstage, stood for a moment, the microphone waiting for him, his tongue thickening, his mouth dry as sand. His soul heavy with dark reminders.

Then he stepped out into the light.

He was greeted by relieved, thunderous applause. The ceiling arched up over him. The audience seats were out in the open, the crowd sitting under a perfect summer evening sky. It was just as the weather stations had predicted, a beautiful night, nearly cloudless, a full blue moon hanging in the sky. Lights began to explode, electric flowers of light sprouting devouring each other over Chris. He sauntered on the tidal waves of applause that crashed into him and images of Momma's milky eyes faded. He crossed the stage, the microphone getting closer.

He could see the vague shapes of human bodies out there, eyes blinking at him in anticipation. On closer inspection, he saw officer Eddie and his daughter, front row privileges. Eddie's daughter, looking to be about twelve or thirteen, was wearing a Chris Flowers t-shirt. She pumped her fist into the air, crying out his name, crying out that he was her hero, while Eddie—wearing civilian clothes—just glanced at her like he felt sorry for her.

Chris tried not to focus on them as he stood in front of the microphone. His lips tingled as he pressed them against it. Lights darted wildly as he stood at the cusp of glory, at the precipice of fame. He felt familiar eyes to his left, turned and he could see a dark shape leaning against a wall on stage left. Squinting, he saw the silver hair, saw Jeff's eyes burning into him.

Jeff nodded at Chris, grinned.

Chris looked away, faced his audience.

Thousands of cell phones were out, filming him. The stage cameras rolled past him, zooming in on his face, his image projected on a giant screen behind him so that people in the way, way back could see his every facial expression. The crowd murmured and gasped as they got a high def close-up of the ruin of his face.

He cleared his throat, his voice quieting the crowd. He gazed out over his people, feeling their love for him, tasting it in the air.

"I know there's been a lot of shit going on lately, but thank you all for being here tonight."

The crowd erupted with approving applause, the sound like rain on a tin roof. Thousands of faces stared at him.

Chris went quiet, swallowing painfully.

The crowd began chattering again.

Chris flicked eyes up at the sound board operator. The sound board operator nodded back, gave his headset a tweak, then started pressing buttons and adjusting levels on the sound board.

The electronic drum track started in.

What am I doing? Chris thought.

The lights strobed with the song. The crowd roared their approval recognizing the tune.

Chris stood frozen at the microphone, lights pulsating all around him, his eyes shut. A part of him still wanted to sing the song, wanted to ignore his shame as he had for years, wanted to ignore Tray's threats.

The music was queued in, but Chris, lost behind his eyelids, heard the sudden roar of disapproval from the crowd. They chattered in confusion again. The song was abruptly ended.

Chris forced his eyes open, the cell phone lights no longer throbbing to the tune. He gulped, turned to look at Jeff's ugly face.

Jeff mouthed the words, *What the fuck?*

Chris shrugged, then sighed and nodded. His lips buzzed and tingled as they touched the microphone. "I messed up. Let me try again."

The audience chuckled forgivingly.

Chris couldn't believe he said it. He wrestled with that small part of him that wanted to keep hidden his dark secret.

He sighed, shut his eyes, and the song started again. The electronic drum track thudded into his heart. The lights pulsated, the music queued in, and his lips parted, the first verse seconds away.

Chris winced as he missed his cue, a rain of boos cascading down upon him.

For some reason, the boos didn't sting so much.

Chris couldn't stop thinking about what Tray had said.

He thought to himself, *Tray's right, isn't he.*

He suddenly realized something. He realized how silly it was, him thinking himself immortal, that his music, his art, his legacy would last forever. How long had he been thinking this way? He realized a million years would pass, a *billion* years, and he knew then...

I'll be forgotten.

The music stopped. The strobe lights stopped dancing.

He didn't know why he was agreeing with Tray, the kid who was threatening Maria. But Chris somehow knew the kid was right about that.

Of course I'll be forgotten someday. No one's immortal.

Just a hot, still spotlight on him now. However, Chris suddenly didn't care if the light was touching him or not.

He gazed out at his confused, chattering fans, fidgeted.

It's gonna be okay, Maria.

He turned to the furious face of his manager who was boiling in the shadows, squeezing his fists and shaking his head.

The fuck are you doing? Jeff mouthed.

"Listen, people," Chris said into the buzzing microphone. His voice boomed and quieted the chattering disquiet. "I need to tell you something. You all remember Tray Mansfield."

The crowd stirred, baffled. Chris chanced one more look at Jeff, Jeff shooting Chris a look of horror, betrayal. He gave Jeff the finger. Jeff turned away, disappeared furiously into the dark.

Chris took a deep breath and faced the audience.

Here it goes.

"Five years ago I hired a man to kill him."

A moment of silence from the audience. A warm breeze blew by, though Chris felt an inner chill that made his skin crawl. The silence hung for a moment longer. Chris wondered if they even believed him.

"I did. I hired Andre Childs to kill Tray Mansfield."

That was when Chris heard the first boos.

Chris's shame-filled face was massive on the screen to his back, seen by the world.

The boos grew to a deafening pitch.

Chris nodded, accepting it.

He chanced a look at Eddie and his daughter. The daughter just stared at him, eyes wide, mouth hanging open. Eddie looked at him with disgust. It was painful watching Eddie take his daughter's hand, the daughter wiping tears from her eyes and looking horrified and betrayed like everyone else, and tugging her away from the stage. As Chris watched the two of them disappear into the rest of the outraged crowd, Chris thought, *I'm sorry. I'm so sorry.*

The boos swelled until they were impossible to speak over.

Daryl, Andre, Marianne, Tray, I'm sorry.

The crowd's faces were mottled with angry and confusion, and they began to raise fists and shout at him.

Chris stood there for what seemed like forever, his fears growing not for himself and his looming destruction, but for Maria.

Please be okay. Please be okay.

Chris's phone was out of control with buzzing. He checked it, hoping one of the endless notifications and texts was Maria's number. He felt his blood run cold when he saw one of the texts was from Maria. The world felt like it was underwater, the crowd's boos fading for a moment, as he checked the message.

She sent a selfie, sitting safely behind the wheel of her Pinto, a happy yet terrified look on her tearstained face. Her text read: *He was watching. He let me go. Turning himself in.*

Just like the kid had promised.

Even as the boos grew louder Chris felt utter relief, shutting his eyes and holding his phone to his chest like he was holding Maria again. He took a deep breath as the world grew to hate him. Somehow, it was all okay. The truth was out, and it felt like a weight leaving his soul. He even smiled, a small smile of relief and resignation, as he was being devoured by the boos.

He hung his head and prepared for the rest of his humbled days.

Printed by Libri Plureos GmbH in Hamburg,
Germany